# THE TINKER'S FOLLY

## A COZY FANTASY CHARACTER TALE

## G. J. DAILY

# WHISPERED THINGS

*Beneath the Raven Light so cold,*
*Where shadows creep and fates are sold,*
*The Raven King, in silence deep,*
*Watches over those who sleep.*
*A Raven Coin, in dreams he brings,*
*A token bound to whispered things,*
*Trade it well, but choose with care,*
*For dreams can turn to dark despair.*

# CHAPTER 1
## THIRTY YEARS AGO

It was night, and sheets of rain blew across the deck of a heavy merchant vessel listing in the wind. A crack of lightning lit the gaping maw of an Eldritch Leviathan figurehead carved into the prow. The ship exuded an air of defiance. Its hull was dark, and it bore the scars of misadventure.

The docks were quiet, but the ship was alive with a motley crew eager to leave port and find open ocean before the full fury of Macpella—the ocean god—could be seen.

The Algi captain, with his translucent, gelatinous body exuding a dim glow from within, paced back and forth along the quarterdeck. "Make ready, and prepare to cast off lines. If he's not here in five minutes, we weigh anchor."

The first mate nodded. His sandy-white fur and thick mane hung heavy with rain, but his stoic manner suggested he hadn't noticed. Then he stepped forward and called out in the deep voice of a lion: "All hands on deck! Man the capstan and prepare to cast off!" as the crew took to their stations.

3

Then, through the darkness came the flicking orange glow of a lamp passing between two tall buildings.

The captain left the ship to meet the cart's driver, a dark figure loosely holding the reins of a pair of pale and sickly empary, creatures akin to skeletal horses with wolf-like maws and slender wings folded against their skin-tight ribs.

"This had better be worth it!" the captain called out against the wind. "It may already be too late to leave port!"

The Dym driver, his skin pale, his eyes dark, and his extremities too long and slender to look natural, said nothing. He climbed down from the driver's bench and went to the back of his cart. As he pulled back the tarp, two children, a boy and a girl, recoiled at the cold rain and squeezed each other tightly. Their skin was sapphire-blue, and they were no older than ten or twelve. Blisters rose on their ankles where heavy irons shackled their legs to the cart.

The captain looked around the dock for prying eyes. While slaves were often sold to merchant vessels, many did not approve of selling children. Selling children this young would surely anger somebody. And children such as these? Someone would have noticed if the dock had not been empty for the approaching storm.

The Dym coach driver unlocked the iron eyelet and urged them down, out of the cart so that the captain could have a look. The boy helped his sister, then lunged at the driver, who kicked him to the ground.

The captain grunted. "He's got fire. I can use that." Then he lifted the boy to his feet with one of his four tendril-arms and pulled up the boy's thin shirt to see if he was healthy. "How much?"

"Two sovereigns a head," the Dym finally spoke. A single gold sovereign was worth ten silver crowns.

The captain grunted again. "I'll give you twelve crowns for the boy. I've no use for the girl."

"No!" the boy cried out and cursed the driver as he and his sister squeezed each other tight.

"Eighteen," the driver replied.

"Fifteen, and I have to leave. Take it or leave it."

The driver nodded, and the captain's light flickered a signal to the first mate, who came down the dock, counted off fifteen silver crowns from a bag hanging at this belt, picked up the boy, and threw him over his shoulder. Then the captain and the first mate turned to leave, as the brother and sister reached for each other.

As they walked, the boy screamed and punched and kicked the first mate's arms and pulled at his mane, causing the first mate to growl low and pull away.

"Stop! Stop," the boy cried, wriggling away and falling to the cracked and weathered boards of the dock. Then he knelt before the captain and pulled at the edges of the coat hanging wide and loose over the captain's gelatinous body. "I'll do whatever you want. Please. I won't fight you. I'll pay for her, somehow. I'll find a way to pay you back for her. Please! Anything. Please. If you don't bring her, you will have to kill me because I will find a way to kill you, but if you bring her, I'll..." The boy stood now and looked up at the lion of a first mate with no discernible fear—rain pressing against his back and running in streams down his jewel-blue skin. "If you bring her, I will kill for you."

The first mate was ready to strike the boy down where he stood, but hesitated out of respect for the boy's passion and strength—something rarely found on the seas. Then he and the captain looked at each other, and with a nod from the lion-like man, the captain turned back to the Dym, who was fighting to re-chain the girl to the cart.

"I'll give you five crowns for the girl."

The Dym turned to him, a leather hood partially covering his face from the increasing intensity of the rain. "Eight."

The captain flicked his light, and the first mate left the boy where he stood and paid the Dym. Then the captain approached the boy. "You were slaves. On my ship, you are free. But. If either of you ever cross me, I'll kill her." Then, he calmly returned to the vessel.

The girl rushed forward, and the two embraced tightly. Then the boy looked at the first mate, who glared down at him.

"This is our home now," Petros told his sister.

She was scared, but she trusted Petros and steadied herself against the possibilities of the unknown. She took his hand as he led her onto the ship.

"All hands! Clear the moorings and weigh anchor," the first mate roared above the sound of the wind.

Then, the boat began to glow from somewhere beneath the choppy water.

# CHAPTER 2
## PRESENT DAY

It was morning. The sky was shades of cerulean, and rose brushed the cheeks of puffy-white clouds like rouge painted on with a fine brush. The air was cool but slowly warming, and the rich, mossy smell of forest was thick.

Andrew always enjoyed mornings—the quiet before the world awoke, so full of possibility. As he rode Brynlee toward Lorna's cottage, he flipped through pages of his leather-bound journal, trying to remember his last lesson with her. He had filled two journals now with charcoal sketches of symbols and sigils of the tiny details he kept getting wrong—pages filled with the true names of elements, plants, parts of the human body for healing, and on and on. His intuition training felt like a dance he couldn't quite master.

Twice, he had accidentally set things on fire with the Warming Rod before finally giving it back to her. It was the word components that frustrated him. He was usually a quick study, but intuition was different. It was based on feelings, emotions, sounds, movement. He wanted structure, something he could measure, something that fit neatly into a box. He couldn't hold intuition in his hand or feel its grain. There were no numbers or precise measurements; no defined parameters.

His growing frustration was causing him to visit Lorna less and less, which was not lost on her. She tried encouraging him and gently nudging him forward, but it wasn't working and she didn't know why. Intuition had come naturally to her—perhaps because she was taught by her mother, who was taught by her mother before her. Perhaps intuition came more easily to women. Perhaps women were more heart-driven and less head-driven. But she saw how much he was trying, and how hard he pushed himself, often to the edge of emotional collapse when things didn't go as he wanted. More than once, he had snapped at her in frustration or come close to tears after failing at something as simple as mending a broken branch.

Still, she was patient. She believed he had the gift, but she didn't want to push him too hard—both for his own sake and the safety of those around him. She tried to keep things simple, repeating the same gentle instructions: "Don't try so hard. Calm your mind. Breathe."

But it wasn't working.

These days, Lorna's cottage looked nothing like it had the first time he had found it. Where a derelict crypt of a spider-web-covered cottage once stood, there was now a beautiful, three-story bed and breakfast wrapping up and around a flowering nightshade tree. It had auburn-red roof shingles against green wood siding that matched the forest's colors while standing out in vibrant contrast. Hand-carved shutters framed lattice windows with heart-shaped decorations. Vines of yellow trumpet flowers climbed the trellises, and a red-brick path led through the fence he had once repaired for her, up to a beautiful door with a hand-painted sign that read: "Eetech Peema," or "The Hiding Place," in the common tongue. While Lorna's incredible intuition had resurrected the old tree and restored her cabin, Andrew insisted on hand-painting the sign.

"Good morning, grandson," Lorna said, still finding so much joy in the sound of that word: grandson.

"Good morning! Are you well?" he replied, climbing down from his dappled horse, Brynlee.

"I am. Have you eaten?"

"Yes, but I could always use a cuppa."

She smiled. "I've already put the kettle on," Lorna said, holding her thick, cream-colored cloak shut against the cool morning air. Well into her seventies, she didn't look a day over fifty, and she might be mistaken for an even younger woman if not for the thick silver curls pinned up into a pile on her head.

Though Andrew was having trouble with his lessons, he felt safer in this place than anywhere else. He could let his guard down and didn't have to hide his humanity with her. Lorna was like him, and he could fully be himself around her. Of course, he also felt comfortable around his father, Lithuel. But since Lithuel was Nimic, Lithuel could never truly understand what Andrew faced nearly every day as a Human—the glances, children pointing and asking why his skin was so pale, women holding their bags tighter as he walked past, the constant sense that he was making someone uncomfortable just for being alive. But in this tiny oasis out in the forest, he had, for the first time in his life, finally found someone else who was like him.

"How's the decorating coming along?" Andrew asked, hanging his coat inside the door and removing his boots.

"Fine. I'm trying to put the finishing touches on a few

things, but I think I'm close. What do you think of the menu?" Lorna asked, carefully filling a purple teapot with hot water and setting it before Andrew.

"What are these?" Andrew asked, looking over a decorative rack of toast and a row of little glass cups of colorful marmalades. Then he picked up the hand-lettered menu and read:

*Eggy toast dipped in a butter batter, dusted with cinnamon & topped with cream and fruit compote.*

*Fresh pelutchi and flavored mendazi buns sprinkled with sugar beside two freckled-lace eggs and sausages.*

*A bowl of overnight oats with brown sugar, seasonal fruits and flowers and optional toast or rincari.*

*Upon Request: Eggs to order, toast and assorted jams, sausages, sunrise rincari, and rashers. Breakfast wine, seasonal juice and assorted hot tea are also available, including the Hiding Place's special blend. A local favorite!*

"I thought you could taste some of my most recent jams and tell me what you think. My favorite is the peach and ginger there on the end."

"You added my egg toast!"

Lorna smiled and nodded. "Are you kidding? It's the star attraction. That and your tea. You really should try your hand at more dishes."

"How close are you to opening?" Andrew asked.

"I'm going to wait until after your big day, but I should be ready by then."

Andrew smiled. "Well, I think it's great, what you've done with the place. And I would never have thought to open a...what do you call it?"

"A bed and breakfast," she said, gently blowing on her cup of Andrew's special tea and taking a slow and careful sip. So perfect.

"And you really think people will come all this way to stay with you?" Andrew asked.

"Oh, I think so. Sometimes, the rich and famous want nothing more than a quiet hole in the wall to escape to. Hey! I've been meaning to ask: Do you think Fey might be interested in helping me with guests sometimes, once we get busy—if we get busy?"

Andrew thought that wasn't a bad idea. "I could ask her, but I don't see why not, now that she and Brutste have finally hired some help at the Hiddy Coo."

Lorna smiled and took another slow sip of her tea. That would be just fine.

# CHAPTER 3

"I can't believe this is happening," Feyloren said from behind a curtain. "I had just about given up, but then... Andrew. He's funny, he's smart, and he really cares about me, you know?"

Brutste held up a white silk shoe and wondered how her foot would ever fit in such a thing. "Well, you sure picked a skinny one," Brutste replied, carefully bending it. "I'm not supposed to wear this, am I?"

Feyloren glanced out from behind the curtain, then returned to what she was doing. "It *would* be nice if my sister, best friend, and the person performing my ceremony didn't have ale on her boots."

Brutste considered again, her look changing to that of contempt. "I didn't even wear this crap at my *own* wedding."

"Humans have different traditions, and if Andrew and I are going to be family, we will all have to learn to flex a little. Bend a little."

"Oh, I can flex," Brutste said quietly, flexing a bicep and

12

kissing it, then twisting the shoe. *How does anyone even conceive of something so ridiculous?* she wondered.

Feyloren pulled back the curtain, and there it was. Now Brutste understood. Her eyes widened. "Sister," she said through a half-whisper.

Feyloren stood in front of a mirror with her back to Brutste. She wore a tight-fitting, cream-colored wedding dress. The back was open in a V down to her waist. Drapes of white organza and silver threaded lace hung from her arms and flowed in a long train behind her. Important scenes of Feyloren's life were embroidered in fine yellow thread along the entire bottom edge of the dress. There was an image of Feyloren on one side of the V opening on the back of her dress and an image of Andrew on the other. Beneath the V, they held hands. The Longbeard people called this a story dress. The white of the dress was very traditionally Human, while the story elements were a part of how the Longbeard people passed their bridal stories down to their children and heirs, each generation wearing the garments of their parents and adding to the story.

Since Feyloren did not have the story dress of her mother, the woman she had worked for had commissioned a new one for her as a wedding gift. Feyloren saw the dress, but she also saw all the space across the train where, one day, her daughters and their daughters would add their own stories to it.

"Is it too much?" she asked Brutste.

For once, Brutste was without words. She just took in how beautiful her little sister was, with her skin the color of copper pennies; no longer the bumbling little girl Brutste had protected their entire life, but a fantastic specimen of a woman. Of course, Feyloren was no spring Lilly herself, but

Brutste had not seen it until now. But here she was. Her sister. In all her beautiful splendor.

Feyloren gently touched the side of her cheek with the back of her hand and tilted her head to one side in the mirror, then the other. She twisted to see her silhouette and ran her hand down the wonderful fabric.

"Sis?" Feyloren asked again, focused on the delicate embroidery. But there was no answer.

She turned.

Brutste's eyes were full, and her heart was fuller still. She swallowed hard, stepped forward, and picked her little sister up in a smothering hug. "By the gods, little sister. You are a *dream*."

Feyloren was surprised, at first by the sight of tears on her never-gonna-cry sister's face, then by the hug. When Brutste didn't let go, she embraced her back, her feet dangling inches from the floor.

Then Brutste set her down and wiped her face on the back of her sleeve. Then she paused for a moment. Something had caught her attention. She grasped Feyloren's shoulders in her hands and looked at her with a newfound curiosity. Brutste leaned forward and smelled the top of her sister's bald head. Then she gently ran her hand over Feyloren's scalp and smelled her fingers. It was a faint honey-like smell that could only mean... Her eyes widened.

"Are you..." Brutste asked.

Feyloren pulled back. She said nothing for a moment but knew she couldn't hide it. Not for long. Not from the women of her clan, who were highly intuitive in such things. Brutste didn't have the same experience, but even a broken clock was lucky twice a day.

A wry smile slowly swept across Feyloren's face.

Brutste laughed so loud that Feyloren quickly looked

around and tried to shush her, but Brutste wouldn't have it. Now she picked her little sister up and swept her around in circles like she was dancing with a doll. Brutste's beard tickled Feyloren's cheeks and the top of her head, and they laughed together.

"My little sister is..."

Feyloren struggled away and put a hand over Brutste's hairy mouth. "Shhhh! You can't tell anyone. I've only just realized a few days ago and haven't had the chance to tell Andrew yet. He's so busy trying to open the store. He's convinced he can get it done before the wedding in two weeks."

Brutste tried to quiet herself and bounced back and forth from her left foot to her right. "When are you telling him?" she loud-whispered.

"Tomorrow night. I've invited him, Lorna, and his father to the Hiddy Coo for a special meal under the guise of wanting to go over last-minute details. I'll tell him then."

Brutste kissed the top of her sister's bald head. "May you be BLESSED little sister!"

Feyloren laughed. "Now, will you please answer my question? Is the dress too much?"

"Pretty soon, it might not be enough," Brutste replied with a huge smile, motioning her hand over her stomach in the shape of a bump.

Feyloren dismissed her sister's joke with a smile and looked back at the mirror, gently rubbing her stomach and considering.

# CHAPTER 4

Lorna and Andrew enjoyed some tea and toast together, chatting about nothing in particular. Then he helped her clear the dishes. As he turned from wiping off plates, he saw that she had laid out the Warming Rod on the counter.

He sighed.

She saw his hesitation and touched his arm. "Why don't we take a day off from the tricky stuff?" she asked.

"Alright?"

"I used to play a game with my mother."

Andrew liked the idea of a game. Then, as they began leaving the cabin, he reached for her staff.

"No, no. We won't need that," she told him.

"But how will I..."

She smiled and took his hand. "Trust me."

Lorna stepped out of the cabin into a sunlit clearing, where the morning light broke through the trees in shafts of golden light. Closing her eyes, she lifted her hands and embraced the warmth.

Andrew followed with arms crossed.

"Intuition is a gift from the Great Ruach, meant to help us live healthier, happier lives," she said, motioning her hands in a slow circle as the thick branches of the nearby hornbeam trees stretched low toward them. "It comes from within. The staff is only a tool. You should learn to listen."

She lifted the back of her robe and sat on a branch. "There are so many voices in your head telling you that you can't. You need to find the still, small voice telling you that you *can*. So, we're going to play a listening game."

"What sort of listening game?" Andrew asked, unconvinced.

Lorna smiled and motioned for him to sit on the branch across from her. He hesitated, but did as she asked.

"Have you ever played *See with Me*?" she asked.

Andrew shook his head.

"No, I suppose you haven't. It's an old Human game. In *See with Me*, one person says, 'See with me something...' and then names a color or shape. The other person has to guess what it is. It's a bit like that, except we'll both have our eyes closed. We start by trying to hear what each other is hearing," she explained. "Then, we take turns creating sounds."

"Creating sounds?" Andrew asked, suspicion coloring his voice.

Lorna smiled a sly, knowing smile. There was more to this game than she let on. The idea was to begin by simply listening. But then they would move on to calling things into their circle, small animals or perhaps a thundercloud. It was more a conjuring game than a listening game, but listening was important.

"What do you think?" she asked.

Andrew sighed.

"I heard that," she said with a smile.

He looked away.

"Do you trust me?" she asked him.

He was hesitant, then replied, "Yes."

"Then, please. Close your eyes."

He did so.

"Now. Listen." She was silent for a few moments, then softly asked, "Do you hear anything?"

What he heard was a thought in his head telling him that this was ridiculous, but he didn't want to tell her that.

"Anything at all?"

He sighed again and decided to try. After all, what could it hurt?

Andrew sat still for several minutes, then said, "I don't hear anything."

"Keep listening."

He took a deep breath and kept listening, but there was nothing. He shook his head. "I don't hear anything. This is foolish."

"You don't hear the finch in the tree above us?"

"What does a finch have to do with intuition?"

"It's not about the finch. It's about quieting yourself—first to hear, then to feel—the intuition surrounding us. It's like music."

Andrew stood up. "I should get going."

Lorna raised a hand. "Please don't." Her voice was gentle but firm. "It's easier for children to learn because their imaginations are so vivid—they're always looking for the unseen around every corner. But you've spent your whole life without this. It might come to you slowly... but it will come."

Andrew ran a hand through his hair. "Have you ever considered that maybe I'm just not intuitive?"

18

Lorna took a breath and let the silence settle between them. "Have you ever considered that maybe you are?"

"But I thought Humans weren't intuitive."

Lorna nodded. "It's true. Most Humans never were, but it isn't because intuition is not available to us, it's just that our people were always hungry for other things. They never slowed down and quieted themself enough to do what we're doing now. After all, I'm Human," she said.

She motioned her hands in the shape of a sphere, took a deep breath, and moved in a way that looked like she pulled something unseen out of herself as the air around her became fog that liquified into a sphere of water about the size of an apple floating between her hands. Her eyes were fierce.

"Nachtanii mel beroshe!" she said as the sphere twisted into the shape of a small elemental water dragon that stretched forth its long neck and wide wings, then shook and screeched. As it stood on its hind legs in her palm, ready to take flight, she pulled her hands apart, and the creature vanished into a splash of water.

Andrew was deeply moved. He had never even heard of such a thing.

"I truly believe you *are* intuitive, but that doesn't matter," she said, sorrow coloring her voice. "*You* have to believe you are intuitive."

Andrew swallowed and played with the possibility in his mind, however remote. Then he sat back down on the branch.

Lorna looked up at him. "Grandson?"

He met her eyes and saw the loving, compassionate look of a mother looking back at him; a look he had always so deeply longed to find; a look that pierced right through him; a look that turned him into that believing little boy once again. "Yes, Grandma?" He had only one other time called her this.

She smiled. "I release you from feeling like you have anything at all to prove to me. Just be. Just...be."

Andrew took a deep breath. Then he closed his eyes again.

For several minutes, he said nothing. It was hard for him to silence the voices in his mind. First, the doubt. Then the list of things he still had to do to open his shop and get ready for the wedding. Then the voice of Lithuel asking him to pick up some bread before returning home. Lithuel. He hadn't seen Lithuel for several days. And Jasper. How was Jasper? He took another deep breath, trying to calm himself and quiet his mind. He was nearly bored before the voices silenced themselves enough that he could hear himself breathing. He began noticing the gentle breeze rustling through the trees and a finch, high above them, singing to the rising sun. Another finch in the distance sang back, with its beautiful warble chirps, so bright and happy. Then he heard a distant deer call through the forest.

"There! I heard that!" he told her.

But there was no reply.

"Lorna?"

She didn't respond.

Andrew slowly opened his eyes. The forest around him was glowing a million shades of iridescence, like the glow of a lantern fly. Lorna looked like she was on fire with wisps of blue and green rising from her skin and hair—her eyes still closed, and her hands stretched to the sunlight pouring down through the glowing trees like a waterfall of thick golden vapor.

Andrew was overwhelmed at the sight that he fell backward off the branch, the vision immediately vanishing. He scrambled to his feet. "What...what was that?" he asked, his heart racing.

Lorna slowly opened her eyes. "What did you hear?"

"I began to hear the breeze and the finch. Then I thought I heard a buck through the trees, but when I opened my eyes, everything was glowing!"

Lorna slowly stood. "Glowing, you say?"

Andrew dusted himself off and nodded. "You were glowing too. It was like you were on fire with blue-green flames."

"You saw this?"

Andrew quickly nodded. "What was it?"

She thought for a moment. She wasn't sure.

"Have you not seen anything like it?" he asked her.

Lorna looked back at him and shook her head. "No. I have not." Then her eyes widened. "Chimcary?"

Chimcary? Where had he heard that word before?

"Perhaps it was chimcary. But that's extraordinary!" she said.

"What's chimcary?"

"It is the intuition that connects all of the natural world. But I've never..."

"I want to see it again!" Andrew exclaimed as he began to realize that maybe he *was* intuitive.

"Okay, let's just take a moment and try to understand what's happening," she replied, but Andrew quickly returned to the tree branch, closed his eyes, and listened again. Only, this time, he was quite excited.

There was no silence; he heard no breeze.

He opened his eyes, but all he saw was Lorna sitting back on the branch with a look of concern. She took a deep breath and held out her hands again, trying to be patient with her grandson. She knew he couldn't force it, but she said nothing.

Andrew closed his eyes again, trying to hear the finch through the trees, but he could not. He leaned forward, grasping at the sound of the distant buck with his ears, but all he felt was tight frustration growing in his chest. A sense of embarrassment and foolishness swept over him again, and he tried to ignore it, but it took root and began to grow.

*Who are you to think you are intuitive?* a voice in his mind asked. *Humans aren't intuitive. Perhaps you were just imagining things. How can a child's game help? You're not a child.*

"Stop," Andrew told himself. "*It is real. Lorna is intuitive.*"

*That doesn't mean you are intuitive,* the voice said back.

"But I used the Warming Rod."

*You nearly burned your house down. Maybe it was the Warming Rod that was intuitive.*

He tried to push the voice away, but it grew louder.

*Nothing but a tinker,* the voice said. *Tinker, tinker, fix yer' wares, 'cause I can't do a darn thing to help anybody, not even myself.*

"Stop," he told himself, gritting his teeth and turning his head in discomfort.

The voices of children began laughing at him in his mind. Housewives pointing. Grown men threatening. *Tinker here. Tinker here. Nothing ever more than a tinker here. Nothing more than a pale white husk of a worthless tinker here.*

"Enough!" Andrew screamed as the adrenaline of the anger and pain flushed out of him, and he fell forward from the branch onto his hands and knees. As he did, a wave of blue light burst from him, knocking Lorna off her branch, which might have killed her if she hadn't shielded herself at the last moment.

Andrew gasped for breath. *Where did that come from?* he wondered.

He slowly picked himself up and looked around.

Every living thing around him for nearly fifty feet was dead, except for Lorna, as a small plume of red and brown finch feathers slowly drifted to the ground around him.

# CHAPTER 5

L orna stepped down from her carriage onto the cobblestone street of Nevarii. She wore a black robe with a high collar, accented with purple velvet and grey lace. Purple beads, sewn into the fabric of her dress in the shapes of constellations, began to faintly glow in the growing moonlight.

She reached into her coach and removed her long, grey staff; its end covered in a small black velvet sack cinched shut. Then she lifted a pale grey stone hanging from a chain around her neck as her coach, driver, and the four, winged skeletal horses pulling it vanished, the pale grey stone becoming a small, intricate replica of the coach and horses —a netsuke, or carved figurine in the common tongue, now slightly warm to the touch.

It was dusk in Nevarii, the time of night when most of the city either locked up for the evening or came alive with the heartbeat of the after-hours Dym trade. This particular street was quiet and in an affluent neighborhood.

Lorna looked to the clouds. The raven moon slowly

crept across the sky like a matriarch ascending her throne. As it did, she felt her robe shifting and coming to life.

A candle in the window of one of the homes flickered in the growing darkness, and a pelmot, with its large nocturnal eyes and fur-covered wings, quietly watched her from a nearby rooftop.

To most, the raven moon was simply beautiful. But to Lorna, the raven light held the possibility of both dreams and despair. She knew that at precisely midnight, for one night a month, and for precisely one second, the threshold between the waking and sleeping worlds was indiscernible and could be crossed. A single second of time might not seem like much, but to the sleeping, a moment could last forever. It is said that a great Magis of the Algi lived an entire lifetime one night a month for decades, amassing such incalculable knowledge through his centuries of study that one day he simply vanished, never to be seen again. Some say he learned to travel entire worlds, and even time itself, through the sleeping, but who can know if such legends are true?

Lorna knew that crossing through the raven light into the dreaming was both dangerous and difficult. She hoped it was worth the risk and she was as prepared as anyone could be.

The street felt both familiar and strange to Lorna. Once, it had been her and her daughter's summer home, but much had changed in the twenty-three years since her last visit. The row of houses remained mostly the same, and the King's Arms carvery still carried the rich scents of roast pork, finger pies, and ale. But a clothier's shop now occupied the place on the street where her home had once stood. She had owned the land, but years of unpaid taxes must have returned it to public holding, which did not concern her. Her mind was set on the far more complicated tasks that lay ahead.

First, she had to find somewhere safe to sleep and around as few people as possible. She had considered an inn, but there was no inn in this part of town. Next, she would cast a complicated stillness word of intuition, which became more difficult and far more dangerous the more people affected by it. Finally, she would pass into the sleeping where she would see and interact with a reflection of the waking world. That was the plan anyway.

Lorna looked around and waited as an elderly man finished crossing the end of the street. Then she took a deep breath. She had sung the spell to herself several times without her staff to make sure she got the notes and timing just right, but she couldn't be completely certain without actually casting it. No more practice. No more waiting. She was running out of time.

"Eem nee lefeem nee. Ez pelculum la feem nee, stillness now," she whispered, lifting her staff above her head.

As she spoke, the flickering candle stopped flickering.

It was quiet now, but it didn't just sound quiet, it almost *felt* quiet, as though she had thick fabric over her ears.

She approached one of the homes with a short, black gate in front of a tiny picture garden, round windows and a brass knocker in the shape of a smoking pipe on the front door. She rapped three times on the door, but there was no answer. That was a good sign. She hoped there would be no answer. If the word of stillness worked, everyone within a two-block radius should be asleep. If it hadn't, someone might think she was breaking into their home. Now, to know for sure. She rubbed her fingers together for luck, then turned the handle. It was locked. She motioned her staff and heard a click, then tried the handle again, and the heavy wooden door slowly opened.

"Hello!" she called in. "I don't mean to intrude, but..." She saw the glowing hearth down the narrow hall in the kitchen. Its flames did not dance; its light did not flicker, so she crossed the threshold and closed the door behind her.

The home was beautiful with furniture half the size of what Lorna was used to. Painted portraits of a Bantam couple and their two small children smiled at her from where they hung, waist high, on the walls. Two comfortable-looking chairs sat in the living room in front of a smoldering hearth that did not crackle, though she could still feel its heat. Next to the chairs were tiny round tables with ash trays holding several smoking pipes. Children's toys and socks lay scattered around the floor. The largest Bantam Lorna had ever met was about the size of an eight-year-old Human child, and she knew them by their more antiquated name of Halfling.

Lorna smiled and continued down the hall, looking for a place to sleep and trying to determine if anyone was still awake. The floorboards did not creak and her staff made very little sound as it touched wood.

She leaned into an office that smelled of leather, parchment, and rich tobacco where a desk held parchments, quills, ink, and what looked like a trade map of the area with well-worn edges. A second table in the cozy office drew Lorna closer. She had always been fascinated by other people's homes—the minutia of their lives. The table was stained brown with rows of jars of dried leaf, each labeled like her jars at home, but these were varietals of smoking herbs. A brass scale with an official seal in its base sat to one side of the desk, and next to it, an odd slender brass pipe with a shallow bowl and a cloth to wipe it clean, stained from countless tastings.

Above the office hearth hung several dozen smoking pipes of every shape, size, and color. One was barely the size of her finger, labeled 'Timar', a race of Pixie from the western country. Another was so large, she thought it half the size of the hearth itself, carved from some dark grey stone, with three large bowls and a large stone fist grasping the stem.

There were three rooms on the second floor. The first had a surprisingly large—considering the couple's small size—four-poster bed with piled blankets and a motionless husband and wife. The wife's head was wrapped in floral fabric, and one of the husband's short legs, with its hair-covered toes, kicked out from beneath the covers.

"Hello?" Lorna quietly asked. There was no answer. "Excuse me?" she asked louder. Having to be sure, she banged her staff against the floor, which made nothing more than a muffled thud. The sleeping couple did not move.

She turned and went to the second room. It was storage, full of various bolts of fabric, sacks of old clothing and currently unused Eden Vale decorations. This wouldn't do.

The third room was the children's nursery, decorated in a cheerful blue-and-yellow happy-dragon theme. There was a dragon-shaped wooden rocker in one corner and a nightstand in the other holding a small oil lamp in the shape of a nest of dragon eggs. Plush dragon toys sat in rows along shelves low enough for the children to reach, and a device sat near a bed in the shape of a baby dragon puffing motionless steam from its nostrils.

On either side of the room, two small beds—painted to resemble dragon nests—held their sleeping occupants.

Over each bed, a mother dragon-shaped canopy stretched her wings wide, watching over two small children curled beneath her in matching winged dragon pajamas.

This seemed like a cozy, happy home to her, but it would not serve her purposes; there was nowhere for her to sleep, so she turned and left.

As she made her way to the second house on the street, she looked again to the sky. It was almost time.

With a wave of her staff, she unlocked the second door and quickly entered. These halls smelled of fabric and glue and looked like the same layout as the first house. Only one armchair sat in this living room, and next to it stood a mannequin draped in a suit of blue floral fabric. The second room on the ground floor had a large, slightly tilted table with a tall chair. Quick sketches of different variations of the same outfit lay scattered on the table next to piles of fabric samples, spools of thread, square pieces of red and green chalk, jars of pins, and a pair of gold, ornately etched scissors. Bolts of cut fabric leaned against a wall, and framed sketches and paintings of gowns and uniforms adorned the walls. Upstairs, where the nursery had been in the last home, was a platform in front of three mirrors with racks of the finest outfits Lorna had ever seen.

As she opened the door to the main bedroom, someone shifted and rolled over in bed. Lorna froze, her heart pounding. It was so dark she couldn't be sure if they had actually moved or if she had just imagined it. And if they had, why? How? Was the spell already fading? If she were caught for being a thief, she could be imprisoned or worse, depending on local law. Even an accusation of thievery might disrupt her standing as a midwife. No court in the area would welcome her again.

As her eyes adjusted to the darkness, she quickly realized it was an Inkling man, probably in his fifties, asleep in the bed. He had gold rings on his fingers, a dark blue kerchief on his head, and a black mask over his eyes. This relieved her and meant this house would not do either; she had to cautiously and immediately leave. She knew Inklings were unaffected by intuition.

The man yawned, scratched his forehead, and slowly sat up in bed.

Lorna didn't hesitate to quickly and quietly make her way downstairs and out the front door, grateful that even if the man wasn't affected by her intuition, the floorboards still were.

Now, back outside, she sighed in relief. This was already proving trickier than she was comfortable with, and she hadn't even crossed over yet.

The color of the gems on her robe and the tingle growing down the back of her neck suggested she could miss her opportunity if she didn't find somewhere safe to sleep in the next few minutes.

The third home was decorated with details of a naval family. A model of a naval man-of-war sat in a glass case in the hall along with a naval captain's hat, coat, and various sealed letters of commendation.

She didn't have much time now, so she quickly glanced around the living room, kitchen and dining room with its large dining table and brass naval-themed candelabra. There were no signs of anyone awake. Moving more carefully this time, she ascended the stairs to a garden room filled with ornate pots and blooming flowers. In the corner, a gilded cage held a small orchid drake with purple and white scales. It sat with one wing over its head as though cleaning itself when Lorna's stillness spell took effect. This was a very good sign. She carefully opened the door to the main bedroom. There was no movement. As much as she didn't want a repeat of the last house, she had to be sure everyone was properly tranquilized, or she would have to scrap her plans and return another night. She could not risk anyone finding her while she was asleep.

"Hello?" she asked.

There was no answer.

She approached a large bed in the center of the room where an elderly Nimic woman lay with her long white hair pinned up in tight curls, and Lorna asked again, "Excuse me?"

Nothing.

She rapped her staff against the floor twice. Still nothing.

That was good enough for her. If her staff could not wake the woman, then Lorna should be able to see to her business and get out before anything else would. There was also a lazy chair near the wall, which might work for her purposes, but she would prefer a bit more privacy if she could find it.

She quickly checked the room where the children had been sleeping in the first house and found what she was looking for. Her robe was beginning to grasp as the doorposts as she passed through them. It was a sitting room with painted art on the walls, a card table in the center of the polished wood floor, and a delicate tea hutch in one corner. Then she found a plush reading chair near a lamp by the window.

*That will do nicely,* she thought to herself. *I should only need it for a few minutes.*

She looked out the window. The raven moon was high in the sky. It was time. The hem of her robe moved around her like the web of a waking octopus. She looked down at the beaded raven moon on her right side. It, too, suggested she only had a few moments left by the strength of its blue-purple glow.

Now for her next trick.

Lorna sat in the chair and removed a small velvet pouch from the inside pocket of her robe. It contained something heavy. She opened the sack and looked in. It was a heavy, white gravestone. She made herself comfortable in the armchair, nestled her staff into the corner of her arm, and took a deep breath. *This is worth it,* she reminded herself. *Come what may, this is necessary. He needs some answers, and so do I. I don't even know if my baby girl is alive.* Then she dropped the heavy stone into her hand and held her hand out to the side of the chair, resting her elbow on the armrest. The moment she touched the stone, she felt its powerful sleep intuition pull at her mind. She could feel her arms becoming heavy, her head leaden, her eyes like sandpaper. She was suddenly so dreadfully tired. She squeezed the stone, but the muscles in her hand trembled. It felt like she hadn't slept in days. She had to hold onto it long enough to sleep deep enough to cross into the dreaming, and then she would have to drop it and hope that she would wake up before anyone found her. If she didn't drop it, she might never wake. She was losing hold of her reason. Where was she? What was she doing in this strange room? Hold on. Just hold on. That's all you need to know. She was becoming nervous.

Then she was gone.

# CHAPTER 6

Lorna now stood in the tea room of the elderly Nimic woman's home, but everything was dark and hazy, and fine details were harder to see. The gravestone hung in mid-air next to her chair, where it had fallen from her hand. She took a deep breath. The spell had worked. She had until the stone hit the ground in the waking world to find out what had happened to her daughter. The stones on her robe shone brightly, illuminating patches of the room like detailed strokes on a blurry painting. She felt lightheaded like she had had a bit too much wine; however, the snug embrace of her robe steadied her, comforting her like a firm hand at her side.

Outside, the candle in the window gave no light. It looked more like an image of a candle than a real source of light, and she knew she could reach through the wall and touch it if she wanted to since the rules here were different than those in the waking world. Everything from the waking world existed here, but it was a blur and unreliable unless it was a part of her memory. If she knew it personally, then her memory would fill in the missing details. If she did not, it was unreliable. She could travel halfway around the world to a mythic mountain, but would the mountain be real or a figment of her imagination? Here, it could be either—or both at the same time. The sleeping world was a place of joy and healing to those visitors whose minds and imaginations were set on positive things—a place where they could explore or visit long-dead family. However, to those whose minds were not set on whatsoever was good and peaceful, the sleeping world could be a land of such incredible tortures of their own making—an oubliette of monsters with unquenchable appetites. And if these dualities were not dangerous enough, beyond the sleepers' own imaginings existed very real beings that might exert their own will upon the sleepers. One such being caused her the gravest concern.

To find what she was looking for, Lorna must steady her mind against her own imaginings and simply observe. If she could do this, she could visit any moment in history and watch it unfold. However, if she engaged with what she was seeing, either mentally or emotionally, it would become unreliable or worse. She might begin to see what she wanted to see, not what had actually happened. Her greatest hopes and worst fears would manifest themselves in this mirror version of her world, which meant she needed to be quick and quiet.

Lorna returned to the corner of the street where her home once stood. The clothier was now gone and her two-story summer townhouse welcomed her with more clarity than anything else on the street since she had known it so well for so many years.

She could hear her and her daughter, Silva, arguing upstairs. This was the last time she would ever see her.

In front of the townhouse, a younger Lithuel leaned into Lorna's coach, wiping down the back seat with a rag where he had just finished setting a row of copper buttons.

She approached him.

He wouldn't know she was there unless she interacted with him, so she just watched him for a few moments with warmth and admiration. The past six months, they had gotten to know each other well over conversations about life and Andrew. She had grown to admire this man's craftsmanship and his unquenchable heart for her grandson. Never having any children of his own, he had taken in the orphan Human child and loved and protected him as his own. As he wiped the handle of her coach door and smiled proudly at the work well done, she wondered how difficult it must have been for him. How would he feed such a small child? What medicine does a Human child need? The constant late-night feedings and nappy changing. He so easily could have left Andrew to die or dropped him at the home of a midwife, but would a Human child survive? Would he be accepted or disposed of?

Baby Andrew cried out from the upstairs bedroom as Lithuel went to the front door of the townhouse and knocked. Lorna followed him.

"Do I have to have Jinto see you to your coach?" came Lorna's voice from behind the door.

"I'm not a child, mother!" Silva yelled. Then the bolt clicked, and the door opened.

Hearing the argument made Lorna's heart sink. If she knew then what she knew now, might she have been easier on Silva, more patient? She hoped she would have, but it's hard not to project one's fears and regrets on one's own children.

The younger Lorna opened the door and brushed a stray hair from her face. "Yes?"

"Oh, ma-lady, I'm sorry to bother. I wasn't expecting..."

"Yes. You will have to excuse me. My manservant is otherwise occupied at the moment. What can I do for you?"

"He's hired me to fix your coach seats," Lithuel replied, stepping back from the front door into the street. Silva watched them from behind sheer curtains on the second floor. Seeing her daughter in the upstairs window for the first time in more than twenty years absolutely tore her in half. She thought she was prepared for this, but maybe she wasn't—maybe she wasn't at all.

As Lithuel and her younger self discussed his pay and the details of his work, Lorna carefully stepped past them and went upstairs. She watched Silva turn from the front window, crying, and it felt like time slowed. The bedroom was just as she had last seen it. Sheets covered most of the furniture.

Silva's bedroom smelled like her, which caught Lorna off guard. She wasn't expecting how visceral and real it would feel—the beautiful lightness of seeing her daughter's face. The tightening in her chest to hold her. Her trembling hands. Her dry throat. So real. Too real. She could get lost in this moment and quickly forget the waking world— the true world—even existed. This place would engulf her, giving her everything she could ever want—very literally anything she could imagine. Somewhere between now and forever, she would forget her cottage, her grandson, and her life as they were. Andrew would change from the shy, confused, and often frustrated young man that he now was into the handsome, confident, and capable leader Lorna imagined him to be. Silva would love her again, never leaving, always agreeing. They could all live together. She could watch Silva raise Andrew and be the kind of mother he deserved. Lorna and her daughter could watch Andrew raise his children or even grandchildren if it pleased her—and it would. However, at the end of the fairy tale, she *would* one day wake in the tea room of a Nimic woman's house with all of the same problems she had now. Only, she would wake with no answers for Andrew or knowledge of where her daughter had gone in the real world.

She stepped back out into the hall and steadied herself against her staff—her robe tightening in a comforting embrace around her as it sensed her wavering resolve. *This isn't Silva,* she reminded herself. *It just looks like her.* But her heart ached to hold her daughter just the same. *This is why I've come. I knew I would see her. Mourn later!* She took another deep breath, shook off her sorrow, and returned to the bedroom.

Silva now sat on the edge of the bed, tucking her long blonde hair back behind her ears.

*She is so beautiful; so much of her father.* Lorna thought to herself as she heard a giggle. She turned to see a six-year-old Silva bound down the hall, into the bedroom, and jump on the bed. Then suddenly, a sixteen-year-old Silva leaned over the dresser, touching her lips with a bit of rouge. All three, here at the same time, in this imagined mirror version of reality.

Lorna squeezed her eyes shut and leaned against her staff again. *Maybe I'm not strong enough. I thought I could do this; maybe I can't.* Then she remembered Andrew. Her beautiful grandson. The man he was quickly becoming. The boy without a mother. She focused on the warmth of her robe and its encouraging embrace. *Focus. You were downstairs with Lithuel as she was about to leave. What is she doing? Where is she going?*

Baby Andrew cried out again.

Lorna slowly opened her eyes, and the two youngest versions of her daughter were gone.

Jinto, their tall, slender butler of nearly twenty years stepped through Lorna like stepping through mist. "The young master is inconsolable, my lady. I believe he needs his mother. Shall I bring him to you?"

"No! No," Silva said, rising and turning from him. "I should finish packing." She wiped her eyes with a cloth from the nightstand.

Lorna watched her daughter twist the cloth in frustration and throw it in the waste bin. Try as she might, Lorna couldn't quite remember what they had been arguing about.

"The coach has arrived to take you and the young master to the wagonway station. Your bags are already downstairs," Jinto said.

"Fine," Silva replied, waving him away. She watched her mother through the front window once more, wiped her eyes, and went downstairs. Lorna followed.

As she began to leave, Silva paused for a moment in the hall and turned to a miniature pocket portrait of herself that her mother had painted when she turned eighteen, which sat in a glass case by the front door. She took the key from the top of the case, unlocked the cabinet, retrieved the portrait, and closed the case again.

Lorna watched Silva avoid the younger Lorna, who still spoke with Lithuel, and quickly entered the waiting carriage. In the waking world, she would never see her daughter again.

Lorna sat down in the carriage next to her daughter and the bundled baby Andrew, who had cried himself to sleep.

Silva watched through the coach window as the young

version of her mother handed something to Lithuel across the street, and older Lorna thought she saw sorrow in her daughter's eyes.

"Very kind of you, ma'am," Lithuel said, petting his horse and climbing onto his wagon seat.

"Where are we headed?" an elderly Longbeard asked from the driver's seat of Silva's coach.

"The wagonway," Sylva replied.

They were leaving the part of town Lorna could remember most clearly and had cast the stillness spell over, which meant she would soon be heavily under the influence of the turbulent sleeping world.

As they rode, Lorna intently watched her daughter, wondering what she was thinking or where she might be going. Or did her daughter even know? She ached to hold her, but every time she felt herself beginning to grieve, she would imagine the emotion as a miniature painting that she would lock in a box in her mind until she could safely sort through her feelings back home in the waking world.

Lorna noticed a scratching sound, a gentle tap, tap, tapping, like a rapping at her door. But she told herself: *Tis the wind and nothing more.*

The coach pulled up to the wagonway station where the faded, dim shapes of well-dressed passengers of every race bustled about trying to catch their transport, talking to porters, and struggling to keep their children away from the massive ferlorn that pulled the two, four, or six wagon chains hovering with a blue glow above stone tracks. Children were always fascinated by the massive, six-legged, wooly creatures because of the much smaller calves that often accompanied them. A porter in navy blue, pinstriped trousers, matching pinstriped hat, and buttoned-up white shirt rolled at the sleeves opened Silva's door, snapped a finger for a younger porter to fetch her bags, and reached for her hand. "Destination, m'lady?" he asked. The porter's face was blurred beyond recognition.

"I haven't decided yet," Silva replied, turning to collect Andrew. For the faintest moment, Lorna thought Silva looked directly at her. Then she took the still-sleeping child and departed the coach.

*Haven't decided yet?* Lorna wondered. Silva was supposed to be taking the wagonway north to the posh Aeltharion Academy in Eldrósk to study diplomacy; however, Lorna knew from contacting the headmaster several weeks later that Silva had never arrived. Then she remembered that they had been arguing about whether Silva could to take care of the baby while she attended school. Lorna wanted Silva to leave Andrew with her; however, Silva wanted to take a year off, but Lorna forbade it.

Lorna was suddenly back in their townhouse—*not* where she wanted to be.

"You don't think I can take care of my own child!" Silva screamed.

"You're sixteen! What could you possibly know about taking care of a baby? I'm simply trying to help," the younger Lorna hollered.

"Then let me stay!"

"If you don't go to school now, you never will. You'll end up as a..."

"A wash woman? Isn't that what you're afraid of, mother? That I'll end up scrubbing socks for a living? And what's so wrong with that?"

"I have fought too hard..."

Silva rolled her eyes. "Oh, cut it, *mother*. You inherited.

40

Heir of the House of Rhenald. Holder of the Sacred Chalice and all that."

"Do you have any idea what I went through to get you into the academy?"

Of course, she knew. Lorna hadn't let a day go by without mentioning what it had cost her calling in old favors.

Baby Andrew screamed from the other room.

Older Lorna closed her eyes and tried to focus—tried to *feel* where she had been, in the coach with her daughter at the wagonway station. Suddenly, it was quiet. She was back in the coach. Lorna tried to breathe through the rising sense of motion sickness, then climbed out.

A raven sat on a stone bust above the wagonway station door, watching Lorna, and when she saw it, she froze. While everything around it was like shifting shades of shape and memory, the details of this dark creature were finer than any detail in the waking world, as though she was seeing it with more than her eyes. Its wings so black they were iridescent purple. Its eyes somehow glistened with knowing.

"Well, hello," a voice like velvet spoke from somewhere unseen.

She looked around but saw only the hustling, bustling shapes of people trying to catch their carriages.

Silva was almost out of sight, so Lorna ignored the bird and quickly followed her daughter into the station. Inside, Lorna couldn't read any of the text on the destination boards or signs hanging throughout the bustling station. They were details too granular for her sleeping mind to grasp, even with the help of the stones in her robe. She watched her daughter wait in line, but just before Silva reached the counter, she stepped out of line and sat down on one of the wooden benches, crying.

"Last call for the Eldrósk 2:15," a wagon master called from somewhere beyond what Lorna could see. "Last call!"

Silva looked up with uncertainty. Then she looked down at baby Andrew, asleep in her arms. Lorna was utterly heartbroken that she had put her daughter in this position. Why wasn't she more patient? Why hadn't she given her more room to blossom? Countless regrets.

Time slowed again. Silva's hair was frazzled and her eyes puffy from the morning's arguing, but she was still so beautiful. Lorna wanted to embrace her—feeling her mind beginning to slip again. She took a deep breath and felt her robe tighten.

*Where are you going?* Lorna wanted to ask her, but interacting with Silva would all but guarantee that whatever happened next wasn't true to the actual events, and she may never find her daughter in the waking. Whether Silva ever got on the wagonway to Eldrósk was one of the questions Lorna came to answer. Did she make it to Eldrósk and not go to school? Had she lived in Eldrósk for some amount of time? Had something happened to her there? Or had she never even made it onto the wagonway?

Time sped up and spun past them—the movement and bustle of the station turned into noise around them. Lorna watched Silva sit with her baby for what must have been hours—holding him, watching him, nursing him after he woke, then back to sleep again. Silva's countenance changed and time normalized when she saw something across the street: a tinker's cart.

Leaving her bags behind, Silva left the station and crossed the street to a tool shop where the cart sat in sharp detail because of how well Lorna knew this particular wagon. It was Lithuel's.

As Lorna followed Silva across the street, a robed figure watched her through one of the station windows.

Silva's eyes welled up with tears as she looked down at the sleeping Andrew and kissed his cheek. "You were loved," she whispered to him, her words catching in her throat. Then she took her miniature painted portrait from her pocket, tucked it into his folded blanket, and laid him in the cart, pulling a bit of tarp over him to hide him. Noticing a piece of marking charcoal, Silva glanced up. Lithuel was still in the shop, so she quickly pulled back the tarp and scribbled something on the back of the portrait before tucking the child away again. "I'll never forget you," she whispered. Then she turned and slipped into a nearby alley, covering her sobs with her hand.

Lithuel came out from the tool shop, set a small wooden box in the back of the cart, and climbed onto the driver's bench.

Silva watched from the shadows as Lithuel's cart left with her sleeping babe hidden beneath a dirty tarp.

*What drove you to leave him with a stranger? Why didn't you just give him to me?* Lorna wondered, but sometimes the most important questions are never answered. Lorna could not hold back the waves of agony. She was losing her daughter and her helpless infant grandson all in this broken shard of a nightmare that cut like a rusty knife.

Then, everything around her became utterly still.

Lorna looked around. All of the movement of the busy street was frozen.

The robed figure watched her from across the street. "What are you doing here?" he asked.

The twilight stones in her robe shone their brightest,

and her robe tightened like a glove around her. However, the figure waved two fingers calmly through the air as the stones went dark, and the robe fell loose like simple cloth. When they did, her mind suddenly listed like a small boat in a violent ocean, and she almost fell over. Panic and confusion engulfed her. Without her robe and the focusing power of her stones, she was at the mercy of the sleeping world. *Where am I?* she wondered. Everything around her shifted so quickly that she felt like she would be sick.

"Why have you crossed through the raven right?" the figure asked.

But instead of answering, Lorna quickly pulled the velvet sack off of the end of her staff as something like bright sunlight shone out of a large amber stone set in its end.

The robed figure shielded his face from the light as he summoned a cloud of ravens that poured over the rooftops like crashing ocean waves, surrounding Lorna.

She stumbled back in fear, almost dropping her staff, but the birds did not touch her, only encircled her in a cloud so thick, the light of her sunstone could no longer reach the robed figure. Then, through the frantically fluttering birds, she could see the figure's visage harden towards her.

*I have to wake up,* she finally realized. She blinked and tried to focus, but the ravens, larger than any she had ever seen, screeched around her, throwing her mind into violent confusion.

*Wake, wake, wake!* she told herself, but it wasn't working. She wasn't waking up! Then, the sunstone at the end of her staff flickered out.

The ravens broke formation and disappeared over the rooftops as the figure stepped toward her. Lorna pulled the sunstone close and blew into it, trying to reignite it, but the robed figure held out a hand as the dim stone suddenly appeared in his fingertips.

"Wake!" she screamed as loud as she could, but wake she would not. Then she bit her lip to bleeding and immediately awoke to the loud crack of the white gravestone hitting the wood floor of the Nimic woman's tearoom where she had fallen asleep—the taste of blood filling her mouth.

# CHAPTER 7

T he following day, the tiny painted portrait of Silva, who Andrew now knew was his mother, sat on a small shelf above his workbench watching him as he held a spiral torsion spring tight with a pair of tweezers that he had fashioned himself. He carefully looked through a crudely fashioned leather magnifying glass and set the spring in place, hoping the wound metal ribbon would steadily power the tiny hands of his timepiece.

Andrew was slender and wore beige pin-striped trousers, his favorite well-worn leather boots, and a dark green vest Feyloren had gifted to him. His hair had begun to show some curl as he let it grow out a little at Feyloren's request. She was fascinated with his hair, perhaps because she had none.

His workroom was cozy and located at the back of his store where rows of tools hung on the walls—tools stained with the oil of Lithuel's hands from years of use. A bookshelf built by Lithuel held sketches, jars of tiny gears, and some heavier tools that didn't make sense to hang. A new harness for Brynlee hung from a leather padded bench, and jars of marking charcoal and oil sat on his worktable next to clay molds of gears of various sizes. A unique brass lamp hung over his workbench fashioned from a stone Lorna had given him as a gift. It was intuitive and would glow brighter or dimmer at his will, allowing for more than enough light to work at all hours of the day or night.

Neither he nor Lithuel had ever heard of a tinker setting up shop since so much of what they did was service and repair metal items that didn't need mending often enough to support a stationary store. Even so, Andrew hoped to make it more than just a corner shop to sharpen knives and mend pots. He wanted to sell some of his and Lithuel's gadgets—maybe even travel to the larger cities once a month to collect useful consumables like teefite. Perhaps he could even return with a small collection of various gift items, like children's toys or etched spoons. He also had the idea of selling miniature versions of Lorna's stone as intuitive lamps. While Jatoba wasn't quite large enough to support the size of his dream fully realized, he planned on finding ways to encourage passersby to explore his offerings and talk about his store in nearby towns. Perhaps even offer discounts to tavern owners in nearby villages to encourage them to chat about his store with their patrons. The possibilities were endless, and he couldn't be more excited.

He hoped to open the store in time for the wedding and wanted to reveal his timepiece at the grand opening.

"That should do it," he said to himself, setting the tweezers aside. He rubbed his fingers together for luck, like his grandmother often did, and pulled a small brass pin that held everything in motionless tension until he was ready for the device to spring to life, and spring to life it did. Four small gears and a larger fifth gear began to spin, transferring energy to a cone-shaped pulley with a spiral grove. Click, click, click, a large central gear with sharper teeth sounded as a small silver arm clicked back and forth, controlling the speed at which the wound spring released its energy.

He turned the clock to see its face and waited. Click. The tiny arm moved, and his heart jumped. Click. It moved again, and his heart jumped again. Excitement flushed over him and he sprang from his stool, knocking it over. He wouldn't know for certain how accurate it was until he measured it against the movement of the sun.

When suddenly there was a loud crash.

He set the monocle and clock aside and ran out to the front of his store where half-built tables sat empty, dust covered the floor, and a partially painted sign leaned against the wall. His front window had a gaping hole, and broken glass lay scattered across the floor.

Andrew ran into the street, trying to see who had smashed his window, but there was no sign of anyone obvious. Then he turned to see the large red mark painted on his door. The offending brush lie in the middle of the street in a splatter of red.

The first time he had seen the mark, he had no idea what it meant. It took him three days to get Feyloren to tell him what it was, and when she did, she only whispered it to him: humatii, a racial slur. She had explained to him that it was a Longbeard word that strictly meant 'pale face' but implied much more. He had since heard it from someone in the tavern, whom Brutste immediately threw out. Andrew had called Jatoba home for nearly six months now, and he thought most of the town welcomed him and didn't care that he was a Human, but clearly, someone cared.

He touched the dripping paint and smelled his fingers. Dread swept over him as he realized it wasn't paint.

He looked up and down the street again, but only a few townspeople were moving about and didn't seem to pay any mind to what had happened. Then he met the gaze of the veg stand owner's wife watching him from across the street. Her face was apologetic as she stepped into the street, carrying a cloth and a bucket of water. She picked up the blood-stained brush, wrapped it in cloth, and splashed away the blood in the street. Then she returned to her store. He could almost hear her heart breaking for him, but she said nothing to Andrew. Her body language told him that she was deeply ashamed that this had happened in her town, but he was still an outsider—still other.

Andrew returned to his shop, found a broom, and began sweeping up the glass. It was the third time this had happened since moving into the shop and the small flat above it.

As Andrew swept, the front door opened.

"I'm sorry, we're closed. Perhaps in two weeks... or maybe never," he murmured under his breath.

"Are you the tinker?" asked an Inkling standing barely the height of a table, with hedgehog-like features and long orange and red braids tied back on his head. He wore a grey coat, a red neck scarf, and a leather harness of pouches. He also carried a bedroll at his side and a traveler's pack on his back. "I'm lookin' for work."

Andrew dumped his pan full of broken glass into a waist pail. "I'm not looking for any help," Andrew replied.

The Inkling looked around. "It looks like you could use some."

Andrew didn't have the time or energy for this. "As I said, I'm closed, and I can't afford you." Andrew leaned the broom against the wall and knelt next to the broken pieces of the sign Feyloren had painted for him to hang above his windows. The rock that smashed his window must have broken it, which was even more infuriating. He picked up two of the largest pieces and tried to fit them together. Perhaps he could glue them.

"I'm not expensive. Somewhere to sleep. A meal. We can start there!"

"I'm sorry, I don't even have that to offer."

"But…"

Andrew held up a hand. "I'm sorry." Then he returned to his workshop, looking for something to cover the window until he could repair it.

"You can pay me later. I'm fast, reliable and my tiny fingers are good with small parts. You'll see," he hollered to Andrew from the front room. Andrew sighed deeply, tore off a long piece of brown paper from a roll, pinched off some sealing wax, and began massaging it in his fingers to make it more pliable. Then he went back up front, where he found the entire floor nearly swept and the window covered with a ridged frame of folded paper like a perfectly shaped origami window patch.

"Impressive," Andrew told him.

The little man finished his sweeping, dumped the pan into the pail and said, "That's nothing. That's just paper. You should see what I can do with a piece of tin."

Impressed as he was, and as nice as an extra set of hands sounded, Andrew still couldn't afford anyone. He wasn't sure if the shop would ever open, much less turn a profit. His daunting list of things to do seemed to be growing, not shrinking. He now had to fix the window, repair the sign, build more tables, set out some goods, create a price list, and on and on.

"I just can't afford anybody right now."

"But I..."

"Please, leave!" Andrew snapped and immediately regretted it. "I'm sorry. Just go."

The little man clenched his jaw, looked down at the broom, then slowly leaned it against the wall. "The name's Tomptee, and I'll be in town for two days. But once I leave, I'm aint comin' back," he said, hoisting his bedroll and backpack over his shoulder.

Tomptee stopped in the doorway, looking at the large red mark. "You need more help than you realize. I know something about being bullied. You can't let them push you around, or they'll never stop."

As Tomptee left, Lithuel rode up to the shop and dismounted the powerful black steed Lorna had gifted to him. He touched the charm around his neck as the steed vanished into mist. Lithuel still hadn't completely gotten used to that little trick. Then he looked at the vandalized door.

Andrew's heart sank at the embarrassment of his father seeing the horrible slur painted in blood.

# CHAPTER 8

A small brass bell tinkled above the front door of Daphne's shop as Feyloren entered. A beautiful glass-wing fairy, barely the size of Feyloren's thumbnail, flew toward her and smiled. She had iridescent-blue wings that were long, slender, and transparent like the wings of a dragonfly, and her skin was a beautiful pearlescent. Her name was Eet.

Feyloren smiled and held out her hand, which Eet landed upon.

"Hello," Feyloren said.

Eet smiled and curtseyed.

"Is Daph available?"

Eet nodded. While her kind had language, it was like butterfly song and couldn't be heard by most races much less understood. Eet flew off through a tiny door in the shop floor near the large windows overlooking Daphnie's arboretum that spread out beneath the herbalist's shop.

Feyloren looked around. The smell of rhumeum blossoms, hibiscus, and damp soil was in the air, which filled her

52

with a sense of joy and possibility. She picked up a small, red clay pot decorated with incredibly detailed designs of pastureland and rolling hills; a beautiful panorama of a land unknown to Feyloren. Tiny cattle and a small farmhouse were etched on one side, where a very small woman swept the front porch. When she saw Fey, she smiled and waved at her. Feyloren smiled and waved back. Fey knew not what sort of intuition this was, but it was beautiful. Then, the carefully sculpted and twisting arestee tree in the pot slowly opened a single eye set deep in a knot in its red bark and blinked at her. "Hello," Feyloren said. The eye slowly closed and reopened in an unspoken 'hello,' then gently closed again.

Feyloren set the pot back on its shelf and continued to look around the store.

Most of the plants had small, hand-written tags hanging from a loop of thread on a branch or tucked into a corner of their pot, but not all of them. The arrestee tree, for example, was too extraordinary of a specimen for Daphnie to ever part with. She would often rotate such unique items up from her arboretum for visitors to gaze at and hopefully talk about to their friends, eventually drawing them into the store for a purchase.

Then Feyloren approached the front counter where a pot about the size of a melon held a single tiny green shoot wrapped in a delicate translucent muslin cloth and tied with a yellow bow. Clippings of leaves, petals, and stems lay scattered around the counter and on the floor.

Daphnie climbed up through a door in the floor and smiled at Feyloren—her hooves glowing faintly. As she did, Fleur di Lis—Daphnie's small Sproutling, with child-like features and small pink flowers—stretched her branches out to pull herself up through the floor and quickly run over to Feyloren. "Fey!" she exclaimed in the beautiful voice of a small child.

"Hello, little one," Feyloren replied with a large smile. She gently picked her up and embraced her. In spring, Fleur di Lis wore a beautiful crown of tiny, freshly sprouted lime-green leaves dotted with clusters of small white flowers.

"Hello, friend!" Daphnie said. "It is getting harder and harder to climb these stairs without the help of intuition." She flattened the front of her dress, covered in pink and green embroidered flowers, and approached the counter. Daphnie was a Minotaur with horns cut short and greying hair braided with flowers. "How does it look?"

"Beautiful!" Feyloren replied, setting Fleur down on the counter and picking up the wrapped bundle.

"And you said that you think your calving date..." Daphnie covered her mouth, and Fleur giggled. "I apologize. Your due date is in about twenty weeks?"

Feyloren nodded. "I think so, but Lorna said she would have a closer estimate when the child starts to kick."

Daphnie nodded and smiled. "This should open just in time. How exciting for you." Then she sighed and touched a carved stone hanging around her neck in a subconscious gesture of self-protection.

Feyloren watched the gesture with compassion, reading the woman's body language and knowing what far too many women know: the quiet, profoundly personal pain of a child gone too soon.

Fleur di Lis looked at Daphnie as her flowers shifted from bright white to autumn sunsets' pale orange.

Feyloren's countenance also softened. She set down the pot and stepped behind the counter. Then Daphnie and Feyloren embraced, pressed their foreheads together, and shared a few tears.

"Her name was Rhea," Feyloren said, remembering her own loss.

"His name was Juto," Daphnie said.

They looked at each other, each wiped their eyes, and Feyloren returned to the other side of the counter.

"This is a special day," Daphnie said gently. "Have you told him yet?"

Feyloren shook her head. "Tonight." Then she picked up the small pot again and looked at it. What a weight of hope and expectation it carried.

Daphnie also knew the thoughts and fears the small bundle brought with it, so she had selected the healthiest blossom to grow for Feyloren. It was a flower the Longbeard people often planted at the news of a pregnancy in the hope of a healthy birth. The large yellow flower that would emerge would be crushed, mixed with butter, beeswax, ashwardicus semen, and powdered silver into a medicinal salve and be spread over the newborn child.

"Would you like me to put it in burlap for you so no one sees it as you carry it home?" Daphnie asked, knowing well that anyone in town who saw the bundle would understand what it was. Fleur quietly nodded at the offer.

"Thank you," Feyloren replied and handed the plant back to Daphnie. Then she removed a silver coin from her purse and laid it on the counter.

With some effort, Fleur di Lis picked up the coin with both hands and hefted it into a box beneath the counter.

Daphnie removed a carefully folded burlap sack from beneath the counter, padded the bottom with paper, gently set the wrapped bundle inside, and pressed more paper along the sides to protect it from getting bumped. Then she cinched the sack shut with twine.

"There. Now, no one should be the wiser," Daphnie

said, sliding it towards Feyloren. "And not a word from you, little one," she added, pointing to Fleur.

Fleur di Lis shook her head and covered her mouth. "Of course not!"

"Thank you, auntie," Feyloren replied—auntie being a term of endearment—and Daphnie smiled and gently bowed her head towards Fey.

Feyloren left Daphnie's shop with a spring in her step. The day was warm. She would stop by the veg stand for some fresh cakes, a loaf of granary bread, and some eggs and drop everything in her apartment before opening the Hiddy Coo for the afternoon lunch crowd. It was going to be a good day.

Unbeknownst to her, three wicked sisters slowly made their way toward Jatoba from their cabin deep in the forest, leaving a trail of dead and quickly decaying plants behind them like a river of rot through the vibrant vegetation.

They were looking for someone, and someone they would soon find.

# CHAPTER 9
## TEN YEARS AGO

A fourteen-year-old Feyloren stood motionless behind the trunk of a great hornbeam. Her arms ached under the strain of the bow string she held taunt. She tried to ignore the pain and focus on the tiwatoo —a flightless bird about the size of a dog—eating white berries from a bush not fifty feet in front of her. The purple and blue bird paused, looked around, and returned to plucking the berries and crushing them with a pop of white juice that spilled down its thick beak.

Feyloren quieted her mind enough to hear her heartbeat. Then she held her breath. Thump-thump. Thump-thump. Thump-thump. Release. Between two heartbeats, she let her arrow fly, but it missed its target by inches, hitting the bush next to the tiwatoo, which flinched and turned to her. But before it could dart off, a second arrow struck its chest hard, sending its immediately lifeless body back into the bush as a small plume of purple feathers gently tumbled to the ground.

Feyloren turned to Perimas and glared at him. "I almost had it."

Perimas smiled back at her. "Yeah, and it *almost* got away. You're not aiming small enough. If you aim at the bird, you miss the bird, but if you aim at its wing or that spot on its back, you might miss the spot but you still hit the bird."

"Yeah, yeah. Aim smaller. I *did* aim at the spot," she replied, following him from behind the tree to fetch the carcass. "You just get more practice than I do."

"Then come hunting with me," the young and beautifully naive boy said to her with a grin.

Feyloren laughed. "I don't think Papa would allow that."

"Have you asked him?"

"Well, no. But..."

"Maybe if I asked," Perimas said, slinging his bow over a slender shoulder, lifting the tiwatoo with one hand, and pulling out the arrow with a jerk.

Perimas wasn't as bulky and tall as the other Longbeard boys his age, which meant he had to learn how to use his speed and agility at a young age to hold his own in tests of strength against the boys in town. While they had learned to wield the axes and war hammers of their fathers, he had learned the finesse of the bow and to carry a long, slender sword at his side that he once saw a traveler carrying who visited Jatoba. Of course, the other boys had mocked him for it until he trimmed one of their nascent beards with a quick flick of his wrist before the offending boy could even lift his axe to defend himself. Their mutual friends laughed it off, and all accepted his bow and blade from then on.

It wasn't long before his best friend, Feyloren, also wanted to learn how to use the bow. For generations, women had not been allowed to learn such things, but the old ways were changing, and Brutste and Feyloren were far too restless of children to care much for baking or weaving. Their father loved them for it, though it was hard for him to completely relinquish the old ways all at once. Brutste could cleave a log better than boys nearly twice her age, and Feyloren was fascinated with the weapons Perimas had chosen for himself.

Feyloren found her arrow, carefully touched the steel tip to ensure it wasn't damaged, and returned it to her quiver.

"Take him this. Tell him you killed it. Then ask if you can come with me. I bet he'll say yes."

"But it's your kill."

He smiled and held it out to her and shrugged. "Invite me over when you cook it, and we'll call it even."

*That's not a bad idea*, she thought to herself, taking the carcass from him.

They walked together back to Jatoba close enough to bump into each other more than once, flirting and laughing about life.

"Do you have chores, or can you come back out?" Perimas asked.

Feyloren smiled. "Still want to see me, do you?"

Perimas blushed and looked away. "I, uh, thought we could practice some more. Clearly you need it."

Fey's eyes grew, and she punched him in the arm. He laughed. "I'm done with housework for the morning," she replied. "Let me see if Papa needs any help opening the tavern."

Perimas nodded. "I'll wait out here," he told her.

Then Feyloren entered her home. "Papa!" Feyloren called out, setting her bow and quiver near the front door.

"I'm here," came the reply of a deep voice from the kitchen.

She went through the front room and found her father, Gaylen, sitting at their kitchen table. He had a thick red beard that hung to the middle of his chest, skin the color of golden amber, and powerful arms and hands; however, she had never known his hands to be anything other than tender and loving towards her, Brutste, and their mother. When she approached him, he looked up at her and smiled.

"What have you there?" he asked.

"I caught a tiwatoo!" she told him. "Well, Perimas caught it, but I was close! He wants me to go hunting with him and thought that if I gave it to you and told you I caught it, you would let me." Feyloren could never lie to her parents.

Gaylen grunted. "Hunting, huh? I think that boy has intentions beyond teaching you to shoot."

Feyloren couldn't argue with that. She felt it, too.

"What are you doing?" she asked.

A steaming brass carafe of hot water sat before him on an ornate tablecloth. Next to it were matching brass cups of fine detail, a small brass bowl with a pour spout, a brass ladle with a long handle, a round brush with long bristles made from reed, and a white and blue lacquer bowl with a lid and tiny spoon.

"This is the ceremony of emsiree tye," he told her. "I am preparing it for your mother."

"Emsiree... you mean..."

He smiled at her. "You have not seen this before, have you?"

"No!"

"Come. Sit. I will show you that you may perform the

ceremony for the one you love one day. Perhaps Perimas," he said, glancing at her.

Feyloren blushed, then took her seat at the table across from him.

Gaylen sat up straight and took a deep breath. "The movement of our hands, the placement of each item, all communicates something to whom we serve. We are precise, because it matters. *They* matter. We slow down, so they may see us. We are quiet, so they may hear the weight of our words." The resonance of his voice, coming from deep within his chest, filled the room with weight and warmth, his large hands moving with delicate grace.

"I will serve you as I would your mother. But as I do, I'll explain to you what I'm doing, though I would say nothing to her until the very end of the ceremony, and only then make my request. She will know what I am asking and how much it means to me to ask by the weight of my precision and how slowly I move. This also gives her time to decide. It is a great dishonor to have no response.

"The carafe is filled before we begin. I open my hands to welcome you. Two even spoonfuls of powdered tea into the pot. One scoop of hot water with the long-handled spoon for you, and one for me, careful to let no drop of water fall to the tablecloth. I then place the scoop back exactly where it was. Notice how it lies facing you as a sign of welcome."

Feyloren carefully watched her father's every move.

This man sitting across from her was Feyloren's ideal man. He was the living embodiment of every good and healthy aspect of masculinity. The good shepherd. The guardian. The protector. The provider. Uncompromising love. Sacrifice. The backs of his hands were rough and scarred from unflinching work to provide for her and their family, but his palms were soft where they held her as a baby. His eyes naturally squinted from years of sunlight but were wide and bright every time they found her or her sister in the crowd. His long, red beard was rough like a horse's main, but somehow soft against her cheek. He was a pillar of absolute granite that went to the bedrock of her life, providing her the stability to fly far and wide and play until her hands ached from the cold night, just to be welcomed and warmed as soon as she came home. She could take risks because he wouldn't let her fail. She could jump off rooftops because she knew he would catch her. She could laugh with the boys and push as hard as she wanted because she knew that if she pushed just a little too hard, all they had to do was look over her shoulder and see him standing behind her. To the world, he was mortal, but to her, he was as immortal as the gods. All she had to do was hear him and her mother flirt and hear his belly laugh to know that all was right in the world. He was her True North. Her guiding light. Her source of direction through this hectic life. And here he was, the poet warrior, unflinching through hardship but graceful enough to pour a perfect cup of tea. A picture of perfect balance she would never forget.

"I stir the tea with the reed brush, tap it once to release excess, and return it to its place next to the tea bowl. I gently fill your cup, then mine, and offer you my service," Gaylen concluded by holding the tea cup out to her on the tips of his rather large fingers. "You accept it, with a slight bow of the head in thanks, and take a sip. If it is pleasing to you, you would gently smile. If not, you do not. This is your courtesy to me to let me know before I ask what your answer will be. This courtesy guards me from the disgrace of an unfavorable reply. If you do not gently smile, I would ask something simple such as: 'Please consider the blossom in spring.' Something you can easily agree to. However, if you smile at the first sip, I would ask..."

A heavy knock at the door interrupted Gaylen's question, and he looked up.

"I'm sorry, Papa. It's probably Perimas. Let me tell him I'll see him later."

Gaylen sighed—an unspoken gesture that said enough.

Feyloren opened the door, ready to dismiss Perimas and tell him she would find him later, just to be met by the fierce gaze of an armored guard. His shoulder pauldron held the crest of Fryowenn. Three other armored guards stood behind him.

"Is this the home of Gaylen of Jatoba?" the guard asked with authority.

Feyloren turned to the kitchen as Gaylen approached the front door.

"What is this about?" Gaylen asked.

"Gaylen of Jatoba, you are ordered to come with us."

"Pappa?" Feyloren asked, but her father silenced her.

"By what authority?"

"The House of Fryowenn."

"I recognize no such authority."

"You will come with us, or we will remove you—and the girl—by force."

"You will NOT touch her."

At Gaylen's tone change, two other guards stepped forward and partially unsheathed their swords.

Gaylen held up his hands. "I relent. I relent."

"Pappa! What's happening?" Feyloren asked, grabbing his shirt.

Gaylen slowly lowered his hands, embraced her, and kissed her forehead. "I'll be home soon," he told her, gently pulling his shirt from her clutching hands and touching her cheek, now wet with tears. His eyes were wide. "Tell your mother and sister that I love them." Then he went with the soldiers.

Feyloren fell to her knees sobbing, confused and afraid. Moments later, Perimas came in, dropped to his knees beside her, and embraced her. She cried into his shirt.

Feyloren would never see her father again.

# CHAPTER 10
## PRESENT DAY

Evening was setting in, and Feyloren could hear the sound of patrons beginning to fill the tavern for their nightly food and drink. A back section of the dining room had been roped off to give her the privacy she needed to prepare for Andrew's, Lorna's, and Lithuel's arrival.

The elements of the emsiree tye ceremony lay before her. Ten years later, she still could not touch them without remembering the look in her father's eyes the last time she saw him.

Gaylen had been preparing the ceremony that day to ask his wife, Feyloren's mother, to bear him a third child. Feyloren had always wondered if he hoped for a boy. Now, she was preparing the same ceremony to give Andrew and his family the news that she was pregnant.

Her hands shook as she nervously moved the cups, mixing brush, and ladle around on the table for the fifth time. Something didn't look right. What was she missing?

Brutste approached Fey, wiping a knife on her apron and sheathing it.

"I want to invite... Would you... Please be with me when..." Fey took a deep breath and glanced up at her sister.

Brutste saw the anguish on her little sister's face. "Hey, hey. What's this all about?" she asked with concern.

Fey rubbed her forehead. "I can't seem to get this right."

Brutste took Feyloren's hands in her own. "It's alright. It doesn't have to be perfect."

But Feyloren remembered Gaylen's words: "The movement of our hands, the placement of each item, all communicates something to whom we serve. We are precise because it matters. They matter. We slow down so they may see us. We are quiet so that they may hear the weight of our words."

"They won't even know if you get anything wrong," Brutste added. "You don't *have* to do the ceremony. It's an outdated tradition anyways."

Feyloren shook her head. "It's part of our story, part of who we are. Andrew and I want to share our cultures with each other and raise our children to know both."

"Do Humans even have a culture?"

"Not appropriate," Feyloren tersely replied.

Brutste apologetically nodded. "Then let me help you."

Feyloren looked at her sister and almost started crying. "Please."

Brutste hugged her.

ANDREW STOOD outside the Hiddy Coo, watching the patrons laugh and drink, some of whom he had gotten to know since moving to town. Everyone seemed so welcoming. Now, he felt like an outsider. Was someone playing pranks, or was this more malicious? A broken window was more than just children's games. Was it only one person, or did more people in town wish he would leave? The tavern no longer felt as welcoming as it had the night before.

"Are you going in?" Lorna asked, walking up behind him and laying her hand on his back.

He turned to her and smiled; hers was a welcome face. Lithuel joined them. Andrew nodded to her, turned, and together they went in.

Tomptee, the Inkling who had asked Andrew for a job, sat at the bar and looked up from his half-eaten bowl of chowder as Andrew entered. Andrew smiled at him, but Tomptee looked away without acknowledging him. Andrew hadn't meant to offend him and decided he would go over and say hello, perhaps buy him a round before the night was over, but he wanted to see Feyloren first.

Brutste smiled at Andrew and her soon-to-be extended family as she exited the back room when suddenly someone outside the tavern screamed: "Fire!" The music stopped, and everyone turned to the front door. An uncontrolled fire in a town like Jatoba, full of wooden buildings, could be devastating.

"There's a fire at the tinker's shop!"

Andrew's heart dropped at the thought of arson, and he glanced at Lorna before running out to the street. Everyone in the tavern followed him as fire light drove away the darkness.

Andrew shielded his face from the intense heat as bright flames rolled out of his shop's front windows and climbed the front of the old wood building. He could hear timbers cracking inside and didn't know what to do. It was already out of control and engulfing the second floor. What could have started this large of a fire so quickly? He had *just* left his shop. Everything had been dark and quiet just a few minutes earlier.

He looked around for a water source as Lorna stepped past him and leveled her staff at the flames.

"Vetcora el empa," she spoke, trying to capture the flames and smother them with intuition, which caused them to shrink, but then they grew even more brightly. She stepped back.

"Shelooma! Reich aleph pelota!" she spoke with authority as water from the fountain rose from behind her and poured itself, like a mighty torrent, through the front window, but where the water met the flames, the fire pushed back in an unnatural way, causing the water to violently bubble and hiss away into steam.

Then, just as Lorna realized this was not an ordinary fire, three figures appeared through the flames, and she lowered her staff as the flow of water fell lifeless to the street with a splash.

"Hello, sister," came the crackled voice of a woman.

"We have no aught with you," another said.

Three women calmly left the burning building with no sign of harm from the growing inferno.

"Who are you?" Lorna yelled over the roar of the fire, holding the end of her staff out before her in a defensive posture.

Orange and red light outlined their tattered black robes and pale skin. Dried flesh clung to tiny bones hanging from their necks and wrists. Dirty stitches unnaturally held shut the mouth of one, the eyes of another and the ears of the third.

Lorna could feel her skin drying and her hair shriveling in their presence.

"We smell the stench of one touched by grace," said the blind woman.

"And we have come for them," said the one who was deaf.

The mute woman held up a finger to Lorna and to the growing crowd.

"But we have no aught with you, sister of earth," added the one who was blind.

Lorna fought the urge to turn to Andrew, who stood just behind her.

"Give them to us," said the one who was deaf. "And we will leave," said the one who was blind, finishing each other's sentences. Then the one who was mute opened her hand and pulled a handful of something unseen slowly towards her face, closed her eyes, and smelled her hand like she was smelling flowers. Her eyes quickly opened, and all three looked at Andrew.

"We can smell the stink of a Grace Giver on you!" she, who was blind, yelled as their robes began to move.

"He is my blood and protected by me. You cannot have him!" Lorna replied with a voice of authority.

They turned to her. "Then you, too, shall die," she who was blind calmly replied.

"Ruach! Em sharee!" Lorna yelled. "Help us now!" And the wicked sisters stumbled back, two of them covering their ears at The Name of The Great Ruach.

The wicked sisters grasped each other's arms and steadied themselves. Then they began chanting. "Eemoo eekoo nooly. Peeshoo teekoo riven," and the one who was mute held out an open hand to the sky as a cloud of biting gnats filled the square, and everyone began screaming and fleeing into their homes.

Lorna lifted her staff and cried out, "Kadosh! A breath of

life, to cleanse the flies!" And a mighty wind blew through town and pushed the gnats into the fire with a violent hiss as they burned away.

The wicked sisters glared at Lorna, and she who was deaf called out: "Stone to stream!"

The street beneath Lorna began to liquify and she started to sink into the street. Then she who was mute pointed to Andrew, as she who was blind focused her attention on him and spoke a crackling curse that hurt Lorna's ears to hear it: "Kreekeck nee flick."

Andrew began choking and felt an unseen hand at his throat lift him from the street.

"Water to ice!" Lorna cried, freezing the street and regaining her footing. Then, she motioned her staff with a word, "Silence!" The one cursing Andrew shrieked in pain and pulled her hand back, immediately dropping Andrew.

The two who could talk felt their throats tighten and their mouths go too dry to speak.

"Binding!" Lorna yelled.

The three felt their arms becoming too heavy to lift, their hands going numb, and their minds beginning to fog. Then she who was deaf, bit her lip to bleeding and spat a spray of red towards Lorna when suddenly flashes of light broke from the heavens and fire rained down on the town.

Lorna's eyes grew. It was no longer a contest of intuitive skill. They were breaking natural laws.

"Ruach!" Lorna cried in fear, unsure what to do next. "Help us now!"

At that, the fire from the heavens burst against an unseen barrier above the town and fell in a dazzling array of harmless sparks.

Then she who was mute, reached towards Lorna, gripped the air and wrenched her hands in a twisting motion causing Lorna's hands to violently shake and cramp with so much pain that she dropped her staff. As soon as she did, Lorna felt the power drain from her. With a flick of her wrist, she who was blind struck Lorna across the face with an unseen force so hard Lorna fell to the street.

The residents of Jatoba cowered in their homes, and Brutste quickly carried her sister into the tavern and closed the door, trying to protect her from the biting gnats or whatever else might come. But Feyloren pulled away from Brutste and ran to the door in time to see the wicked sisters reaching for Andrew, who lay prone in the street. As they did, a bright green light emanated from him with such intensity that it forced the wicked sisters to shield their faces.

Feyloren grabbed the bow hanging behind the tavern door and drew a single arrow. Time slowed as she stepped into the street. Though she had not touched the weapon in countless seasons, its soft leather grip and smooth curve brought back her muscle memory, and she took aim.

Andrew felt something strengthening his resolve, and he slowly rose to his knees.

"*Aim small,*" Fey remembered Perimas telling her when she was young, like a whisper in her ear. So, instead of three, she aimed at one; instead of one, she aimed at a tiny skull hanging around the mute woman's neck standing in the middle.

Thump-thump. Thump-thump. Her heart beat.

The wicked sisters slowly turned back to Andrew, now all three raising their hands towards him.

Thump-thump. Thump-thump.

*One shot. Make it count.*

Feyloren held her breath as the taught strand of sheep gut bit into her fingers.

Thump-thump. Thump-thump.

Release.

Flying close enough to brush his hair, the green light emanating from Andrew ignited the arrow, and it found its mark.

She who was deaf burst into bright-green fire and fell back. Her sisters screamed and reached for her, casting intuition to extinguish the green flames.

As soon as the fire was extinguished, she who was deaf turned to Feyloren and spoke a biting curse that caused a sharp twisting cramp in Fey's stomach that raced up her back and down her legs, causing her to drop the bow, clutch her stomach in agony, and fall onto her hands and knees.

Brutste rushed out of the tavern and covered Fey's body with her own, and Andrew screamed until his face turned red, reaching for Feyloren. Then he turned to the wretched sisters and picked up Lorna's staff. "Tannish ee looma!" he yelled.

Lorna reached for him. "No! Andrew, don't!"

"I bind you!" The green radiance left him as anger poured forth.

The sisters tried to scream, tried to curse him, tried to do something, but they could not. They had never felt power like this. Their robes became heavy, and their limbs turned to stone. With the last of her strength, she who was blind plucked a dried rat's foot from her sleeve, ran through with a rusted needle, and cast it into the street as a raven swooped in, grabbed it, and fled away.

"I rebuke you!" Andrew yelled for all the times he had been bullied, for all the times he had been spat on and kicked, for all the times he had turned the other cheek. Well, not this time, not here. Attacking his family was too much. "I cast you into the place of forgetting!" he cried out, pouring something from inside of him out through his hands and Lorna's staff, which radiated incredible heat.

"Don't!" Lorna screamed, "Please!" But it was too late.

The fervor of Andrew's hate flashed brighter than the noon-day sun for a white-hot moment, scorching his hands.

Then they were gone.

Andrew dropped the staff, which broke into pieces, and he fell to the ground unconscious.

As soon as he had heard shouts of intuition in the street, Tomptee had hid beneath a table in the tavern and tucked himself beneath his cloak. Now that it was quiet, he crawled out from his hiding spot and found Brutste shielding Feyloren with her body and Andrew lying unconscious in a flash-burn that splayed widely across the stones beneath the broken staff.

There was no sign of either the wicked sisters nor Lorna. All four of them were gone.

THE RAVEN LANDED SOMEWHERE deep in the forest and violently pecked the ground. Once it broke the soil, it dropped in the rat's foot pierced through with a rusted needled, and flew to the roof of a nearby cabin.

Moments later, the ground beneath the rat's foot rose and broke open like a wound in the soil.

# CHAPTER II
## TWELVE YEARS AGO

It was spring, and a visit to the large city of Nevarii had proven profitable for Lithuel. A Longbeard baker, who had owed him money since last Eden Vale, finally paid him and tossed in a dozen nintoo cakes and a small jar of honey as an apology for the late payment. Evening was setting in, and Lithuel was ready to head home, but he had one more stop to make.

Andrew, only six, sat next to his father on the driver's seat of their tinker cart with crumbs of cake on his chin. He was wrapped in a large blanket to shield him from the cooling evening air.

"Last stop. Stay and finish your cake. I'll only be a minute. Do NOT leave the cart. Hear me?" Lithuel asked, kissing the top of Andrew's head and climbing down from his tinker cart.

Andrew, with his large brown eyes and the ears he may never grow into, nodded. He was lost in the small, flower-flavored cake sticking to his little fingers like clay. He had even managed to get a large crumb on his forehead.

A bald boy across the street, with saffron-yellow skin, nudged his two friends. "Look. It's a Human!"

They smiled.

As soon as Lithuel entered the vet clinic, the yellow boy whistled to Andrew, trying to get his attention. He didn't want to get too close because he could see Lithuel through the store's large front window.

At first, Andrew didn't notice, but then the yellow boy whistled louder, which made Andrew look up from licking between his fingers where he chased the last of the deliciously sticky crumbs.

The boy motioned Andrew to come to him, but Lithuel had told Andrew not to leave the cart, and Andrew didn't want a discipline, so Andrew stayed put.

Deciding to up his game, the yellow boy flicked a firework of intuition into the sky that popped into a rain of colorful lights.

Andrew's eyes grew.

Minor, flashy cantrips were the full extent of the yellow boy's intuition, yet they kept him at the top of the food chain on the streets of Nevarii. Now that he had Andrew's attention, he pointed to his left hand, cupping it as blue light began to glow between his fingers. Then he signaled for Andrew to come closer.

Andrew looked for his father, who he could see through the front window, and decided that it couldn't hurt to climb down and have a look.

The two Longbeard teenagers exchanged a subtle nudge.

The boy with saffron-yellow skin held out his hand, slowly opening it to reveal it was empty before quickly seizing Andrew and carrying him into a nearby alley.

Lithuel left the vet clinic with a small pot of medicine

for Mayloy. His heart stopped as soon as he saw the empty blanket lying on the bottom of the cart. Andrew was gone. He tore back the canvas hoping Andrew had gotten bored and crawled into the back, but there was no sign of him.

"Andrew!" he yelled, looking up and down the street, but there was no answer.

The three boys heard Lithuel hollering, and Andrew struggled, but a yellow hand was tight over his mouth. They ran down the alley, around a corner, and squeezed through a crack in a low stone wall that they covered with wooden crates behind them. Now they were in their world, the hidden underworld of back alleys and sewers where the rules were different, where they called the shots.

"Look at the humatii!" the yellow boy laughed.

"I've never seen one before," one of the Longbeard boys said.

The yellow boy shoved Andrew to the ground, and Andrew cried out in pain, scraping his palms against the street.

"Look at his skin. It's so pale, like he's dead," another laughed.

Andrew tried to crawl away, but the yellow boy grabbed him by the leg and pulled off a shoe. "The bottoms of his feet are soft!" he said, stabbing a finger into the center of Andrew's foot, causing him to scream in pain.

"I wonder what his pisser looks like," one of them replied.

The yellow boy smiled. "Let's see!" Then he picked Andrew up by the arms. "Pull down his pants!"

Just then, a heavy hand slapped across the back of the yellow boy's bald head, knocking him forward and causing him to drop Andrew. He turned, ready to curse whoever had hit him, then realized it was the man with sapphire-blue skin dressed in expensive robes and jewel-encrusted rings. Standing beside him was a half-man, half-lion guard with a sandy-white mane and a scar on his neck.

"Petros!" the yellow boy stuttered. "I was just..."

Petros calmly grabbed the yellow boy by his testicles and squeezed so hard that he cried out, green tears immediately filling his eyes.

"What's going on here?" Petros asked, squeezing tighter.

The boy struggled but couldn't answer. His friends took a step back but knew not to run. There was nowhere to hide in Nevarii from Petros. If they were squires and footmen calling the shots on the streets of Nevarii, Petros was king.

"I've told you before, no children. I don't care who you mark as long as they aren't smaller than you. If they are, they belong to me. Do you understand?" Petros calmly asked, squeezing tighter.

The yellow boy quickly nodded, bile rising in the back of his throat from the pain. Then Petros released him.

Lithuel's calls drew closer, and Petros sighed. He nodded to the boys with a look of disdain who quickly ran off. He reached for Andrew, but Andrew winced and pulled back. Petros signaled for his lion guard to pick up the tiny shoe lying in a puddle of water, and he gently took up the crying child in his arms, who struggled. Then he carried Andrew out of the alley, towards Lithuel's frantic voice.

When Lithuel saw the men carrying Andrew, he ran to them and jerked Andrew away.

"We found him crying in the alley," Petros said.

Lithuel glared at the two men and quickly took Andrew back to his cart, who buried his little face in his father's shirt.

"He's safe now. No one will bother him," Petros said, handing Lithuel Andrew's shoe.

"Was someone botherin' him?" Lithuel asked, setting Andrew on the seat and wrapping the blanket around him.

Petros was intrigued by the Human child. Lithuel clearly was not Human himself, so Petros asked, "Where did you get him?"

Lithuel ignored the question and pulled the canvas tight over his cart, eager to leave the wretched city.

"Did you buy him? I'd be willing to pay you twice whatever you paid for him," Petros offered.

Lithuel turned and punched Petros across the jaw hard enough that most would have crumpled like paper to the tinker's blow, but Petros knew how to take a punch.

Petros' guard drew a blade, but Petros signaled him to stand down. Then he slowly wiped away the drop of blue blood rising on his lip. "It was an honest offer. No need to make it personal," Petros said, clenching his jaw.

Lithuel climbed up onto his cart and flicked Mayloy's reins.

As the tinker's cart quickly trundled down the cobblestone street, Petros signaled two of his men to follow the tinker out of town.

# CHAPTER 12
## PRESENT DAY

Brutste had carried Andrew up to the guest room where he now slept. She had also helped Feyloren to a separate room, trying not to disturb Andrew while Daphnie stopped Fey's bleeding and checked on her child, whose heart was strong—for now.

The faintest blue from the earliest kiss of morning rimmed the dark tavern windows as Tomptee rummaged behind the counter, trying to find something to eat. Inklings don't sleep as long as most races and need several smaller meals throughout the day. He was hungry, but he needed no light. His eyes were well adapted to seeing in almost complete darkness and his nose was well developed, though Inklings refrained from fully rooting around like dogs or hogs when in the presence of other races, often overly self-conscious of their smaller size.

"What are you looking for?" Feyloren asked from the stairs, leaning against the railing and protectively covering her stomach with a hand.

Tomptee looked up from behind the counter. "Oh, I'm sorry, I shouldn't be..."

"It's okay," she said with difficulty.

"I was looking for food."

Fey pointed. "There's bread, fruit, and more in the larder."

He nodded. "I can smell it, but it's locked."

She slowly sat at the bar. "The key is behind the jug," she said, pointing to the shelf where barrels of wine and whiskey sat waiting to be poured.

It was too high for him, so he pulled a barstool over, climbed up, and found the key. "Why are you awake?" he asked.

"I couldn't sleep. My night visions trouble me. I've came down for a cuppa tea."

His eyes grew with excitement. "Let me brew you some!" He dropped down from the stool, darted across the tavern to the hearth, stacked some wood and tinder, and quickly used the hanging striker to rain sparks onto the pile until the fire sprang to life. Then he shot across the dining room with pot in hand, filled it with water from the spout behind the bar and back to hang it above the fire; all done before Feyloren had time to object—though she had no energy to object.

Daphnie's herbs had stopped the bleeding, but Feyloren still ached in a way that made her nervous.

"How far along are you?" The tiny man asked without hesitation or reservation.

She furrowed her brow at him. "How do you..."

He smiled and tapped his nose.

"Ah."

With a rag, he took the kettle of hot water from the fire and poured the steaming-hot liquid into a cup sitting on the bar in front of Fey. "Where do you keep your leaves?"

Fey winced and pointed to a stone jar above the wine barrels.

Tomptee climbed back up the bar stool and onto the bar, reaching with tiptoes up to fetch the jar and carefully handing it down to Fey. Then he unlocked the larder and disappeared into the dark room while she carefully pulled the cork lid off the jar and scooped two piles of dry, crushed leaves into her cup. She pulled the cup close, took it in both hands, and lifted it to her nose—warm steam rising and blanketing her face. The dark, herbal smell calmed her.

There was a knock at the tavern door.

Feyloren painfully turned to the door as Tomptee came out of the larder with an armful of bread, fruits, and vegetables as a bright purple apple fell from his elbow and bounced across the floor. Before Fey could rise to see who it was, Tomptee set the pile on the bar and went to the front window to peek out into the darkness and see who would possibly come at such a time as this.

"A Longbeard man with wild hair. Want me to send him off?"

She shook her head.

Tomptee unlatched an iron lock, and set his foot hard behind it in case of hostility. Then he opened it a few inches and peeked through.

Fey blew on her tea and slowly took a sip. She felt its warmth travel all the way to her belly, warming her from within. Then she heard a voice from the other side of the door that somehow sounded familiar.

"Fey?" the voice asked.

Her mouth went dry, and she nearly fell off of the barstool. "Perimas?" she whispered; the boy who taught her to shoot, strengthened her when her father was arrested, and held her hand at her mother's funeral. Her first kiss. Her first crush. Her first of many things. The boy she married far too young, in a field down in the valley on a cool spring evening with no one to witness other than Bruste and a few friends; the boy she buried two years later.

Perimas smiled his beautiful smile and approached her. "Hey! There you are," he said, casually embracing her. "What happened to your hair?" he asked, looking at her bald head.

She was stunned. Confused. Even scared.

Fey pulled away. "Who are you?"

Tomptee didn't like the look on Fey's face and reached for a finger-length blade, sharp as a razor, hiding in his belt.

"What's wrong?" Perimas asked, confused. "What do you mean, who am I?"

Fey looked around, then back at Perimas. She touched his shirt, which hung loose and ill-fitting, then his hands and face. She wasn't sure if she was dreaming, hallucinating, if this was some form of dark intuition, or if he was real and actually standing in front of her. There was dark soil underneath his nails, and his hair was damp and more unkempt than he usually wore it, but he did, in fact, look like her long, lost husband.

He smiled a questioning smile. "Why are you looking at me like that, and what happened to your hair? Did you cut it? Why are you bald?" Then, his countenance slowly changed. "Are you ill?" he asked, touching her cheek. "Why do you look older? What's happened?"

Her eyes widened. That was it! That was one of the many unsettling things about what she was experiencing. Perimas looked like he did the last time she saw him—*just* like he did the last time she saw him, five years ago. He looked like he hadn't aged a day. He was a year and a half older than her, but now he looked younger— even younger than Andrew. Could he still be seventeen? She shook her head. How could that be?

"Peri. I haven't seen you in five years."

Fear and confusion swept across his face, and he stepped back. "That's not possible. I've only been hunting a few nights."

She looked at him as all of the sorrow and heartache of losing him came flooding back, and she swallowed. "Where have you been?"

He looked around, trying to remember. "I... I was just... Well, I'm not sure."

"Where did you come from just now? Before knocking on that door."

He turned to the door. That was a good question. Why couldn't he remember? He shook his head. "I was walking... It was dark. Then I came up the street and knocked on the door," he shrugged. "I can't remember where I was before that."

Tomptee stepped closer. He didn't like the sound of any of this. His father had taught him and his prickle of siblings about shades and ill spirits that come in the form of a long, lost love to tempt, trick, or lure someone to their death. However, since he was almost entirely immune to intuition, such a vision would not likely work on him, and this person looked—and smelled—entirely real. Real or not, Tomptee still didn't trust him.

Confused and overwhelmed with emotion, Fey embraced Perimas.

# CHAPTER 13

The morning was quiet and still.

It had only been a few hours, and already the townspeople had tried to cleanse the square of spirts by encircling the site with sweet petal, salt, and some sort of fragrant liquid Tomptee didn't recognize, all a sign that they had no idea what they were dealing with. Fingers of smoke rose from small bags of incense, filling the square with fragrances of mend mum, lavender, myrrh, and xe so thick it was nearly noxious. Worthless luck charms in the form of coins with a square hole in the center, often carried in the pockets of maidens or tied to horses' bridles, lay in growing piles, and there was even a child's stuffed Minotaur doll, which Tomptee found a novel addition.

He had seen sites like this before where innocent lives had been lost or some evil—real or imagined—had been vanquished. While salt might help with garden snails and lavender worked to discourage blood wisps, Tomptee knew most of this was worthless. There was superstition and then there was intuition, and what Tomptee had witnessed the night before was old intuition. Fire from heaven?

Protection from The Great Ruach himself? No. This was well beyond garlands of dried flowers and salt circles.

Tomptee stepped across the circle of protection where Lorna's staff still lay in pieces; no one had dared touch it. He surveyed the charred stones—blackest where Andrew had stood—and knelt. What extraordinary power could burn the surface of rock? He removed his leather glove and laid his hand flat against the street pavers. He felt no cold nor heat but rather the static tingle of a residual intuitive force. A small handprint remained in the black soot when he lifted his hand. The very surface of the stones had turned to ash.

He rubbed his fingers together and smelled his fingertips. *What an odd, earthy smell*, he thought, surveying the sight of sorrow.

A blue-black raven sat on an awning overlooking the square, clutching a small frog in its claws. A dire omen.

Seeing it, Tomptee slowly rose.

The raven watched Tomptee closely, then tore the frog's head off and swallowed it.

Tomptee glared back at it in disgust. Then he slowly removed a leather sling and a smooth stone from a pocket in his cloak and gently loaded the sling behind his back, trying not to startle the bird.

It jerked its head back and forth, as ravens do, and swallowed the rest of the frog, then took to the air before Tomptee's stone could find its mark.

Tomptee didn't like the look of that at all, but the bird was gone now, so he sighed and turned to wash his hand in the fountain, which still flowed from deep within the mountain.

There, beneath the clear water's surface, was an oddly shaped stone. Of all the worthless trinkets lying around the square, Tomptee knew that flowing water was quite powerful at cleansing impurity, binding darkness, and creating barriers between opposing forces—both intuitive and corporeal. The black rock, about the size of his small hand, stood out in sharp contrast against the cream-colored stone of the fountain. He leaned in closer, curious where it had come from and why it was in the fountain but unwilling to immediately touch it. It looked like a carving, but the bubbling surface of the flowing water made it hard to see clearly. He reached into the water and poked at it. Nothing extraordinary happened, so he picked it up but did not yet take it out of the water. He could feel the same tingling energy in his fingertips that he had felt in the street, and as he turned it over, he saw the intricate shape of four women: three wicked sisters and one tinker's grandmother. The sight of the women startled him, and he dropped it. It fell hard and fast through the water and rolled out of sight. Just then, Tomptee heard a loud cry and turned.

Andrew knelt at the outside edge of the circle of protection and wept bitterly. His hands were wrapped in gauze from where Lorna's staff had burned them. "What have I done? What have I done!" he cried out so loud that the pain of his sorrow echoed across the square. Lithuel knelt next to him and pulled him close. "This was not your fault," Lithuel tried to assure him, but Andrew wouldn't have it.

"I killed her!"

"You couldn't have known. You couldn't have," Lithuel replied, but his words were lost beneath Andrew's anguish.

Andrew pulled at his hair and fell to his face on the ground, lifting handfuls of ash and pouring them onto his head.

Tomptee's heart broke for Andrew, but he didn't want

to intrude on this deeply personal moment, so, in respect, Tomptee quietly disappeared into the shadow of an alley, pulled the hood of his intuitive camouflage cloak up over his head, and became entirely indistinguishable from the wood and rock behind him.

For several minutes, Andrew cried aloud in the street while people watched from their windows and doorways, Lithuel never leaving his side. When it seemed as though Andrew had no more tears to cry, Lithuel helped him to his feet and suggested he eat something, but Andrew said nothing.

With slow, heavy steps, Andrew approached his shop. It was charred and black, all the way back to the field on the other side. The shops and top-floor apartments on either side were half gone, now leaning in like they could collapse at any moment and forever bury his dream of owning a store; of ever settling down; of ever belonging anywhere outside of a cursed swamp. What awful curse had he brought upon this once quaint and quiet village?

Lithuel said nothing, only gently touched his son's shoulder.

Andrew pulled away.

"This isn't your fault," Lithuel whispered.

Andrew slowly turned to him, his face wet and black from the street. "Not my fault? Not my fault! I might not have done this, but I did that!" he pointed to the street. "And they came for me! This is exactly, entirely and completely my fault!"

Lithuel shook his head. "You couldn't have known."

From the shadows, Tomptee watched Andrew's face slowly change from sorrow to something else entirely.

"I knew."

Lithuel's eyes rose to meet his son's. "What? What do you mean?"

"When I picked up Gran's staff. I knew. Something tried to stop me. *She* tried to stop me, but I knew. Somehow, I knew that what I was saying would kill them. But I didn't just want them dead. I wanted them to suffer."

Lithuel shook his head. "You don't mean that. You were hurt. You were just defending yourself."

"And not just them, but everyone who has ever hurt us... hurt you! I wanted them all to suffer!" Andrew cried out so loud that the fateful word "suffer" rang across the square. "And so, I killed them," he screamed, no longer caring who could hear. Then his posture slumped, and he began crying again. "And I killed her."

Now, residents of Jatoba were standing at a distance, on the edges of the square, watching and listening, when one of them yelled, "Leave!" Then others began murmuring. "Go home. Leave us alone!" And through the voices, a single word rose above the rest, clear as crystal: humatii.

Andrew clenched his teeth, and Lithuel's heart broke.

# CHAPTER 14

Three doors down from the corner of Laughing Cow Lane, Perimas stood in front of the home he had grown up in and where he had brought his young wife. The door had once been red and was now yellow, with a half-circle window and large iron knocker. Flowering vines had grown up from window boxes to the round windows on the second floor, and there were children's toys lying on the stone steps, which was odd, but perhaps they were the neighbors.

Perimas tried the handle, but the door was locked. No problem. He dug around at the base of the rose bush and found his hidden key, which was now quite rusted but worked, so he let himself in. It was good to be home. He took off his boots and ran a hand through his long hair. He could use a bath and some sleep. It also felt like he hadn't eaten in days. He paid no attention to the scattered toys in the main room or that none of the furniture belonged to either him or Feyloren.

As he entered the kitchen looking for some food and water, a woman screamed.

Perimas stumbled backwards. "Who are you?"

"Demas!" The woman cried out, quickly rising from the kitchen table where she had been having a rest after cleaning up breakfast. The babe at her breast that had been sleeping startled awake and began to cry. "Demas!" she cried out again.

"What are you doing in my house?" Perimas asked.

Just then, a Longbeard with thick black hair and powerful arms came down the stairs. "Aye! What's this?" he asked with anger and surprise.

Perimas eyes grew. "What are you all doing in my house?"

Demas grabbed Perimas by the shirt and pulled back to punch him, but Perimas shielded his face and cried out, "Stop. There's been a mistake."

"Aye! You bet there 'as. Breakin' into my house and commin' at my wife!"

Perimas pulled away and fell backwards over a toy cart. "I thought this was my house!"

Demas stepped between the intruder and his wife and took a knife from the counter. "You've got three counts to get out or I'll open you wide, right here on ma' kitchen floor!"

Perimas scrambled to his feet and fled the house, nearly knocking Feyloren over who had been looking for him outside. Perimas hugged her. His heart was beating violently. Then he turned to look back at the house. One, two, three doors down from the corner. It was yellow now, but it *was* his door—the key had worked. But who was living in his house? He looked at Fey and hugged her again, but this time she pulled away.

He was confused. "What's wrong? What's going on?

Who's living in our house, Fey!" he asked, pointing and starting to get both angry and a little scared.

Fey's face read like a woman trying to help a lost child. "We need to talk."

"Talk about what? Just tell me what's going on, Fey!"

She held up her hands and glanced around. Demas, the man she had sold the house to years ago, was watching from the front window, still holding the kitchen knife. Fey looked at him apologetically, which calmed him a bit since he knew Fey well; everyone in town did. Then, there was a sharp pull of the curtain and a loud click of the lock.

Fey took a deep breath. "Peri, you've been gone nearly five years. Five this Autumn."

Perimas pulled back from her and tried to process what he had just heard. Then, he slowly began to shake his head. "No, no. That's not right. That can't be."

Sorrow swept over Feyloren's face. "I buried you. We held your rites. The whole town came."

"What!" he retorted sharply, walking partially down the street in confusion, then turned and walked back to her. "That's absurd! I'm not dead, Fey! I'm right here."

Fey didn't like how angry he was getting with her. She was trying to give him a measure of grace to process what she was saying, but she was also still in pain and exhausted enough that her patience was wearing thin.

She squeezed his hands to reassure him. "I *know* you are here, *Perimas!* But where have you *been*? Do you remember the last time you saw me?"

"Yes! We got upset at each other and..."

"You yelled at me and stormed out of the house."

He ran a hand through his hair. "I'm sorry. I shouldn't have raised my voice. I was just so..."

Fey shook her head. "Peri, that's not the point."

"Okay? Then what is the point?"

She spoke softly now as she gently touched the cheek of the man she had so dearly loved for so long, who now looked strangely out of place and time. "That was five years ago. Five."

Perimas shook his head again.

She took his face in her hands. "Look at me. Look at my face. Am I the girl you left that night?"

She was right. Where he had left a girl, a woman now stood in her place. Her eyes were the same, but now they were framed in gentle creases he didn't recognize. Her hands were still the hands he fell asleep holding every night, but they were now somehow more firm. And where had she gotten that scar on the back of her thumb? She had never been a good liar, and she never lied to him. He didn't know what to say.

She could see that only now was he beginning to finally hear her. "Where did you go that night?"

He looked away, trying to remember.

Daphnie left a house across the lane. "Thank you, we'll talk again soon," she said to the woman in the home who looked like she had been up with a sick child all night. When Daphnie saw Feyloren, she smiled. "Hello! Look who's up and around. How are you feeling?" she asked, gently touching Fey's elbow in concern.

Fey did not immediately answer.

Daphnie read the situation and discerned that Fey was in the middle of a difficult conversation. Then she turned to Perimas, unsure of who he was, trying to piece together what might be going on. "Hello."

Perimas looked away, not in the mood to meet anyone right now but not wanting to be rude either. "How do you do?" he said with forced courtesy, tipping his head toward her.

"I'm Daphnie. Are you new to Jatoba?" a ridiculous question since Daphnie knew everyone in town.

Perimas shook his head. "No. I grew up here. Jatoba is my *home*," he punctuated with more vinegar than he had intended, looking at Fey, who defensively rubbed her shoulder.

The wise elder woman read all of this with clarity as feelings of protectiveness for Feyloren began rising within her.

Daphnie smiled and calmly took Perimas' hands in friendship. "Ah, so you are the one everyone is talking about."

"Talking about?" Perimas questioned.

"The long lost son of Jatoba, back from the dead," she replied nearly in jest. Then she casually turned his hands over and looked at his fingernails. Seeing the dark soil deep under each nail, like black crescent moons, surprised her.

Seeing the look on her face, Perimas jerked away, and Daphnie covered her mouth with a hand.

The three stood looking at each other long enough for Perimas to become more than uncomfortable. Then, without a word, he turned and left.

Daphnie's stunned silence was cut sharply by the caws of a flock of ravens watching from the rooftops—an ominous sight that made the hair rise on the back of Daphnie's hands.

She reached for Fey's hand. "Come, child. Let's get indoors. It is an ill morning, and I want to check your bleeding."

Fey agreed and followed Daphnie back to the Tavern.

# CHAPTER 15

Behind closed doors, Daphnie asked Feyloren to lie back on the bed and knelt beside her. Then she touched a small wooden icon to her lips that hung from a simple cord around her neck, and began praying.

"Great Ruach. I beseech your goodness and mercy. This is an ill time, and we need Your peace. Please fill this place with Your presence." As she spoke, Daphnie's fur began to rise gently from her body, and Feyloren felt a sense of calm fill the room.

Fey took a deep breath.

Daphnie rose. "Protect these walls from prying eyes and ears or anything that would mean us harm," she softly spoke as she touched the door and each wall. Then she returned to Fey with a smile. "There. Now, that's better. How are you?"

"Struggling."

Daphnie nodded. "I bet. How's your pain?" she asked, setting a towel and washbasin on the bed next to Fey.

"I still have a deep ache."

Daphnie nodded, gently laying a hand on Fey's stomach. "The child's heart is strong."

Fey sighed a sigh of relief.

Daphnie took a small jar from her purse and rubbed its contents on Fey's stomach and chest. The herbal aroma further calmed Fey.

"I need to check your bleeding. Is that alright?"

Fey nodded and turned her head, then winced.

"My apologies. Are you alright?"

Fey nodded.

"Your bleeding has stopped. The babe within you has its mother's fire. Even still, try to take it easy for the next few days," Daphnie said as she rinsed her hands in the washbasin and dried them on the towel.

Tears streamed down Feyloren's cheeks.

Daphnie took Feyloren's hand in her own. "Go on, child. It's okay. Let it out."

Fey covered her mouth with a hand and cried. "I don't understand what's happening."

Daphnie began a soothing low and asked, "Have you told Andrew about the baby yet?"

Fey shook her head. "I was going to last night."

"And what about your husband?"

Feyloren looked at her.

"Your husband has returned to you," Daphnie said.

"I buried him! My marriage ended that day."

"Did it? Did you bury him, or was the grave empty?"

The question stung, even though Daphnie only gave voice to what Fey was already feeling. "But I'm pregnant with Andrew's child."

Daphnie did not reply.

"I waited for Perimas. For months, I waited. And when he did not return to me, we held his rites. His own mother had given up on him long before I did. In some ways, I never stopped mourning for him," Fey added, gently touching her smooth scalp.

"You did far more than any wife could be expected to do. No one would question that."

They sat quietly until Daphnie broke the silence. "I think it best you stay inside and try to keep away from others for a few days."

"Why?"

"Something is happening in town. I'm not sure what it is, but I've been to three homes just this morning where children are not waking."

Fey sat up. "What do you mean?"

The look of concern on Daphnie's face was alarming. "All three very young; one Minotaur and two Longbeard clan. When their parents could not wake them, they sent for me. I tried touch, sounds, strong herbs, and even a word of intuition, but nothing could rouse them."

"What do you think it means? Could it have something to do with last night?"

Daphnie shook her head. "I do not know, but I've never even read of such a thing. I've already sent Eet with a message to a friend at Lincarna Academy asking for help, but until then, I can't discount anything. And I don't want to take any chances with you and your child."

There was a knock at the door, and Daphnie rose. She looked at Fey, who covered herself and nodded.

"Come in."

Andrew slowly opened the door.

Fey smiled and reached for him, and they embraced.

"I will leave you two," Daphnie said, then left.

"I've come to say goodbye," Andrew told her.

Feyloren slid to the edge of the bed and sat next to him. "Why?"

"This is all my fault, and I don't want anyone else to get hurt."

Fey shook her head. "But it *isn't* your fault! Those horrible women attacked you."

"But If I hadn't been in town..."

She took his face in her hands and kissed him. Then she looked at him. "You were the victim of a horrible evil. You are not at fault. You should not have to run or hide simply for being who you are."

Andrew felt anger rising in him. "But I killed my Gran!"

Fey pulled back in astonishment. "What a lie! What a total lie! You did no such thing! They were literally burning down the town. They called fire from the heavens! They were going to kill ALL of us. You saved us, Andrew. You stood when everyone else fled. You fought. You did the only thing you could think to do. It is NOT your fault! We are all alive because of you."

"She's dead because of me!" he barked at her, tears flowing once again.

She grabbed him and embraced him. Though he tried to pull away, she held on, and together they wept.

As they began to calm, Fey wiped her face. "I need to tell you something. I was going to tell you properly last night, but it can't wait any longer."

Suddenly, something smashed through the window, startling them both.

# CHAPTER 16

Andrew rose and went to the window as a blue piece of fruit splattered against the glass startling him. Several townspeople gathered in the square in front of the Hiddy Coo and called for Andrew to leave town.

As Andrew and Fey went downstairs, Brutste motioned them to wait inside while she tried to sort things out. Then she went out to the crowd.

"Aye! What in the nine hells is this then?" she asked, looking up at her windows.

The crowd fell silent.

"Minter! Are you throwin' fruit at my tavern?" she asked.

The crowd parted, and everyone looked at a cowering teenage Minotaur with blue hands holding several pieces of rotting fruit. He shook like a mouse before a lion.

"What would your Da say?" Brutste asked.

"I'm here, and we've come for the boy," an older Minotaur spoke, stepping next to the boy in a show of protective agreement.

Brutste crossed her arms and flexed. "Minetin, you old

heel sore. *What* are you goin' on about? There's no boy here."

Minetin snorted a counter-challenge to Brutste's flex and stepped forward. "We know the tinker is here."

Brutste took another step forward. "Oh, you mean the one who will soon be *my* brother? He's no boy," she calmly replied, slowly drawing a carving knife from the back of her belt and leveling it at Minetin and the crowd. "And you know that, same as everyone here."

At the sight of the blade, the crowd stepped back, but Minetin did not flinch. The crowd was a dozen or so who had now been joined by another handful standing at the edges of the square watching the commotion.

"Look at the birds. It's a bad omen!" Minetin said, pointing to dozens of ravens sitting on rooftops, windowsills, and doorposts around the square. Brutste looked around and said nothing. She, too, didn't like the look of the birds.

"We don't want trouble. We just want him out of our town," Minetin said.

"Oh, wet dog's hair! You always want trouble. Like last week when you stumbled out my tavern and decided to lock horns with Deelo's prize bull."

"So, that's how it broke a horn!" Deelo hollered from the back of the crowd.

Minetin's eyebrows rose and he glanced over his shoulder.

"Or when you were so drunk you fell off my barstool thinking someone pushed you, and when you rose, you challenged your own reflection in my bar mirror."

Minetin snorted a laugh and tried to regain his composure.

Brutste put her knife away, and Minetin relaxed his

shoulders. Then Brutste spoke to the crowd with open hands. "Look. Friends. I *know* last night was scary. It was scary for all of us, but the worst is past, and we will rebuild. We've done it before."

"How do you know the worst is past?" the tanner's wife called out.

Brutste didn't have an answer.

"Because I'm leaving," Andrew replied, standing behind Brutste.

Brutste looked past Andrew to the sight of broken sorrow painted in tears all over her little sister's face. But Feyloren did not object.

# CHAPTER 17

Andrew's ride out of Jatoba was slow and heavy. The weight of the attack, the town's anger, and the loss of his grandmother pressed against his soul so much that even Brynlee could feel his despair. He had told Feyloren that he would return in a fortnight, but he was trying to make her feel better. In truth, he was unsure if he would ever return. Lithuel had tried encouraging him before he left—offering him his old bedroom—but Andrew just wanted to be alone.

Without the power of her intuition, Lorna's cottage had returned to its derelict state. The garden was still manicured and white flowers bloomed in the trees around it, but his sanctuary was gone. The cottage itself looked like the hallow visage of a long-dead corpse. Was his sense of safety and security as artificial as this ramshackle hovel? Was he as quickly forgotten as its trestles and painted shutters? If he disappeared into the forest, would anyone even remember that anyone had ever existed by the name of Andrew? It was a fitting place for him to wallow.

Andrew pushed open the door with difficulty and went

inside. The air was stale. The floorboards were so warped they were difficult to walk on, upturning at their corners until they pulled up their rusted nails. A death shroud of thick webs blanketed Lorna's wall of medicinal herbs, and the jars holding Andrew's special blend of tea looked like they had cracked and rotted into oblivion more than a century earlier.

He turned to where Lorna's breakfast menu was still lying on the kitchen table; only now, it was so old that it crumbled at his touch. No one happening upon the cottage would believe just how beautiful and full of life it had been only days earlier. And where had Vetta gone? Oh, how Andrew longed for the company of that ornery sparrow or the tiny breakfast mouse that often lazily joined them for tea, but the cup it usually slept in was empty. Only a crust of dust and dirt remained. Did all of the cabin's regular inhabitants somehow also know that Lorna was dead?

Andrew slumped back in the thick armchair by the cold, dark hearth. He could really use the warmth of a fire, but there were no strikers, and he didn't have the strength to rise.

The sound of gentle rain began tap, tap, tapping on the cabin's loose panes of glass, and Andrew could hear the growing wind through the cold chimney. The sound of rain comforted him, and he closed his eyes and remembered the old woman with the bird in her hair who saved his and Brynlee's lives from a blizzard; the day the children had mocked her in the market; how she had almost killed him with fire the morning she woke to find him—a total stranger at the time—making her tea in her kitchen; Vetta on the fireplace mantel defecating in annoyance at his presence; the journey he had undergone into the Kilo Kan forest to help restore her memory; the Igbaya.

Before he knew it, he was asleep.

After some time, Andrew slowly woke to the warmth of the fire and the crackling hearth. He rubbed his eyes and his stiff neck.

Tomptee knelt before the fire, adjusting the logs with a long stick.

"What are you doing here?" Andrew groaned.

The short Inkling glanced over his shoulder. Without his cloak and bags, Andrew could now see more of his clothing: well-worn leather boots with brass buckles; brown adventurer's trousers with extra miss-matched pockets sewn up the legs; a warm-looking flannel shirt over a cooler undershirt all beneath a leather shoulder harness with brass hooks that helped him balance the weight of his bags; beautifully crafted leather gloves missing the tips of the forefingers and thumbs—tinker's gloves.

"Door was open. You didn't answer when I knocked. You were shivering in your sleep, so I lit a fire."

"Thank you, but you should go," Andrew said, sitting up and rubbing his face.

Tomptee shook his head. "I can help. You'll see."

"There's nothing anyone can do now."

Tomptee ignored the comment and lifted a kettle from the fire that Andrew had not noticed, took a flat metal disk from his shirt pocket, flicked his wrist so that the metal disk telescoped into a cup, and filled it with hot water. He returned the kettle to the fire, opened a small brown sack the size of a coin purse, dropped in a compressed ball of tea leaves that sank to the bottom, and handed the cup to Andrew.

The aroma was intriguing.

Andrew reached for the cup and winced. His bandaged hands badly ached from the burns.

Tomptee was concerned. Burns lead to infection, and infection can quickly turn into deadly fever.

Andrew cautiously took the cup and was momentarily distracted from his pain by the cup's unusual design. Then he smelled the liquid. Its fragrant steam immediately calmed him. It was like rich leather and ocean waves and tobacco. His eyebrows raised, and he took a sip. The rich, dark liquid was laced with the cool, clean flavors of eucalyptus and mint.

"What is this?" he asked, sitting forward to take another drink.

Tomptee smiled. "Momma's recipe. I've got just the thing for your hands."

Andrew almost said it wasn't necessary, but he was lost in the hot drink warming him from within, which caused his skin to tingle like a gentle touch at the back of one's neck.

Tomptee returned to Andrew with a dented, scratched, flat metal jar about the size of his palm with a screw-top lid. He pulled off his gloves, twisted off the top of the jar, and scooped a finger-full of salve that he held up to show Andrew.

Andrew looked at it suspiciously.

"If you like the broth, you'll love this. Trust me," the Inkling said in a high, child-like voice.

Andrew did love the broth, so he took another quick swallow and set the cup aside. Then he held his trembling hands out to Tomptee.

In the dancing firelight, Tomptee gently unwrapped Andrew's hands to find a channel of dark red blisters across each palm and the middle of his fingers as though Andrew had grabbed a narrow, red-hot iron and refused to let go.

"Please be careful," Andrew gently spoke through his vulnerability.

Tomptee nodded with a veil of deep concern covering his face. He rubbed the balm in his hands to soften it and very carefully applied it to Andrew's blisters, always careful to let the balm touch the burns for a few moments before beginning to massage it into Andrew's skin.

The balm melted away the bright pain and deep ache like wax before firelight. Andrew felt the sharp pain drain from his palms and watched the blisters shrink into pink flesh that turned firm and healthy.

"I really *can* help you," Tomptee told him.

"I can't pay you. I have nothing left. Nothing, except this place, I guess."

Tomptee scooped up more salve and massaged Andrew's hands more vigorously since they were now completely healed. "Don't worry about that, Andrew, son of Lithuel," Tomptee said, wrapping Andrew's hands in fresh gauze, even though Andrew wasn't sure he needed them. "What is this place?" Tomptee asked, looking around with mild disgust, his twitching nose searching for unseen clues.

"It was my grandmother's home."

"How long ago did she live here?"

"Yesterday."

Tomptee looked at him in disbelief.

"It looked much different when she was alive," Andrew said, picking up the cup for the last of the soothing elixir. "She was a woman of powerful intuition, and I think it somehow kept this place alive. It was beautiful and vibrant just a few days ago."

Tomptee quietly considered this.

"Where did you get this?" Andrew asked, carefully looking the cup over.

Tomptee smiled and lifted his nose with pride. "Made it, I did!"

"Really?" Andrew asked, turning it over. Then he gently pressed on its rim as it collapsed back into a disk of concentric metal rings. "You built this?"

"Sure did!"

"It's so simple, yet so effective. The rings are tight enough not to leak."

Tomptee smiled larger. "That's just a cup. Take a look at this," he said, removing a filigree dragonfly from his bag and handing it out to Andrew.

Andrew leaned the beautiful creature towards the fire, made of the most intricate filagree of brass wire and enameled glass. The dancing firelight made the iridescent glass wings shimmer with green and yellow life. Then Tomptee twisted a tiny lever at the back and let go as wings flicked to motion, and the dragonfly took off, darting around the room.

Andrew's eyes grew. "It's extraordinary!"

"Thanks!" Tomptee said, following the clockwork insect around the room until it finally stopped in mid-air for a few seconds, where Tomptee held out his hands, and it dropped lifeless into his hands.

"You're a tinker?" Andrew asked.

Tomptee looked fondly down at the dragonfly. "I do, yes. Tinker here and there, with this and that, but not like you! My uncle told me about you," he said, carefully returning the insect to his bag.

"Oh, who's your uncle?"

"Pectree. He works for a Scritt named Elrift."

Andrew fondly remembered Daphnie's friend Elrift, and the grumpy Inkling who slammed the door in his face. "I'm surprised he remembers me. He didn't seem to like me much."

"I'm not sure he likes *anybody* that much. I've also heard about some of the things you've built, and I wondered if you might be willing to teach me."

"Teach you?" Andrew had never thought of himself as having enough experience with anything to be a teacher.

Tomptee nodded. "The dragonfly isn't the only thing I've built!" He returned to his bag and took out several items that he laid out, side-by-side on the table. There was a folding multi-tool, some brass precision measuring instruments, a small bell, and a brass box about the size of Tomptee's hand. He smiled large as he handed the brass box to Andrew. The firelight made the box glow.

Andrew gently lifted the lid as a lullaby began to play, and a tiny dancer rose on a spring and danced around a tiny dance floor. His eyes grew. Then he carefully examined the box, trying to ascertain where the music came from.

"Here," Tomptee said, taking the box from Andrew, turning it over, and opening the bottom. "A spring turns a small disk covered in carefully placed bumps. These protrusions pluck a metal comb, and it's the comb that plays the music," he said, pointing to a small metal comb with teeth of different lengths.

Andrew gently plucked one with a fingernail, and it played a single tin-sounding note.

Andrew smiled. "I've never seen anything like this."

"Then you'll teach me?"

Andrew's heart sank, remembering his shop.

"I have nothing left to offer you. I'm sorry."

Disappointed, Tomptee returned his trinkets to his bag. "I have something that belongs to you," he said, removing a

G. J. DAILY

roll of fabric from his backpack, bound by twine, and set it before Andrew.

Andrew studied the Inkling's face, trying to discern what this was all about but couldn't. So, he carefully pulled the twine and unrolled the bundle. It held the broken pieces of Lorna's staff. Seeing the staff made his hands ache again even though they were healed.

He gently touched the wood with his fingertips. "Why did you bring this here?"

"It's yours."

"No. No, it's not. It was my grandmother's," Andrew replied.

"But I saw you use it."

"And it KILLED her!" Andrew snapped, but Tomptee didn't flinch.

"I don't think it did," Tomptee calmly countered.

It took a moment for Tomptee's words to penetrate Andrew's anger.

Andrew swallowed. "What?"

Tomptee lifted a fold in the fabric Andrew had not yet fully unwrapped, revealing the black stone figurine of fine detail Tomptee had found in the fountain.

108

# CHAPTER 18

"**W**hat is this?" Andrew asked, carefully picking up the tiny statue.

"The word of intuition you spoke was a word of binding, and I found this in the fountain. I don't think she's dead. I think she's captured in the stone."

Andrew's heart raced at the possibility, and he gently touched his grandmother's robe who was reaching for him and still trying to stop him. He could feel a static energy like it was humming. It was also warm. The three wicked sisters were also there, faces twisted in anguish.

"How do you know this?" Andrew whispered.

"I'm an Inkling. My people often have a nose to help the powerful with their work because intuition rarely affects us. We aren't sure why. Perhaps the Great Ruach knew someone had to clean up everyone else's mess," he added under his breath, partially referring to Andrew.

Tomptee's words stung, but Andrew did not reply.

"I was raised on stories of such things, and I've seen figurines like this before. They're called netsuke, often holding animals or powerful elemental spirits, but I've never seen one used to bind a foe before. Though, a lot happened last night beyond me. That fire from the sky..." Tomptee's mind wandered off to somewhere distant. "That was... well, I'm not sure exactly *what* that was."

Andrew carefully studied every curve, line, and detail of the statuette. There were no scoring marks, scratches, or any indication of tool work of any kind. It was both beautiful and horrifying—that fateful moment captured in incredible detail, from Lorna's delicate fingernails to her flowing hair. He could see the stitches closing one of the sister's eyes and silencing another's mouth. Something about it made him uncomfortable, and he set it on the table in front of the fire.

"You think she might be alive in there?" Andrew asked.

Tomptee nodded.

"How do we get here out?"

"I don't know. But I think I know someone who might," Tomptee replied.

"Who?"

"A wise Nimic woman with a shop in Nevarii."

Andrew sighed. Nevarii. Racist shopkeepers. Racist guards.

Tomptee could see that Andrew didn't like the sound of that. "My family's there. We can stay with my parents. Don't you worry! I'll get you through this. You wait and see."

Andrew's shoulders relaxed a bit at that. "You never told me your name," Andrew said, checking the cup for any remaining broth.

"Tomptee. It's nice to properly meet you," he said, jumping down from the chair next to Andrew, taking the cup from his hand, and filling it again with hot water and another bouillon ball.

Andrew smiled and gently swirled the hot liquid in the cup, watching the dark ball slowly melt into broth.

Just then, Vetta, Lorna's sparrow, flew in through a crack in the ceiling and fluttered around the cabin.

Andrew was excited to see the little jerk. "Hello! Where have you been?" he asked, rising to meet him, but the sparrow didn't immediately stop its frantic flight around the cottage. Twice, it fluttered past Andrew like it was looking for Lorna, confused why she wasn't there, when it finally landed on a bookshelf and hopped nervously back and forth, looking around the cabin.

"She's not here," Andrew told him.

Vetta cocked his head at Andrew and shot a streak of white liquid down the wall.

Andrew nodded. "It's nice to see you too."

Tomptee laughed a bright laugh at their interactions and removed a meal sack from his backpack where an elbow of bread and a knob of cheese had been hiding. He broke off a large corner of the granary crust and slowly set it on the shelf next to Vetta, who watched him carefully. Then Vetta hopped over and began pecking at the bread.

"Was this your grandmother's familiar? It doesn't seem to like you much."

"We've never quite gotten along. What's a familiar?" Andrew asked.

"What's a familiar? Did your grandmother not teach you anything?" Tomptee asked, making a clicking sound with his cheek as his backpack began to move.

# CHAPTER 19

A small grey creature with large eyes and even larger ears poked its furry head out of Tomptee's bag and clamored across the wood floor to his open hand. It had soft, silver-grey fur, webs of skin between its front and back legs, and a short nob of a tail that flicked with excitement.

"A familiar is a creature that someone has an intuitive connection with. This is Nelot. I'm not intuitive, so he's not technically my familiar, but he is my friend," Tomptee said, breaking off another corner of bread and handing it to Nelot.

Then Tomptee held his open hand out to Vetta, who looked at him cautiously before hopping down from the bookshelf and into his palm.

*Little kocker*, Andrew thought to himself. "So, what are you really doing here? Surely you can see that everything I had has turned to ash. Why are you trying so hard to help me?" Andrew asked, watching the young adventurer, barely the height of Andrew's waist, finish hand-feeding both Vetta and Nelot, who climbed up Tomptee's back and curled up on his shoulder once its furry belly was full.

Andrew's question washed away Tomptee's convivial demeanor. Then he sighed and said, "My Da kicked me out. He said I was worthless. 'I don't want to see your snout again until you've made somethin' o' yourself.' So, I left. Ma thought it too soon, probably 'cause my quills haven't come in yet," he shrugged and slumped back in his chair. "But I didn't have much say."

"Why would he say something like that?" Andrew asked, undoing his boots and making himself comfortable in the armchair next to the crackling hearth and the sound of the growing rain outside. He was enjoying the comforting broth, which he savored more slowly this time.

"He wanted me to work with him at the academy," Tomptee said, rolling his eyes. "But how *boring* would that be! My uncle's a scribe. My Da is a professor's assistant. My Pa was scribe to The House of Elnor, and at least two of my brothers went on to work at the academy with Da. Everyone expects me to become someone's assistant some-where, but I don't want to write down everyone else's stories. I want to create my own!" Then he quieted himself as he remembered. "When I was a pup, Ma and Da took us to Quincary for the Firelight Festival," he said, smiling and petting Nelot, who was now asleep in his hands. "Jugglers. Fire breathers. So many candles. I felt like I was in a trance. We had spiced drinking chocolate and gooey, pepper-dusted popcorn balls and cinnamon bubble candy!" Nelot was beginning to purr.

"It was one of the best nights of my life. I remember Da putting me on his shoulders to watch someone touting themself as a fire mage of the highest order," Tomptee said, waving a hand through the air like he was motioning to an

113

overhead banner. "But he wasn't intuitive. His sparks and puffs of smoke were just special effects. And even though the crowd was oohing and ahhing, Da could see right through them and whispered to me how they worked. 'Look at the brown tube in his sleeve; it's a smoke charge,' he'd tell me. And you'd think that somehow took away from the magic of the moment, but it didn't. I was more enamored with Da for knowing how it all worked than the phony fire mage.

"Later that night, after we were all half drunk on sweets and the crowds were dying down, we came across this tinker calling out to the crowd, 'tinker, tinker, fix yer' wares. Mend yer' pots, sharpen yer' shears!'" Tomptee said, smiling fondly at the memory. "But most of the crowd was either tired or had already been dazzled enough for one night 'cause few paid him any mind. But my Da was curious, so we went to his cart.

"He was Nimic, with the most beautiful white tattoos all over his arms, hands, and face."

It dawned on Andrew who Tomptee was referring to.

"And he and Da started talking. He took this long metal tube with long legs out of a box in the back of his cart and set it up.

"'Have you ever seen the raven moon?' he asked.

"'Of course,' Da replied.

"'Ah,' the man replied, holding up a finger. 'But have you ever *really* seen the raven moon?'

"Da didn't know what he was talking about. The man just pointed to the end of the tube." Tomptee chuckled. "And when Da looked through the glass eyepiece, what he saw scared him so bad, he fell backwards, and ran behind the cart. I had never seen anything scare him like that. But the tinker assured him it was alright.

"I didn't know what was happening, but my Da slowly came out and looked again. And the look on his face..." Tomptee said, gazing into the firelight like he was in a trance of memory. "I can still see it so clearly." Then he looked at Andrew. "It was a..."

"Telescope," Andrew finished his sentence, smiling.

"Yes. That's what he called it. How do you know that?"

Andrew smiled. "That tinker is my father."

"Really?"

Andrew nodded.

"Does he still have the..."

"Telescope? Unfortunately, no. He hurt himself a few seasons back and had to sell some of his things to keep the cupboards stocked. But I remember the telescope well. Crowds loved it."

Tomptee nodded. "That was it! That's what made me want to become a tinker. It was real! It wasn't a trick of light or some tube up a sleeve. When I saw just how much awe and wonder it created in my Da, I knew it must be special, and I wanted to build something like that."

Andrew laughed. "Wow. What a world, huh? Yeah. I remember that telescope. We used to lay out on a blanket on warm summer nights and take turns looking up at all the stars or making up stories about the moon. I remember the day he told me he sold it. I was heartbroken, and I think he was too, but he just touched my cheek and said, 'It's worth it,' and we never spoke of it again."

The cabin door started to rattle in the wind and swung open. Tomptee jumped up to secure it and paused, leaning forward into the night. His low-light vision could see clearly through the dark forest. "There's someone out there," he told Andrew, who rose to have a look.

Even without low-light vision, Andrew could make out

the faint orange glow of a campfire fighting to stay alive in the pouring rain. Save for the leaks in the ceiling, the cabin was warm and dry. At first, Andrew was hesitant to go out into the rain, but then he turned his attention to the place, just beyond the fence line, where Lorna had gone out into the blizzard to save his and Brynlee's lives. So, he sighed, pulled one of Lorna's dusty cloaks over his shoulders, and went out to see if the stranger could use a dry place to sleep.

# CHAPTER 20

The rain was heavy and quickly soaked through Andrew's cloak, with fat drops falling from the edges of his hood.

A Longbeard at the crest of adulthood sat in the bend of a leaning tree that protected his campfire from the wind just enough to keep it alive. In the tree above him were the vine-covered and leaking remains of a hunter's hide that Perimas had built years earlier.

Andrew stood a stone's throw away, waiting for acknowledgment, as was the custom when approaching a stranger's campsite.

The Longbeard looked up from his fire. "Who goes there?" he called out through the rain. He sat with arms crossed near a bedroll, bow, quiver of arrows, and leather sack. He looked surprisingly dry. Much more so than Andrew.

Andrew approached with both hands open to show that he had carried no weapon and intended no ill will. "Greetings!" he called through the rain. "My name is Andrew, son of Lithuel. I saw your firelight through the darkness and came to invite you in from the rain. I have a cabin just through that thicket," he said, pointing.

The ranger looked past him towards the cabin. "Thank you, but I've already made camp for the night," he called back.

"But it's cold and wet out here, and the wind could shift at any moment and extinguish your fire!"

The ranger looked towards the sky even though it was dark. "I think not. The wind is steady through the valley. I've hunted these woods since I was a lad and am accustomed to the weather."

"Are you from Jatoba?"

The ranger smiled. "I am! Grandfather built one of its first homes."

Andrew nodded. "I'm also from Jatoba! Come, come then. The hearth is warm, and I have a kettle on. Besides, with those cursed birds around town, it is an ill night!"

The ranger thought for a moment. "I *could* use a hot cuppa."

Andrew smiled.

The ranger kicked enough dirt onto the fire to snuff its few remaining embers, picked up his things, and followed Andrew back to the cabin.

"Are you the one everyone's talking about?" Andrew asked.

The ranger sighed. "Afraid so. I'm Perimas, and you must be the Human."

"Afraid so," Andrew replied. "What are you doing out here?"

"Everyone's acting like I was dead and come back to life! Brutste was so happy to see me that it was drinks and roast meats for everyone, but it was getting to be a bit much. I was never comfortable in crowds. I'd rather be out here, rain or no."

Andrew nodded, sharing the sentiment. "You know Brutste?"

Perimas nodded. "Aye. Since I was a child. She's my sister."

Their voices were thin through the wind, and Andrew didn't hear Perimas' last comment.

"You don't look dead to me," Andrew said as they kicked their boots against the doorpost and entered the warm, dry cabin to a waiting Tomptee who took their cloaks and hung them by the fire. "This is Tomptee."

"How do you do?" Tomptee asked.

"A bit wet, but otherwise well. And yourself?" Perimas asked.

Tomptee nodded.

"Can you pour our friend a cup of your broth?" Andrew asked Tomptee.

Tomptee paused momentarily and looked back at Andrew, a bit annoyed that he had offered away his broth without asking, but said nothing and nodded again.

"A party, huh? Yeah, that sounds like Brutste. Any reason to drink," Andrew said to Perimas as he shook the water from his trousers.

Perimas laughed. "Truer words, my friend. Truer words." Then he approached the fire, picked up the figurine, sat back in Andrew's chair, and put his muddy boots up on the hearthstone. "What's this?" he asked, rubbing the stat-uette of Lorna on his wet trouser leg.

Andrew reached for it. "Uh, a family heirloom, and it's a bit fragile if you don't mind." But Perimas didn't respond. Instead, he looked down at the black stone figure in his palm, and his left eye twitched ever so slightly.

"Can I just...get that from you?" Andrew asked, taking a step closer.

Then, as if out of a stupor, Perimas snapped to, smiled, and tossed it to him. "Never can be too careful."

Andrew juggled it in his arms, almost dropping it, and looked at Tomptee, horrified.

Tomptee returned the sentiment and handed Perimas a cup of broth.

"Appreciate ya," Perimas said, leaning forward and taking a drink. Then he winced. "What is this?"

"Family recipe," Tomptee replied.

Perimas glanced at him, adjusted his demeanor and quickly swallowed the rest with a gulp as if he were shooting whiskey. Then he tossed the cup back to Tomptee. "So, this is home, huh?" Perimas asked, arms crossed behind his head and leaning back in the chair.

"My grandmother's. It was anyway," Andrew replied.

Tomptee offered Andrew the second armchair nearest the fire, but Andrew declined.

"Yeah, rough business, that," Perimas said.

*Rough business?* Andrew thought to himself. *It was more than just rough business.* Then he sat on Lorna's bed in the corner of the main room, not far from the fire's warmth.

The rain let up a bit and quietly droned against the windows. The cabin was dark save for the outline of fire-light on the dusty heirlooms, but it was dry, warm, and cozy.

The hearth's crackling fire entranced the three, and they said nothing more to each other.

Andrew rubbed his forehead and felt the veil of exhaustion closing in around him; however, he couldn't sleep in Lorna's bed. It was too soon. So, he excused himself and went to the once dusty, and now dusty again, bed in the guestroom at the back of the cabin.

For a while, he tossed and turned. Though he was exhausted, sleep evaded him. The words of the wicked sisters haunted him, and he couldn't get Lorna's face, or her reaching hands, out of his mind. "Don't," she had pleaded with him. "Don't!" And each time he began to doze, he startled himself awake—heart beating and in a cold sweat. Eventually, Andrew sat up again on the edge of the bed and rubbed his face.

Tomptee slept in one chair, with Nelot and Vetta both curled on his lap, and Perimas snored loudly from the other, with a leg up on the hearthstone and arms hanging from either side.

Andrew was beginning to feel claustrophobic. He needed some air, so he rose and left the cabin but didn't go far. It had stopped raining, and the smell of the wet forest was thick. He looked on at Brynlee, who slept near the fence. Though he longed for company, he chose not to wake her. She was getting older, and she would need her strength for their return to his childhood home in Aitechem Tioram in the morning.

He stood just outside the cabin's front door, closed his eyes and breathed deeply of the fresh, cool air. Then he decided to try listening as Lorna had taught him to do that last morning they were together. At first, all he heard was his own anxiety. But slowly, the sounds of the night began to calm him. There was a buzz somewhere near the door. A ribbit deeper in the forest. The call of a distant Cervinae, perhaps an elk or deer.

He sighed. Now he was getting cold, so he returned to the cabin.

The hearth was growing dim with smoldering coals, so

he removed a log from the pile Tomptee had brought in before the rain grew heavy, laid it on the embers, and gently blew, trying to bring the few smoldering embers back to life. As he did, the orange-red heat grew in intensity against his face, causing him to squint. He blew harder and quicker until the flames sprang to life and engulfed the log. The warmth felt nice. He rubbed his hands together and sat for a few minutes on his knees, letting the heat of the hearth warm his heart and the movement of the flames entrance him.

Sleep called to him again, but he feared the blurred edge between waking and sleeping, where the blank canvas of his imagination painted nothing but sorrow and pain. His growing sleepless exhaustion was turning his sorrow into physical anguish. Now he understood why she had kept her bed so close to the warm and comforting hearth. He wanted to roll into it and pass out, but that still wasn't an option. So, with heaviness, he returned to the barren womb of the cold, dark guest room and sat on the edge of the bed. The small, black effigy of his dead grandmother sat next to him on the nightstand like the rotting finger of a loved one. He didn't want to touch it. What was he supposed to do with it? Bury it? He rose to find something to drape over it so he wouldn't have to look at it but found something else instead: the Igbaya.

The intricate, grey chest hadn't reverted to the same state of decay as the rest of the house. Perhaps it had its own intuition. It was like a masterpiece painting still hanging, untouched, on the burned-out walls of a museum. The full moon—known as the raven moon—set in deep relief on its lid, still shone brightly, and the tree holding it in its once barren branches now shimmered with a crown of vibrant leaves, full and rich. It was vibrant and alive in the sarcophagus of a cabin like a single rose growing in the middle of a graveyard. How could he ever have mistaken it for anything other than a living creature? And to think that he nearly killed it to save Lorna's life. Perhaps it could save her again.

Andrew knelt before it and gently ran his hand along its edge, like a lover touching the leg of a mistress. And at his touch, the leaves of the world tree shimmered and its roots flexed like muscle. Was it purring?

"Hello, old friend," he whispered. He may not have known it long, but he knew how much his grandmother loved it. He took a deep breath. "She's gone," he whispered. He swallowed. "And she's not coming back."

At his words, the leaves of the world tree began to dry and fall, like a scene of autumn on the lid.

He wiped a tear from his cheek, his throat tightening.

"Three women came to town looking for me, and she defended me," he took a deeper breath. "And I cursed them. And the word of intuition hit her as well."

He laid his hand flat on its side.

The last leaves fell into a pile at the foot of the world tree, and the raven moon began to dim.

Andrew rose, took the black figurine from the night-stand, and brought it to the Igbaya. "This was left behind," he said, holding it up.

As he did, the carving of the raven moon on the lid became cloud-covered, and the color of its light shifted to a rust red, rimming the edges of the world tree in a light that looked like blood.

Andrew watched with confusion, not knowing what it meant. But then, the Igbaya slowly opened, revealing the trove of Lorna's most prized possessions: shelves of books, small boxes, ornaments, and artifacts of the most incredible power and memory. Andrew had seen it open. His gran had introduced him to it and explained the purposes of two or three items, but she had made him swear by oath never to open it or touch anything inside without her.

"You were wise to have considered destroying it," she had told him. "Without me, much of what is contained herein is lethal...or worse."

Worse? When she said it, he couldn't comprehend what could possibly be worse, but then he looked at the oddly heavy figurine in his palm and began to understand what she might have meant.

Then, a thin volume slowly slid out from the other books.

It was a strange tome, with a spine of five hard circular discs resembling thinly carved bone. Each page was wood about twice the size of his hand, with a thin leaf of gold overlaying one side where a strange script Andrew didn't recognize had been pressed into the soft metal. Why would someone create a book in such a way? It would be quite inconvenient to travel with—always a concern for Andrew.

He tried to recognize a word or even a character and couldn't. The writing ran vertically down the page in columns. The top of each column had a character with a line descending from its center. The lower characters were then written in various ways across those lines. Five columns per page. Five pages. A pattern not lost on Andrew, though he didn't know what it meant. Lorna had taught him that intuition is much like poetry or music. It is not just the words one speaks that are important, but the shape of the words, their rhythm, timing, tone, and intonation. The more tightly the word of intuition was patterned, the more tightly it held together—like a carefully crafted box, which made more sense to him than the music analogy. Some boxes are poorly crafted, with loose seams and poor material and will eventually fall apart. Others are so finely crafted, with oiled wood and perfectly shaped seams, that even without wax, they can hold water and last a lifetime. This made perfect sense to him. Carefully spoken patterns. Music in the text. The most powerful intuitive masters must be extraordinary. Lorna was.

And the thought broke his heart all over again.

Then his thoughts slowly wandered across some of the other weird and wondrous items in the chest: a ring of grey filigree wire twisted and wrapped around a naturally shaped pink pearlescent stone; a wisping, hand-painted chart inside the lid of the Igbaya of the phases of the moon —the full raven moon at the apogee; a small stack of letters bound by twine from someone in Nevarii. Then, there was a shelf of figurines not unlike the graven image he held in his hand. One was an odd-looking, tiny house; another, a lily. There was a carved bead inside a carved sphere inside a carved polygon inside a carved cube, all freely floating as though they were in some form of unseen liquid. There was also a small carriage pulled by four empary—winged, skeletal horses—the likes of which Andrew had never seen before. Finally, a single-stem rose sat in a small vase, barely the size of his forefinger, carved from the most beautiful alabaster stone.

Andrew did not touch the items, aware of how powerful and dangerous each one might be, but one in particular gnawed at his curiosity. On the shelf of the figures sat a purple silk sack cinched shut by a silver cord. Purple was exceptional. Purple fabric or ink was nearly impossible to come by. He had only seen genuine purple cloth a handful of times, always in Nevarii, always in the hands of the wealthy, and always a watered-down or muted hue. This sack was a dark veronica. He could not imagine its value.

He set the book down and gently touched the smooth, silken fabric. It was sensual, intriguing. Inside was a finely carved jade statue of a twisting dragon. The stone was translucent, like emerald green glass. He felt his heart racing. As he slowly lifted it to look at its scales and claws more closely, something moved just beneath the surface of the stone, which startled him in the twilight of the room, and he quickly put the statue back in the bag and cinched it shut, returning it to the Igbaya. Then he quickly closed the chest and took a deep breath.

As he calmed himself, he picked up the golden book and wondered: *Might Tomptee recognize the script?*

Andrew went to the main room to wake Tomptee and ask about the book, but the small Inkling slept so quietly that Andrew decided he could ask him in the morning. He spent a while longer looking over the script by firelight, then returned to bed.

# CHAPTER 21

Hundreds of ravens watched an enigmatic figure walk the streets of Jatoba. His face was white as starlight, and his lips and eyes black as a crow. He wore a headdress and robe of long black and white feathers that dragged along the ground behind him like a royal train.

He stopped outside a dark herbalist shop where a garland of dried oranges, cinnamon, mend-mum, and zephyr bulbs hung from the doorposts. Most of the trinkets around the square were rubbish, but this was for him. He lifted it to his nose, smelled it, and smiled. He paused for a moment to take in the citrus, spice, and floral fragrances; to feel the dried rind in his fingers; to remember the Uptee who first offered him garlands such as this many millennia ago. Then he whistled through his teeth as the ravens sitting on the rooftop of Daphnie's shop scattered to other buildings.

With a thought, he was now in the tavern, reaching behind the bar and lifting a bottle to his nose. *Interesting fragrance,* he thought as he took a mouthful and considered the honey and yeast. Then the hearth awoke and filled the cozy dining room with light; old chairs worn crooked; walls stained from many years of merriment and mirth. He set the bottle on the bar, slowly and precisely turned it just so, and reached for the next.

Black raven claws tipped his unnaturally long fingers, which tapped the glass of a broad green bottle with a red wax seal that Brutste had been saving for a special occasion. He looked at it closely and followed the shape of the seal with his fingertip, then broke the seal and pulled off the cap. *Apples, lito spice, and marcom peppers,* he considered and took a drink. "Oh, that's good," he said, holding it up to let the firelight dance in the liquid, then took another drink.

"What are you doing here?" Feyloren asked from the stairs through a dreamy, sleep-like stupor.

He did not turn to her. She was why he came. He was just giving her a moment to rouse.

"Listening. And tasting your lovely beverages," he replied, setting the green bottle on the bar and reaching for the next. "Can I offer you a drink?"

"Pass," she mumbled.

"Are you sure? This one is especially good," he said, pointing to the applecary.

Suddenly, she was across the tavern and sitting at the bar, though she didn't remember crossing the room, and he was sitting next to her, his long feathers splayed out around him like a gown. Two wine glasses sat on the bar between them. He pulled the cork off a wine bottle and smelled it. "Fruit of the vine. Favored in so many places." Then he poured them both a glass and slid hers toward her.

Fey steadied herself against the bar. She wasn't quite sure where she was or how she got there.

He held up a glass at the base of the stem and swirled

the blood-red liquid, watching its color closely. "If you're worried about your child, there's no need. This won't bother her here."

Fey protectively covered her belly with her hand. *Her? Did he say, "her?"*

He looked up at her from the wine with the herky-jerky motions of a bird. "Oh, you didn't know, did you? You're having a girl."

*A girl?* Fey thought she should be excited, but everything she felt was somehow muted like she was still half asleep.

"Please, drink with me. I insist," his voice becoming unnaturally deeper, punctuating his final word.

Almost without control of her faculties, she slowly lifted her glass as he lifted his. Then she took a drink as he did and savored her wine as he savored his, though she never had a taste for wine.

"See. Nothing to fear."

*Fear.* As he said it, her heart beat faster.

"What do you want?" she asked.

As he finished his glass, she finished hers, tasting but not tasting the tannic liquid, almost like she was fumbling with the memory of drinking a glass of wine.

He carefully lined the bottle up on the bar next to the others. "I'm looking for someone. A young man recently seen in your town." When he said, "Your town," she felt farther away somehow. *Where is Jatoba?* She couldn't remember. *Where am I?* She didn't know.

He wiped a drop of wine from his lip, and she, too, felt a drop of liquid on her own and touched her lip.

"Perhaps you can help me find him," he said, turning toward her as his black eyes became starlight. "You've been dreaming of your child's future, until last night. Fear has not let you sleep—not deeply. I can help with that. I can let you drink deeply of the night; savor its quiet," he said with a long, slow sigh. "I can take away that nightmare; all of your nightmares; heal your dreams. But first, it's important to me that I find who I'm looking for. Very important."

"Very important," she whispered. *Is he here for Andrew?* she began to wonder through her confusion.

He leaned towards her with eyes that held galaxies. "Yes. That's right. Remember."

She could feel him somehow with her in her memories and was afraid for Andrew. *The witches. The fire.* She struggled against him, becoming agitated and rubbing her legs to comfort herself.

"Don't fight it. Give yourself to me," he told her, gently touching her tender cheek with his sharp fingertips.

*The arrow shot. The curse. A visitor.*

The light in his eyes grew brighter.

She did not know it, but Jatoba was breathless and unmoving. The hearth did not dance. Even the ash from the previous day's fire, wafting in the cool breeze, hung motionless in the night outside. But before she could continue, Andrew entered the tavern.

The stranger felt an unexpected change in the room and turned his head towards the door as a raven would, his eyes returning to eternal black, but he could not see Andrew.

"Hello?" the stranger asked.

"Leave her alone," Andrew replied.

The stranger rose. "Who's there?"

"I said, leave her alone," Andrew replied. He wasn't sure how he got there, but it didn't matter.

The stranger stepped towards the sound of Andrew's voice and squinted as his eyes returned to starlight, the feathers on the back of his neck rising like an agitated bird.

He tried hard to see through the room, through the tavern, through the town, but he could not see Andrew. "Why can I not see you?" he asked through clenched teeth.

Andrew didn't understand what was happening, but he didn't want a repeat of the previous day's attack, so he put himself between Feyloren and the stranger.

"What's your name?" Andrew asked. Lorna had taught him that there is power in one's name, and to be cautious of those who will not readily share theirs.

The stranger turned again to the sound of Andrew's voice, and he approached Andrew with movements like a bird. He could no longer see those parts of Fey behind the unknown voice, as though someone or something unseen blocked her from his view.

"I compel you to tell me your true name," Andrew said.

With a short bird squawk of a laugh, the stranger replied, "I am not easily compelled, nor do I take kindly to manipulation." Then he slowly reached for Andrew, but his hand moved through him like a hand through vapor. "You see, some of your tricks and trinkets were dreamed of by me, and just because you find them useful does not mean they are not still mine. And it appears you may not be easily manipulated either. Interesting. I can't even see you; here I can see everything, which must mean..." He reached into his robe, revealing the iridescent black skin of his arm for just a moment, and plucked a small bone from heavy clusters of chains full of bones hanging underneath his robe and around his neck. Then he crushed the bone in his hand with its unnaturally-long fingers and blew the bone dust at Andrew. A green fire burst forth so bright that the stranger stumbled backwards, shielding his face from the light.

Just then, Andrew awoke.

# CHAPTER 22

Andrew jerked the covers back and quickly crawled out of bed. His heart was racing.

The first kiss of dawn was drawing back the curtain of the night, and Andrew smelled something cooking in the kitchen.

Tomptee was humming something to himself over a sizzling pan of rashers.

"Good morning! I found some salted pork in the larder and..."

"I need to get back to Jatoba," Andrew said, frantically packing his rucksack and tying his boots.

"What's wrong?" Tomptee asked.

Andrew took a deep breath. "I'm not sure exactly, but I think Fey's in danger."

"Did you say something about Feyloren?" Perimas asked, rising from where he sat in front of the hearth, smoking a narrow pipe about the length of his thumb.

Andrew nodded. "I had a dream that felt more real than dream."

132

"Let me just wrap this all up, and we can eat it on the way," Tomptee replied.

Andrew shook his head. "I'm leaving straight away and don't want to wait for anyone. I hope you understand."

"I won't hold you up," Tomptee said, tossing the last of the bacon in a cloth, cinching it shut, and tucking it in a shirt pocket. Then he pulled on his leather duster. "We should take that with us," he said, pointing to the pieces of Lorna's broken staff still lying on fabric on the kitchen counter.

Andrew shook his head. "I won't touch it." Then he left the cabin.

Tomptee turned to Perimas, who just shrugged. Then he paused for a moment, weighing the pain he heard in Andrew's voice against the possibility of what might come, and decided to carry it himself. He wrapped the pieces in the fabric, tied them shut with twine, and tucked them carefully in his bag.

Outside, Andrew mounted Brynlee, and Perimas mounted his nicatoo—a gazelle-like creature with tall, twisting, narrow horns often ridden by smaller races and mocked by Longbeards and Minotaur. There was no mount in sight for Tomptee.

"Do you need a ride?" Andrew asked, a little confused how Tomptee had traveled to the cottage.

"No need," Tomptee said, holding up a hand. He pressed two fingers against his lips and whistled loudly. Through the forest came a gold and brown xenophon—a giant land frog—about half the size of Brynlee, who backed away from the creature as it hopped up to the fence gate.

Tomptee smiled and pet the xenophon beneath her chin, which made her close her eyes and let off a long, contented croak. Then he climbed onto a leather saddle with low-hanging stirrups that he cinched up to the length of his legs with the pull of a leather cord and settled into the well-worn saddle. "This is Marta," Tomptee said, rubbing the top of her head. Then he whistled through his teeth as Marta leapt off into the forest.

Andrew looked at Perimas, who shrugged. Then Andrew pulled Brynlee around and urged her on to Jatoba.

# CHAPTER 23

As the riders approached Jatoba from the valley road, they saw a black blanket of ravens covering the rooftops in the distance, which gave them pause.

"What happened here?" Perimas asked, the sight of the ravens making him nervous.

"Two nights ago, three women came to town," Tomptee began.

"Looking for me," Andrew interrupted.

"Why?" Perimas asked.

"They said they could smell a Grace Giver on me," Andrew replied.

Tomptee turned to him with a questioning look. He knew they had come for Andrew, but he hadn't known why.

Andrew returned to him an unspoken "you heard me" look.

"A Grace what?" Perimas asked.

"A child of Elohaynu, a being of myth and legend, powerful beyond finding out. Older than the world itself. It is said that a Grace Giver spoke the world into being. That they exist outside of time. In some places, they are worshiped. In others, feared. It is also said that they grant wishes, but never without a cost," Tomptee said.

Perimas chuckled. "Child's stories. Fey tales. I think I've heard that one. It's ridiculous."

"Except I've met one," Andrew said.

Tomptee looked at Andrew with astonishment. "What?"

Andrew nodded. "And the part about them granting wishes—*a* wish—but not without a cost," he looked away. "Well, apparently that part is true."

"How do you know this?"

Andrew didn't reply to Tomptee's questions but turned again to Perimas. "The women came to kill me. And I think I somehow caused this," he said, pointing to the birds.

Perimas looked up the hill to the town covered in a quilt of moving feathers. Something deep within him gave him great dread at the sight of the birds. "Grace Giver or no, I might try to find us some fresh game."

Andrew nodded. "Then peace to you."

"And you both," Perimas replied. Then he turned his mount and returned to the forest.

Andrew and Tomptee looked at each other, sharing without words the dread they both felt, then urged their animals forward.

JATOBA WAS QUIET. Hundreds of ravens sat atop every roof in town like funeral mourners.

There was no usual hustle and bustle of shops opening, morning chores, and people preparing for the day; there was no smell of baking bread or warming breakfast; no birds singing; no cattle in the pastures. It was a grey morning.

Andrew and Tomptee said nothing to each other as they quietly crossed the cobblestone streets. Save for the ravens, nothing was out of place, but the town didn't feel right. It felt more like a graveyard than a village.

As they entered the square, they looked around. Stores should have been open and preparing for the day, but they were all closed and quiet.

Tomptee felt like a mouse crossing an open field and wanted to hide, while Andrew's thoughts were for Fey.

As they dismounted, Daphnie came out to meet them.

"Daph!" Andrew exclaimed, happy to see anyone, especially her. "I've had such a dreadful vision in the night. Why is Jatoba still quiet? Have you seen Fey?"

Daphnie's eyes were heavy. She was draped in long grey robes and a wide hood covering her horns. "I'm glad to see you. I feared the worst."

Her forlorn countenance worried Andrew. "Why? What's happened?"

She led him to the small flat above the tavern where Feyloren slept. When Andrew saw her, he embraced her, but she did not wake to his touch.

Daphnie approached her bed and clapped loudly, which startled Andrew. Fey did not rouse or move. Then Daph shook her by the arm. "She will not wake," Daphnie said.

"What do you mean?"

"It started before you left. First, with the children, falling asleep and not waking. Their parents were doing everything they could: noise, movement, cold baths. But nothing worked. Then others. I'm the only one left," she told him gravely. "I've spent all night going from home to home, looking for anyone who might still be awake, and there is none. So, I've done what I can to quiet still burning hearths, lay children in their beds, and wrap as many in blankets as I can," she said, touching her throat as though it had been quite an ordeal.

"You must be exhausted," Andrew told Daphnie, touching her hand.

Daph gently smiled at his courtesy, but did not disagree.

Andrew then looked at Fey. She seemed so peaceful. "Do you know what's causing it?"

"I think you should come with me," Daphnie told him.

Andrew kissed Fey's forehead gently and followed Daph to her shop.

"Excuse me, friend, but I have to ask you to remain here while I speak with Andrew," she told Tomptee as the three entered the store.

Tomptee looked at Andrew, who nodded.

Daph lifted a small green stone hanging around her neck and kissed it as the front counter moved to the side and the glass floor opened to the vast arboretum below. Andrew followed her down a set of newly created stairs to the forest floor.

"These are new," Andrew said.

She nodded. "I'm getting too old to climb ladders."

There was no sound of bird song or leerie flies. No crickets or piquets croaking in the distance.

"Why is it so quiet?"

The look of concern on Daphnie's face disturbed Andrew.

"Please remove your shoes," she asked him, so he unlaced his boots and pulled off his woolen socks, leaving them draped on the bottom step of the stairs. The moss was soft and felt spongy beneath his steps as he followed her down the path he had walked with her before. Only this time, as he passed the small pond where she had planted the brynlee phalaenopsis he had given her when they first met, there was no stirring animal life. A plump, yellow Sproutling, twice the size of Fleur de Lis, slept on its stomach along the pond's edge, snoring loudly, with a hand branch hanging lazily into the still water.

Up top, Tomptee was fascinated by Daphnie's store. To most, it looked like a simple herbalist shop, with shelves of basil, lemon grass, and bilac lace, but Tomptee saw something else entirely. Braided sweetgrass slowly smoked near the door as incense for purification and calm, its smell reminding him of when he was a wee hoglet in his mother's kitchen, tasting and smelling different herbs.

"These are for flavor, these are for health, and these are for power," he remembered her saying, pointing to a page in one of her books, its margins full of handwritten notes. The book was beautiful, with frayed edges and wrinkled pages dotted with stains from her work.

"What is a small purple flower, seven petals, with white veins?" she asked him while stirring a pot of soup simmering on the hob. "And no peeking!" she verbally poked at him with a laugh and a shake of her head.

"Oh, I know this one. Don't tell me!" he said, barely tall enough to look over her table. He must have only been three or four. "Pu, puuu, passion in the night?"

His mother laughed a warm laugh and shook her head. "No, silly! Love in the mist. What is it used for?"

"Synthesize it into a tincture, then aromatize it into an ampordeze..."

"Aphrodisiac. Good!," she corrected.

Tomptee smiled at the memory. Time with his mother had always been special. With so many brothers and sisters, he rarely had one-on-one time with her. He missed her.

Then he continued around the shop, quizzing himself on the name and use of every plant. The small, deep-green shrub with purple berries and bright yellow flowers sitting in a pot by the door was known in the common tongue as night wort. Its roots were lethal, but its berries were the main ingredient in a powerful healing salve. *Purple needle causes sleep*, he thought, pointing at a pot hanging on the wall. *Astrazenus is a stabilizer in elixirs and tonics. Elmoree tastes like honey and is often added to cookies and cakes.* His eyes widened and he smiled. *Fromp!* He said to himself with excitement as he knelt next to a wood box holding a plant with long fronds of slender brown leaves shimmering with an oil-like, red iridescence that he gently touched with an open hand. When dried, crushed, and added to smoking herb, it created a sense of weightlessness and happiness. *Only a pinch*, he thought to himself, wondering the price of a few leaves. And at that thought, he started keeping a mental shopping list.

Back down below, Daphnie quietly led Andrew further down the mossy path, which branched off several times into entire groves of trees and swaths of prairie grasses of different varieties, surprising him at the incredible spaces hiding beneath her store. Then he and Daphnie stepped from the main path and wound their way through a blooming hedge that opened into a wonderful private garden dotted with an array of fragrant flowers. A bed, a desk and shelves of books were hidden in the glade. The cozy little garden was Daphnie's bedroom; her sanctum sanctorum. Andrew paused at the entrance out of respect.

Several cute and furry creatures slept around the room. A golden fairy with butterfly-shaped wings slept on the back of a deer. A slender, light purple Sproutling snored beneath Daphnie's desk. An entire family of bunnies—two adults and at least eight babies snuggled together by the door. Then he saw it: A long, snow-white, fur-covered neck wrapped beneath Daphnie's bed, heaving slowly back and forth as it breathed. Daphnie casually stepped past the sleeping menagerie to her bookshelf and took a strange tome off the shelf.

"What is that?" Andrew asked, kneeling and looking beneath her bed of intertwining tree roots covered with moss and lichen, draped with a simple, hand-made quilt and a few scattered pillows.

She turned to him and smiled. "That's Felecium. He's a luck dragon. They're born as twins only once every seven-hundred and forty-two years in the dark spaces amongst the stars. Every night, I travel the raven light with him—the land of the dreaming. He is exceptional. He is the only one of his kind in our world."

"But I thought you said..."

She approached the sleeping, dog-like dragon and ran her hand along the soft, downy fur on his neck. "We still visit his brother when we travel together through the raven light, but his brother is on a different world, far from here."

"Another world?" Andrew asked, rising and looking at her. "There are other worlds?"

She sighed. "You are young," she said, shaking her head and continuing to pet Felecium. "There are so many layers of truth. I don't want to overwhelm you. I would have preferred your grandmother teach you these things, but I fear there isn't time to introduce you to everything slowly. So, what I say next, I need you to believe."

Andrew's eyes widened. "I'm listening."

"There are many worlds scattered all across the heavens, including at least one where your kind is the only species that is self-aware."

Andrew's eyes grew wide. "Where is it? Have you seen it?"

Daphnie nodded. "Once. In the dreaming."

"What were the people like? How big was it, how many..."

She stopped him. "I'm sorry. I would love to discuss this with you, but we haven't much time, and there is much for me to explain if we have any chance of helping everyone. I fear you and your friend will soon succumb to the same sleep affecting the rest of Jatoba."

"How are you not affected?" Andrew asked.

"What do you know of the raven light?"

Andrew's mind raced across some of the stories his grandmother had shared with him. "It's a kind of passageway to the land of the dreaming."

Daphnie nodded. "A reflection of our world that can be manipulated by the dreamers asleep in this world. And not just us, but all dreamers in all worlds—a kind of shared reality."

"How is that possible?"

Daphnie's brow raised. "Is it so different from our own? This is my home, but if you set it on fire, wouldn't I now live in a reality that you have manipulated?"

Andrew considered this.

"The Great Ruach appointed children to set the worlds across all of His creation in order."

"Grace Givers," Andrew whispered.

Daphnie nodded. "Yes. They are known as Grace Givers here, but they have many other names on other worlds. One such being sets in order the land of death and dreaming. When the children would not wake, I thought that perhaps those pythonesses—those horrible *women*—had hexed the entire town, an incredible feat but not impossible considering some of the intuition they worked. Then I found some of my friends here beginning to sleep as well, some of whom are quite resistant to intuition. It wasn't until Felecium fell asleep that I knew something much deeper than intuition was at work. He is a part of both the waking and sleeping worlds and is entirely immune to intu-ition. I have tried everything in my power to wake him, but nothing has worked. Not even this," she said, rising and reaching towards the head of her bed as the vines opened and revealed a dark purple stone about the size of her hand. It was dull and opaque, like a large drop of purple smoke. "This is a Raxion—a sleeping stone not of our world but of the dreaming—that grants me travel between the waking and sleeping worlds. I should have been able to wake him with it, but I could not. Felecium exists beyond our intu-ition. While I must use the Raxion, he always exists freely in both places. And so, I tried to go into the dreaming to find him, but I could not enter it. The Raxion should be nearly clear as glass, but you can see that it is not." She took a deep breath. "It seemed that something was at work so powerful it could affect Felecium, powerful enough to cloud my Raxion. I sent Eet with a message to a friend at the Lincarna Academy, and she returned with this," and Daphnie handed Andrew a small, rolled-up piece of paper on which was written: *Consider the Tales of Trevalis*.

"What does it mean?" Andrew asked.

Daphnie approached a book lying open on her desk.

"Trevalis was a traveling scribe who lived during the time of the Elves, an ancient race who left our lands long ago. One of his stories speaks of a strange traveler who entered a wealthy and powerful city looking for something he had lost. Trevalis says that this traveler wore incredible robes of feathers and bone and spoke like a monarch. But when the king of the city would not grant him an audience, the city began to fall into a sleep without waking."

Daphnie quieted and turned to Andrew with a look that caused fear to rise within him.

"It began with ravens. Countless ravens covered the rooftops—watching and waiting. Then the children began to fall asleep, and soon the elders. Sound familiar?"

Andrew slowly nodded.

"Before long, there was no one left to grant the stranger's request, so the city slept... for three *hundred* years."

Andrew's mouth dropped. "What?"

Daphnie nodded, then she took out a pair of reading spectacles, rested them on the bridge of her nose, and began reading.

*Surely, even a child could have overthrown the entire city's standing army if it were not that the few who remained who knew of the city's location were so afraid of the curse covering it to barely speak its name above a whisper. Only through the drunken ramblings of an elder did I receive the name of the mountain upon whose cliff the once great kingdom of Emporium now stood. Many nights I tried to convince myself it was a fay tale of a once great kingdom from a bygone era, but my night visions would not leave me. It was as though Emporium beckoned me to find her; to visit her; to embrace her as a lover returning from war. So, to the cliffs I traveled. And there I found her, like a sleeping maiden, waiting for me; however, it was not just a maiden but an entire kingdom built of stone in quiet slumber. Towering edifices so exquisitely carved from the mountain face that one might have thought they were fashioned of the hands of the gods themselves. Marble statues sixty feet high, if one. Streets paved of white marble. Gardens once beautiful, now brambles and weeds. Into the homes I carefully went, and it was just as the tales had said: Everyone, from man to child, wealthy noble to the poorest pauper, lying in a sleep so powerful no sound or touch would cause them stir.*

Daphnie paused for a moment, trying to find her place and running her finger quickly down the page to the point in the story that she felt relevant to the circumstances at hand. "Ah, yes. Here we are," she said.

*As I entered the throne room, surrounded by armed guards sleeping so soundly that thick dust had entirely hidden their faces, I found one who was not asleep but sat on the throne of Emporium lazily like a jester mocking the court, and as I approached, he leaned forward. He wore a long, white robe of feathers that spread out around the stone chair. His hands were narrow and calculating, and his face painted white and black.*

*Did she say white and black?* Andrew asked himself as he listened to Daphnie.

*"Who are you?" I asked.*

*"I am king of this land now," he told me, then he proceeded to tell me of my life and all my most hidden passions—nay, my very dreams.*

*"How do you know such things?" I asked, to which he smiled and said, "Because I see you when you dream."*

*After some discourse, he told me his story, how he had come to the king seeking an audience, but the king refused. Then he stood, and in a voice of power and authority unlike any I had heard before or since, he said, 'And to deny me audience! A king of kings? A prince of Elohaneu! What fools these mortals be."*

*His words darkened my heart with fear and made me wish I had not graced these cursed stones with my shadow. But I did not dare flee, for if he could do what I saw with my own eyes, surely his power was great. So, instead of fleeing, I chose to use my gifts* of eloquence and engage this so-called king. "What is this thing you seek?" I asked him, unsure if I could help him, but knowing now that I was in the presence of power beyond even the most powerful elven wizards.

The stranger leaned forward. "You and your people dream of each other more than any food or found thing. Why?"

I considered his question for a moment. "Perhaps it is because we are fond of each other."

"But aren't you fond of your animals? Fond of your drink?"

"Yes, but our fondness for each other goes deeper than such things."

"How do you mean?" he asked.

"Well, it is true that a rider can be deeply fond of a mount he has raised by hand since it was fresh from its mother's teat, but that animal cannot speak with him, argue with him, laugh at his absurdities."

"So, you dream of others like you because you need to be laughed at?"

His questions were odd to me. Why did he not know of such things personally? But again, I chose to be careful in the presence of such power and felt little risk to try to answer. "Yes, but that is not all. What I mean when I try to describe such things is that perhaps we need someone who understands us. Someone who might empathize with us. Who shares our story. We need someone like us. And when we find them, some hidden part of us becomes attached to them in a way that goes deeper than reason."

At this, his shoulders dropped and he turned away. I thought, for a moment, that I had offended him.

"Is this what you call love?" he asked.

I nodded. "Yes. I suppose it is."

"So, to love, you need something...someone who is like you?"

*"Yes. I think so. At least enough like us to understand our hopes and fears."*

*Now, I could see the stranger's countenance fall. "Then I can never truly understand this love of which you speak, because there are none like me."*

*And as he said it, the guards sighed deeply and began to move. At that very moment, everyone in the kingdom began to wake. Then, the stranger rose from the throne. "You have done me a kindness scribe. And so, too, I will repay you kindness for kindness." And he reached into his robe and removed a coin from a pouch of blackened skin. "One favor," he said, then he tossed the coin to me and was gone. But within my heart, I heard him whisper, "Spend it wisely."*

*The coin was solid gold, with the visage of a raven pressed into it.*

Then Daphnie slid the book towards Andrew and showed him an ink sketch of the coin on the page. Then she closed the book.

"I considered the coin as I went from house to house. I had heard of such a coin but could not remember where. Then I remembered," she said, as she reached for another book lying on her desk beneath a garland of mend mum bulbs. This one a dreadful tome fashioned from gravestone clay. On the left side of the cover was a raven skull closely resembling the one on the coin, with a garland of dried oranges, cinnamon, mend-mum and zephyr bulbs hanging around its neck. On the right side was a strange image of a barren landscape with a high waterfall, and in the fore-ground fluttered a blue and black dire butterfly often found in graveyards.

She touched the skull on the cover, which closely resembled that which was on the coin sketch and took a deep breath. "This came into my possession by one who swore me never to open it. It is a tome of death and dreaming. Much of what is kept within these pages is not of our world. Things we are not meant to know. The Great Ruach wishes we were naive to some of these things, but alas, we lust too deeply for that which is not ours."

Her words resonated deep within Andrew's soul, as he remembered the archon's warning who protected the entrance of the Grace Giver's cave:

"Be wise, Andrew, son of Lithuel. Do not hunger for more than you can eat. Do not reach for more than you can carry. Do not lust for more than is yours. Or you will be consumed."

Andrew shuddered at the memory.

As Daphnie slowly opened the hard, clay pages of the book, Andrew saw that they contained some of the same script he had seen on the golden pages of Lorna's book in her cottage; the book the Igbaya had nudged towards him. Then, several of the creatures asleep around them began to stir and whine as though they had just entered a collective nightmare. Seeing their reactions gave Daphnie pause, and she looked at Andrew with concern, then she whispered a prayer of protection and continued.

"I cannot read most of what is written here, nor would I want to. It is the language of the dreamer, full of dire warnings and incantations to speak with the dead, even raise the dead; descriptions of things worse than death."

Andrew's body began to feel heavy, and it became difficult to understand her, but he thought he had heard this before... somewhere. "What could be worse than death?" he whispered.

"The flesh can be twisted only so far before it breaks, yet the mind... the mind can be twisted ad infinitum—again and again, forever." Suddenly, a wave of vertigo flushed over her, and she had to sit down.

Andrew reached for her. "Are you alright?"

She took a deep breath to steady her resolve and nodded—turning to a page pressed with the image of a raven's skull and a set of skeletal scales. She whispered another prayer of protection, then read, "The few words I can make out speak of one who governs the world of the dreaming. A... Raven King," she said, touching the page.

Andrew remembered the man in his dream with the long cloak of raven feathers.

"To some, he is a friend. To others, the worst kind of foe. A being of shifting shades. Ancient," she said, picking out a word here and there from the vertical lines of text. And as she did, her nose began to bleed.

"Daph!" Andrew said, pointing.

She gave him a questioning look, touched her face, and was surprised at the drop of red on her lip.

"We should stop," he told her.

"Please. It's important," she replied and continued.

The shape of the raven coin was pressed into the clay on the next page.

"Something about coins. Favors. Wise to distrust the raven," she said as her finger tried to follow the scratchy, broken lines. Then she shuddered, her head swayed, and it was all Andrew could do to stop her face from crashing into the corner of the desk as she passed out and fell to the floor, dropping the book.

"Daphnie!" Andrew called out, trying to help her to the soft, mossy ground. The sleep had not affected her, but the book had.

Then, he made the fateful mistake of picking up the book.

# CHAPTER 24

Andrew hears something—a gentle low like cattle in the fields with their spring calves.

He looks around, unsure where he is. It's the glade. It's Daphnie's glade. He's alright.

He sighs.

Daphnie sits at her desk with her back to Andrew. She's working on something, perhaps knitting something.

He approaches her to see if she's alright after her fall, but when he does, he sees she has no face, which startles him and he pulls back. His heart is beating heavily.

*Something doesn't feel right. Where am I?* he questions.

She doesn't notice him but keeps lowing to herself and knitting. Then he realizes she's knitting the skull of a raven into grey fabric with thread from the veins in her wrists.

He turns and flees, but as he crosses the threshold, he steps onto the cobblestone street of Nevarii in front of the townhouse his grandmother owned many years ago.

Andrew is confused, and his heart is racing now.

A narrow brownstone. Two stories. Someone is arguing inside. A cart. A tinker's cart.

150

It's Lithuel's cart!

Andrew quickly crosses the street and calls out: "Father!" But Lithuel doesn't hear him. "Father, it's me!" Andrew calls again, touching the man's arm, but Lithuel doesn't respond. He continues wiping off the end of his spanner, sets it in his toolbox, and turns to the house where the arguing grows louder. Andrew watches Lithuel knock on the front door and speak with a young Lorna about the work and the price of the buttons he has mended on the seats of her carriage. Andrew never knew his gran at this age. Then, a much younger woman looks out from the upstairs curtain, and Andrew's heart stops.

*Mom?*

And just as he is about to dart into the house, his gran walks past him into the brownstone, following her younger self up the stairs. Now, there are two of them.

Andrew swallows. *What is she doing here?*

As he crosses the threshold into the townhouse, Andrew is suddenly upstairs in his mother's bedroom where she frantically tries to calm a baby. Her face is red and wet with tears. His grandmother is standing in the hall watching, her face painted with worry and sorrow, but she doesn't see him. "Gran?" he asks, but she doesn't respond.

*Is that me?* Andrew wonders as his mother watches the younger Lorna pay Lithuel through the window, then his mother turns and leaves the room. As she does, she passes through him like stepping through vapor.

He follows her. Only now, he steps onto the street across from the wagonway station. His mother is crying again and squeezes the baby as she quickly tucks him under the tinker's dirty tarp.

The older Lorna leaves the shadows of a nearby alley as

Lithuel pulls away, and as she does, everything on the street becomes entirely still, except for her and Andrew.

"Gran, what's happening?" he asks, but she doesn't hear him.

Something is coming.

The hairs raise on his arms, and he can feel himself beginning to panic.

A tall, gaunt figure draped in a train of black feathers and wearing a large black raven skull begins to step across the street towards Lorna. "What are you..." the figure starts to ask, then stops. He slowly turns towards Andrew.

Lorna stumbles and leans on her staff for a moment, then reaches to remove the velvet sack covering the end of her staff as the figure holds up a long, black, clawed finger, and Lorna freezes.

"I have felt you before," the stranger says to Andrew. "In the tavern."

Andrew flees down an alley and around a corner when suddenly he comes upon three boys, one with yellow skin, mocking a small Human child.

"Look at the humatti!" the boy with yellow skin laughs.

"I've never seen one before," his friend says.

This seems somehow familiar to Andrew, but he's unsure why.

Then the yellow boy grabs the young Andrew by the foot, pulls off his shoe, and stabs Andrew in the center of his tiny foot with his finger so hard that the younger Andrew screams in pain, and the older Andrew winces at the memory that now crashes into his mind like a punch in the gut.

"Hey!" he calls out, now remembering the abuse. And this time, he's much larger and much older than the bullies. "Leave him alone!" he screams, fury rising in him.

Then the boy's faces change, and they unnaturally shake their heads and slowly turn towards the older Andrew. Only, now they wear the same ash-black raven skull the stranger wore in the street.

Andrew's eyes widen, and he takes a step back and turns to flee, but the stones beneath him become wet sand. The way from which he came is gone. His alley has become a long, narrow path of shifting sand, surrounded by towering buildings on every side. The stranger stands at the end of the now-closed alley—calm and unmoving.

"Who are you?" the stranger asks. "I could not see you before, but I can see you now."

Suddenly, Andrew is holding the graveyard book, which he drops into a splash of water rising through the sand. He feels himself sinking and looks back at the boys who are not sinking but approaching him with the herky-jerky movements of birds.

Andrew has nowhere to run. He tries to pull his feet out of the sand but sinks deeper with every step. The water is now up to his waist, his chest, his neck.

The stranger slowly approaches him, standing upon the water, pulling his long train of black feathers behind him like royal robes.

"Take my hand. I can help you," the stranger offers, reaching into the water.

The quicksand holds Andrew's feet firmly. He sucks in one last breath as the water engulfs him.

"Let me help you," the stranger says.

Andrew's heart pounds with every passing moment of tightly held breath. He tries again to pull away from the sucking grip of the sand, but the sand holds him fast.

*Do not trust the raven,* he remembers Daphnie telling him. *There are things worse than death.* Is this it? Is this the end? The faces of his loved ones flash in his mind like bright lights: Feyloren, Lithuel, Lorna, Daphnie, Brutste. He never had the chance to know his mother. Does Fey really know how he feels? How much she means to him? How hard he tried?

When Andrew finally opens his eyes, he can see the stranger standing above him upon the water along with the three boys who mock him as he struggles.

Andrew finally frees himself and begins to swim. Only now, the surface is gone completely. There is no sand or ground beneath him, no surface above him. He hangs motionless in an infinite void of dark, cold water—a liquid oubliette. But he is not alone.

The stranger is here before him in the infinite void of liquid darkness; motionless; calm and terrifying. His robe of feathers gently floats around him in two separate pieces of cloak, spread wide like the incredible wings of a raven; his exposed feet are black and clawed, and draped upon his narrow form is a garment of countless tiny animal-like bones.

"I am not here to hurt you. You can trust me. I am the Ancient of Days, and I can free you from this watery tomb. Just tell me your name, and take my hand," the raven says with a soothing voice; however, Andrew feels a strong revulsion and shakes his head as the stranger speaks that name: Ancient of Days. It's a lie. He doesn't know how, but he knows as clearly as he knows his own name. This person, this *creature* in the water before him, is certainly *not* the Most Ancient One.

Without thinking, Andrew releases a bubble, which, for a long moment, does not move in the water. But it does draw Andrew's attention. Then, the bubble slowly... sinks.

Andrew's calculating brain latches onto this tiny detail

and he releases a few more precious spheres of air and watches them sink as well. *I'm upside down!*

Andrew quickly twists in the water and swims with the rising bubbles as his panic crests. The bubbles he released were the last exhale of someone who could do nothing else but gasp for a lethal, final lung-full of cold ocean water. And at the very last moment, just as he convulses to inhale, his face breaks through the water surface, and instead of cold ocean water, Andrew sucks in the life-give grace of fresh, fragrant air.

Andrew splashes at the water's surface, grasping at air and life, as his hand finds the stony floor of a cave. He pulls himself towards the edge, props himself up on his arms, and struggles to catch his breath. Once he does, he looks around.

*Where am I now?* he wonders—his mind reeling from the quickly changing landscapes through which he has been fleeing. But this place... somehow, this place feels welcoming and familiar.

A green glow kisses the surface of his skin.

# CHAPTER 25

Andrew pulled himself out of the water with great difficulty and rolled onto his back, still gasping for air and trying to understand what had just happened and where he was. Then he slowly sat up.

A gnarled hornbeam covered in blinking eyes watched him as a young girl stepped out from behind the tree. Her white hair was so fine that it rose ever so gently in the air like a halo, and her dress was a sheer blush linen with a green sash tied around her waist. Her feet were bare.

Andrew sighed a deep sigh of relief.

The young girl walked slowly around the tree and climbed a low horizontal branch, she tucked her thin legs beneath her dress, and sat.

"I'm so glad to see you!" Andrew exclaimed, calming himself and rising.

"Please, remove your shoes," she gently asked.

"Oh, yes. Of course," he replied, kicking off his now completely dry boots and pulling off his socks. He looked back toward the water and saw the darkened, distant shape of a raven deep beneath its surface.

"What have you done?" the girl asked.

The question sank in Andrew's heart. "What do you mean?"

The young girl buried her head in her hands and began to cry in a way that tore Andrew's heart in twain. He wanted to approach her and try to comfort her, but he dared not. Then he realized that the eyes of the tree had turned away from him.

"What *have* I done?" he gently asked.

She looked up at him with deep sorrow and pain painted across her face. "Have you any idea how long I waited for you? I dreamt the dream of you; one whose heart might be like mine; one who might sit in my presence and not demand trinkets and gifts. When you came, you did not come for selfish means but to help another. And so, you found favor. Then this," she said, pointing.

Andrew turned to see a vision of himself standing upon the water. It was the night the wicked sisters had attacked him and Lorna in Jatoba. What he could not see then, but he could see now with the help of the Grace Giver's vision, was an unseen hand like smoke slowly stretching from one of the sisters' mouths, squeezing Andrew by the throat, and lifting him off the street until Lorna's word of silence broke its grasp and dropped him. Then, from the ether, stepped the little girl. In the vision, she was a being of green glowing light, and she put her hand on Andrew's back. He remembered the strength and resolve he felt in that moment, helping him to rise. He didn't know it at the time, but it had been the Grace Giver's hand of protection upon him.

As the three wicked sisters reached for him, the vision slowed.

He watched as the arrow left Fey's bow and passed

him close enough to brush his hair. The unseen girl raised her hand and the arrow passed through her palm, which ignited the arrow in green fire that exploded on impact, knocking she who was deaf back and dispelling fog surrounding the sisters. Then one of the sisters cursed Fey, a curse that took the form of dense black smoke pouring out of the sister's mouth, but the girl in green dispelled most of it before it hit Fey, striking Fey with illness instead of death. Then the girl stepped between Andrew and the wicked sisters, her form changing from the image of the young girl into that of a tall and powerful woman of almost terrifying radiance and beauty. In her hands was a spear of pure light the length of a weaver's beam, which she lowered at the three women.

And then, the vision froze.

"I was prepared to fight for you, but something in you changed. You could have asked for help. You could have spoken a word of protection. You could have pleaded with them. Anything. But instead, you chose... *hate*." A word that caught in her throat, making her touch the hallow of her tender throat.

Andrew watched himself scream and lift Lorna's staff. In the vision, there were now dozens of people standing in a long line behind the wicked sisters as the embodied forms of distant memories. There was an adolescent boy from Jatoba painting humatii in blood on his shop door; an elderly Minotaur woman spitting at him when he had first arrived in Jatoba; the city guard who mocked him; the boys who attacked him as an infant and on and on. When Andrew lowered Lorna's staff at the three, he wasn't merely defending himself or his family; he wasn't even trying to stop them. He was trying to *kill* them and repay all the pain he had suffered because of the color of his skin. And in that moment, just as in the present one, he knew this was true.

Once again, the vision came to a standstill.

Still moving freely within the vision, the Grace Giver turned to the vision of Andrew and touched his chest. "You don't have to do this," she whispered to him. "You are more than this. Do not repay evil for evil. I lay before you life and death. Choose life!" But alas, he did not. Andrew chose death.

"Tannish ee looma!" Andrew yelled as Lorna cried out to stop him. "I bind you!" And as he said those words, the tall and beautiful woman vanished, and a glow of blood red grew from within him and poured through his mouth and hands at the wicked sisters like liquid fire. "I rebuke you!" he yelled over the screams of the women. In the unseen, he saw the fire engulf them and pass beyond them to those standing behind them in the near and distant memory. For all the times he had been bullied, for all the times he had been spat on and kicked, for all the times he had turned the other cheek. Well, not this time, not here. Attacking his family was too much. "I cast you into the place of forgetting!" he screamed until his throat went dry, pouring that fire from inside of him out through his hands and Lorna's staff, heating it to the point of burning and dropping it to the ground.

The last thing Andrew heard before the visions faded was the sound of Lorna screaming, "Don't! Please!" Her final word unnaturally echoed around the cave, somehow mixing with the voice of the Grace Giver as though it was not just his gran pleading with him but both of them.

Andrew hung his head low. "They attacked my *family*," he whispered under his breath.

The girl sensed a change in his heart toward her. She

159

was becoming his adversary. "But that is *not* why you did it."

It was true. He had been ridiculed so fiercely his entire life that when he had the power to stop it, he used it, and he did not regret it. She saw that in him.

"Evil will never vanquish evil. Do you know why I chose this form to speak with you?" she asked, sorrow streaming down her cheeks as she looked at her frail hands. "It is not just for your sake—because you could not look upon my true nature and survive—but because I find it beautiful. You are beautiful and precious to me. You who are the least amongst your brethren."

*Beautiful? How could I possibly be beautiful? My pale skin. My hair that will not straighten. My weak arms and unintuitive nature. I have never been beautiful, not once. I am humatii. Pale face. Other.*

Her eyes returned to him. "You are *not* other," she replied as though he had said these things directly to her. "You are my child, and I created you. I fashioned you by my hand! I chose your humanity! You cannot see this now, but I *shaped your brokenness!* My fingerprints are all over your life. What you call weak, I call tender-hearted. What you see as unintuitive, I see as a wonderful opportunity to slow down and be creative, like me. Humans are the *most* compassionate and creative of all my creations. You lead with your hearts, and I love that so much about you," she said, looking at him, now with sorrow for herself and him.

Her words were weighty and confusing to Andrew. *There are others like me? Where? Fingerprints all over my life? What could this all mean?* He had never heard such things. But one word did ring true: Other. He hadn't realized how he had been tormenting himself until he heard that word, which rang in his ears, in his mind, in his heart and soul like the tinkling of a bell. It *felt* like a summary of his entire life. *Other. Yes, that's it. I am other.* The realization of it swept over him like clearing fog. He had seen himself as other more than anything else. He had so deeply internalized the lies that they soon sounded like his own voice. He no longer knew where those voices stopped and his own began. But here in this place, somehow, she knew. She saw all of him, exactly as he truly was. Past his facade and beyond the lies and pieces of his broken past, she saw the perfect and innocent child struggling to find meaning and purpose in life.

However, even in the presence of Perfect Truth, those other voices were not gone.

"But you have never protected me," he said, narrowing his gaze at her.

Her look became stern, and he felt himself beginning to cross a line.

"Your father was not supposed to be in Nevarii that day. He had a dream that night, reminding him to repair a broken tool, so he went. And there he found work at a woman's house whose daughter would soon hide her child in the back of his cart. It was I who spoke to Lorna through the wind and snow to come find you. And the night you went out onto the lake, looking for the night flowers? It was I who summoned the elotoo to rise from the depths where it slept, to strike out and catch the dragon who found you on its island. It was I who led you into the shepherd's field near the mouth of this cave. It was I who hid you from my brother last night in the tavern! I *have* protected you. I have drawn you to me your entire life! I have wanted you to draw near to me; to *choose* me."

He remembered his dream. "If this is true, then I have not felt it. I have not seen you. You have remained silent my *entire life!* And now, you say that you want me to choose you? This sounds like a game. Well, it wasn't a game to me. They attacked my family! You might be able to stand by and watch, but I could not! If this is what you call love, then I reject your love," he snapped, and as soon as he said it, he realized it was a mistake. Andrew looked away in shame. "You could have come to me so many times in the midst of my darkness and despair. My suffocating loneliness. My sorrow. You couldn't possibly understand," he whispered.

She rose, and the image of the small child in the blush linen dress faded into that of a tall being with flowing hair and robes of radiant light. "Can't understand? I can't *understand*? How dare you speak to me with such insolence! I hold every sick child and weeping mother. In horror and anguish, I watch countless mortal beings scattered across the heavens kill and plunder by the multitude, hearing every single heartbeat as it beats its last. Not a single prayer to me in the secret places is lost. I mourn deeper than you could ever imagine!" As she spoke, the sound of countless voices filled the cave. "Their voices may fall silent to you, but they never fall silent to me. I STILL hear them, every single one of them. You have no idea..."

"Then where were you!?" Andrew cried out. "Why watch them suffer!? Where were you when my mother cast me aside like rags!?"

"I could erase the very memory of you from history. I could pluck your entire family tree up by its root and cast it aside. How dare you question my compassion or my resolve?" she spoke as her voice rose like the sound of mighty waters, and her light shone so bright that even the shadows ceased to exist. "Am I not the one who set time in motion? Who gave you bread to fill your belly and rain to feed your crops? Am I not the one who causes kingdoms to rise and fall at my will? Just because you found favor with me once does not mean I am a child to be corrected. If you knew with whom you speak, you would silence yourself. I AM the Ancient of Days."

*Ancient of Days.* He had heard that before in the mouth of the trickster raven. "Are you?" he asked, turning again to her. "That's what *he* called himself," he said, pointing into the now dark water. "Or is this also a trick? Am I dreaming? Do you know these things about me because I know them about myself?" And he started laughing. "I am not afraid of you. I AM NOT AFRAID OF YOU!" he screamed and slapped his chest, his words echoing around him.

At that, the brilliant light dimmed, and the tree was gone. Only the little girl stood before him, brokenness on her face.

"Andrew, son of Lithuel. I dreamt the dream of you and have loved you with an everlasting love, but because you have rejected me, My Spirit has departed from you. I will not strike you down because I remember that you are but dust. As such, you and your friend will leave Jatoba safely, not because of who you are but because of who *I* am. But you must never return. If you do, you will surely die."

Now, *this* scared him. But she was gone.

And suddenly, Andrew woke in Daphnie's glade.

# CHAPTER 26
## THIRTY YEARS AGO

The bald boy with sapphire-blue skin leaned against a bulkhead as the ship listed in a storm that had been blowing violently for the past two days, with no sign of relenting. There was an unnaturally low fog on the water, which made the superstitious crew nervous. Visibility through the fog was now barely two cable lengths from the forecastle—a quarter mile. As the storm approached, they made out to sea, but no one knew how close they were to Dead Man's Reef just south of Eetoomba.

For two days, the ship groaned, timbers creaked, and waves crashed as the crew worked with careful urgency to tie down sails and lash the bow against the wind and waves. They gripped rope and rail with white knuckles, trying hard not to get swept overboard with every gust that threatened to wipe the deck clean of anything and everyone not lashed down.

Below deck, the hold sloshed with seawater and various ephemera such as stray papers, globs of tar knocked loose, and bits of rotting food. There was nowhere on the ship to hide from the constant drip, drip, drip of cold saltwater.

Meals had been scarce since no one had time to eat. Now, Petros's sister Sa-uree, pried open a barrel of dried peas to add to the portion of ship's biscuit and salt beef that the captain had instructed her to give to each crew member. As she did, the men watched her with hungry eyes.

Everybody was exhausted and on edge, their skin raw and eyes burning from the constant spray of salt water.

Each man took their portion and quietly stepped aside until a bald Longbeard man objected, who wore his beard so long it wrapped around his neck.

"I lost my best mate today. I'll take his portion as well."

Sa-uree didn't even look at him. "A biscuit, a strip, and half a handful o' peas, each man. Those are the orders."

He grabbed Sa-uree's wrist. "I'll have his portion as well, or I'll have somethin' from you."

She jerked her hand away, casting the Longbeard's food into the mucky water several inches deep on the floor.

Petros saw the exchange, drew a blade, and lunged at the Longbeard, who was ready for the fight, just as the lion guard stepped out from the shadows and laid a large hand on the Longbeard's shoulder.

"You heard the captain's orders," he said with a low, slow growl. "Are you questioning them?"

The Longbeard looked at him and knew.

Just then, there was a deafening crash and the ship jerked forward, sending everyone tumbling across barrels and into bulkheads as water poured into the hold. Everyone rushed to the top deck, and Petros reached for Sa-uree, helping her to her feet.

"All hands on deck, I say, all hands!" the captain cried from the top of the stairs.

"Go!" Sa-uree told Petros, "Go."

He hesitated. He wanted her with him; however, he knew the work would be hard and that it was much safer for her below deck during the heavy storm.

"Stay near! I'll return for you," and he pressed the handle of the shiv into her palm. She tucked it beneath her coat and nodded to him. Then, he joined the rest of the crew.

The anger of Macpella blew with ferocity, but the ship did not move in the waves as it had. Something was holding it fast until an errant wave of incredible size crashed into the side of the ship, dislodging it from where it had caught on a reef, spinning the ship around, and dashing it against a dagger of rock jutting out from the violently frothing surf. As it did, Petros and at least a third of the crew went careening overboard into the dark water, some of whom were immediately torn apart by the razor-sharp reef.

Petros' heart pounded as he fought for breath but only found a mouthful of water. Then, something struck his shoulder and pressed against him. He instinctively grabbed for it and held it tight. It was the barrel of dried peas his sister had opened moments earlier, now empty and rising from below the waves with him in tow. The moment he felt his face touch air, he gasped in a lungful with everything he had. Then, he tried in vain to gain his bearings.

"Help!" he cried out, "Help!" But his voice immediately disappeared into the cacophony of wind and rain.

The barrel was almost too large for him to wrap his arms around. It was bobbing violently, so he removed his belt, tossed it around the barrel, tied it tight, and wrapped

166

his arm in the length of leather as many times as he could, which turned him into something of an anchor that kept dragging beneath the waves. Just as he would find a moment to pull his head out of the water long enough to breathe, the barrel would spin and plunge him beneath the water again. After several minutes, he repositioned his hands on either side of the barrel, pulled it to an angle that used its awkward shape in his favor and kept his head above water. Then, something in the darkness grabbed his shirt. He turned to see the grasping hands of the first mate fighting for life.

For a moment, Petros considered if he should try to help him or let him disappear beneath the waves. Especially since an attempt to help him might pull them both under. But he couldn't do it; he couldn't let the first mate drown. He grabbed the lion's wrist and helped him find the mouth of the barrel where he could pull himself up and out of the water enough to breathe.

As lightning flashed, Petros and the lion looked at each other, fighting to survive. They gripped each other's arms and held on. Petros pulled the lion's paw-like hand to the leather strap and secured it as best as he could.

Before long, the lion growled through the sound of the wind and pointed to the faint sliver of a shore peeking through the fog. Together they started kicking. Through floating wreckage, they fought to make their way to ground. When their feet touched sand, they released the barrel and splashed through the waves until they made the beach and fell onto their backs. Petros struggled for air until he vomited a lungful of water onto the sand. Then he passed out.

When Petros awoke, it was morning, and the sun was starting to burn his tender skin. He shielded his face with a hand and slowly lifted himself to his feet. Ill from being tossed overboard and without his "land legs," he could barely stand. There was no sight of the ship on the horizon, and the beach was scattered with pieces of wreckage that had washed ashore during the night, including the lifeless bodies of several crew members. The lion first mate he had saved in the night was lying on the sand not far from him.

After struggling with his first steps, Petros found the lion breathing, so he slowly began walking the beach, looking for any sign of either his sister or the ship.

There was none.

# CHAPTER 27
## PRESENT DAY

Andrew shook himself loose from the clay book and quickly rose to his feet—the image of the raven skull on the cover now terrifying him. *How long have I been lying here?* he wondered, running out from Daphnie's glade, across the moss-covered path, and up the stairs to where Tomptee lay sleeping in the corner of the shop.

"Tomptee!" Andrew called, but he didn't move. Then Andrew shook him hard, and the furry Inkling gently stirred.

"By daisies, where are we?" Tomptee whispered.

"We have to go," Andrew replied.

"Where?"

"Anywhere but here. I've made a terrible mistake, and we aren't safe. We must go. Can you walk?"

Tomptee rubbed his face and slowly rose. "I think so." He felt drunk.

Once outside, they found that the animals, too, were sleeping, but Andrew's touch was enough to rouse them. And together, Andrew and Tomptee fled Jatoba.

ALONG THE ROAD out of Jatoba, down through the valley, Andrew and Tomptee found a well-used campsite where—by the sight of the volume of ash in its pit—a fire had been fed and burning for days. Two deer pelts hung on hand-built wooden frames leaning against a tree. Perimas's mount grazed on wildflowers freely nearby.

"Welcome!" came a holler from up in the tree. "I almost gave up on you two. What took you so long?" Perimas asked, climbing down through the branches.

Andrew and Tomptee dismounted.

"Where has the night gone?" Tomptee asked, kneeling by the fire to consider why it looked so used.

"Night? Which night?" Perimas asked.

Andrew took a deep breath, remembering the stories. "How long has it been since we last saw you?" he asked Perimas.

"Nearly three days."

Tomptee rose and looked at them. "This can't be."

Perimas looked confused. "Why? Where were you? When you did not return, I assumed things were well and you were resting. I was waiting for you to send word. Is something wrong?"

"Have you anything to eat?" Andrew asked.

"Of course," Perimas replied, motioning them to join him by the fire.

Together, they ate some venison and wild potatoes Perimas had collected. He had also managed to brew a handful of coffee beans. It was thin but hot, and that was good enough for Tomptee.

"Brutste packed me some essentials before I left town," he told them.

Brutste. Feyloren. Now Daphnie. Everyone was gone. Everyone except...

Andrew sat up, realizing that through all of the commotion of the past few days he had completely lost track of his father.

"Tomptee?"

"Hmm?" Tomptee asked, from where he leaned against a tree, savoring a hot cup of coffee with both hands that looked much too large for him.

"Do you remember back in the tavern?"

Tomptee nodded.

"There was a man with me."

"Aye, the Nimic."

"You don't happen to remember seeing him leave town, do you?"

Tomptee took a long drink of his coffee, wiped his wet, furry mouth with the back of his hand and shook his head. As he did, Nelot, his grey furry friend, poked its head out from the inside of Tomptee's jacket and sniffed at the cup of coffee. Tomptee smiled and poured a few drops into the palm of his gloved hand, letting Nelot have a taste.

"I need to go home," Andrew told them.

"Where's home?" Perimas asked.

Andrew hesitated. Just then, a large raven landed on a branch in the tree just above them, which made the hair on the back of Andrew's hands stand on end. Perimas didn't like the sight of the bird but wasn't sure why. Tomptee, on the other hand, was entirely unwilling to sit around and let the dire creature ruin his cup of coffee, so he slowly set it aside, rose, and took a sling from a pouch without taking his eyes off the bird. Neither Andrew nor Perimas was paying any attention to what he was doing until a small stone he had found at the base of the tree turned into a lethal projectile and struck the bird dead true, sending its motionless corpse to the ground in a falling plume of feathers.

Andrew turned to Tomptee in horror.

"And I've got more than enough stones for the lot of 'em," he replied, mostly to himself, and sat back to enjoy his coffee.

The now-dead creature lay on the grass in front of Andrew, wings spread wide, and all Andrew could do was remember the shape in the water. Nothing that had happened to him was fading as dreams do. No, he could remember every detail. The graveyard book. The sleeping animals. The stranger in his dream. Or was it a dream? The water. The Grace Giver. The warning that he should never return to Jatoba.

Andrew set his coffee down as his two compatriots watched him with trepidation.

"What's happening in Jatoba?" Perimas asked.

So, Andrew told them.

# CHAPTER 28

A ndrew told Tomptee and Perimas about Daphnie and how there was something greater than a curse upon Jatoba, yet he omitted what he had experienced in the dreaming, which wasn't difficult since he wasn't quite sure what had been real and what had been his own imaginings anyways.

"I don't know how to help our friends, but I know this: If we go back, we may never be able to leave again. And that's why I want to know if my father is safe."

"Then we're off," Perimas said, rising, kicking dirt onto the fire, taking down the now dry pelts, which he rolled and tied onto the back of his mount, and prepared to leave camp.

"I've been meaning to ask: How do you know Feyloren?" Perimas asked Andrew.

Andrew checked Brynlee's straps to make sure everything was still snug. "We are soon to be married."

Perimas shook his head. "I'm sorry, you're what?"

Andrew looked up over Brynlee's saddle. "In two weeks. Do you know each other?"

"I'm her husband!"

Andrew stepped back. Surely, he misheard. "What? Her husband? That can't be. She's never been married."

"We've been married two years, and she's pregnant with my child."

Andrew shook his head. "Then we can't be speaking of the same person."

Tomptee stepped towards them as Perimas approached Andrew. Andrew wasn't sure how to read the situation. It must be a misunderstanding, yet Perimas was becoming agitated.

"Feyloren of Jatoba?" Andrew asked.

"Yeah! Feyloren of Jatoba."

Andrew's mind raced. "There's no way. Fey and I have been together for nearly a year. She's never said one word about having ever been married, and I can assure you: She is not pregnant."

Perimas leaned towards Andrew in a hotly aggressive posture, but Tomptee stepped between them and pushed Petros back. Andrew still didn't understand what was happening.

"My fiancé is bald and owns the tavern," Andrew said, taking a step back, trying to dispel the confusion.

"That's my wife!" Perimas snapped and shoved Andrew to the ground.

"Stop!" Tomptee hollered, caught between the two men.

Andrew scrambled to his feet. "She can't be your wife! I've never seen you! If you're married, where do you live?"

"In Jatoba!" Perimas said, pushing against Tomptee, more in show than an actual interest in hurting Andrew since Tomptee was little match for Perimas' size, agility, and the blade that hung at his side. "My family practically *built* that town."

Andrew dusted himself off. "Then why have we never met?"

Perimas couldn't answer this. Why was everyone acting like he'd been gone for years instead of days?

"My Feyloren is Brutste's sister," Andrew said.

"Daughter of Gaylen," Perimas replied. "Who was taken from her as a girl. Yes. I know. I was there the day they took him. I taught her how to shoot. We were married in the valley, and she is pregnant with my child. And she's *not* your Feyloren. She's *my* Feyloren," Perimas said, pushing Tomptee's hands off his chest and nearly knocking the Inkling to the ground.

Andrew tried to fit what Perimas was saying into what little he knew of Fey's past. "She is Gaylen's daughter, but she's never told me what happened to him. How can this be? Why have we never met?"

Perimas turned in frustration, drew his sword, and struck the tree.

"Wow, wow!" Tomptee exclaimed. "There's no need for that!"

"What is happening!?" Perimas screamed, fighting against the rising sense of helplessness from his lack of memory and whatever it was that was going on.

Andrew held up his hands, trying to calm Perimas. "Please. Put the blade away. There has to be some misunderstanding. Are you sure you were married?"

Perimas slowly turned to him and leveled his blade at Andrew.

"Alright, alright. You were married. There has to be an explanation. I'm sure Fey can clear all of this up when..."

Tomptee looked at Andrew and saw Andrew's shoulders drop. He knew she couldn't answer anything until the curse was lifted. Then he turned back to Perimas. "Help us."

Perimas glared at the squat little man. "Why would I help you?"

"Help Fey," Tomptee said.

Perimas's countenance softened ever so slightly, and Tomptee saw it.

"Something big is happening, and she's caught in it with the rest of the town. Clearly, you can hunt. You know these woods. Help us help her. I'm sure we can sort this out once the curse is lifted."

Perimas wanted to kill both of them, but his better self stopped him from doing that. His next instinct was to turn and walk away, flee into the solitude of the forest as was his way, but instead, he sighed, sheathed his blade, and ran a hand through his hair in frustration.

"Normally, I would kill you where you stand," he said, then looked away for a moment. "But something is happening. And not just to my home." He looked again at Andrew. "I can't be certain where I was before I returned to Jatoba. In truth, I seem to be missing at least a few days." And he pointed at Andrew. "And that alone wouldn't be enough, but when I saw her, somehow, she was different. I don't know how..." He clenched his teeth. "But it scares me. You say you know my wife?"

Andrew wanted to immediately object to that label, but he could see fear and confusion in Perimas's eyes. So, he just nodded.

"I will come with you, for Fey's sake," he said, pointing again. "But if I find that you have dishonored her in any way, I swear by the gods, I will kill you."

Andrew could see Perimas's resolve and nodded.

Tomptee sighed a heavy sigh of relief. He waited a

moment longer for Perimas and Andrew to mount their animals before mounting Marta. Then he asked, "Where are we headed?"

Andrew could feel his body cooling after the adrenaline-fueled encounter, and he wasn't feeling up for a ride, but he was worried about his father, and there was nothing they could do for Fey at the moment. "My father and I have a cabin in Aitecham Tioram," Andrew replied, expecting some level of protest, but neither of his companions said anything. "Aitecham Tioram," Andrew said again, this time more slowly. "The Dry Places."

Tomptee looked at him and nodded.

"Does that not scare you?" Andrew asked.

"Should it?" Tomptee asked.

"Yes!" Andrew replied with a flourish of his hands.

"Why?" Perimas asked.

"Because it's dangerous! Deadly creatures. One false step and your entire mount could be lost in the dark water."

"I assume you know the way if you live there," Perimas replied begrudgingly.

"And Marta here can swim!" Tomptee added. "Can't you girl." And he leaned down and petted what looked like a large ear hole. Marta closed her eyes and kicked her back leg. Andrew could swear she was smiling.

"People often think the place is cursed," Andrew said.

"Is it?" Perimas asked.

"Well, no..."

"Good, then lead the way!" Tomptee replied. "Besides, most curses don't bother me," Tomptee added with a shrug, and together they began to ride.

THEY RODE without a word for more than an hour as Andrew tried to process everything. There were so many broken pieces. It was hard enough to know what was true and what was a dream. Now this. He felt sick. Could Fey have been lying to him? She was older than him. He had always thought of her as wiser and more experienced, but he assumed it was because of her age. He had often asked her about her past and family, and she didn't exactly try to hide anything from him, not that he knew of anyway, but her answers were always short and direct. What happened to your father? "Arrested." What was your youth like? "Bruste and I took care of each other." He never pushed for more. He figured it was her story to tell, and she would share it with him when she was ready. Besides, he loved her for who she was today, not whoever she had once been. But her being married? That was more than just a story from her adolescence. And pregnant? There was no way. Then what was Perimas talking about? And where had he been until several days ago? Perhaps something was affecting his memory so much that he *thought* Fey was his wife. Andrew had heard of people whose minds had been so affected by a fever that they would talk to themselves, bark at the moon, or even cut themselves with pieces of broken clay. Was the curse on the town somehow affecting Perimas's mind? Whatever it was, there had to be a rational explanation.

The possibility of Perimas having some illness put his mind at ease enough that Andrew finally broke the silence. "Why don't most curses bother you?" he asked Tomptee.

"My kind are immune to most forms of intuition."

"Really? Interesting."

Tomptee smiled. He had never been called interesting before and thought it was quite clever.

"Is that why you weren't afraid to cross the circle of protection back in Jatoba?"

Tomptee nodded. "Aye. Though it wasn't going to be much protection. Most of what was there was old wives' tales and superstitions. Nothing intuitive; however, what your friend... what was her name? In the shop?"

"Daphnie," Andrew replied. Saying her name made him sad.

Tomptee nodded and lit up like a candle. "Her shop was something else entirely! I found a Sproutling asleep in a pot on her counter! And an incredibly mature one was in a clay vessel on the wall."

Andrew smiled. "Yeah, the young one is Fleur de Lis. She's a proper cutie, that one, and very polite."

"You spoke to her?" Tomptee asked with surprise.

"Yeah. I get the feeling that Daph raises them. Cultivates them? Whatever you do with them."

"Wow," Tomptee slowly replied, sitting back in his saddle, considering. "I've read about them, but I've never seen one. I'd LOVE to meet her one day."

"Well, if we get through all of this, I'd be happy to introduce you."

Tomptee smiled.

"How did you know that most of what happened back in Jatoba wasn't intuition?" Andrew asked.

"My father is assistant to the Professor of Astral Intuition at Lincarna Academy," Tomptee replied. "And my family has a great deal of experience with such things."

"Professor of Astral Intuition? Now, that's a title if I've ever heard one."

Tomptee nodded, not impressed. "Yeah. Big titles tend to accompany big egos. Don't get me wrong. The professor's actually a pretty decent lady..."

"But?" Andrew asked, seeing how there was something Tomptee wasn't saying.

"But... she's the reason my da was always gone. He looked up to her so much, I think in some way he resented not being intuitive himself."

"Ah."

"He would quiz us at the supper table every night, my brothers, sisters, and I: 'What is a stable base for intuitive concoctions?' Bilac lace. 'What is the key to summoning a creature?' Its name. 'What do you use to keep away night-mare flies?' Table salt. And on and on. He wanted each of us to work for a great house one day, like my uncle, like him. Helping someone intuitive. Journal their work. Mix their potions. Bind their books. Why should I write someone else's story when I could be out writing my own? Besides, I've always liked building things."

Now, this was something Andrew could understand. He might not have had a father breathing down his neck to be something he didn't want to be, but he *did* love to build things.

"I built the dragonfly for him because he loves dragon-flies. But when I showed it to him, he didn't even look at it. Instead, he said, 'Is this what you've been wasting your time on?' And that's when I told him I wanted to be a tinker."

Andrew waited, but Tomptee was quiet. So, Andrew slowed Brynlee and climbed off to let her have a drink and rest by a slow creek. Then he broke off a piece of bread he had brought from Lorna's house and asked: "What did he say when you told him?"

Tomptee didn't immediately respond. Instead, he slowly took the bread from Andrew and gave a knob of it to Nelot, who then raced off into the trees to find her own food. "He told me that no son of his would ever want to be a worthless tinker."

Worthless. That's a new one. Andrew filled his canteen with water from the creek and took a drink. "I'm sorry. That must have been hard."

Tomptee didn't reply.

"For what it's worth, I was raised by a tinker, and I've seen some things. But I've never seen anything like your dragonfly or that music box," Andrew told him.

Tomptee slowly looked up at him.

"Would you show me the dragonfly again?"

Tomptee reached into his coat pocket, took out the golden dragonfly, twisted a tiny nob at its back, and lifted it in the palm of his hand as its wings began to flicker to life and it took flight.

Perimas whistled when he saw it, which made both his mount and Brynlee look up from where they drank. "Well, now I've seen it all," Perimas said. This made Tomptee smirk; then he walked up to where he knew it would slow and let it fall into his hand.

"Can I give it a go?" Perimas asked.

Tomptee and Andrew looked at each other.

"It's a bit fragile," Tomptee replied.

"Oh, I don't mind. Do you think I could?"

*No!* Tomptee wanted to say, but he didn't. Instead, he quietly handed it to Perimas, who looked it over for a minute and began winding the nob.

"Not too much," Tomptee said, nervously reaching for it.

"Yeah, yeah. I got it," Perimas replied, then held it out as the gold insect took flight and fluttered around them as it had for Tomptee. Then Tomptee held out his hands and let it fall into his palm once again.

"See. No trouble," Perimas said.

Tomptee just looked at Andrew, who could see Tomptee's trepidation.

Then Tomptee clicked twice, summoning Nelot from the trees, and the three returned to the road and continued on.

# CHAPTER 29

As the forest gave way to marsh grasses and swamp, Andrew explained to them both how they should follow behind him carefully and described some of the dangers that lurked beneath the tea-colored waters, such as ghost snakes that were nearly translucent in the water, with a bite that would paralyze before they started feasting. He also told them about his experience collecting the Brynlee flowers for Daphnie and how the Ape Dragon had almost killed him until something much larger came out of the water, grabbed it by the throat, and pulled it in. What he didn't add was that it was by the hand of Grace that he had been saved that night and probably would have died otherwise. Perimas and Tomptee heeded his words and quietly followed close behind him as Brynlee carefully navigated the dark waters.

As they rode, Andrew wondered how many other times in his life he had come to the bleeding edge of life and death just to be saved by Grace, and now Grace had left him. This made him nervous. Aitecham Tiorem was his home. He had never feared it. It was where he had learned to walk and ride Brynlee and go fishing with his father, but now... now he felt incredibly vulnerable, the way prey must feel when hunted.

He looked back at Tomptee, who was incredibly attentive to every step Marta took, and watched the waters on either side of them closely for any movement.

"Are you alright?" Andrew asked him.

He shot Andrew a nervous look, nodded his head, and then went back to watching the dark water.

It wasn't long before they came to Andrew's cabin nestled in the thicket of trees on a small patch of stable, dry ground, and seeing his home filled Andrew with a sense of warmth and joy, though he was keen to find Lithuel.

"Father!" he called, but no one answered. "Father!" he cried again, but no one came.

Andrew dismounted Brynlee and ran inside.

The smell of cooking stew greeted him at the door, and Jasper nearly knocked him over as he walked in.

"Hey, boy!" Andrew said, laughing.

Lithuel stood at the hob, leaning over a pot, lifting a spoonful to his mouth and blowing on it. "Hey! There he is! What are you doing here?"

Andrew couldn't be happier to see anyone in all the world. Lithuel was safe. Andrew ran to him, hugged him, and almost started crying.

"Hey, hey now. That's alright," his father said, reading every move and nuance in his son's body language, which spoke more to him than any words. "What's all this about?"

Andrew wouldn't pull away. He just squeezed Lithuel harder.

"Okay. Okay. That's alright. You go on then. I'm here. I'm still here. I'm not going anywhere. You just let it out, you hear me." And at that, Andrew properly broke down and cried.

Lithuel lifted him off the ground and held him like Andrew was only six again, and Andrew let him. He had never needed his father more than he did right now, and finding him here healthy and happy meant, if only for a moment, Andrew could stop carrying all the pain and loss and grief and sorrow that he hadn't even realized he had been carrying like a lead blanket for the past few days. Now he was home, and he could rest.

At supper, Andrew shared with Lithuel some of what he knew, but he wasn't comfortable sharing everything, what with Perimas and Tomptee present, and Lithuel could tell he was holding something back. But the hearth was warm, the food was comforting, and Jasper never left his side, all of which was like a balm to his soul. Tomptee enjoyed exploring the many gadgets around the tinker's shack, and Lithuel was happy to chat about how he came up with the design for his sheers and to show Tomptee the leg brace Andrew had once built for him to support a leg that was now stronger than ever. Tomptee let his dragonfly buzz around the cabin, to Lithuel's amazement. But all the while, Lithuel could see his son was suffering.

That night, sleep did not come easily to Andrew, though it was good to be back in his own bed, and it was now the very early hours of the morning. Andrew sat on the edge of his bed, trying to decide what to do next, looking up at the last few lantern flies buzzing about his window, casting the last of their light before dawn would send them home. It was quiet save for Jasper snoring from Lithuel's room across the rustic cabin. Andrew was shrouded in a numbing sense of loss, lack of direction, and fear. Every time he set down one horrible thought, another sprang up to suffocate him. He was exhausted. He remembered how it felt to only worry about opening the store in time for the wedding and wished that was all he had to worry about now. What seemed insurmountable at the time was now small and insignificant.

He decided to put one foot in front of the other and get to work.

Outside, the air around the cabin was always so rich and fragrant, and the soft, spongy soil comforted him.

Andrew poured grain into Brynlee's trough and checked her water for anything that might have found its way in during the night. Then he brushed her and spoke softly to her, which comforted them both. He wanted to feed Marta and Perimas's mount, but he knew nothing about either of them and understood the principle of not feeding someone else's animal without their direction, so he let them both sleep—Marta off to the edge of the property where the land gave way to water. As he quietly checked on her, he paused to consider her form.

Marta looked like an ordinary land toad, only much larger, and she was the color of autumn foliage—toasted orange and mossy green. Tomptee had called her a xenophon—a creature Andrew was unfamiliar with. Her saddle and reins looked well crafted and well suited for her. Curious. She had no bit in her mouth, which would make her difficult to control if she were a horse. Perhaps Tomptee didn't use the reins to control her. Perhaps he communicated with her some other way, a touch or a heel tap? Andrew would have to ask.

As he walked the grounds looking for any sign of unusual animal activity and letting his mind wander, he gently ran his hand through the tall marsh grasses. The sky was just barely beginning to show morning's glow.

Through an opening in the trees, in a narrow stretch of dark water not a hundred feet from his home, Andrew saw a magnificent garzetta nivea sleeping on a single slender leg. It was a tall snow-white bird with long plums of feathers hanging low onto the water like a bridal dress of lace. Beneath its feathered curtain slept half a dozen chicks. In a mud flat behind the cabin, a large mud crawler hid behind one of the cabin piles, with hundreds of babies surrounding her in the moist, dark soil. They were so much smaller than her that Andrew could barely see them save for the blanket of movement around her. In the distance, he heard the call of a marsh elk. It was good to be home.

Having finished his leisurely tour of the grounds, he went inside to start breakfast and perhaps fidget with one of his many unfinished gadgets.

Jasper greeted him at the door with a lazy yawn and pressed his aging head into Andrew's side. Andrew smiled.

Andrew opened the small, heavy door of the tiny two-burner hob, stacked three pieces of narrow timber inside its cast iron belly, and remembered his Warming Rod—another link back to Lorna. He sighed, struck a match, and lit the stove.

"Morning," came the comforting, gruff voice of Lithuel from his bedroom door. "Wanna go fishing?"

"I thought you'd never ask," Andrew replied.

# CHAPTER 30

A ndrew and Lithuel said not a single word to each other as they prepped their flat-bottom boat. Andrew collected the rods and capture basket, Jasper jumped into the raft, and Lithuel took a short-handled shovel out towards the water's edge and dug until he found a couple of handfuls of purple mud worms. Then they pushed off.

A curious yellow snake followed them along the surface of the water for a few minutes while Lithuel gently paddled out to a slightly deeper piece of water where he set the oars aside and let the boat freely drift.

As Andrew began to prepare, Lithuel didn't bother lifting his rod. He wasn't out to catch anything. He was there to be with his son, and he never pushed, never asked, never said anything. He knew well that the heart of a young man sometimes needs space to find itself and come home before it can be tended to, and he could see that his son was wandering far and wide within himself. He also knew that sometimes the hearts of men need no words. It is not easy for men to be together, especially when they are suffering, and strength leads to strength if it is given enough space to draw in. Lithuel knew that what his son needed was for his hands to be busy: busy with details, busy with tying knots and hook, busy casting a line and watching the pole's end for a nibble, busy doing nothing at all important. Though his hands needed activity, his mind needed the vast empty spaces across the marsh flats that calmed the soul. Save for their two house guests, Lithuel and Andrew were alone in every direction for miles. They always had been, and they absolutely loved it. The solitude meant that they were safe as long as they remembered and respected the wetlands and the creatures living within. No greed or malice could be found anywhere across the dark water. That nonsense was for the outside world, and this world, this kingdom of solitude some thought cursed, was a sanctuary of life for them they could get lost in for time immemorial. Lithuel had never told Andrew that he had originated some of the best local legends about the dark water's curses to protect his son from the cloying and clawing outside world until the day Andrew would become a man and find his own way.

Lithuel watched the young man sitting next to him and remembered the boy when he first caught and landed his own fish: a red, deep-throat bass. Then he conjured the memory of the even younger child more playing than fishing, swinging a stick with a line and cork attached, as though he were fishing like his daddy and properly scaring away every living creature within a hundred feet for the constant splashing, but Lithuel couldn't have cared less. At the time, Andrew had been with him for nearly a year and was starting to feel like his own son. Now look at him: grown and soon to be married.

Lithuel watched Andrew stand at the front of the well-worn craft and lean towards the line where grass and open water met, carefully looking beneath the water's surface for streaks of red or grey. He was hunting for bass or anything else that might be worth a fight and make a good meal. Then, Andrew slowly lifted his rod high in the air and, with a roll of his wrist, gently cast his line across the water with a narrow loop that dropped his hook in an opening of reeds barely the size of a wagon wheel. The form, accuracy, elegance, and grace of this young man now before him was a thing of beauty, and he felt his eyes water.

In a moment, there was a flick of the rod tip. Andrew drew the rod high to set the hook, and the fight was on. Lithuel smiled as he watched the line race back and forth as the hooked fish fought for deeper water, but Andrew would not let it run, not too far. He gently held the line taut with one hand and the rod high with the other, forcing the fish to struggle against the bend of the wood. When it pulled so hard the rod might break, Andrew would lean the rod towards the water so that the tension didn't break the line, but every time the fish paused to rest, Andrew lifted the rod again and shortened the line. Dip and rise, dip and rise, the fish slowly drew closer to the boat and eventually tired enough for Lithuel to reach into the water and simply lift it out.

Andrew was beaming. Lithuel laughed.

Andrew removed the hook and held it up for a moment. It was a beautiful red deep-throat like the one he had caught on his own as a child, but this one had a sack of eggs deep in its gullet.

"She's pregnant," Andrew said, looking at Lithuel.

Lithuel said nothing. It was a beauty. There would be no judgement from him if Andrew kept her, but he knew his son wouldn't.

"Be well, mother," Andrew told the fish, then gently returned her to the water.

*What a beautiful heart,* Lithuel mused.

Andrew rinsed the fish grease from his hands in the water and baited his hook again.

The sun had properly risen now, and the morning was warm, but neither of them felt any rush to go anywhere. Small clouds of tiny nymph flies hatched from the grasses in the warmth and looked like gold dust floating in the morning sunlight.

"I don't know what to do," Andrew finally broke the silence.

"Is there anything you can do?"

"Maybe."

Lithuel decided it was time he bait his own hook and let it casually sink into the water with no real interest in catching anything. The yellow snake passed by them again, this time with a stomach full of breakfast.

"I hurt a lot of people. Those women came looking for me. What if they aren't the only ones? How am I supposed to protect my family?" Andrew asked, looking off across the marsh.

"You can't," Lithuel replied, watching the tip of his rod.

Andrew turned to his father.

Lithuel let that sink in for a moment, then said it again: "You can't. Not always."

"But I have to try."

"I know you do. But you also have to forgive yourself because, son, perfect don't exist. This broken world don't give you the same room to make mistakes that it gives some of us, and I see that. I seen that since you was a boy. I've watched you try so hard, but I fear that somewhere along the line, the weight of being everything to everyone will one day crush you. Maybe it's time you just be you."

Andrew carefully considered what his father was saying. "I'm not sure I understand."

Lithuel nodded, slowly lifted his line from the water, and cast it to the other side of the boat. "Who are you when no one's watchin'?"

Andrew didn't respond.

"Is that who you are when everyone's watching?"

No. No, he wasn't. But he hadn't realized anyone had noticed. It's easy for children to not realize that their parents sometimes know more about them than they know about themselves.

"How did you feel finding your grandmother?" Lithuel asked.

"Wonderful."

Lithuel nodded again. Then he turned his eyes to his son. "How did it make you feel about yourself?"

Andrew was quiet. "Found," Andrew finally replied.

His father smiled gently. "Found. With your grandmother, you was finally with *your* people."

"But you are my people," Andrew replied, once again trying to protect his father.

His father's chin slowly dropped, and he held up a stout hand. "Don't do that. You don't need to protect me. Don't you see? Bein' fully you don't diminish me. Stop thinkin' about me or anyone else, and think about yourself. When you was with your gran, you was with *your* people. True or not true?"

This was beginning to reveal something profound Andrew hadn't given words to. It was just as the Grace Giver had said: with his gran, he was not "other." With his gran, he felt like he finally belonged.

"True," Andrew whispered.

"There's nothing wrong with that. It's as it should be. A part of me feels that whatever it's goin' to take to help your gran will call on every part of who you truly are. Perhaps you were born for such a time as this."

Lithuel was giving Andrew permission to be his complete self. In so doing, a sense of freedom washed over Andrew like warm water after a hard day's work. What does it mean to be fully accepted, fully seen? No more hiding. No more apologizing.

"I don't know how to be that person," Andrew replied.

Lithuel nodded again. Gently drifting his line to a patch of reeds near the back of their boat. "I can't give you that. I wish I could, but I'll never be Human," Lithuel said. "But there is something I can give you."

"Oh?" Andrew turned to him.

"I haven't always been completely honest with you."

"What do you mean?"

Lithuel's tattoos began to glow deep blue. "When I found you, you was so little. I never raised a child before. I didn't know how to be a father, but I knew the world, and I knew there was no place in it for a Human baby with no parent to look out for it, so I held a part of myself back to try to give you as much of a world that looked like you as I could. But that means I wasn't always fully me, either."

"I don't understand."

Lithuel nodded. "Hear me now. I am more a part of this place than you know. Aitechem Tiorem is where my people come from, and we are as much a part of this land as the land is a part of us. My tribe was driven from these waters long ago, but I returned when I knew you needed somewhere safe."

Then Lithuel rose and removed his shirt. As he did, his

tattoos began to pulse with life, and the water around them began to move. Fish circled the boat. Golden nymphs surrounded their shallow-bottom craft, and their little snake friend returned. Then something large slowly moved through the grasses.

"Stay calm," Lithuel said. "It's time you know what it means to be fully yourself." Lithuel lifted his hands as a marsh dragon twice the size of their cabin lifted its head out of the water. It was the same creature that had saved him from the Ape Dragon months earlier.

Andrew fell back in the boat.

"It's okay. She won't hurt you," Lithuel said. "She is queen of this land and has wanted to meet you for some time."

The Marsh Dragon had a long face full of hanging whiskers that nearly touched the water. It had two sets of eyes. One large and knowing, a second small and set further back. Its skin was like a fish, smooth and the color of iridescent wheat. Andrew could only see its large head and neck because most of it disappeared beneath the water.

"I chose to be less of myself so that you could grow up with someone who was as much like you as I could be, but you're grown now and there is so much more that I can teach you. But first, you have something you need to do.

"You and your gran have something special. If you can help her, don't you think you should try? Don't be afraid of who you really are. Sure, some will fear you because you are different—in more ways than you realize now, but different isn't wrong. Different is beautiful. You are a part of all of this, and you have a place. Go find that place and know you can always come home." As Lithuel spoke, the Marsh Dragon reared its head and called out a deep guttural harmonic that echoed across the wetlands.

Suddenly, Andrew awoke back in his cabin. Jasper was asleep on his legs. Jasper never slept with Andrew, not if Lithuel was home. *Had it only been a dream?* Andrew felt as though something had been stolen from him; a special moment with his father. Yet, the dreaming held the power for two to connect beyond life, time or distance.

Andrew quickly climbed out of bed and went to his door, then stopped. Jasper wasn't moving. Something wasn't right.

Jasper was quietly snoring his old dog snore, but when Andrew gently ran his hand over his tattered grey neck, he did not wake. Andrew gently shook him. Nothing. Andrew turned and ran through the cabin, past Perimas and Tomptee who slept near the quiet hearth, to Lithuel's bedroom, which was empty, cold, and dark.

Andrew returned to Tomptee and spoke his name, but Tomptee didn't rouse. Then he shook Perimas by the shoulder, and he, too, did not wake. His heart dropped. Had the curse found its way to Aitecham Tioram?

Andrew went out into the humid night air, looking for his father's wagon, but it was not there. Then he looked around, trying to gain his bearings. He was overwhelmed with that shifting sense of confusion that lay between waking and dreaming. What was real? What had actually happened? Where was Lithuel? Then he felt something begin to pull at his mind.

Something powerful in the marsh.

# CHAPTER 31

An autumn-gold raven moon hung low in the sky, casting an orange glow on the trees. Through the trees, Andrew could see the moon's reflection on a slick of dark water. There was an unusual silence in the swamp. No cricket, toad, or rustle of leaf could be heard. Everything was completely still.

He didn't know why, but something was drawing him into the moonlight.

Andrew had no coat or boots, but it didn't matter to him now. He calmly walked barefoot through the skeletal branches that embraced the raven light. In the center of the moon's reflection was a large stone, and on the stone perched a peculiar figure. Andrew approached until he stood ankle-deep in the histic peat.

"Is this another dream?" Andrew asked.

The stranger, squatting low on the stone like a bird, flicked his head towards Andrew with the same herky-jerky motions as before. He wore a gown of bluish-grey linen hanging low to the water and the mask of The Poet with simple features and a lifted brow line. "No. It's been a long time since I visited Aitecham Tiorem," he said fondly. "I've decided to come to you here and speak with you plainly."

"Then why the mask?"

There was a long pause, then a slender reply: "Dreaming is my nature, and part of dreaming is nightmare. This mask is a courtesy."

This unsettled Andrew. "How did you find me?"

There was no reply.

"Have you come to kill me?" Andrew asked.

The stranger cocked his head to one side. "Why would I want to do that? You will join me soon enough."

"Then what do you want? Why do you torment Jatoba?"

The stranger looked down at the reflection of the moon on the water. "What an interesting word: torment—to twist or tear the mind. I know it well, but they are not in torment. They are only sleeping." Then he lifted his gaze again to Andrew. "I've come because I think you can help me."

"Why would I do that?"

"I have gifts," he said, his mask now The Merchant with a calculating smile and whisper-thin mustache. "What do you desire? Sex? Money? Tell me. What do you dream about?" And as he asked, his eyes became starlight, trying to see Andrew beyond the surface of the waking world.

"I don't want anything from you. Just leave me and my family alone," Andrew replied.

The stranger squawked like a bird, and his eyes returned to solid grey. "Interesting. I see why grace was upon you, but you Humans always want something." Then, the stranger's mask became the maiden, with gentle eyes and slender lips painted crimson. "We haven't been properly introduced. Your people once called me The Raven

King, which I thought had a rather nice ring to it. And you are?"

Andrew took another step closer. "You know other Humans?"

Andrew could not see the dark smile slowly rise behind the mask. "Ah. There it is. I'll give you this one for free—call it a gesture of good will. The history of your people is written in the Book of Elyon."

"Where can I find this...book?"

The stranger squawked and held up a slender, unnaturally black finger. "Now, now. The first one was free. The next one will cost you."

Andrew swallowed. "What do you want?"

The stranger's mask returned to that of the merchant. "Nothing of value to you. I've lost something I want back, that's all. A trifle. A trinket." The Raven King carefully watched Andrew's reaction, gauging the negotiation. "Would you trade the knowledge of the history of your people for a simple bauble of wood or clay?"

"Perhaps," Andrew replied.

The dark smile behind the mask grew. "And what if it was a some*one* instead of a some*thing*? Would you help me then?"

Andrew knew he was in a terrible position. While Daphnie's story told how unwise it was to trust the trickster raven, there was also no question that he was in the presence of an ancient power, and the hand of grace was no longer upon him. He couldn't say yes, and he couldn't say no. How do you negotiate with a dream? He considered again that word: torment. Had it come from him or the raven? Andrew wasn't sure. The word in his mind felt like a bloody ax sitting on his dinner table. Then he remembered Daphnie warning of things worse than death. What if things worse than death waited for every man, woman, and child in Jatoba if he didn't give The Raven King what he wanted?

"Who?" Andrew asked.

"Someone youthful. Out of place."

Andrew took a step back. *Tomptee?* "I don't want anyone getting hurt."

The Raven King's head jerked, and his mask became the Elderly Maid with puffy cheeks and a kindly face. "It's nothing like that. Tell me: Have you seen any wayward strangers lately?"

"No one that I can think of. I travel a lot. So many traveling the roads. What do you want with them?"

"You don't need to concern yourself with that. It's time they come home. That's all."

"Where is home?"

The Raven King leaned back and basked in the moonlight. "Through the raven light."

"And what would I do if I found them? How would I contact you?"

The Raven King opened a black-skin bag hanging from his belt, took out a solid gold coin, and flicked it to Andrew. "Spend it wisely," The Raven King replied. Then he was gone.

Andrew looked at the heavy coin rimmed in moonlight. It was twice the weight of a solid gold sovereign. One side of the coin was the same raven skull Andrew had seen on the cover of the graveyard book. On the other were the words:

A raven coin
in raven light
for The Raven King

# CHAPTER 32

Andrew returned to the cabin to find Tomptee awake and feeding Nelot, his furry pocket friend. Nelot and Jasper perked their heads up as Andrew came in.

"Where have you been?" Tomptee asked, looking at Andrew's bare feet, caked with mud up to the ankle.

"Out for a walk, I guess," Andrew replied, filling a bucket with water.

Tomptee shook his head. "You must be comfortable here. You wouldn't find me out after dark in this place," he said looking around.

"Have you seen my father?" Andrew asked, fairly sure he knew the answer.

Tomptee thought for a moment. "No. Can't say I've met your father. I know you hoped he'd be here. I'm sure he's safe."

"So, you didn't meet him here yesterday? Show him your dragonfly? Talk for over an hour about our tools?"

Tomptee slowly shook his head. "No. When we arrived, the house was empty. You said you were worried about him and that he must not have made it out of Jatoba in time, then you cooked us a meal. You don't remember any of that?"

Andrew carefully washed his feet and wiped them dry. Then he sighed. "I've been having some powerful dreams lately, and I'm not entirely sure what is real and what isn't." Then Andrew felt the weight of the coin in his pocket and took it out. It glistened in the light of the hearth.

Tomptee immediately took notice of the raven skull in its center. "Where did you get that?"

Andrew ran his thumb along the coin's edge, feeling its cold weight. The line between reality and dreaming was a blur, but this was concrete. If their fates were intertwined, Tomptee deserved to know, so Andrew told him everything. He told him about his first encounter with The Raven King, how the Grace Giver was real and how she—or it, he wasn't sure which—had taken her hand of protection off of him, how he had dreamt of talking to Lithuel and going fishing with him, and how The Raven King had come to him in the swamp.

"He said he's looking for someone," Andrew said gravely, the coin lying on the table between them.

Tomptee listened carefully, and Andrew watched his reactions to see if he could discern any reason Tomptee might know of why The Raven King might be looking for him. But there was none.

As fascinated as Tomptee was with the coin, he wasn't willing to touch it.

"I think I know someone who might be able to help," Tomptee said.

"Who?"

"The professor my father works for, which works well

because the person who might know something about your figurine is also in Nevarii."

"Another professor?"

Tomptee shook his head. "No. She should be, but no. Her experience is less... formal."

*Curious*, Andrew thought.

"We can stay with my family, but quarters might be a little tight for you and..." Tomptee pointed at Perimas. "But I have to admit, I wish we could go alone." Then he lowered his voice. "I don't trust him. He doesn't smell right."

"I'm not thrilled with the idea either, but he might be able to help us. And right now, I'd work with a wild badger if it meant helping Fey and the rest of Jatoba."

Tomptee sighed and watched Perimas by the fire.

"Besides, people don't always trust me," Andrew said, showing signs of discomfort at the thought. "For now, I think our fates are intertwined."

Tomptee couldn't argue with that, even though he wanted to.

Andrew fetched a small box from the mantle containing pipes, put one in his mouth and offered Tomptee the second who happily accepted. Andrew packed them both with damp brown leaf, used a reed to draw fire from the hearth to light them, and handed one to Tomptee. Then they sat together and watched the fire as fruit-laced tobacco smoke filled the cabin.

Neither of them knew that Perimas was awake and quietly listening.

# CHAPTER 33
## EIGHT YEARS AGO

"I wish you wouldn't go," Feyloren said, standing barefoot at her kitchen table, splashing some milk into a pot of porridge and placing it on the lit hob. Perimas pulled on his boots.

Fey didn't want to push. She knew things were touchy between them and didn't want to upset him, but she really didn't want him to go. Not right now. Especially not for several days. She rubbed her enlarged belly, exposed to the morning light. Then she leaned against the counter. Even cooking a pot of porridge was a lot for her at the moment.

"We could use some meat, and if I wait much longer, all the game will move into the low country until Spring." This was just an excuse. Perimas wanted any reason to get out of the house—get away from her.

She turned to him. "We'll be fine. The larder is stocked with autumn vegetables, and the Hiddy Coo just got a new shipment of..."

"I don't need your sister's help feedin' my family!" he snapped at her.

Her eyes welled up. "That's not what I meant."

Perimas didn't mean to snap and wanted to apologize, but a wall of frustration was high and heavy in his heart, so he said nothing. He grabbed his coat, slung his bow over his shoulder, and turned to leave.

"When will you be back?" she asked, wiping her eyes and trying not to fall apart in front of him.

"I don't know," he said, then slammed shut the door, causing her to jump.

Their fight that morning wasn't even about anything important. It was just a small thing piled on top of a much larger wound growing unspoken beneath the surface of both of their hearts; misunderstandings and unmet expectations that festered. Jabs at each other about things like how she didn't respect him anymore or how he didn't love her. Then, one night, he slept in the guest room, which became three months. Just when their fledgling marriage needed them to come together the most, Feyloren found out she was pregnant and began paying less attention to her struggling husband and more attention to their upcoming addition. Now, Perimas felt deeply frustrated, horny, unheard, unloved, and unable to argue with the needs of a baby over his own.

She would have said so many things if she had known this was the last time she would ever see him. She would have stopped him from leaving. Whatever it took.

Perimas mounted his nicatoo and fled to the solitude of the forest, where there was no argument or judgment. The trees were his compatriots; the falcon his friend.

Hoarfrost glistened in sunlight. He didn't care where he was going. He just rode out his frustration until his nicatoo slowed from exhaustion, and he stopped to let his mount rest.

He rubbed his face and screamed as loud as he could, startling his animal. What was he supposed to do? No one had taught him how to be a husband, much less a father! He didn't *want* to be angry at Fey. He kept telling himself that everything he needed wasn't necessary, but then they would spring up again and bite him like a snake in a thicket. Couldn't she see how hard he was trying—how he was suffering? Did she know that he needed her more than just once a month? He tried telling her that more than once, but perhaps she wasn't listening; perhaps she didn't really care. And why was she always trying to control him? Of course, she wasn't, but it felt like she was. He was a grown man, and he could take care of himself. He was fully capable of providing for his family. So what if he had caught nothing more than a sprained ankle the last two times he had gone out hunting?

As he slowly calmed down, he looked around and realized that he was in a part of the forest he hadn't been in before. How far had he ridden? It didn't matter. It was good to get lost once in a while, and if he needed to, he knew how to wayfind.

Then he heard something, and his nicatoo lifted its head from grazing.

Now, the forest was quiet. A morning breeze through the leaves. Two grey squirrels chasing each other high above in the branches.

There it was again. A voice. A woman's voice.

Perimas mounted his nicatoo and listened more carefully, trying to discern what he was hearing and where it was coming from.

"Help!" A voice broke through the branches more clearly this time. He turned slightly and quickly made his way in its direction. Not much farther ahead, the trees opened to a small lake where he heard the cry for help again and saw someone splashing near an upturned rowboat out past a dock.

He swiftly road to the dock, dismounted, dropped his boot knife and bow, and dove into the water.

Barely a stone's throw from the dock, a young woman splashed violently in the water and struggled for air before sinking beneath the surface and not returning. Perimas quickly took in a deep breath and dove into the dark.

The water was cold and murky. He found her hand, pulled her into an embrace, and swam to the surface. As they broke through, the young woman gasped for air and squeezed him tightly.

"It's okay. It's okay. I have you," he assured her as he put his arm underneath hers and swam to shore.

She did not struggle and weighed very little compared to the carcasses he was used to carrying. Once back to the muddy bank, he pulled her onto the beach and leaned on an elbow, trying to catch his breath.

The young woman coughed up water and rolled towards him, embracing him.

"Thank you! Thank you," she gasped. "I thought I was gone for sure."

"What happened?" he asked, breathing heavily and wiping water out of his eyes.

She did not reply.

As his senses slowly returned, he took in the situation. She was Longbeard clan with skin the color of crystal quartz, and she wore the thinnest of white gowns that clung to her body with one breast partially uncovered and a second clearly visible beneath the wet fabric. But she didn't seem to notice at all. She was just happy to be alive.

Perimas tried to look away from her nakedness and sat up on the beach.

She clung to his arm. "What a thing to do for a stranger. Jumping into that cold water. I owe you my life," she said, watching his mouth.

"You owe me nothing," he replied, glancing at her. She smelled like something wonderful he couldn't place.

Just then, two women came running from a cabin sitting high on the hill above the lake. One with hair black as coal, whose skin was the color of ocher, and another whose hair was red as firelight with skin the color of pale emeralds. One of the sisters led the other by the hand, for she was blind.

"What's happened?" the blind one called out to her sister. "I heard you scream."

The one who led her nodded with concern and agreement but said nothing.

They, too, wore whisper-thin gowns that nearly blew open as they ran.

The one the color of quartz waved to her sisters and squeezed Perimas' arm tighter.

"I overturned the boat, and this wonderful hero dove in after me without hesitation. He saved my life!"

"I'm not sure of all that," Perimas said as the two finally approached them and helped him to his feet.

"Wonderful! Wonderful! What would have happened if you had not come?" she with black hair said, gently touching his face, which made him slightly uncomfortable. Then she with hair like flame, touched his cheek and slid her hand down his neck towards his chest. This startled him, and he stepped back, but she just smiled.

"I owe you my life! How can I repay you?" she asked, watching his mouth.

Perimas shook his head. "That's not necessary."

"Please. We are simple women and don't have much. The least we can do is feed you and let you dry by the fire," the woman with black hair said.

Perimas was about to say no again, but then that peculiar smell caught his attention again, just long enough to distract him. It was strong now. Perhaps it was emanating from all three of them. Something sweet and woodsy and sensual. Something that reminded him of Feyloren after a hot bath.

He swallowed. He was starting to *really* miss his wife.

"I can see you're cold, and the day is growing colder still. Please. Come in. Let us warm you," she said with white hair and crystal skin.

"The hearth is warm. We already have bread done baking," she said with the midnight black hair. "Can't you smell it?"

Now he noticed the smell of fresh bread, which he hadn't before, making his stomach grumble. Perhaps he shouldn't have left home before breakfast.

"But my..." he began to say, pointing to his mount.

The sister he had saved from the lake took his arm again. "Don't worry. We will take care of it," she told him and pressed her pelvis against his hand.

The sharp details of his reason were softening. He felt his hunger grow, both for bread and for flesh.

As he walked with them towards the house, the one with red hair said no word to him; she only smiled a delicious smile. He couldn't stop looking at her mouth. Halfway up the hill, he paused and turned. "But Fey," he mumbled.

"Who's Fey?" she, who was blind, asked.

He couldn't remember.

As they entered the cabin, the one he had saved from the lake, who was also deaf, said, "Don't worry, kind hunter, we will feed your hunger. Then you will feed ours."

Then she closed the door.

# CHAPTER 34
## PRESENT DAY

As they approached the gates of Nevarii, Andrew felt his chest tighten and his breath shorten as a heavy dread rose within him as though he were about to have a tooth pulled.

"I'm not sure about this," he told Tomptee and Perimas, directing Brynlee out of the steady traffic that flowed in and out of the city's gate. Memories of harassment flooded over Andrew. Name-calling children. Abusive guards. Constantly being less. Constantly being other. Here more than anywhere else.

"What's wrong? We need not stay long," Tomptee said. "Do you want me to go on by myself?"

Andrew shook his head. "No. No. I need to do this." But what he didn't say was that he didn't want to let the figurine out of his sight.

Nevarii was draped in ribbons and flags the color of wine. It was the first day of The Festival of Ny Fødsel—or New Birth in the common tongue—and the city was bursting at the seams with visitors from all over the land.

Andrew thought this influx would help him more easily disappear into the crowds, so he pulled on his hood and lowered his head, but one of the guards at the gate stopped them before they entered the city.

"Say, what's your business here?" the guard asked, pulling them aside. As he spoke, two other guards approached them.

Perimas sighed, then feigned enthusiasm. "Friends!" he said, raising his hands. "We're here to have a little fun and spend a little coin."

"My father is employed by the academy," Tomptee added.

"And what about you?" the first guard asked, stepping towards Andrew. "Speak up!"

Andrew looked at him from underneath his hood. "We're here for the festival."

"Pull back your headcover and let me see your face," the guard pushed.

Tomptee and Perimas glanced at each other.

Andrew slowly removed his hood.

"Do I know you from somewhere?" the guard asked.

Andrew shook his head. "I'm not a resident. I'm just a lonely tinker who passes through now and again when I need supplies." At first, he also thought he recognized the guard from somewhere until he remembered that it was this guard who had given him a hard time when he was last in the city looking for the grounds keepers' wife.

"From where do you hail?" the guard asked.

"Jatoba," Andrew said.

The first guard turned to the other two. "Do either of you recognize this humatii from anywhere? Perhaps the interest posters?"

One of the other guards grunted and smirked at the question.

"Dismount your horse," the first guard said.

Tomptee didn't like where this was going.

"Friends! We've an appointment to keep," Perimas said with an even bigger smile. "It's clear you've been working hard all morning. Let me buy you three a round at the tavern."

The three guards looked at each other, and two seemed to like the sound of a drink over bothering with some Human. But the first was undeterred.

"Oy! Are you deaf or just daft, humatii! I said dismount."

Andrew slowly dismounted Brynlee.

"I'm pretty sure I know you from somewhere. What's your name, boy?"

"Andrew, sir."

"Don't lie to me!" the guard said, reaching for the sword hanging at his left hip.

"He's not!" Tomptee hollered. "My father is Wilkers. He works for Professor Lyra Luminara at Lincarna Academy. She's professor of Astral Intuition."

The guard's face hardened. "I don't give a flying pig lump who your father is. If you speak again without be'in spoken to, I'll cut this humatii's manhood off."

Tomptee swallowed hard and looked away.

The crowd began to slow and watch the goings on, making Andrew even more self-conscious.

Perimas climbed down from his mount with his hands open wide. "Friends. Is this really necessary?"

The first guard turned to Perimas. "I wasn't talkin' to you either."

Perimas didn't move for several long heartbeats, then—careful not to look aggressive—slowly unsheathed his sword and showed them the shimmering blade.

They took a step back.

"We're sorry to have bothered you, sir," one of the lesser guards said nudging his friends. Then, two of them returned to their post by the gate. The first guard, however, looked away for a few more heartbeats and turned to Andrew.

"Even so, you're not welcome here, humatii. Best you move along." Then he, too, returned to his post by the gate.

Perimas sheathed his blade, and he and Andrew remounted their animals.

"What just happened?" Tomptee asked Perimas.

"Let's go," he said, staring down the first guard who watched them with disdain.

The three rode away until the gate was out of sight.

"I know another entrance, around the east side by the academy. A shepherd's gate," Tomptee finally said, angry for Andrew. "I'm sorry..."

Andrew cut him off. "I'm not sure this is a good idea. I don't want to get either of you into trouble."

Perimas shook his head. "That wasn't you. That was all him. What an absolute turd stain."

Tomptee nodded in agreement.

"It doesn't matter. And it's not just him. This city has never welcomed me. Most places don't," Andrew said.

"Why?" Perimas asked.

Andrew didn't respond. Why? was the question he had struggled with his entire life. Why is anyone ever horrible to someone simply because they are different? What's so wrong with different? Of course, it's because different can be scary, and bullies like the guard are cowards hiding behind some thin veil of power, trying to overcompensate for their inadequacies. "I still don't think it's a good idea," he replied.

"The gate is near my family's home, and we can get to the academy grounds without going through the city. I doubt many will see us, and there are no guards on the academy grounds," Tomptee tried to reassure him.

Andrew thought for a while then simply nodded, and Tomptee led the way.

"What did happen back there?" Andrew finally asked Perimas as they rode.

Perimas took his sword from its sheath and held it up so they both could see a small sigil, faintly glowing blue, etched into the bottom of the blade near the hilt.

Tomptee whistled through his teeth, causing Marta to turn her head towards him. "That's the mark of Emberholt!"

"What is Emberholt?" Andrew asked.

Tomptee replied, "Emberholt is an elite, secret order of magi, which means that sword..."

Perimas looked at it fondly. "Is intuitive. Yes. It was my father's. Its blade can never dull nor break, and it can rend any metal in twain."

"Armor?" Tomptee asked.

Perimas looked at him. "Cut like cloth. And it cannot be taken from its owner, only given. Here, try," he said, sliding the blade back into its sheath and moving his nicatoo closer to Tomptee so he could reach.

Tomptee looked at him and smiled, game to try. He took the sword by the handle and casually tried lifting it, but it not only did not move, the sheath didn't even swing at Perimas' side. Tomptee tried again, this time with both hands.

Nothing. It felt like he was pulling at a tree root. Then Perimas casually removed it from its sheath and handed it to Tomptee who looked at him with hesitation. Perimas urged him to take it, so Tomptee did. It was quite light, perfectly balanced, and so clean that it almost looked white. As Tomptee held it, the blade changed in size to fit his hand. "Incredible," Tomptee said in awe.

"It has a name, if you can believe that," Perimas replied, reaching for it again. "Tyrfing."

Tomptee playfully pulled back. "What if I didn't give it back?"

"Well, then it's yours and they will bury you with it after I dispatch you with my boot knife," Perimas replied jokingly.

Tomptee grunted a laugh and handed it back to Perimas, who looked at it again and returned it to its sheath.

"Then the guards knew the sigil. I thought it was supposed to be a secret society," Andrew said.

Perimas nodded. "Stories like those of Emberholt tend to get traded like trinkets among soldiers who have nothing to do for hours but stand around and guard a gate."

"And your father was one?" Tomptee asked.

Perimas shook his head. "Saved a member's life who gave it to him in thanks. Three years ago, my father fell in battle, betrayed by one of his own men, and it was returned to me at his funeral."

"How? If it can only be given?"

Perimas looked away. "His last words to the Longbeard who gave it to me, were that it was for me."

Tomptee had so many questions, but they would have to wait. They had just arrived at the shepherd's gate, a small, cast-iron gate covered in rust set into a brick wall covered in beautiful green vines probably ten feet high, running the entire length of this part of the narrow and overgrown path they had turned down. Near the path was a low hedge surrounding a large field of grazing sheep.

Tomptee climbed down from Marta and approached the gate. The lock drew Andrew's attention. It was a clever tube-like mechanism that required no key, only the knowledge of the code by those who regularly used the unassuming entrance.

Tomptee turned and moved the row of dials until the gate released, which groaned as he swung it open with some difficulty. Then he pulled a bar holding the second half of the gate shut, which made the entrance wide enough for their animals to pass through. Once through, Tomptee re-latched and relocked the partially hidden entrance.

On this side of the wall, the academy grounds were impeccable. Orange and yellow flowers bloomed along the banks of a narrow creek flowing underneath a red-brick walkway. An old stone fountain stood in the center of the private garden surrounded by old wooden benches and tables. Tall, stone buildings rose high above with diamond-shaped panes of multi-colored glass looking down on the courtyard. On one side of the courtyard was an incredible hornbeam with beautifully reaching branches and a perfect canopy of deep green leaves. On the other side of the courtyard was a tall hedge shaped into a wall with a semi-hidden entrance.

Tomptee led Marta through the hedge into a second private garden with a waist-high black, rod-iron gate. Beyond the gate was a two-story cottage with a narrow finger of smoke rising from the chimney, well suited for Tomptee's smaller size. The cottage had a red, mushroom-shaped roof, small windows, and even smaller flower boxes

THE TINKER'S FOLLY

on the windowsills, with a dozen different kinds of cooking and medicinal herbs. The delicious smell of baking bread was rich in the air.

Tomptee tied Marta up to a stable post where two ponies casually ate mouthfuls of hay. He then proceeded to the house. Andrew and Perimas followed.

# CHAPTER 35

Tomptee knocked on the front door, which Andrew thought was odd.

There was a rustle of feet behind the door. When it opened, a small, black nose poked through the crack and sniffed the air in their direction. Then the door swung wide and a young hedgehog-looking child screeched in excitement. "Tomptee! It's Tomptee! Tomptee's home!" Then, the young one burst forth and dove at Tomptee, who laughed and lifted the child into his arms.

"Hello, Tivee!" Tomptee exclaimed as three more children, near Tivee's age, poured forth from the cottage and tackled their older brother. Tomptee laughed and nuzzled each of them in their neck with his nose causing them to squeal with delight.

Tivee, who was the smallest of the group, tugged at Andrew's trouser leg and enthusiastically sniffed up at him. "Who are you?" she asked in the voice of a very young girl.

Andrew smiled and knelt to speak to her. "I'm Andrew."

"Are you friends with my brother?" she asked.

"Yes. I suppose you could say that," Andrew replied thoughtfully.

That was good enough for her. She climbed into his hands and nuzzled her nose into his neck with the biggest hug she could muster. As the rest of the children saw that Andrew was safe, they wanted him and Perimas to pick them up, causing Andrew to laugh harder at the inundation of such innocent affection.

"Now, children. Give our guests some room," an older Inkling woman said, wiping her hands on a floral print apron. Her fur greying at its edges, and her quills pulled back and tied with a bright purple band. She had the warm, knowing smile of a mother, which welcomed Andrew without a word and immediately touched his heart in a way few ever had.

"Hi, momma," Tomptee said, embracing her warmly.

"My boy," she replied, holding him for a long while with eyes shut and in a slow rock back and forth like she was coddling a baby.

When Tomptee finally let her go, he turned to Andrew and Perimas. "Momma, these are my friends, Andrew and Perimas. Andrew, Perimas, this is my momma, Nizzle."

Nizzle smiled large, approached Andrew, and took his hands in hers. "Welcome. Welcome." Then she turned to Perimas. As she did, there was a momentary change in her demeanor, then it became warm again. She took Perimas' hands in her own. "Welcome." She turned back to Andrew. "Come. Come. Come inside and rest yourselves. I've just taken some bread from the oven."

Tomptee smiled large.

Andrew ducked as he entered the cozy cabin, but it wasn't so tight as to make him uncomfortable.

There were tiny flower details hand-painted in the

corners of the rafters and on doors. Watercolor portraits of Tomptee's family adorned the living room walls. A particularly large one hung above the hearth of his mother, his father, Tomptee, and fifteen other siblings of various ages. Well-loved, hand-made toys were scattered around the living room floor; the house was otherwise carefully kept. A small desk sat at the corner of the living room with writing instruments, overlooked by three rows of narrow shelves bowing from the weight of hand-bound books smaller than standard books by a third. Herbs grew in the kitchen in window boxes, jars along the walls, and baskets hanging from the low rafters. And in the center of the otherwise tight kitchen was a beautifully hand-carved table with seven chairs, the perfect height and dimensions for Tomptee's family.

"How are you, son?" Tomptee's mother asked. "How long will you be staying?"

"Not long. Perhaps the night, if you have room.

"Of course! Of course. We have plenty of room. Tivee and Willa can sleep on the couch, and Pimble and Wimble will take the floor.

"Yes! Campout!" Pimble exclaimed, throwing himself over the back of the couch in the main room.

"Is father here?" Tomptee asked with trepidation.

"Not yet. Afternoon lectures aren't done for another hour. Why?"

"There's been an incident, and Andrew needs help."

"Go see him. He'd love to see you!"

Tomptee looked away. "At the academy? I don't know about that."

She smiled. "It's settled then. But first, toast."

Tomptee knew that meant he was going to see his father whether he entirely wanted to or not.

His mother removed a beautiful, golden loaf of bread stuffed with dates and nuts from underneath a tea towel where it sat to cool. She took a long, well-worn blade out of a pantry drawer and sliced off three large pieces that steamed in sunlight pouring in through the small kitchen window. Then she scooped a healthy dollop of butter from a small stone bowl sitting on the counter and slathered each piece, handing them to Tomptee and his friends.

"Come. Sit! Tell me of your travels," his mother said, motioning them to the kitchen table.

Tomptee's voice raced much faster and much higher in pitch than Andrew had ever heard, and he would often slip into long bouts of Inkanee, the Inkling's native language. He told his mother about meeting Andrew, looking for work, the incident with the witches, and details of their travels together.

"May I see them?" she asked Andrew. "The staff and the simulacrum?"

Andrew carefully removed the staff from his bag and laid the bundle on the kitchen counter in front of her as several of the littles gathered around to see it, though they all kept their distance, having been taught well not to touch such things.

With a look of calm resolution, she gently unwrapped the bundle and let the broken pieces lay out in front of her. They looked like little more than kindling.

She went to the living room and brought back a small brass box and a grey candle in an ornate candlestick holder. She opened the box, took out what looked like a small, silver eyeglass the size of her thumb, and set it on the counter. Then she struck a match and lit the candle. The dancing yellow flame turned a steadier red as she moved the candlestick over a small ring on her left finger, and she nodded. As she moved the candle along the staff's broken handle, the dancing yellow flame tightened to a steady purple. It then became a tiny, bright blue flame over the staff's head.

She nodded again.

"It still holds power, but you have to repair it. And take note that a simple mend will not do. You have to properly *heal* it."

Heal it? Andrew didn't know what that meant.

She blew the candle out and set it aside. Then she took the small eyeglass, held it close enough to her eye to touch her brow, and leaned towards the breaks in the staff, again, careful not to touch it.

"The breaks are clean. The wood is not desiccated, which is good. Very good," she said, following the wood to the staff's head with her eyepiece as her nose worked twice as hard as her eyes. "Someone skilled in skog innblikk, perhaps."

"Forest intuition," Tomptee whispered to Andrew.

Andrew nodded as his mind raced, wondering who he knew who could help, and then it hit him. His shoulders dropped. Of course, he knew *exactly* who could help. Unfortunately, he was forbidden from ever seeing or speaking to that person again.

"And the simulacrum?" Tomptee's mother asked.

Andrew withdrew the small, tightly wrapped bundle that held the figurine from an inside coat pocket and handed it to her, but she held up a hand and refused to take it. "Please, just set it on the table."

He carefully unwrapped it and set in on the worn wood before her. Her children, including Tomptee, leaned forward, but she held up a hand, and they all leaned back.

She leaned towards it, studying the black stone and intricate details with her looking glass and nose.

As she did, Perimas felt his hands begin to shake. For a reason he could not describe, he was drawn to it. He wanted to hold it—take it. He squeezed his leg and felt himself beginning to sweat.

"It stinks like burnt coffee and bitumen. It's an angry piece. Beautiful. Dark. There is no etch or sign of tooling. The detail is exquisite." Then she looked up at Andrew. "They're moving."

"What?!" Andrew asked, picking up the figurine and studying it. He hadn't looked at it since Tomptee had given it to him, but she was right! When last he looked at it, Lorna had been prostrate on the ground a distance from the other women who pulled back from Andrew's curse. But now, the four were locked in a motionless battle of anger and hate with the wicked sisters pulling at Lorna's hair and robe as she held her hand high with her mouth frozen open as though she were trying to cast some ill-attempted word of intuition that would never leave her sealed throat. Their motion so slow that it was indiscernible to the unaided eye, like the growth of a plant, but it was true.

Andrew's heart sank further than before. What if Tomptee was right? What if his grandmother wasn't dead and she was trapped in some nightmare place with those horrible women forever trying to torment her.

Torment.

That word pulled at his mind like an anchor.

Tomptee's mother could see the anguish on his face. "There is hope," she assured him.

He looked at her with tears in his eyes.

"I don't think this is a lifeless figurine. I think it's a heltebilde."

"What's that?" Andrew asked.

She thought for a moment. "I don't think it has a direct translation in the common tongue. It's like a living stone—a statue in-dwelt by a spirit or creature of power. I think your gran..." Then she paused. She almost said she thought his gran was alive, but she hesitated since she couldn't be certain. "I think there *is* hope." Then she turned to Tomptee. "But you should absolutely take this to your father. Sooner than later." Then she lit the candle again and held it over the stone figure. Its flame shrunk from dancing orange to a small black flame that kicked off hissing yellow sparks.

"Curious. I've never seen any color other than that from orange to blue." And as she set the candle on the table near Andrew, its flame turned pale green and leaned towards him. She and Tomptee looked at the candle, then at each other. They turned to Andrew, who looked back at them, unsure what it meant.

"Would you mind?" Tomptee's mother asked, lifting the candle again.

Andrew nodded.

"Please, hold out your hands."

Andrew did so, and she held the candle over them. The candle's flame became an unmoving emerald color. Then she set the candle stick in his palm, and as she did, its flame became a green starburst.

"Extraordinary," she whispered. "I think it's time you speak with your father."

Tomptee finally agreed with her.

As they finished their toast, Tomptee's mother asked to speak with him privately, "But first, I will speak with Andrew," she said, dismissing the children.

"I sense a heaviness on you," she told Andrew.

Andrew didn't reply.

"You think this is your fault."

Andrew wrapped the staff and the figurine and tied tight the twine.

She gently touched his cheek. "I see you," she told him. "I see your pain. I don't know your story, but I see you. If it is fear, do not be afraid. This is a safe place, and you are safe here. If it is loneliness, you are *not* alone. You have family with us now. If you are lost, you belong."

Andrew's eyes widened.

"Ah. That's it, isn't it? You don't know where you belong."

A tear streaked down Andrew's cheek and his hands began to tremble.

She rose from her seat and took his face in her hands. Then she gently lifted his face and looked up.

"Great King. This child is lost and does not think he belongs. But You made him just as he is. Great Ruach. Remind him who he is in You. Draw him close to You. Be a shield to him. Let him know..." and she looked now directly at Andrew and paused so that he could hear her words well, "that he *is loved*." At that, tears poured down Andrew's cheeks and wet her hands. She pulled him close and held him as he wept.

After a long moment, Andrew wiped his face and thanked her.

"I meant what I said. You are family now. Whatever happens, you have a place here. You *belong* here."

Andrew nodded.

Then she went to the main room, where Tomptee was waiting to speak with her. "Now you."

Tomptee followed her upstairs to a cozy bedroom that was the epitome of warmth and safety for him. It was the

225

bedroom where he was nursed and sang to as a pup. It smelled like his mother's robes and homemade perfume of lavender and vanilla. Thick blankets lay in a disheveled pile on the bed, and books lay open on the floor, such as *The Sacred Garden: Healing Herbs and their Mystical Properties* and *The Cosmic Song: Seeing Beyond the Veil.*

"How have you been?" his mother asked, gently closing the door as Tomptee sat on her soft, round bed.

"Alright. I made a little money mucking stables outside the city for a couple weeks before finding my way to Jatoba."

She smiled a gentle smile. "Andrew?"

Tomptee stood. "He's not just a tinker! He builds these fantastic devices! A tool for cutting cloth he calls scissors, and a pencil! It holds carbon in the wood, which makes it stronger, and you can easily carry it in your pocket," he said, taking a pencil out of his pocket and handing it to her. "When the nub wears down, you just use a knife to sharpen it."

She was impressed. She could easily see the usefulness of such a device over constantly having to dip a pen in ink.

"And that's just the beginning! There's talk he's designing a device to track time without water, sand, or flame. He hasn't shared that with me yet, but I'm waiting for the right time to ask him about it. I think we'll be able to build some really interesting things together."

"And he's offered you gainful employment?"

His shoulders dropped. "Well, not yet. I'm sure he was going to... if his shop hadn't been burned down." He sat again on the edge of the bed.

"Are you eating? Your face looks thin."

"I'm fine."

"That's not an answer. Do you have any money?"

"Momma, I'm fine," he replied a bit too sharply.

She sighed and let him have a moment to compose himself.

"I'm sorry," he finally said. "I have a few coins."

Without another word, she went to a small box on her nightstand, took out two silver crowns, and pressed them into his palm. "Take these."

"But momma..."

She held up a hand. "It's settled."

"Will pappa mind?" he asked, looking at the coins.

She grunted. "It's my money, and I'll be damned if I let my littles go hungry. He can sleep in the garden if it's a problem."

Tomptee grinned at her swearing and at the thought of his father in the garden. He knew deep down that though she smiled and often did what his father asked, she was the quiet rock their lives were built upon, and he loved her so much for it. "Well, thank you," he said, nuzzling her neck with his nose and leaning into her embrace.

"Always, my little. You may grow, but you will *always* be one of my littles. You hear me?" she asked, taking his head in her hands.

He nodded.

"There is one more thing," she told him. "I know you think your father hates you, but he doesn't."

Tomptee took a deep breath and gently pulled away.

"He loves you very much and just wants you to succeed."

"That's not how it felt when he kicked me out of the house."

"He leads with his head and thinks that if he is... structured with you and your prickle mates, it will prepare you for the real world, and he isn't wrong."

227

"But he wants me to be something I'm not!"

She nodded. "I know. I understand. But we *all* need room to grow…"

"But that's what I'm trying to do!"

"Including, your father," she said, lowering her gaze at him in a knowing motherly way.

Tomptee didn't reply. The thought of his father being mortal and making mistakes was hard to accept. Of course, it made sense. No one was perfect. But growing up, he had always considered his father a bastion of wisdom and strength. It was hard to think of him as anything less than heroic.

"I'm not sure he'll see me," Tomptee replied.

"He will see you."

"How do you know?"

She went to his father's side of the bed and, from beneath the mattress, removed a dark green folio held shut with a length of red twine. She handed it to Tomptee.

Tomptee carefully untied the twine and opened the folio. Inside were charcoal sketches of himself. He carefully lifted a page covered with powdery black lines of his eyes at different angles and sizes. Another was his hands. Yet another was of him smiling and laughing. Then there was one of him holding a tiny clockwork dragonfly with a smile that beamed brightly.

"What are these?" Tomptee asked.

His mother smiled. "Every night since you left, your father has sat up here for hours sketching these. He's hurting. He's sorry. He just doesn't know how to say it."

"Why can't he just say that he's sorry."

"It can be quite difficult to apologize. It means that some part of you has to change, and that can be painful, especially for a man who has spent his life trying to learn a set of principles that will protect and provide for his family."

Tomptee considered this as he looked at another sketch of himself several years younger.

"Give him a chance," his mother said. "Please."

Tomptee looked at her. "I'll try."

"And I want you to promise me one more thing...even before I ask, I want you to promise me."

"Okay?"

"Promise me that if you end up without food for more than a day, you will send word."

He hesitated and looked away. When he turned to her again, he saw her eyes beginning to gloss over, so he agreed.

# CHAPTER 36

Tomptee opened the heavy wooden door to Professor Lyra Luminara's classroom, hoping not to interrupt a lecture; however, the open door spilled light into the dark classroom from the hall.

"Close the door!" a loud whisper commanded.

Andrew and Tomptee quickly snuck into the room and closed the door behind them.

Perimas was not with them because he had decided to go into town for some supplies.

Andrew couldn't see anything as his eyes tried to adjust to the darkness, so he followed Tomptee to a seat towards the back of the class, who had no problem seeing in the dark.

"They are older than we know," said a woman's voice through the darkness. "Possibly older than we can imagine. But that does not mean that we should consider them out of reach. The celestial bodies that govern the night sky have so much to teach us and so much to give."

As Andrew's eyes adjusted to the darkness, he saw a beautiful woman with delicate deer-like antlers and a long robe covered in star patterns standing in the middle of a circular room, surrounded by rows of desks where more than a hundred students looked up at the dome-shaped ceiling full of constellations that moved at the motion of the woman's lifted hand.

"We have texts that speak of some who have traveled to other worlds through the raven light."

Andrew heard several students gasp.

She nodded. "It is true. One such work has quite detailed accounts. Then there is Fostrus Lyricus, who tells of how his master traveled to other worlds during the waking. He spoke of gates that connected our world to others, known as mortal gates."

There was an audible rustling in the room as many shifted in their seats and began murmuring to each other.

Students whispered and asked each other how that might be possible.

The professor held up her non-controlling hand to quiet the room. "I have no more information on such things at this time, but to underscore my thesis that these points of light in our sky do not just twinkle at night but hold life, I want to show you all something very special." As she said it, she drew her right hand towards her like she was drawing the fabric of a blanket, and one particular star quickly drew close enough to stand as a floating orb in front of her, lighting her face in its glow.

Now Andrew could see that she was exceptionally beautiful, reminding him of his sleeping beauty back home.

The sun that now floated in the professor's open hands like a ball of fire grew as she opened her hand to get a closer look at the surface. "There. Do you see them? I had hoped that today would be the day."

The students in the front row covered their mouths

with their hands and leaned forward. Most of the rest of the class was having trouble seeing.

She pulled at the surface again, and again the surface grew closer. Then, students began laughing and hollering and standing to their feet. None of them could believe what they were seeing. They couldn't be real. This had to be a trick.

The professor smiled.

Two red dragons, with their long bodies entwined, flew through a bursting arch of fire erupting from the surface of the sun. And as they flew, one of them shook its body and cocked back its head in what looked like a violent cry that the students could not hear, as a baby dragon was birthed from under its tail into the warmth of the sun's fire.

"What a special privilege to witness such an extraordinary event," the professor said, clearly as astonished as the students, if not more so, though she kept her composure. "Vulkanas Normas. The adults are likely between 300 and 500 years old and easily thrice the size of our planet. Exceptional."

Then, the family of dragons flew into the sun and out of sight. The professor opened her hands, and the image of the sun and stars vanished.

"Curtains, please," she said, as heavy curtains were pulled back and the light of day flooded in again. Everyone but the professor shielded their eyes and winced at the daylight. "That's all for today. I want your reactions on my desk by Friday. And don't forget that your astrolabe quiz is next Wednesday."

As students collected their things and made their way out, Andrew saw an Inkling with thick, grey fur and heavy glasses rise from a smaller desk next to the professor's and collect some papers into a leather satchel. Then, the professor closed a heavy book and left the lecture hall through a narrow back door. The older Inkling—Tomptee's father—followed close behind her.

Andrew and Tomptee followed them up a circular set of stone stairs worn smooth at their center from centuries of use. A narrow door was at the top that looked like it never closed, through which was the professor's study.

Andrew stepped into the first of two connected rooms while Tomptee remained in the doorway, pulling at the corners of his coat, hesitant to approach his father. Here, Tomptee's father—Wilkers—had a desk perfectly designed for his smaller stature; wood polished so dark its mirror-like surface was nearly black, which held several glass jars of different colored inks, stacks of papers, and a charcoal sketch of Tomptee's mother from fifteen or twenty years ago.

Andrew decided to give Tomptee time alone with his father as his eyes raced along shelves of books bound in leather, wood, and metal. He then stopped at a row of books chained to a top shelf and locked with a bar with titles like *Into the Void* and *Raven Light Visions* pressed into the spines in gold leaf and dark red ink. He then quietly meandered into the second, larger room that was the professor's study where a larger desk held various brass instruments of measurement, and star charts lay scattered across the table. Andrew approached a beautiful brass and leather telescope standing near an open window. A stone basin of water, probably five feet wide carved from black stone, sat near a second window used to observe the passing moon in the reflection of the water, making measurements and calculations more manageable. Then Andrew turned to a rolling staircase leading up to several large brass dials built into a wall, the largest of which was at least fifteen feet in diameter. Ropes and weights lie in piles on the floor. Marks of lunar phases and time covered the dials' mirror-like surfaces.

"Hello," came the elegant voice of the professor as she took a piece of bread from a tray on her desk piled with apples and cheeses.

Andrew turned to her. "Hello."

"Office hours are Thursdays and Fridays."

"I'm not one of your students," Andrew replied.

"Oh? Then how can I help?"

Andrew turned to the large dials on the wall. "I've never seen anything like this."

She walked up next to him and offered him a piece of apple, which he took and ate. "No one has. It's a novel invention of my own design, but it doesn't work."

Andrew took a step forward. "It's beautiful. Did you build it?"

She laughed. "No. I'm more of a... thinker than a builder. A friend of mine in the school of metallurgy and some of his students built the components. Once I had the measurements, he used intuition to etch the dials. It's supposed to..."

"Measure the phases of the moon," Andrew cut her off, stepping towards it.

She smiled. "Well, yes. Well done."

"What's wrong with it?" Andrew asked, approaching it and leaning down to look up behind the dials.

"I'm not quite sure. It seems to work for a few days then the ropes get caught on something in the back there and I have to have one of the students come up to sort it out. Then I have to wait until the moon comes back into view to make new calculations and..."

"It's an interesting design, but I don't think it will ever work correctly," he told her.

She took a bite of apple. "Really? Pray tell."

He reached up behind one of the smaller dials. "It's not the ropes. The teeth on the gears are getting caught. They should be beveled so they don't catch on each other."

She considered. "Interesting. Please, continue."

He stood up, brushed his hands on his coat, and approached her desk. "Do you mind?" he asked, reaching for a sheet of paper.

She motioned him to proceed.

He took one of his pencils from a coat pocket and began drawing a gear.

"What is that?" she asked, stepping close enough to brush his shoulder.

"Oh, this? I call it a pencil. It's just a bit of graphite in wood so that I can write without ink."

"May I see it?"

He took a second one from his coat and handed it to her. "You can have this one. When the tip blunts, just sharpen it with a knife."

She used it to sign her name in looping lines of lovely script on the corner of the paper he was using. "This is incredible. Do you have more?"

He smiled. "I have a couple more back home. Why?"

"You could sell these in the student dispensary."

*That's not a bad idea,* he thought to himself. Then he handed her the paper, which now had three quick sketches. One was two gears connecting with square teeth, one was two gears connecting with beveled teeth, and one was something that looked like a wound ribbon with a small hook at one end.

She studied it. "This is a beautiful facsimile. Are you an engineer?"

"No, ma'am. Just a simple tinker," he replied, pointing to the first diagram. "This is how your gears were fashioned. When the teeth come together, they catch. If they were fashioned with beveled corners like these," he pointed to the second diagram. "They would easily slide into each other without trouble."

She nodded. "Of course. What an elegant solution."

"But that will only fix your current problem. It won't solve the bigger issue."

"And what might that be?"

"The weights pulling your dials will only last for so long before you have to reset it."

She nodded. "I planned on winding it once a rotation."

He shook his head. "That would be fine for something that doesn't need precision, but the winding has to be done at precisely the same time each month, else it will become inaccurate. If you are off by even an hour..."

"By month's end, it could be off by days," she completed his thought.

He held up a finger in agreement.

"I hadn't thought of that," she replied with disappointment.

"What you need is this," he said, pointing to the third sketch of the wound ribbon.

She picked up a pair of spectacles lying on the corner of her desk and put them on. Then, she leaned the sketch closer to light from the window. "What is this?"

"This!" he emphasized with excitement, "is a novel invention of *my* own design. I've been working on a device, not entirely unlike your own. Mine is meant to tell time without using consumables. The idea is a round face with twelve numbers and a hand moving through a full rotation twice a day. The challenge has been keeping a steady force applied to the gears. To overcome this challenge, I designed a series of flywheels and gears about two years ago that can take a force and apply it at an even rate, but it also used weights and pulleys to move the device, which was fine at a large scale, but I wasn't content with that. I spent the next two years considering how to apply a constant force *without* ropes or weight because I wanted something small enough for a woodworker..."

"Or tinker?" she interrupted with a smile that suggested she had an idea where this was going.

He tipped his head in agreement. "For someone to use at night in a shop or kitchen and take with them while traveling. Then I found it! In a toy shop in Quincary. The toymaker had used a small ribbon of metal, wound with a key mechanism, to create motion in his toys that lasted all day. I know because I bought one and timed it. Then, after some testing of different metal blends, I finally designed such a ribbon that would last nearly two days..."

"Allowing you to rewind it once a day without losing motion. Fascinating."

Tomptee's conversation with his father was getting heated in the other room, and Andrew turned to their rising voices.

"Was that you who interrupted the professor's lecture?" Wilkers asked as he sorted through a stack of papers without looking at his son.

"We didn't think..."

"That's right," Wilkers interrupted his son. "You didn't think. I *really* wish you would more often."

Tomptee swallowed. "This was a mistake."

Tomptee's father turned to him. "You're here, aren't you? What do you need?"

Tomptee pulled at the edges of his jacket, wanting to flee, but he knew that Andrew needed answers, so he held his ground when the professor spoke up from the other room.

"Wilkers. Come take a look at this."

Wilkers looked at his son over the top of his thick reading spectacles for another long moment before sighing and entering the professor's study. Tomptee followed.

The professor handed Wilkers the sketch. "I think our young...*engineer*," she said, smiling at Andrew, "might have solved our lunar dial."

Andrew felt his cheeks brighten, but he held his breath and his composure.

Wilkers looked at Andrew skeptically, then took the sheet of paper from the professor and considered the designs carefully.

"Why are we discussing gears?" he asked.

"Because you don't have a rope assembly problem, you have a gear problem," Andrew replied, then explained the difference in ease of movement between the two designs. And as he did, Wilkers' stern look slowly melted away.

"What's this?" he asked, pointing to the ribbon design.

"Something your son was going to help me with."

One of Wilkers's brows raised, and he glanced at his son, then back at the design.

Andrew explained the higher-level problem with their moon-phase mechanism, how he was working on a time-keeping mechanism much like theirs, and how this solved their problem. He also took the time to say how impressed he was with Tomptee's ideas and how confident he was that Tomptee would help him immeasurably advance his work, never mentioning that they hadn't yet actually worked together. It was a friendly gesture meant to draw Tomptee back into his father's good graces and show Wilkers how Tomptee's mechanical inclinations could be of great use.

"The steady force of the ribbon, combined with my gear and flywheel assembly, fairly accurately applies a constant and even force. It's not as precise as I would like yet, but it's nearly there!"

"I think this is what we need!" the professor exclaimed, tapping the paper.

Andrew smiled large. "Tomptee and I could build you such a device. It would have to be larger, but I think it might work. Some of the alloy mixes I found, unwind very slowly. Finding the right balance would take some trial and error, but..."

"You're hired," The professor exclaimed.

Andrew's eyes grew. He didn't know what to say.

Wilkers hesitated to respond before considering the matter further. He was always fast to consider and slow to respond. But the design did appear to be sound—on paper.

"And your time-keeping device...what did you call it?" Wilkers asked.

"A clock."

*From klokke or bell,* Wilkers thought to himself. *Good name.* "And your...*clock*...keeps accurate time?"

Andrew sighed. "Well, I'm not sure. I have been iterating the design. Phase one was to design the dial. Phase two was to get the dial to properly work. Phase three was to find a way to move the dial with the wound springs. I have completed all of these. Phase four—testing and adjusting its accuracy—had not yet been completed before we were attacked and my shop was destroyed in a fire."

The professor's face fell into a look of horror, and she touched Andrew's arm.

"That's what we came to talk to you about," Tomptee sheepishly told his father.

"I'm not sure we've met," the professor told Tomptee.

"This is my third eldest son," Wilkers told her.

"Wilkers! Why didn't you tell me? I'm constantly asking you to bring your family around." She shook Tomptee's hand enthusiastically. "Welcome! I've only met one of Wilkers's children. Please. Do tell us how we can help."

Wilkers's nose twitched in disapproval at the thought.

For the next short while, the four of them sat in a circle of chairs in the center of the professor's study while she listened with horror to the events leading up to Andrew cursing the women, which he let Tomptee tell since some of the details were still fuzzy and very raw.

"May I see it?" she asked, referring to the tiny black simulacrum of the four women.

Andrew removed it from his coat pocket, unwrapped it, and handed it to her.

The professor took a deep breath and held it gently as she considered its shape and implications. "I have heard stories of wondrous items but never such a thing as this. It's warm," she told Wilkers. "I'm afraid that I have no great wisdom here. Perhaps you could ask around and see which professor might know of such a thing. I also belong to three different guilds. We should inquire," she told Wilkers, offering him the small figurine for his own consideration, but he declined to take it, believing—as he had taught his family—that it was not safe to touch such things. Instead, he nodded and said nothing, deeply considering his son's words.

"There's more," Tomptee added, speaking more to his father than the professor.

His father looked at him.

"The curse was bad, no question, but I think that what came next is the real problem."

"Oh?" the professor asked.

"That night, the town fell into a sleep without waking, beginning with the children."

The professor's and Wilkers's eyes began to grow.

"Dozens—soon hundreds—of ravens descended on Jatoba. Then Andrew began having dreams of a raven."

The professor covered her mouth with her hand.

"A wise friend of mine, skilled in intuition, met me in town when I returned," Andrew added, "and took me into her...private study...where she showed me a book with a skull on the cover."

"What book?" Wilkers finally asked, breaking his long silence.

Andrew fought to find the words to describe it. "It was thick, like stone or clay, with a waterfall and a..."

"Raven skull?" the professor asked.

"Yes!"

She and Wilkers looked at each other. Then she rose and went to a corner of her office that looked like nothing but a stone wall. "Eech teech teeloom-lay," she spoke, waving a finger through the air as the wall vanished and revealed yet another bookshelf, this time full of tomes of all sorts of shapes and sizes, one of which was glowing with a strange green light like Andrew had seen emanating from the Grace Giver. She whispered something that Andrew couldn't hear and pulled the air towards her like she was opening an invisible drawer, and out of the invisible drawer, she took something wrapped in cloth. Then she moved her finger through the air again, and the bookshelf, once again, became a stone wall.

As the three joined her, she approached her desk and unwrapped what looked like a cracked and broken clay tablet, careful not to touch the clay but only the cloth wrapping it.

"Did your book have a cover like this?"

Andrew looked at the pieces of clay lying in front of him. The waterfall. The dire butterfly. The raven skull. Seeing it made his throat go dry. He did not speak. He simply nodded.

She picked up a piece of the now broken cover and showed them how it was once attached to something that looked like the spine of a book.

"Did you open it?" she was hesitant to ask.

Andrew nodded.

She sighed deeply. "What happened?"

"My friend was forbidden from reading it, but she thought she had no choice. She thought it was the only way to help Jatoba, but when she read it, she passed out. I tried to catch her when she fell and accidentally touched it."

The professor turned to the window for several moments, then back to Andrew. He could see the fear on her face, which was now rising in both him and Tomptee.

"What happened when you touched it?" she asked.

"I must have blacked out or something because the next thing I knew, I was dreaming and..." he stopped. He was suddenly having trouble remembering what he was about to say.

"And...?" the professor asked, anxious for more details.

Andrew looked around. He wasn't sure where he was.

"Are you alright?" Tomptee asked.

Andrew looked at his friend, but he wasn't sure who he was. The room shifted. Nausea rose within him, and he started getting dizzy. Something in his pocket grew warm. The next thing he knew, his face slammed into the wood floor.

# CHAPTER 37

THE TINKER'S GIFT

"Are you all right?" Tomptee asked.

...looked at his friend, but he wasn't sure who he was. The room shifted. Shadows crept within him, and he started getting dizzy. Something in his pocket grew warm. The next thing he knew, his face slammed into the wood floor.

ndrew picked himself up off the professor's floor. There was no sign of Tomptee nor Wilkers. The professor was the only one in the room now with Andrew. She stood at her desk, with her back to Andrew, gently holding the clay book cover.

"What happened?" Andrew asked, rising to his feet and rubbing his cheek where he hit the ground.

The professor did not respond, nor did she turn to him.

"Where's Tomptee?" Andrew asked, trying to gain his composure. "Professor?"

The professor gently ran her fingers over the details of the clay surface, which was now wholly unbroken.

"Professor?" Andrew asked again, taking a step towards her.

Then, a voice that was not the professor's voice came from the professor. "What do you think you are doing?"

Andrew was confused. "What do you mean? Tomptee and I came seeking advice." He glanced into the other room, but the office door was now closed, and there was no sign of either Tomptee or his father. "Where's Tomptee?"

The professor ignored his question. "Our dealings are not meant for public consideration. Even mentioning my name to any of them puts their lives at risk. Is that what you want? To tell them all about who I am and what you've seen, forcing me, one night when they are asleep, to climb into their skin and slowly pull them apart from the inside out?"

Fear paralyzed Andrew. He knew that voice. "You never told me not to tell anyone."

The professor slowly turned to Andrew. Her eyes were starlight, and her fingers were long, black, and clawed at the tips. "I am telling you now."

Andrew swallowed.

"Have you found what I'm looking for?" The false image of the professor asked.

Andrew didn't respond, realizing he had mistakenly spoken Tomptee's name to The Raven King. His lack of response made The Raven King stand immediately next to him. "What about me?" he asked in the professor's smooth and alluring voice. "Would you help *me*?"

Andrew turned his face away.

"My *engineer*. Help me fix my broken machine, and I'll be more to you than just a friend. Perhaps I'll give you a *treat* in return," The Raven King said in a slow flirtation, gently touching Andrew's neck, causing him to blush and begin to sweat. "I could *teach* you all sorts of things."

Andrew suddenly awoke, with Tomptee and Wilkers kneeling over him and the professor standing tall with a purple jewel in one hand and completing a word of intuition that she spoke with authority, her hair gently floating back down to her shoulders.

"Are you alright?" Tomptee asked, helping Andrew to stand.

Andrew's head was throbbing. "Yes. Yes, I think so. What happened?"

"You passed out," the professor replied. "You were just telling us what happened when you touched your friend's book."

Andrew glanced at her, then glanced away. "What book?"

"The book that looks like this," she said, turning to the clay book cover on her desk, now a single, solid piece—startling everyone except Andrew.

"What's happened?" the professor asked to no one in particular, approaching the cover but now afraid to touch it.

Wilkers, however, was not looking at the book cover. He was watching Andrew.

Andrew looked back at him sheepishly.

After several more attempts from the professor to get more information from Andrew, who claimed that he could not remember what they were talking about and denied any knowledge of any book with a skull on the cover, the professor sighed a heavy sigh and accepted that the conversation wasn't going any further.

She gave him some ground herbs in hot water to dull the pain in his face and promised to look further into the circumstances surrounding Andrew's figurine. He assured her it wouldn't be necessary, which only strengthened her suspicions that something had, indeed, happened when Andrew had passed out, but she could not help him if he wasn't willing to let her.

"If I do hear anything, I will let Wilkers know," she told Andrew and Tomptee.

"Thank you," Andrew replied. "You've been very kind. I'm sorry we disrupted your day."

"Not at all," she assured him, touching his hand, but he jerked it away without meaning to.

Wilkers offered to see them out, and the professor agreed.

As they were about to leave the school, Tomptee's father stopped him and handed him a small, folded piece of paper. "Take this to the utskåret kunst shop, just beyond the covered bridge near the northern gate."

Tomptee opened it. It said: "Help my son, and consider our business settled," and it was signed by his father.

Tomptee looked at his father and considered his father's eyes, which were now soft towards him in a way Tomptee had not seen in a long time.

"And come home for some supper tonight, you hear? Safe!"

Then Tomptee and his father embraced each other warmly.

247

# CHAPTER 38

The Festival of Ny Fødsel was a three-day-long celebration of fertility, death, and rebirth at the apex of the raven moon's annual cycle. During the festival, wine flowed freely, attendees wore decorated masks, and offerings were made to the god of death and dreaming.

The first day of the festival—known as krukkeåpning, or jar opening in the common tongue—was marked by Nevarii's Governor opening the first jar of new wine of the season, tasting it, and declaring it good. Then casks of wine were opened for everyone across the city, with attendees symbolically tasting the wine by taking only a spoonful, showing how "temperate and self-controlled" they were.

However, on the second day of the event—known as drikkedag, or drinking day—the scales were tipped as far in the other direction as physically possible, and nearly everyone throughout the city and surrounding villages, including children, drank until they passed out. Participants wore garlands of oranges and mend mum bulbs and masks of the caricatured royal household, including the fool, the old woman, and the poet, amongst others. The masks symbolized the shifting nature of dreams and how the possibility of the idealized life was always close at hand, which the royal household represented. There was music, dancing, and drinking contests throughout the day. Whoever vomited up their wine the fewest times was crowned the winner and declared the most fertile of the season—enjoying all the benefits of such a title.

The third and final day—known as gryteoffer or pot offerings—was unsurprisingly somber. Unofficially, it was probably due to the massive hangover felt by nearly every man, woman, and child, but officially, it was a day to remember loved ones lost. Offerings of wine, seed, and grain were made to The Raven King, and his good graces were beseeched for the growing season ahead.

Now, the opening of the consecrated cask was only an hour away, which sat on a table in the city center, draped in burgundy fabric, piled with mend mum bulbs, and guarded by Andrew's favorite city guard. Thankfully, the academy grounds were closed to outsiders, and the pressing throng of festival attendees was outside the academy gates, but things were getting busy.

Andrew and Tomptee returned to Tomptee's family home, where Perimas was waiting for them on a bench near the cottage. He appeared to be napping.

"Find what you're looking for?" he asked as they approached, half opening one eye.

"Not really," Andrew replied.

"But we have a name. Someone who might be able to help," Tomptee said, still untrusting of Perimas, though his trust was slowly building after Perimas had helped Andrew with the gate guard.

"How about you?" Andrew asked.

Perimas sat up. "Prices are higher than I remember. Much higher. Perhaps for the festival. So, I kept to the basics. Just some salt, coffee, strikers, and a few other bits and bobs. When do you want to go see your contact?"

"Straight away," Andrew replied.

~

NEVARII WAS DRAPED in marbled hues of burgundy and mauve. Festival participants wore garments stained with old wine, making the city look like the streets were flowing with the crimson elixir.

Andrew did not want to go through the city center, so the three took a longer route around the outer edge, through seedier neighborhoods and back-alley passages where it looked like many had begun day two of the festivities early. The smell of fresh-baked bread and pastries spilled out of shop windows and kitchens everywhere they went. Big, puffy loaves of granary bread. Small, cinnamon and sugar-coated pinwheel cookies. Crackers, muffins, and cakes. It was all making the three terribly hungry.

Entering the Bantam quarter calmed Tomptee's nerves considerably. This is where Bantam and Inkling moved about freely with little thought of being bothered by the larger races since most didn't bother trying to navigate the smaller stalls, purchasing shot-glass-sized cups of wine, or squeezing through the low doorways.

In one tea shop, Andrew was fascinated at the sight of a Bengari family, who were all short, fat, and bald, with four arms and spotted green skin. Even the youngest of the twelve children wore gold rings on each finger and gold loops in their ears. They were accompanied by a tall, finely dressed fae guard—though Andrew didn't know how he was so large since the only fae Andrew had ever seen could fit in the palm of one's hand. He wore a solid-gold bangle on each arm and a jewel-encrusted blade at his side. When he moved, it looked as though he phased in and out of reality, correcting the children with a touch and a whisper. Andrew considered the family's bodyguard for a moment and realized that perhaps he was not phasing at all but moving so fast that Andrew could only see his blurred shape.

As they turned onto a quieter side street—if there was such a thing during Ny Fødsel—they found a bookshop that filled one entire side of the cobblestone road. Through the windows, Andrew saw a beautiful Inkling woman answering customers' questions. A Scritt, with transparent skin, sat motionless underneath a set of bright lights towards the back. Tomptee knocked on the front window. The Inkling woman looked past her customer, smiled, and waved. Tomptee waved back.

"My sister," he told Andrew and Perimas, then pulled tight his gloves and continued on.

Navigating the throng, they drew near the wagonway station where the smell of ferlorns, and their distant low bellows, immediately reminded Andrew of his childhood visits to Nevarii with his father. He wanted to see a baby ferlorn as he had so loved doing as a child, but the station was too overcrowded to approach. Then he saw, sitting on the sidewalk at a busy intersection, a child with twisted legs and a sign that read: Coin, please. Andrew watched two other boys lift valuables from the pockets of anyone who dropped a coin in the boy's cup. Then, one of the pickpockets slipped through the crowd, dropped something into the palm of a man with saffron-yellow skin, and disappeared into the ocean of travelers. The color of the man's skin looked familiar, but Andrew didn't know how, and for several minutes it gnawed at the back of his memory.

As they crossed the covered bridge near the northern gate, the smell of curry and exotic spices made Andrew's mouth water and his belly grumble.

"This is it," Tomptee said, nearing a shop entrance beneath a wood-carved sign that read: Utskåret kunst, or carved art in the common tongue.

A middle-aged Nimic, with hickory-colored skin and light grey tattoos on the backs of his hands, stood in the doorway, surrounded by baskets of wood-carved jewelry. He wore piles of carved, wood-and-bone beads on his wrists, and at least a dozen carved-bone necklaces hung around his neck.

"Welcome!" he said with a large smile as the three approached.

Perimas stepped forward before Tomptee had a chance to present his father's note. "Hello, friend. We've traveled far and have come to ask you some questions."

"Oh?" the Nimic immediately looked skeptical.

Perimas smiled. "Nothing like that. We've traveled from Jatoba with an ornament we'd like you to consider."

The Nimic man looked at them hesitantly, then invited them into his boutique.

Carvings of wood, bone, stone, ivory, antler, and several other materials Andrew didn't recognize filled the stall. Wooden plant pots sat on the shelves next to little rows of stone statues. There were wood plates and eating utensils next to white and black stone boxes the size of Andrew's thumb. He even found a beautiful set of polished lechtfelt nesting jars.

"How can I help?" the Nimic asked, stepping behind an old table made of driftwood.

Perimas motioned Andrew to hand him the figurine. Andrew slowly did so, not comfortable letting it out of his possession.

As Perimas took it from Andrew, his hands began to tremble ever so slightly, and his mouth went dry. He slowly unwrapped it and held it for a moment. They were right, it *was* warm. And beautiful. So precious. He turned it over in his hands. Hurting. Scared. Not Lorna, the wicked sisters. He wanted to help...

"Perimas?" Tomptee asked.

Perimas snapped out of his momentary stupor and shook his head. Then, he slowly set it on the table in front of the Nimic.

The shopkeep haphazardly picked it up and ran his fingers over it. "Mighty fine piece, that is. Who carved it?"

Andrew and Tomptee looked at each other but said nothing.

"Look like volcanic rock, maybe." He felt its weight in his palm. "Ain't a big one, but dere's quality, yeah." He glanced at them, reading their body language, then shrugged. "I've got a dozen already." He held it up in his thumb and forefinger. "Maybe I could find somebody who'd wanna buy it. I'll give ya four silver crowns for it."

"We're not here to sell it," Andrew replied.

"Oh? Then what y'all here for?"

Tomptee was about to speak, but Andrew stopped him. "Have you ever seen anything like this before or know anything about it?"

The shopkeeper shrugged. "How I'm s'posed to know anythin' about it?"

"We were told you'd know something about intuitive artifacts," Perimas replied.

Andrew glanced at Perimas, wishing he would take a

more discrete route through the conversation. Where Andrew preferred caution, Perimas was bold—tool bold for Andrew's comfort.

The shopkeep smiled large, revealing a chipped tooth on one side, then laughed out loud. "Nah, dis ain't intuitive. Too small. Intuitive icons, they rare as fire in snow. I seen one, maybe two, in all my days, and only home to great creatures, you know? Dis here, it's a house idol maybe. Nothin' more. Tell ya what—I'll give ya five crows for it, an' not a penny more. Call it for yer trouble."

Andrew began reaching for it, but the shopkeep's smile slightly lessened, and his grip tightened. Then he sighed and looked at it once more. "Now, if ya tink it's wort' more... let me ask 'round, see if I can't find a buyer. We split whatever profit comes. Leave it wit me, and I'll see what I can see."

Andrew was getting nervous and wanted to leave when an elderly woman with dark black skin and eyes as white as quartz pulled back a curtain behind the shopkeep.

"Julio, who's there?" the old woman asked in a high, uneven voice.

"No one, Jadati. Just some folk lookin' to deal."

The woman's eyes looked off in the distance for a moment, then squinted and began searching until they found Andrew. Though the woman had been blind for more than half a century, she looked right at him. "It's you."

She slowly moved her hand towards the shopkeep's table, and Julio helped her find its edge—all of his charismatic salesmanship now gone. She could not see the table, but somehow, she could see the figurine, which she gently picked up and held in her arthritic, knotty fingers. Then she looked directly at Andrew again.

"Come with me."

# CHAPTER 39

There was no light in the space behind the curtain. The shopkeeper lit a candle, which cast a low, warm glow across hundreds of carved figurines. Rows and rows of wood, stone, bone, and tusk took the form of dragons or small children playing. Fish swam, birds flew, pigs rolled together in mud, and ivory trees grew, bearing exquisite tiny fruit so small Andrew had no idea how anyone could even see such fine detail, much less carve it. The images were not like those in the front of the shop, which looked like quickly cut children's toys or knick-knacks for traveling tourists. These were priceless works of art, and there were countless many.

In the center of the room sat a small carver's desk, scratched and cut from decades—perhaps centuries—of use. There were rows of tools, and piles of dust climbed the desk's spindly legs.

The old woman did not need to feel her way around in this space; this was her space. She knew the precise location of every figurine, rasp, and file.

"Leave us," she told her grandson.

"Yes, Jadati," he replied with a bow, closing the curtain as he left.

She sat behind the small table and studied the simulacrum's every edge, surface, and detail with hands like gnarled wood, never looking down at the figure but staring unblinkingly at Andrew.

Andrew gently touched her desk. He had never seen most of the tools standing upright before him in small, wooden cups, and his mind raced at each possible use. His finger found an old knot on the desk's edge, and he picked at it.

Tomptee suspected she was blind, but he wasn't sure, so he quietly waved a hand through the air. She did not respond.

"What have you done?" she finally asked.

Andrew swallowed. "Can it be undone?"

The woman's bottom lip was larger than her top, which stuck out in a kind of pout as she considered. She turned her head to the side as though she were listening for something, then looked back at Andrew. "You carry with you something more dangerous than this," she told him.

Tomptee and Perimas looked at Andrew, who wasn't sure what she meant. "We have my grandmother's broken staff. She was a powerful..."

"Not a staff," she interrupted. "A coin."

Andrew's eyes widened. "I'm sorry. I don't..."

"He's after you, isn't he?" she asked.

Andrew said nothing.

She lifted a small silver charm in the shape of a key—one of dozens on her spider web of silver necklaces—and kissed it, then spoke a series of guttural clicking sounds perhaps no one else could ever hope to emulate as the wall behind her ever so slightly draped like fabric.

She rose and pulled the wall back like a painted curtain, behind which stood a door that looked like it was carved of a single, large pearl. She motioned them to follow her.

"Not you," she told Perimas.

The three looked at each other, but Perimas motioned them to go ahead without him.

The woman's curved stature straightened as she stepped through the door, and her hands loosened. Her hair fell into long, beautiful black braids across her shoulders, and her eyes became bright. She was still older than Andrew could guess, but in this place, she was healthy and strong. Her Nimic tattoos of power now glowed so brightly that Andrew could see them through her robe. Thin twisting glyphs up the center of her back and down her arms. She also had one behind each ear and a large design on her scalp that glowed through her lush hair.

They were now standing in a museum of carved artifacts and bone with a ceiling probably seventy feet high full of beautiful stained-glass windows. The walls were carved with every kind of creature, from land sharks rising in a field at a herd of jumping elk to the image of a vintnew thirty feet high with wide, gently glowing antlers, which turned its head and watched them as they walked past. Thick, towering columns rising to the levels above looked like the trees Andrew had seen in the Ki Lo Kan Forest, with stone branches holding different creatures, including three tree horses. High above them hung the skeleton of a giant turtle with trees growing out of its back.

"Is that a..."

"Archa tenech? Yes."

Andrew shook his head. "I know someone who would *kill* to see this place," he said as they followed her across the foyer to a marble staircase.

257

The old woman glanced at Andrew. "Oh, there are many who would kill to see this place."

"Where are we?" Tomptee asked, turning in circles, trying to take everything in.

"A distant moon, actually."

"Then it's true! There *are* gates to other worlds," Tomptee exclaimed.

She nodded with a smile.

"Your necklace..." Tomptee began.

She shook her head. "My necklace isn't the gate. *I* am the gate."

Tomptee didn't understand. "But..."

Andrew gently touched his arm. "I don't mean to seem ungrateful, Jadati, but..."

She smiled at Andrew. "Jadati means grandmother. My name is Nomi, but you may call me Jadati if you like."

A laboratory was on the second floor with wide tables, glass, brass, and metal instruments, and shelves of jars full of countless specimens of plants, liquids, and animal parts. Some of the jars glowed, and other jars moved.

She took a transparent box off a shelf and set the simulacrum inside. Then she turned to Andrew. "May I see the coin?"

Andrew took a deep breath.

"It's alright, child. You are safe here."

Andrew cautiously took the coin from his pocket and set it on the table.

"No one can take it from you. You know that, right?"

"I did not," Andrew replied.

She did not touch the coin at first but instead motioned her hand as three chairs walked over to the table, and everyone sat down. "Tell me everything."

So, they did.

# CHAPTER 40

Once they finished telling Nomi everything they both knew, from when Tomptee first stepped into Andrew's shop until now, Nomi had sat quietly considering, having asked no questions nor saying a word during the telling. She just listened and periodically looked at the simulacrum and coin in front of her.

She sat the coin on its edge and spun it on the table. "I've seen counterfeits. Never a real one. But yours isn't counterfeit, is it?"

"How would you know?" Tomptee asked as the coin spun.

"Because I can see it, and because..." she said, pointing to the coin, which should have at least slowed by now but just kept spinning. "It isn't a part of our world, so it isn't bound by the rules of our world. If none of us stop it, it will spin until we are all dead, buried, and long forgotten."

"You can see things that are intuitive?" Andrew asked.

She nodded. "But this isn't intuitive like so many pieces in my collection. It's something else entirely. You see, nuqṭat quwwa—or points of power, if you will—are imbued with their own intuition. They can be buried, forgotten for centuries, and still be dangerous. This...this is *a part* of Malik al-Ghurab. I suspect he gave it to you to see you in the waking."

Andrew looked at Tomptee.

"Why would he need a coin to do that?" Andrew asked.

"He's not omniscient. That's why ravens followed you until he gave you this. I suspect you haven't seen any since."

Andrew hadn't considered that.

"Then we need to get rid of it!" Tomptee exclaimed.

She shook her head. "Not necessarily." She picked up the coin and read the back. "The coin, like the trickster raven himself, has a dual nature, you see. Horror on one side," she showed them the skull of the raven, "and hope on the other." She turned the coin over and read: "'A raven Coin, in raven light, for The Raven King.' Why did he give it to you?"

Andrew looked at Tomptee.

She, too, looked at Tomptee, trying to understand what Andrew's body language was communicating.

"He said he lost something...someone, and he wants me to help him find them," Andrew told her as his shoulders dropped like a child who had just got caught with his hand in the cookie jar.

"Why you?" Tomptee asked.

"I don't know," Andrew replied.

"Legend tells that whoever possesses a coin of The Raven King—a true raven coin—will be granted a single favor."

"A favor?" Tomptee asked.

Andrew turned away from them as he said, "Ever since he gave it to me, he's been trying to offer me things."

"What kind of things?" Tomptee asked.

Andrew was ashamed to answer, remembering his last dream in which the image of the professor had made him all sorts of tawdry promises.

"I would not be quick to discard it if I were you. Not only does it have more value than possibly anything else in my collection, but the favor of a god is no small matter." She motioned her hand over it, changing its appearance to that of cracked wood. "I wouldn't let anyone else know you have it. Entire cities have been razed to the ground for far less than this."

"You said no one can take it from him," Tomptee replied.

She nodded. "That doesn't mean they can't try."

"You take it!" Andrew exclaimed.

Her eyes grew.

"I don't want it. Hide it away in this fortress of solitude," Andrew pleaded.

*What an intriguing idea,* she thought to herself as she gently touched the coin's raised edge. *I've only ever seen counterfeits. To have and to hold such an exceptional piece. I wouldn't have to use it. Just keep it. Look at it. Protect it. I would be doing the child a favor.* She licked her lips, and Tomptee saw it.

"Are you sure, Andrew? We might need it?" Tomptee said, slowly reaching for it.

Then Nomi blinked and smiled. "Of course not. As I said, it has a dual nature. It brings both blessing and cursing to whoever possesses it, or whomever *it* possesses, as the case may be."

Andrew didn't like the sound of that. "Very well," he sighed, sliding the coin back into his pocket.

"But perhaps I can be of some help with this," she said,

taking the glass box holding the simulacrum and setting it in front of them.

They watched as she held her left hand open next to it and spoke: "'Arni nafsak alhaqiqia."

Inside the box, as though through a fogged window, they saw images of the four women appear who were screaming and cursing each other, though no words could actually be spoken, which meant that no intuition was being cast.

"They are still alive. They might not even know what's happening. Something akin to sleepwalking."

"Or sleep fighting," Tomptee said.

*Quaint turn of phrase*, she thought and nodded.

"How do I help my grandmother?"

"You can release them, but you would need both the staff that cast the word and memory of the word itself. You see, intuition is like music. It's not just the words you speak but how you speak them. Your emotions, your passion, your *rage* can all affect the outcome. Do you remember what you said?"

Andrew shook his head. "I thought I was casting a word I had heard my gran speak before."

"But the result was quite different, wasn't it?"

He nodded.

"Tell me how you *felt* when you spoke it."

His face went white, and she could see his shame. She reached over and took his hand. "There is grace for you. But I need to know, if I am to help you."

"I was scared at first, but then they tried to kill my fiancé, and I just... had to stop them."

"Is that all you were trying to do?"

For a few long moments, he did not respond. Then he shook his head.

Words weren't necessary. She knew.

"It was a powerful word. A dangerous word." *A word meant for death,* she wanted to say but refrained.

"Do you still have the staff?" she asked.

Tomptee nodded and began reaching for it.

She held up a hand. "That isn't necessary."

"Can you fix it?" Andrew asked, slightly perking up in hope.

She shook her head. "I'm sorry. No. My intuition is not with wood itself else, I would not need to carve it." Then she had an idea and turned to the door. With hands outstretched, she spoke the title of a book as it flew to her from a library on the other side of the building. She gently fingered through its pages and lay it open in front of them.

"Have you heard of the Shimar Etsell?" she asked.

"I've had some dealings with them," Andrew replied.

She nodded and rose from her desk. Andrew and Tomptee followed her.

"They are skilled in such things. Return to them, and perhaps..."

"I can't," Andrew replied.

"Why?" she asked.

"Because I overstayed my welcome last time I was there," Andrew replied.

"You've seen their lands?" Nomi asked.

He nodded.

*Incredible.* "Find a way," she told him.

*Just add it to the list of impossible things I need to get done,* he thought to himself.

As they followed her back down the marble staircase, Andrew asked, "Have you heard of the Book of Elyon?"

She thought for a moment, then shook her head. "I'm sorry, no. Why?"

"No reason," he replied.

Then, as they were about to return to the shop through the pearlescent door, Andrew said, "One more thing..."

Nomi turned to him. "Yes?"

"When I was in the front of your store, you said: 'It's you.'"

She nodded. "I have seen you in my night visions. You and your mother."

"I'm sorry, me and my *mother*?"

She nodded. "Why?"

"I do not know my mother. I was abandoned in a tinker's cart as a baby."

She touched his arm. "I did not realize."

"Could it have been my grandmother?"

"A woman, perhaps in her thirties, with long blonde hair?"

"I don't understand," Andrew replied.

Nomi thought for a moment. "I *have* seen you in several night visions. One of you in a swamp at dusk. Another as a babe in a pram at the wagonway station. The woman is holding you and crying." She thought again, her finger touching her chin. "Another in a home. You are talking to her, and she is holding a very small child. Someone else is there..." Nomi tried to remember. "A beautiful bald woman with copper skin."

Andrew got goosebumps. "Holding a small child?" Andrew asked.

She nodded. "Do you have a child?"

Andrew shook his head. "No. But the woman I will soon marry has skin the color of penny coins."

"There was something else," she added. "A sound... maybe a bird song? Then the woman with the blonde hair smiled at the child and said it was time for tea."

*A bird song*, Andrew wondered.

"Perhaps the visions are not for me," she told him as they stepped back through the door into her shop.

"I have something for you," she handed Andrew a small, carved cube of green jade on a whisper-thin necklace.

"What is it?"

Now elderly once again and unable to look directly at him, she smiled and replied, "It will loosen your tongue and help you speak words of intuition more clearly."

He thanked her and put it on.

# CHAPTER 41

Andrew still had so many questions, but he also had hope for the first time in a long time. Even the *possibility* that his mother was alive somewhere meant they may one day be reunited.

Outside the academy gates, the city was tasting and tasting and tasting again the freely flowing wine. However, Tomptee and his family had never taken part in the revelries, and the grounds were quiet as beautiful glass lamps began to light from some unseen source. One of them came to life right next to Andrew, who wanted to know how it was lit and looked at Tomptee, but Tomptee just smiled. It was an academy of intuition after all.

By the time they returned to Tomptee's home, the air was rich with the smell of cooking butter and fats and baking spiced cakes. Tomptee's mouth watered at the smell of cottage pie—his favorite—a treat always reserved for guests, baked with diced root vegetables and cubed meat in a thick brown gravy.

"How did your fortunes fare?" Nizzle asked as they put down their things and came in.

"So, so," Tomptee said, pulling off his boots and making his way into the kitchen to get a snout full of all the lovely fragrances.

"Our journey didn't end with her, as I hoped it would, but she did point us to someone who might be able to help," Andrew replied, slumping down onto a chair in the main room.

"Well, that's something, right?" she tried to encourage him, wiping her hands on her apron.

Tomptee took a spoon and pulled a piece of meat out of the pot, blew on it, and tossed it into his mouth. His mother gently tapped the back of his hand with a smile. "Not until we're all together!"

Tomptee smiled and bumped her with his shoulder.

Wilkers came down from the upstairs bedroom in a loosely tied robe. He wiped his spectacles on the corner of his collar and put them on. "Was she able to help you?"

"Not as much as I would have liked."

Wilkers nodded. "Her shop is something, isn't it?"

Andrew leaned forward. "It was incredible!"

Wilkers sat at the desk near Andrew.

"Are they *all* intuitive?" Andrew asked.

"I don't know," Wilkers replied. "At least a few of them are. But either way, her work deserves to be in a museum. She should be teaching at the academy."

"Why isn't she?"

Wilkers looked away. "No telling. I stop by every once in a while, and I asked her once, years ago, but she just waved me off."

"Have you been in her back *back* room?" Andrew asked.

Wilkers looked at him over the top of his spectacles. "Her back *back* room?"

Andrew smiled an I-know-something-you-don't-know

smile and glanced at Perimas, who was helping pour cups of juice in the kitchen. "She touched a charm on her necklace and almost *sang* a word of intuition, and all her shelves changed. Behind them was this beautiful jewel-like door leading to a vast stone building with high ceilings, rooms, and galleries of creatures and artifacts. The walls were carved with moving creatures, and an entire skeleton of an archa tenech was hanging from the ceiling!"

Wilkers listened intently. "Behind her shop?"

Andrew shook his head. "No. Not exactly. The door appeared at the back of her shop, but she said the building was on some moon somewhere?"

"What? A moon, you say?"

Andrew nodded with excitement. "Do you remember the professor talking about gates?"

"Mortal gates?"

Andrew nodded. "She said she *is* one!"

Wilkers stood and slowly wandered around the room, considering what he was hearing.

Andrew lowered his voice again. "I'm not sure how much of what I saw she wants me to share. She said some would *kill* to see her collection, and she wouldn't let Perimas go through with Tomptee and me."

Wilkers looked into the kitchen at Perimas, who was laughing at the table with two of Wilkers's youngest. "Any idea why?"

Andrew shook his head.

"It is wise of her to be cautious. The professor's research on mortal gates has led her to countless dead ends. It's almost impossible to find anything about them, and the little we have is mostly myth and legend; however, it does appear that they were highly coveted by some."

"Tea time, boys," Nizzle called from the kitchen.

Wilkers and Andrew took their place at the kitchen table, which was cramped but cozy.

With difficulty, Willa pushed her chair over next to Andrew.

Andrew watched in envy as Nizzle and Wilkers scooped portions of food onto the plates of each of their children, wordlessly handing plates and cups back and forth to each other like a dance they had danced together for years. Each of the littles began to take bites and reach for juice as Nizzle told them to wait for their guests. The warm and inviting family atmosphere the two had created for their children in this home, made Andrew miss his own. His wasn't the same as this, but it was something and it was his. Lithuel. Jasper. The rich, brothy smell of cockles boiling on the hob as Lithuel stirred them gently. Summer nights in the swamp, with the sound of crickets and the glow of lantern flies on the marsh. He missed home.

"Where are you?" Nizzle asked Andrew with a gentle smile.

Andrew shook his head. "Excuse me?"

"Just now. You were somewhere else. Where?"

"Home."

She smiled and touched his hand. "Will you tell us of your home?"

"Yes, Andrew, share!" Willa exclaimed in her gentle voice, crawling onto his lap, and the other littles nodded with agreement. Andrew smiled at her.

He took the slice of buttered granary bread Wilkers handed him and considered. "You live in this beautiful place, but I live in a swamp," he said, and the children gasped. "But the swamp isn't what you might think. You know the garden you have just past your bushes?"

The children nodded.

"Well, I, too, have a garden, but my garden is full of water and trees with branches that hang so low their leaves touch the water. Countless fish dart back and forth through grass growing out of the water, and at night, these beautiful tiny bugs glow, called lantern flies. Their light pulses just as the sun goes down on the marsh, and if you watch, you can see that their light begins to flash in unison. All across the water, for miles, there is this amazing synchronized dance of light, like the entire marsh is one big living thing."

"Lovely. Thank you," Nizzle told him. "Alright, whose turn is it?"

"Tomptee's!" Pimble said with excitement.

Tomptee sighed and looked at his father, who nodded in agreement. Then he lowered his head, and everyone held hands.

"King of kings. Thank you for hearth and home. Thank you for bringing me home safely and for my new friends." Then everyone squeezed hands, and Wilkers said: "Let's eat."

Perimas wanted to help clean up after dinner, and Andrew was tired, so he followed Nizzle upstairs.

"Will this work well for you?" Nizzle asked, showing Andrew to the boy's room where four small beds sat neatly made along the walls. "They will be a bit small for you, but we've had guests before put three together and lay across them corner to corner."

Andrew smiled. "This is fine. Thank you for your hospitality."

"My pleasure. It's good to meet some of Tomptee's friends. He hasn't had many." She handed him a plush blanket and closed the door behind her.

Andrew looked around the room. Various toys lay scattered about. A little family of wooden ducks was painted in faded yellows and greens, and each bed had a somewhat threadbare stuffy leaning against its pillow.

Andrew had never known a home like this. His toys were rasps and spanners. Lithuel had built several clockwork devices for him, but Andrew had *never* had anything soft to cuddle with other than Jasper. Perhaps that's why he loved the old codger so.

One bed, slightly dusty, lay beneath sketches of horseless carts and gear shapes pinned to the wall. This must have been Tomptee's bed. Andrew picked one other than Tomptee's, sat, untied his boots, and reached for the figurine in his pocket to tuck it safely beneath his pillow.

There was no figurine.

He quickly stood and searched the rest of his coat but didn't find it. He frantically pulled everything out of his trouser pockets, dug through his jacket again, and then dumped his rucksack onto the floor. Nothing.

He ran downstairs in his sock feet and found Tomptee sitting by the fire with his parents nursing a cup of something hot. Two of the older children, who had not yet fallen asleep, sat up, all of whom were lying in front of the fire.

"What is it?" Nizzle asked.

"Have you seen the figurine?" he asked Tomptee.

"Not since the store. Why?"

Perimas came down from the other room where he had been given a bed. "What's the trouble?"

"I can't find the figurine," Andrew panicked, looking around the kitchen table and floor.

"Have you seen it since the store?" Perimas asked.

"No! I had it when we were with Nomi, but I haven't seen it since! I got so distracted with supper I didn't even think about it."

"Perhaps you dropped it," Tomptee said. "I'll go out and see if I can find it."

"I'll help. I bet that shopkeep lifted it before we left!" Perimas said.

"We'll join you," Wilkers said, looking at Nizzle, who nodded in agreement.

"Tivee, Pimble, you two keep an eye on the littles till we get back, you hear?" Nizzle told them, pulling a warm shawl over her shoulders, not so much to keep out the cold for the evening was lovely and her fur was warm, but more to provide a sense of safety against the dark. City Inklings never found themselves out after dark if they could avoid it. Though their ancestors were nocturnal, city life was far more dangerous after dark than their secure homes.

Through the streets they went, retracing their path from the academy to the charmer's shop. The city had now taken on a new life. Many were stumbling around from the effects of the wine while the Dym population began their nightly routines. Though the streets were dark, the Inkling's eyes were sharp, and their noses sharper still.

By the time they returned to the charmer's shop, it was locked up for the night and they had found nothing.

Andrew circled the squat masonry building, looking for any sign of his simulacrum or Nomi and her grandson, but there was nothing but an old Longbeard passed out in the back alley.

Perimas pounded on the front door.

"We can return at first light," Nizzle said, but that wasn't good enough for Perimas. He looked in through the front window and decided he was getting in one way or another, but as he picked up a rock and approached the glass, Andrew stopped him.

"Not like this."

"I think it's in there," Perimas replied.

Andrew shook his head. "I don't."

"But..."

Andrew interrupted him. "If he had taken it, Nomi would have seen him."

"Seen him? I thought she was blind as a bat."

Andrew nodded. "Oh, she's blind, alright, but she can see intuitive objects. I don't know how, but she can, and I trust her. I don't think they have it."

Perimas looked back at the window, unconvinced but willing to let Andrew make the call. So, he sighed and put down the rock.

Then a thought dawned on Andrew that made his face flush.

"What?" Tomptee asked.

"Do you remember the boy at the wagonway station earlier today, holding the sign?"

Tomptee nodded.

"There were boys in the crowd picking pockets."

"I noticed that too," Tomptee replied.

"What if..."

Tomptee checked his pockets. Everything was there. "Are you missing anything else?"

Andrew felt for his coin purse, but its weight was still on his hip, and the pull of the raven coin was in his pocket. "No."

"Why would they steal that and leave your purse?" Tomptee asked.

Andrew didn't have an answer.

"What if someone overheard us talking to the shop-keep?" Perimas asked.

Andrew considered. He could have dropped it, but he had been so careful with it. He didn't think Nomi or her grandson would have taken it, leaving a pickpocket as the next most likely possibility. Perimas had been so quick to rush in and ask the shopkeep about intuitive items. Someone could have overheard them. Perimas just *had* to hold it and negotiate with Julio. Even then, Andrew had wished he hadn't been so straightforward with Julio. They could have explored possibilities more discreetly. Had Perimas's foolish big mouth gotten them robbed?

He grit his teeth in frustration.

"You just had to argue with Julio, didn't you?" Andrew snapped at Perimas.

Perimas looked at him, confused.

"There was no reason to tell him it was intuitive. There was no reason to even show it to him! We could have inquired more discreetly."

Perimas held up a hand. "Well, I'm sorry for trying to help! I have some experience with these sorts of people."

Andrew furrowed his brow. "What sort of people?"

Perimas didn't answer.

A long string of expletives ran through Andrew's mind, but he said nothing.

Tomptee heard the exchange and chose not to approach. Though his feelings about Perimas had often been mixed on their travels, nothing indicated this was intentional. It was just someone who thought he always had the answers rushing in to help when help was unnecessary and—in this case—hurtful.

They looked twice as carefully on the way home, but the streets were getting more rowdy as the night grew late, and there was no sign of the carved black stone.

The hope Andrew had felt just a few short hours earlier was now crushed. He had absolutely no recourse to find out if or who might have taken the figurine, the last chance he had in all the world of bringing his grandmother back. The bitterness of her loss returned with so much venom it made his throat burn with heartache, anger at Perimas, hatred of this wretched city, and shame for what he had done to put all of them in this position. The night was darkest now, and all was lost.

Wilkers and Nizzle wanted to offer some words of encouragement, but they had none. They knew more than the rest how relentless and unforgiving the city streets could be, making them even more thankful for the gates of the academy that had provided a haven for them to raise their family.

Andrew felt utterly defeated, and everyone saw it. No one said a word to him as he quietly went to bed.

That night, Andrew tried to sleep, but sleep eluded him. Instead, he tossed and turned, going back over the day's events in his mind, trying as hard as he could to remember if maybe he *had* dropped it or somehow set it down some-where. He had it with Nomi. He could clearly remember her giving it back to him. No. Something must have happened to it on his way back to Tomptee's home.

Then, a thought occurred to him through the thick darkness: the raven coin.

# CHAPTER 42

Andrew sat up in bed and took the heavy coin from his pocket. Was this the answer? Could it be that simple? But what would it cost him? The Raven King had told him to spend it wisely, asked him what he wanted, and he had said nothing. But he *did* want something. He wanted his grandmother back. Perhaps he needn't bother with the figurine at all anymore. Maybe he could ask The Raven King for his grandmother directly. He had already taken a great risk helping his grandmother last year when he went to the Grace Giver, but this didn't feel like a risk; this felt like a trade—one life for another. Or perhaps, The Raven King had taken it or done something to it to manipulate Andrew into needing his help.

He held the coin up to the moonlight spilling in through a tiny, single window in his room. Its blue-grey light traced the coin's rim and the edges of the raven skull rising from its center, and though the coin now looked like wood— thanks to Nomi's word of intuition—it somehow still glinted like gold.

The Raven King was looking for someone. Andrew

thought that was Tomptee, but the raven had never specifically said. How was Andrew to know for sure? But what if it *was* Tomptee? What would the Raven King want with Tomptee? He had said that he had lost something—someone. What did that mean? How would he have lost Tomptee?

Andrew considered the words on the back:

A raven coin
in raven light
for The Raven King

Andrew didn't know what that meant. Was The Raven King watching him right now, through the moonlight, while he held the coin? The thought made him uncomfortable, so he slid the coin back into his pocket and went to the window where he looked out across the school's private garden. He had a beautiful view of the grounds. And that's when he heard a click of tin through the slightly cracked window; he'd recognize that uniquely sharp sound anywhere. A small flame illuminated the face of a stranger standing in a dark corner of the courtyard. The stranger, with a puff, lit the end of a cigar. Then, with the next puff of brightness, Andrew saw that the stranger was Human!

Andrew quickly pulled on his boots and quietly snuck past the pile of snoring children asleep in the front room and went out into the darkness.

"Who's there?" he whispered.

The stranger stepped through a wafting cloud of smoke. "A bit late to be out, in' it?"

"You're Human!"

The old man pulled the cigar out of his mouth, its end now wet and chewed. "Ey, so are you, by look of it," he replied. He wore single-piece overalls Andrew had never seen before, with straps pulled up over his shoulders and clasped in the front. They had a large pocket on the chest that held several small, well-used hand tools. He also wore a pair of cracked and faded black leather shoes and a chocolate-colored canvas jacket. A blue-striped hat was pulled down over matted tufts of slate-grey hair, and he had a knotty, uneven nose. With one good eye, he looked at Andrew and asked: "You ain't from 'round here, is ya?"

"What is that?" Andrew asked.

"What?"

"You used to light your smoke?"

"Ey, this?" the man asked, taking the lighter out of his pocket and tossing it to Andrew.

"How does it work?"

The man grinned and didn't reply.

Andrew turned the small tin box with a hinged lid in his hands. He slowly pulled back the lid and saw a tiny chimney with holes holding a wick. Near it was a wheel of some sort. Andrew smelled it. It smelled like some sort of strong, metallic fluid. Then he turned the wheel as little sparks hissed forth, igniting the wick.

"What do you call this thing?" Andrew asked.

The man held up a hand as though he were about to bestow some ancient wisdom. "A lighter." Then he laughed and slapped Andrew's shoulder.

"Where did you get it?"

"Made it," the man replied.

"You made this?"

The man's thick eyebrows raised, and he grunted a laugh. "Surprised?"

Andrew was actually, but he said nothing. Then the man held up a hand, revealing fingertips died dark purple.

Andrew looked down and rubbed his own purple fingertips.

"Same stains as you. Potash from solderin' joints. Cost a workin' for a livin'."

Andrew handed the lighter back to him, but he held up a hand, indicating Andrew should keep it. "You go to school here?" the man asked, tucking the cigar back into his cheek.

"No. I'm staying with a friend. We came looking for answers."

"Find any?"

Andrew looked at his boots.

The man nodded with understanding. "Wilkers? Good people," the man replied, changing the subject.

"Do you live here?" Andrew asked.

"Ay. Me and the misses. Been keeping these grounds more than fifty-two years."

"Is your wife also Human?"

The man shook his head. "Nay, Nimic. Good woman."

"Can I ask where you're from?"

"Madina. Left to find my fortune 'bout your age." He grunted again. "Found a dose of reality instead."

"Madina?"

The man's brows raised again, and he pointed the wet end of his cigar at Andrew. "In't that where you's from?"

Andrew shook his head. "I've never heard of it. Are there other Humans in Madina?"

"Ay. Only Humans," the old man replied.

"Really!? How many? Where is it? How far?"

The old man studied Andrew for a moment. "Didna' your parents tell of it?"

Andrew looked away sheepishly. "I wasn't raised by Humans."

The old man's eyes grew, and he shook his head. "Hells. A Human child grown 'round those *things*."

*Things? Poignant word*, Andrew thought. He had never heard anyone in Jatoba called a *thing* before.

"Come on then," the man said, motioning Andrew to follow him.

Andrew looked around. The grounds and Tomptee's cottage were all dark and quiet.

"Not for long," Andrew replied. Then he followed the old man behind a low hedge to a moss-covered hatch. The man took a key from a ring of keys on his belt, unlocked the heavy door, and opened it to reveal a dark set of stone stairs. He held it open for Andrew, pulling one more long drag from his cigar then flicking it into the bushes.

"Where are we going?" Andrew asked.

The old man just smiled and touched his nose.

# CHAPTER 43

"What is this place?" Andrew asked as he followed the old man down the old stone steps beneath the academy grounds. The air was metallic and earthy.

"There used to be nothin' round these parts but some villages and an old Nimic shrine. The school was built on it; then a city grew up 'round it. But not up there. Up there is only a few hundred years old. Down here is the original city." The old man pointed down a long tunnel from which Andrew could hear the sound of something in the distance. Then the old man stopped before a narrow, heavy-wood door, took another key from his ring, and unlocked it. "These old tunnels used to be roads," he said, tapping old pave stones with his foot.

The door opened into a small room, barely twice the size of a broom closet, and the old man turned a dial on the wall as a string of glass bulbs flickered to life and began to glow.

Andrew squinted and looked around. It smelled of grease and stale tobacco smoke. A dozen different spanners, hammers of various shapes and sizes, measuring instruments, and blades hung on the walls from metal hooks. Jars of glue, grease, and paint sat on a shelf with handwritten labels, and a small, wood-carved bowl sat on the side of one of the benches piled with spent cigar butts. Andrew thought he had seen such a bowl in the trinket shop earlier. There were also dozens of contraptions, both finished and in pieces, lying scattered across one of the work tables; however, Andrew was first fascinated with the electric lights.

"How do you power these?" Andrew asked, looking at one of the small glass bulbs hanging from the ceiling.

The old man smiled, took off his coat and hat, tossed them over the back of his work chair, and tapped on the glass of a large box screwed into the wall. Through the glass, Andrew saw a colony of ants. The same ants Lithuel had used back home to keep Brynlee's fence safe from predators.

"The power they produce can be harnessed for some usefulness. It moves through those strands of copper to the bulbs," Then he took another cigar off the shelf, patted his front pocket looking for his lighter, and remembering that he had given it to Andrew, took a second lighter off the shelf and lit the end. Then he offered Andrew one, but Andrew declined.

"Incredible," Andrew said, putting the puzzle together in his mind of how the ants produced the electricity, how it was harnessed and carried through wires traveling across the wall to the dial, then up to the lights. It was a function he was familiar with because of his experience with the fence Lithuel had built to protect Brynlee, but Andrew had never considered it for anything other than deterring predators in a swamp.

The old man took a folded paper off a shelf and handed it to Andrew.

"What is this?" Andrew asked.

"Ay, you tell me," the old man said, blowing a mouthful of smoke onto the page.

Andrew opened it. It was a bill of lading from Madina to Eetoomba.

"This looks like a shipping receipt," Andrew told him.

The old man shrugged. "It's from when I left home years ago."

Andrew looked at it more closely. Then Andrew read, "One rite of passage aboard the Algi ship, Macpella's Grace, bound from Madina to Eetoomba."

The old man nodded. "Always wondered what it said."

"Can't you read it?"

The old man shook his head.

"You live at an academy, and you can't read?"

"You think anyone up there wants to teach us anything? That ain't for us. If we ain't useful to them, we ain't nothin' to them. Besides, at least I know where I come from."

*Truer words were never spoken,* Andrew thought. "Sorry."

The old man didn't look bothered. He took the paper from Andrew and looked it over like he was reading it. "I recognize the word 'Madina,' and the numbers are clear enough, but the rest...just chicken scratch." Then he put it back on the shelf and turned to Andrew. "You said you come lookin' for answers. About what, exactly?"

Andrew sat on the single chair in the small room and told the old man how he had come with his friends to the city to learn about a valuable figurine he had inherited from his grandmother and how it had disappeared last night; however, he didn't get into the details of how it was intuitive or much else about his journey from Jatoba.

He didn't have the strength, nor did he feel it was necessary.

"Is that who raised ya?" the old man asked as the small room filled with smoke.

"Mind if I crack the door?" Andrew asked.

The man motioned him to do as he pleased.

"No. I was abandoned as a baby and raised by my Nimic father, who is also a tinker. I never knew my family."

The old man shook his head and snuffed out his cigar. "Shame. Do you know *anything* about your people?"

Andrew shook his head. "Can you tell me?"

The man raised his eyebrows. "How long you got?"

Andrew smiled. "All night. I'm Andrew, by the way."

"Noah Oliver," the old man said, reaching for Andrew's hand.

Andrew was confused.

"Take it, and shake it. We Humans shake hands when we meet. Sign of friendship."

Andrew held out his hand as Noah Oliver shook it warmly with the grip of a man who knew how to hold a hammer. Then he removed some tools from a wooden crate and motioned Andrew to trade seats with him, which he did, and the old man crossed his arms and leaned back in his chair while Andrew sat on the crate.

"Our people were once a proud and powerful people, ruling the entire country of Renfall. Our lands prospered, and there was peace until the Great War. We fought hard but could do little to stop their parlor tricks until we discovered iron. Their *intuition,*" he spat the word, "could do little against it. It's counterintuitive, you see; strong but brittle, 'less ye mix it with something. So, we built our weapons and war machines out of it, and the tides began to turn in our favor. Then the dragons came.

284

"They waited until the first snowfall, then attacked. In a single night, entire armies of good men were wiped from the land, leaving nothing but nursing mothers and old men to stand. But they didn't just take our boys; they destroyed our fields, our storehouses." His eyes glazed over like he was remembering the night himself. "Those bastards wanted us to starve to death." He looked at Andrew. "Have you ever seen the hallow, haunted look of a mother walking empty fields, clutching a child to her breast that will never wake again?"

Andrew said nothing.

"Those who survived scattered. But hunted they were. For nearly a hundred years, we lived like rats in caves. Some were kind, taking in the wayward orphan," he said, motioning to Andrew. "But most still hated us. Not much has changed."

Andrew calculated. "Was that four hundred years ago now?"

"Ay, maybe five."

"Why did they hate us?" Andrew asked.

The old man looked at him. "We're different. Simple as that. We don't rely on tricks. We use tools. We build machines." Then he touched his nose again like he had a secret to tell. "And legend has it that some of them machines could think for themselves, they could." He pointed to the door. "These kids up there... they can light a candle from across the room but can't change a wagon wheel to save their life."

Andrew looked at the lights. *But grandmother is intuitive,* Andrew thought but did not say. *And I, too, have felt power.* "Where is Madina?" Andrew asked.

"Don't know the way by land. Took the first ship

leaving home and found port in Eetoomba. I never planned on goin' back."

"Why?" Andrew asked.

"No reason to return. Mother raised me but was sick in the head. The day they put her in the ground, I packed a bag and never looked back."

"Have you heard of The Book of Elyon?"

Noah Oliver scratched his forehead. "Can't say I have. But I've got a mind how you might find that trinket you lost. If someone *did* lift it, he'd know."

Andrew leaned forward. "Who?"

"Up there, the governor and her henchmen guards run the city, but down here...down here, Petros is king and country."

"Can you take me to him?"

Noah Oliver shook his head. "Nay. Don't know him, only *of* him."

Andrew's shoulders dropped.

Then Noah Oliver took the now short cigar from his yellowing lip and pointed it at Andrew. "But I think I know someone who might."

He rose and took something from a small wooden box on his top shelf.

# CHAPTER 44

A ndrew followed the old tinker down the long, dark tunnel by the light of a single candle. As they walked, the sound of that strange something coming from the distance grew louder.

They stopped at a rusted iron gate where the old tinker took his keyring off his belt, clanged the ring loudly across the bars, and blew out the candle.

In the darkness, they waited.

Andrew grew uneasy, his ears reaching for any sensory detail.

"Who are we waiting for?" Andrew whispered, but the old man shushed him. Then he clanged his ring across the bars again. It was so loud that Andrew almost felt the metal reverberate down the tunnel in both directions.

And they waited.

Andrew would have thought he had been left alone in the tunnels if not for the sound of the old man breathing a heavy, rasping breath from too many years of too many cigars and the rustling of the old tinker's coat as he found a new cigar, removed his lighter and clicked it to life. And as he did, the light of the lighter lit the face of a Dym standing immediately on the other side of the bars, startling Andrew so badly he fell backward.

The old tinker didn't even flinch. He just pulled a long drag and handed the cigar to the Dym on the other side of the gate.

The Dym, with his necrotic-colored skin, reached through the gate bars with fingers twice the length of Andrews, slowly took the cigar and put it in his mouth. He wore nothing save for a frayed strip of cloth tied around his waist. He had no shoes, robe, or staff. His features were unusually long, with eyes three times the size of what Andrew thought was natural, an adaptation of life in the tunnels, and his white, whisper-thin hair floated like a cloud around his head.

Andrew lifted himself off the ancient street and dusted off his trousers.

The Dym watched him with those large, unblinking eyes as he slowly breathed the smoke of the cigar in through his mouth and out his nose without removing it from his lips, like some smoke-filled breathing apparatus.

"My friend here lost something. Can you take him to Petros?" the old man asked, not extinguishing the lighter.

The Dym just watched Andrew, his long arms hanging loosely at his side.

Then Noah Oliver took a polished corner of tin from his jacket pocket, punched through with a bit of twine, and let it hang loosely from his fingers—its movement reflecting the glow of the lighter.

This caught the Dym's attention, and his eyes widened.

The old tinker held it out towards him, and the Dym reached for it, but the tinker pulled it away. "Take him to Petros?"

The Dym nodded, and Noah Oliver handed the shiny bobble to him.

Andrew knew it had no value other than it shining like a fish lure, but the Dym held it like one might hold a pearl of great price.

The old tinker unlocked the gate and opened it for Andrew. Andrew passed through, and the tinker locked it behind him.

Andrew turned. "Aren't you coming?"

The tinker shook his head. "Nay. Not my world." He took another cigar from his pocket, lit it and the candle, and flicked the lighter shut. "Not yours either. You'd be smart to remember that."

Then he turned and disappeared down the dark tunnel, leaving Andrew with the Dym, who Andrew could only see by the cigar's ember glow.

# CHAPTER 45

A latticework of hidden tunnels and rooms ran for miles beneath Nevarii, most utterly devoid of light.

Andrew followed the Dym, who never said a single word. The cigar's ember produced just enough light for Andrew to follow until the old road eventually began to slope down and around a corner, where Andrew's eyes finally found light once again. The sound he had heard in the distance was the sound of a busy street.

Still underground, the tunnel dumped into an old alley between two stone buildings whose backsides were built right into the old stone walls. The Dym continued down the alley between two leaning, white-masonry buildings until he came near enough the street to see passersby while remaining at a safe distance.

The street was full of makeshift stalls and carts selling everything from food to weapons. One vendor had cages of fairies and other winged creatures, while another stirred a bubbling pot of something with black fur in it. There were hanging bones and meat and stalls of simple potions, both real and fake. Near one stall, a Nimic child with the most snow-white skin and pale-blue eyes played with a dire cat twice her size, lazily pawing a ball back and forth to her. Another stall, beneath a stone arch, sold skins of every kind, including lizard, gorilla and tiwatoo. A horse head sat on a table, and the bottom left jaw of a terrible lizard hung on the back wall with curving viper-like teeth.

Beyond the street, layers of homes were carved into the stone above, where a little boy looked down from a wooden porch and smiled and waved at Andrew. Colorful fabrics and drying laundry hung from railings.

This was the underground that greased the wheels of the world above. Every city had its version, some more vibrant than others; Nevarii's was one of the oldest, making it one of the most colorful, with races and species from all over the known and unknown worlds. It had traded hands over the centuries from one gangster family to the next until Petros.

There were no guards, no aristocracy. Children were safe to play in the streets, and there was only one law: An eye for an eye. Any sign of organized crime was ruthlessly and publicly dealt with before it could get a finger hold. Down here, Petros was king, country, law, judge, and executioner. If you stole from above, you paid tribute to Petros. If you stole in the underground, then like kind would be taken from either you or your family. If you hurt someone in Petros' underground, payment was due. No one even bothered to try to keep anything of material importance from him. Either you chose to be a part of Petros's underground city, accepted the way things were, and enjoyed a life of freedom, or you stayed the hell out. Live and let live.

As Andrew tried to take in everything he saw, an entourage of two heavily armored Longbeards and a nearly naked Nimic woman covered in white tattoos walked next to a bald man with sapphire-blue skin and arms heavy with bands of gold and jewels. Petros was also accompanied by a woman with white skin, white robes, and white hair nearly long enough to drag on the ground. A band of rusted iron covered her mouth. The sixth in the entourage was something Andrew had never seen before: An old lion guard with light leather armor and a braided grey mane with one paw-like hand resting on the hilt of a rapier. A scar parted his fur along the left side of his neck.

The Dym, who Andrew had been following, pulled the now stubby end of his cigar into his mouth with his lips, chewed it, and swallowed it, then slowly pointed to the man with the blue skin before turning and returning to the tunnel.

"Is that Petros?" Andrew asked, but the Dym didn't bother to reply. He just disappeared into the dark tunnel.

Andrew watched Petros from a distance as Petros browsed the various wares with little interest, casually eating a piece of green fruit from a basket. The shopkeeper just permissively nodded. Then Petros stopped at the small child playing with the dire cat, who smiled and ran to him when she saw him. Petros returned the smile and picked her up. His group paid little attention to what he did. Instead, they watched passersby. The girl enthusiastically hugged Petros' neck, and he began speaking with the old woman, who was a race Andrew didn't recognize. The old woman smiled and nodded, and she and Petros spoke for a moment when she touched the side of her head with a look of concern. Petros leaned forward and signaled the beautiful Nimic woman with him, who approached and smiled at the old lady. Laying hands on either side of the old woman's face, the Nimic woman lifted her head and closed her eyes. Circular tattoos on the backs of her hands began to glow, and the old woman's eyes widened and she hugged Petros. Petros hugged her back, and his entourage continued on.

As they approached a stone archway beneath a tinted yellow window at the end of the street, Andrew left the alley and approached him.

"Are you Petros?" Andrew asked as one of Petros' guards quickly drew a blade.

Andrew held up his hands and took a step back. "I'm not looking for trouble. Something was stolen from me, and I was told you could help."

The woman in white pushed down the guard's blade, slowly approached Andrew, and gently touched his face with her hand. She had a look of concern that shifted to surprise. Some sort of horrific, rusted iron contraption was strapped across her mouth and around the back of her head. Her delicate skin was cracked and sore along its edges. She also had two pupils in each eye.

Petros took another bite of his fruit and watched their interaction. Then the woman in white nodded to Petros, and they walked on. Andrew followed.

"Have we met?" Petros asked Andrew as they passed beneath the stone arch and up a set of stairs to a steel door with no handle that opened as Petros approached it.

"I can't say that we have," Andrew replied.

They were now in a large workshop with tables, shelves, and glass cases filled with an array of beautiful, strange, and unique items. A tall and slender, elderly Nimic man with thick glasses bent over a large leather book next to a short, squat, Bantam man with grey hair pulled back in dreadlocks who stood on a bench at the same table using a set of small picks and tools to work the lock of a silver, jeweled box. In the back corner was a hole in the wall where tiny, purple-feathered dragons barely the size of Andrew's hand flew in and out, dropping coins into a large pile on the floor.

Petros studied Andrew's face. "You look familiar, and I tend to remember a face. From where do you hail?"

Andrew decided not to obfuscate his lineage. "I grew up in Aitechem Tiorem but now live in Jatoba."

"The Dry Places?" Petros asked with surprise. He removed the cork from a crystal bottle of purple liquor and poured himself a glass before sitting in a plush chair in the corner of the workshop. "No one lives in the Dry Places, do they?" The lion guard and the woman in white stood on either side of him.

Andrew nodded. "My father is a tinker and fisherman, and we have a small cabin just south of the marshes."

"And you've come to ask about stolen goods? Who told you I'd know anything about it?"

Andrew considered his answer and looked at the woman in white. She looked sad, defeated. Then it dawned on him: She was Shimar Etsell, the race of forest-dwellers he had encountered last winter when trying to help his grandmother!

"What is she doing here?"

Petros took another slow drink from his glass but didn't answer Andrew's question. Instead, he said, "Tell me about the statuette."

"Who told you it was a statuette?"

Petros smiled and turned to his lion guard. "Would you retrieve it for us, and a table?"

The lion signaled a boy, barely twelve, who ran off to a glass cabinet at the back of the workshop and returned with a small box as one of the Longbeard guards set a small wooden table between Petros and Andrew.

Petros leaned forward and gently opened the filigree box. From it, he removed a bundle of cloth, set the box aside, and tossed the layers of fabric back, revealing the small black figurine. Then he held it up and looked at it closely.

"Now, this *is* unique, isn't it? Where did it come from?"

Andrew took a step forward, but as he did, the lion made a very low, slow chesty growl, causing Andrew to step back.

Petros looked up at Andrew. "They're alive, aren't they?" he asked with fascination.

How does he know that? Andrew studied Petros, trying to decide how to navigate the situation. Then he slowly nodded.

Petros caressed it with his dark-blue fingers, his jeweled rings dancing in the room's light. "Who are they?"

"One of them is my grandmother," Andrew replied.

The woman in white winced, sorry to hear that.

"Interesting," Petros said, drawing the word out slowly. "Tell me about it."

Andrew didn't reply.

Petros looked at him. "You know, for someone who came here wanting my help, you don't seem terribly willing to reciprocate."

Andrew took a deep breath, deciding he would have to give Petros *something* if he wanted his grandmother back. "Those women came to my home and tried to kill me and my family, so I cursed them."

Petros's smile grew. "Really? A Human. Using intuition. Now, that *is* interesting." And he looked at the figurine again.

"Why? What do you know of my people? We are more powerful than you might think."

Petros burst out laughing, and he shook his head. Then he snapped his fingers and spoke a few words in a language Andrew didn't recognize.

The old man who had been studying the hefty leather tome slowly approached Petros with a small, yellow book and handed it to him.

Petros laid it open on the table next to the simulacrum and fingered through the pages.

"Have you ever seen one of these?" Petros asked. "I doubt it. It's a rare history of the Human race." He picked up the book and read the spine. "The Book of Elyon." Then he laid the book on the table and carefully ran his finger down the page until he came to the passage he was looking for. "Fascinating. An entire race completely devoid of intuition," he paused momentarily to read Andrew's reaction. Then he continued. "So much so that they fear its presence and effects. Any wayward visitor to their camps exhibiting the slightest intuitive inclination is cast out or worse. One elderly woman in a nearby camp used an unknown medicinal herb to cure a small child of a fever, and they thanked her by burning her alive." Petros closed the book and tapped its cover. Then he picked up the simulacrum again and used it to punctuate his words: "A Human using intuition like this is interesting indeed. What form of intuition are you skilled in?"

Andrew shook his head. "Believe it or not, nothing."

"Uh uh," Petros shook his head. "False modesty won't help you here."

"I'm not trying to be modest. My grandmother is the intuitive one. The curse was an accident."

Petros narrowed his gaze at Andrew, trying to determine if this Human before him was lying or just naive as hell. Then he looked at the woman in white and motioned her to approach him. She squeezed the sides of her robe and didn't move.

Petros clenched his jaw and said a few heavy words to her that Andrew didn't understand.

She swallowed and slowly approached Andrew. The look in her eyes—so full of sorrow and pain—broke Andrew's heart. Why was she so sad?

She cupped his face in her hands and gently touched his ear lobes as tears streaked down her cheeks, which she quickly wiped away.

Petros rose. "Do you two know each other?"

"No?" Andrew replied, but Petros didn't believe him and nodded to the lion guard, who grabbed Andrew's shoulder and slammed him down onto the table, laying a hand-length blade across the back of Andrew's neck.

"Cut off his balls," Petros said, and Andrew screamed.

"No! Stop! I don't know her! I swear! She's Shimar Etsell. I know her people."

Petros held up a hand.

The strength of the lion guard was terrifying, and Andrew's heart raced.

"Pick him up," Petros told the lion, who lifted Andrew to his feet with little effort.

After a few moments of reflection, Petros took a deep breath and poured himself a second cup. "Do you visit Nevarii often?"

"I honestly avoid it as much as possible, but I've come with my father a few times when we needed supplies," Andrew replied trying to pull away, but the lion held tight.

Petros approached Andrew, gripped his chin, and studied his face carefully. "Who's your father?"

Andrew didn't want to say anything, so he jerked his face away, but the lion squeezed Andrew's arm so hard that he thought it might pull out of its socket.

"A simple man. No one you would know," Andrew replied.

"A tinker, you say?" Petros asked.

Andrew nodded.

Petros grunted a laugh. "Now I remember," he said, pointing. "You were a very small child when last I saw you."

Andrew didn't know what he was talking about.

Petros nodded for the lion to release Andrew, and Andrew rubbed his shoulder. Then Petros sat back in his leather chair, casually letting his crystal glass swing in his fingers.

"Oh, probably fifteen years ago now, give or take, I came across a couple of my boys teasing a Human child. I had never seen one before... or since to be fair."

Andrew's eyes grew. "That was you?"

Petros lifted the glass to him. Then he sighed. "That shouldn't have happened. They paid for it, but you... you were unique." He leaned forward. "I didn't understand why some Nimic tinker was with a Human child." Then he shot back his last swallow and set the cup aside. "I offered to buy you from him."

"Buy me?"

Petros nodded. "It's not what you think. Most of us are orphan scoundrels and outcasts ourselves," he said, waving his hand through the air. "And I've made a home for us here. Somewhere safe where they, up top," he spat, "are usually smart enough to keep clear of. He shrugged. "We grift. We lift. We hustle, but we mostly keep to ourselves. Down here, my kids are safe."

Andrew shook his head. "Ever the hero, huh?" his question full of accusation.

Petros pursed his lips and his eyes narrowed, trying to understand Andrew's meaning.

"And all you get out of it is a measly little fortune," Andrew said, pointing at the rings and bracelets.

Petros sat up. "Oh, these?" He asked, sliding his bracelets off into a pile on the table. "These don't interest me. They serve as a sort of..." he waved his hand like he was trying to pluck the words from the air. "Protection.

"Protection? For who?"

"For my family!" Petros spat. "Do you think I care about gold? Here. Take it! A gift," he said, picking up a heavy bangle and tossing it at Andrew's chest, who let it drop to the ground. "I have gold," he said, pointing to the pile at the back of the room that continued to tink larger and larger, one dragon-dropped coin at a time. "And this is just the first day of the festival! I literally have more gold than I can carry. Gold is easy. I *only* care about this filthy lucre because *they* do!" he snapped, pointing to the ceiling. "It's all they know! Half the take will pad the Governor's pockets. They don't care about us! You and me. If we are poor, they will take the little we have and let us starve. But... if I wear these shiny baubles," he said, slowly picking one of the bracelets up and sliding it back onto his arm. "Then it is like a shield of protection for *all* of us. Now they see us; now they listen. They don't see me; they see the shine. If I drop them trinkets like treats for a dog, they let us live!" he said, pounding his chest. "And if not! They don't!"

Andrew had no idea.

"You and I, we're not so different, Human," Petros said, his voice softening. "I offered to buy you, to protect you. I was afraid..." Petros stopped. He felt hidden pain rising in his chest like a sleeping bear, and Andrew saw his countenance change. Andrew thought he saw sorrow in Petros's eyes for the briefest moment. "Let's just say I have some idea how the world treats those of us who are different."

Of course. Petros's blue skin. *Where is he from,* Andrew wondered. *What had he been through?*

"I'm so sorry," Andrew said.

For a fleeting moment, Petros looked at Andrew with soft, wet eyes. Then, his resolve hardened again. He cleared his throat and looked away, back to business.

"What's the figurine worth to you?" he asked.

Andrew considered. It was worth everything, but he couldn't say that. He was afraid that if he offered all he had in all the world, Petros would want more.

"I don't have much money."

Petros stood with his back to Andrew, poured himself a third glass of liquor, and quietly replied: "You weren't listening, were you? I don't care about coin."

"What else do you want?"

Petros turned to him. "Something unique. Something as rare as a Human casting intuition. If you want your grandmother back, it'll cost you something worth more than gold."

Andrew didn't know what that meant. Was Petros saying that he wanted Andrew? He *had* tried to buy him once before. His mind raced. Lorna's staff was still with Tomptee. His grandmother's cabin had a host of unique items in her chest. Perhaps the chest itself. Then it dawned on him.

"Have you heard of a raven coin?"

The woman in white and the lion guard looked at Petros, who turned to Andrew with eyes wide.

300

"I have. Are you telling me you know the location of such a coin?"

Andrew reached into his pocket, and the lion guard reached for his blade. But Petros held up a hand. Andrew held out the coin to show Petros the skull on its face.

Petros laughed. "It doesn't even look real."

"It's real. It just looks like wood to protect it."

Petros stopped laughing. He approached Andrew and tried to pull it away but couldn't. Then he motioned the lion guard. "Take it from him."

The lion stepped forward, grasped its edge, and pulled. It would not move, and Andrew wasn't even trying. The lion pulled again, this time with both hands, and he may as well have been pulling at a mountain's mighty face because Andrew's hand didn't even sway against the lion's strength.

Petros glared at Andrew, then motioned to the woman in white.

She approached the coin but did not want to touch it. To her, if it were real, it was unclean, unholy. Instead, she held up a hand, quickly turning its appearance back to gold, and felt something unlike she had ever felt before. It was heavy. It was dark. It was shifting and unstable. It was not intuitive but also not a part of her world.

She turned back to Petros, shrugged, and nodded, indicating that she couldn't be sure that it was a raven coin, but it was something alright, which intrigued Petros, and he calculated his options. Even if it were not a real raven coin, something about it was unique. At the very least, gold is gold, and intuitive gold was worth more. Worst case scenario: He could sell it. Maybe he could even convince someone in the academy to think it *was* a raven coin and trade him for something worthwhile. On the other hand, he didn't imagine the black stone having much power or value beyond this boy's interest. It was worth something to Petros for novelty's sake but not much more. Then a thought occurred to him: Every counterfeit coin he had ever seen was either blank on the back or had the same raven skull in duplicate.

"Show me the back," Petros said.

Andrew turned the coin over and revealed the simple poem:

A raven coin
in raven light
for The Raven King

Petros swallowed. *Could it be?* he wondered. "Let me see it."

Andrew pulled it back. "Uh uh, no chance. Not until we have a deal."

Petros finally nodded. "Fine. The coin for the stone."

"And her," Andrew said, pointing to the woman whose eyes grew wide.

Petros clenched his teeth. He did *not* want to lose his seer. But he *had* received much from her over the years and often had second thoughts about keeping her against her will. He had grown fond of her, perhaps some part of him even loved her, but if the coin *were* real, he could become a seer himself. Just imagine, with the favor of a god, he could ask for power beyond imagining. In truth, he had been looking for a raven coin ever since his scribe translated parts of a scroll that spoke of a traveler to an entire city caught in endless sleep. Many nights, Petros had imagined what he would ask for if he ever found such a coin.

"*If* it's real. Then you have a deal," Petros replied. "And if it's fake, I keep *you.*"

"And the book!" Andrew quickly added, now feeling like he really was reaching.

Petros smiled. "And the book, but...if you ask for anything else, I will slit your throat where you stand and figure out a way to pry the coin from your cold fingers."

Andrew nodded and held the coin out to him, but Petros declined.

"Spin it," he told Andrew.

"Excuse me?"

Petros glared at him. "Spin. It. And hope it doesn't drop."

Andrew's throat went dry. He had never actually spun a coin before. What if he messed up and spun it off the table or somehow didn't get it right?

He looked around.

Everyone in the workshop who had been busy and seeming to ignore their conversation was now standing around and watching this deadly serious child's game.

Andrew knelt before the table and carefully moved everything out of the way, desperately wanting to snatch the simulacrum and run. However, he knew that was impossible and set the coin on its side—standing it on its edge with a finger.

He took a deep breath and flicked the coin.

# CHAPTER 46

Andrew's beating heart punctuated every moment that the coin spun.

Everyone in the room watched in silence.

Every second that passed, Andrew became more nervous that it would drop, and Petros became more excited that it had not yet.

And they waited.

After more than a minute, just as Andrew was about to ask how much longer he had to wait, the coin kicked a knot in the wood and flicked off the table. There was an audible gasp from everyone watching, but the coin didn't stop spinning. Instead, it hung in thin air, spinning just as fast as when Andrew had first set it in motion.

Petros knelt in front of it, eyes as wide as the coin itself, with mouth agape. Then he slowly reached out and took it from the air. Without taking his eyes from it, he said, "Go."

Andrew scooped up the simulacrum and the book. "And what about her? We had a deal."

Petros slowly looked up at him. Then he nodded to his lion guard.

The old lion approached the woman, his eyes soft to her for the first time that Andrew had seen, and he unstrapped the muzzle across her mouth. She shuddered as it fell with a heavy bang to the floor, revealing a mouth full of broken and weeping sores.

She looked down and screamed. Then she turned to Petros, who was still kneeling. There was so much she wanted to say. She wanted to curse him, make him pay for all the years of her captivity, make him suffer. But she knew he was a dangerous man and had seen him bring his vengeance down on the families of those who had wronged him many times. So, instead of turning him into stone, or worse, she glared at him and said: "An eye for an eye."

Petros knew what that meant and could not blame her.

Then she turned to Andrew. As she did, her mouth healed, her robes became the color of the deep forest, her skin darkened to glorious emerald, and her hair went black with that same beautiful green shine Andrew had seen in the hunter's hair the night he had first met the Shimar Etsell.

She threw herself into his arms.

"Thank you, Child of Grace," she whispered in his ear so no one else could hear, which made the hair on the back of his neck stand on end.

Petros rose and squeezed the coin in his palm. Then he smiled a showman's smile, "Now that our dealings are done, I hope you will feel welcome in my city."

*How do you act in the presence of a king?* Andrew had once asked himself. *Circumspectly.*

"Thank you, sir. I think, for now, we'll just be going," and he gently bowed his head.

Petros didn't argue; he just let them leave.

As quickly as he could, Andrew led the young woman

back through the tunnels to Tomptee's home, using the flame of the lighter the tinker had gifted to him as a simple torch through the darkness. There was no sign of Noah Oliver.

Andrew found Perimas asleep against a tree as he crossed the academy grounds.

"What are you doing out here?" Andrew asked.

Perimas opened one eye. "Claustrophobic, I guess."

"Well, we have to go."

"Why?" What's wrong? Who's she?" Petros asked.

"I'll explain later. Ready the mounts," Andrew replied, then he turned to the woman. "Stay with Perimas. I'll be right back." But she shook her head and gripped his arm. "Fine. Come with me, but we have to be quiet."

Perimas readied the mounts as Andrew had asked.

Andrew quietly opened the front door of Tomptee's cottage. Tomptee was asleep on the couch with his two youngest siblings tucked up next to him.

Andrew gently touched his shoulder.

"What's wrong?" Tomptee asked, rubbing the sleep from his eyes.

"We have to go," Andrew whispered.

"Why?"

"I'll explain later."

"Who's the girl?"

"I will explain later!" Andrew loud-whispered.

The littles shifted and turned, but none woke. Tomptee pulled on his boots, gloves, and coat as Wilkers and Nizzle came down the stairs.

"What's going on?" Nizzle asked as Wilkers put on his thin spectacles, and they both looked at the woman.

"While I am grateful for your hospitality, I'm afraid we must leave," Andrew told them.

"Why?" Nizzle asked.

"What's happened," Wilkers added.

Andrew held up his hands to calm them. "Everything is fine, but we have to go. I found the figurine and was able to get it back..."

"Where was it?" Tomptee asked.

Andrew held up a hand. "But *the coin* is gone."

Tomptee and Wilkers considered what that meant, but Nizzle was confused. She knew nothing about any coin.

"My friend here needs a ride home, and we must be going," Andrew added, looking at the woman still holding his hand.

"Very well," Wilkers said with a sigh.

"Let me pack you some nibbles for the road," Nizzle replied. But before Andrew could decline, she was in the kitchen tossing a fresh loaf of bread into a sack, along with a clay jar of milk, some cheese, and a few apples.

Wilkers approached Tomptee. "I'm sorry we didn't have more time. There's so much more I wanted to say."

Tomptee hugged him. "I understand. I'll return soon. I promise."

Then Wilkers looked at his son in a way that made sure he was listening. "I'm proud of you."

Tomptee hugged him again. Then, they quickly mounted their animals and departed through the shepherd's gate.

Wilkers and Nizzle leaned into each other as they watched their son ride into the darkness.

# CHAPTER 47

The Ki Lo Kan Forest was a hard day's ride from Nevarii, and Andrew hadn't slept, so they rode as they could and periodically stopped along the way. First light was just beyond the horizon, but the raven moon was still large in the sky, and its presence made Andrew nervous. No one asked what had happened during the initial ride because of the heavy traffic going in and out of Nevarii, but the questions were mounting.

After a while, Brynlee began to sweat and toss her head, signaling she was ready for a break, so Andrew pulled off the road near a quiet stretch of chalk stream where they could let the horses rest and drink. As he climbed off Brynlee and helped the woman down from where she sat in front of him, he knew he had some explaining to do. However, no one said a word.

Both Brynlee and Perimas's nicatoo took heavy mouthfuls from the creek as small golden trout darted back and forth, but Marta didn't hesitate; she climbed right into the cool water, letting it run over her back and soak Tomptee's saddle.

Perimas offered his water skin to the woman, but she turned away from him and wouldn't take it.

"It's alright. This is Perimas and Tomptee. They're friends," Andrew told her. She nodded to Tomptee but didn't even look at Perimas, which Andrew found odd.

Andrew broke off a piece of the bread Tomptee's mother had sent with them and handed her a piece, which she declined. Then he had an idea. He reached deep into the bottom of Brynlee's saddle bags and found the last remaining piece of oatcake Petook—the elder Night Watchman—had given him the winter before and offered it to her.

Her eyes grew, and she took it and ate. It was a taste of home, and it warmed her heart. *How does this boy have kero cake?* she wondered and watched Andrew check on Brynlee and hand some bread to Tomptee and Perimas, who were more than happy to partake.

"Are we going to discuss what happened?" Tomptee finally asked.

Andrew sighed. He wasn't sure where to start. He told them about meeting Noah Oliver and the "strange figure" who led him through the old tunnels into Nevarii's underground. Then he described his interactions with Petros.

"He was fascinated with the figurine and knew they were still alive."

"How?" Tomptee asked.

"Her," Andrew pointed.

"Who is she?" Perimas asked with a whisper-thin smile.

"I don't know. But she's Shimar Etsell."

They all tried not to stare at the stunning woman with crumbs on her lip sitting on a rock along the creak's edge, but it was hard not to, for so many reasons.

"What's a shimmersel?" Perimas asked.

"Shimar Etsell," Tomptee corrected. "Also known as Night Watchmen. A reclusive race of forest people known for their exceptional craftsmanship. They used to serve wealthy families, but none have been seen for centuries. Some have even thought they were actually a myth."

"Oh, they're no myth," Andrew replied wide-eyed.

"Yes. You mentioned you've had some dealings with them in the past," Tomptee said.

Andrew nodded. "Last winter. I needed one of them to help me open..." he considered how to describe his grandmother's sentient chest and remembered that Tomptee had seen it. "The chest at my grandmother's cottage. A craftsman came to me where I camped in the Ki Lo Kan Forest. He helped me at grave risk to himself."

"Why?" Tomptee asked.

Andrew shrugged. "He had already had some dealings with the outside world and seemed gracious. Or perhaps he was just curious. I'm not sure. We had little time to talk before I fled for my life."

This part of the story caught Perimas's attention, who had been paying too much attention to their new guest to hear most of what Andrew was going on about.

Andrew read the look on his face. "Yeah. About that. Petook, the craftsman who helped me, made me swear never to return. He said that it was forbidden for anyone to enter their homelands, and I would be killed if they caught me."

"Let me guess... that's right where we're going," Tomptee said.

Before Andrew could reply, the woman spoke up. "You are correct. It is forbidden for anyone from the lowlands to enter my home."

"Why?" Perimas asked.

She turned away from him and directed her answer to Andrew. "Many seasons ago, my people served royal families all across Middengare, but some began to take... advantage," she said, squeezing shut the top of her robe in a kind of protective posture. "We are a highly... sensitive... people. Our elders decided that we would depart from the lands beneath and never return."

Andrew didn't blame them, based on how Petros had treated her.

"I'm taking her home. But you both should stay behind," Andrew told Tomptee and Perimas.

"Sod that! What about Fey?" Perimas objected.

"Nomi said we'll need the staff, and I think the old man who came to me can fix it—or *heal* it—as Nizzle said. That's where I'm taking her. We can meet at my gran's cottage in two days."

Perimas shook his head. "No offense, but I'm goin' with you. We still don't know what's happening to Fey, and she might not have much time. I have a feeling she's all I have left."

Andrew looked at Tomptee.

"Just 'cause I'm small doesn't mean you should underestimate me. You might need my nose in a pinch!"

Andrew chuckled. "Very well. The decision is yours, but we should get going."

As they began to remount their animals, Tomptee nudged Andrew away from the group and quietly asked what had happened to the coin.

Andrew looked at him with uncertainty. "I had to trade it for the simulacrum and her freedom."

Tomptee shook his head. "By daisies, do you think that was wise?"

"Why do you think we're in such a hurry!?" Andrew

shot back with a sharper whisper than he had intended. "I think the..." he paused, not wanting to speak his name aloud, "you-know-who is coming. And I'd like to get her home and help my grandmother before I'm forced to face him again. I think the craftsman can repair the staff, and I'm hoping that maybe, just maybe, taking her home will keep me from being gutted before I can even ask."

Now Tomptee understood. "So, you're trading her for his help."

Andrew shook his head. "Not exactly. I knew she was one of The Shimmering, and I could see she was suffering. I wasn't sure he'd let her go, but I had to try. And I'm starting to think there's no such thing as coincidence. Maybe I was supposed to help her. She called me a Child of Grace."

Tomptee's eyes grew. "How..."

Andrew just shook his head. "I don't know. I don't know what's happening, but I have to do something, so I will take the next step and see what happens. Unless you have a better idea."

Tomptee considered this and shook his head. He didn't have a better idea, and he did have more questions—he *always* had more questions—but this would do for now.

# CHAPTER 48

**B**ack in Nevarii, a dark figure walked the streets freely. With pleasure, he watched the drunken revelries and throngs of people adorned in masks and feathers. He knew each and every one of these foolish mortals and looked forward to the festivities every year. He was dressed in opulent silk robes the color of wine that actually did flow around him, and he wore a simple, white paper mask that only covered his eyes and cheeks.

On one street corner, he stopped by a Nimic man and Longbeard woman leaning passed out against each other. He knew both of their names, their hopes, and their fears. Just that summer, she had taken three other lovers, but he was faithful and kind. She dreamt of shiny things, while he dreamt of one day having children. It was a beautiful dream actually, and The Raven King wondered what the man's life might have been like if it wasn't his time, but it was. The king of dreaming waved a hand over the man's slowly breathing chest as his heart stopped beating. Then he rose and continued on.

The Raven King did not often walk anywhere, but he

was enjoying all the little details of the night: The cool air across his skin, the hard, cold stones beneath his bare feet, and the sound of friends laughing together. And often, he would pause to collect another silent soul.

He found the charmer's shop quiet and dark, but this did not deter him. He passed through the walls and explored the various knick-knacks on the shelves. Behind the curtain, he found the old woman's table and trinkets. He was impressed with her craftsmanship; the way a snake coiled or a calf jumped. He remembered finding her in the dreaming many decades earlier when she had first begun her studies and watched her dream about carving an entire mountain into a nested eagle that came to life and flew through the air with her on its back.

He smiled at the memory.

Then he realized he had not seen her in the dreaming for many seasons.

The Raven King's eyes became starlight as he looked into the dreaming to see what Andrew had discussed with the blind old woman. He watched as her fingers studied the figurine's edges, and she told Andrew that he had something even more dangerous with him. Andrew did not respond at first, but then she told him it was a coin and that someone—The Raven King—was after him. But before Andrew said anything else, she opened a mortal gate, which angered the old raven because he knew he could not follow her through it. It was a safe place beyond his prying eyes, invisible in the dreaming.

"Peemah!" The Raven King spat an ancient curse and flung the old woman's workbench across the room, sending her tools scattering across the floor. His mask turned from that of simple, white paper to a heavy, black leather shroud.

Suddenly, every wall in Nevarii was invisible to The

Raven King, and his eyes raced from room to room, through every home, inn, and tavern in the entire city in a moment, looking for where the old woman might be sleeping. But he could not find her, and he screamed a shrill, bird-like screech that startled several passersby on the street. He should not have trusted the boy. He thought he could be reasoned with, but clearly, he was wrong. He had to have told the old wench about their dealings, though he couldn't be certain.

Then he stopped.

He walked back to the store's front room and, in the dreaming, looked closely at the younger man who stood behind the front counter—the old woman's grandson. The raven's eyes searched every bed in a fraction of a moment and found him. Not a hundred yards away, passed out near a hearth in a small home with an empty wine glass in his lap.

The Raven King smiled, and in a heartbeat, stood next to him. With starlight eyes, he looked through the waking to see where the younger man was in the dreaming. He was laughing with a Longbeard woman he had met earlier that night in a tavern just down the street.

Everyone in the tavern vanished as The Raven King sat beside him.

Julio turned to him, wondering where everyone had gone. Seeing him, he had an idea who he was. "What you want, hoodoo man?" he asked.

"Where is your Jadati?" The old raven asked.

The man shook his head. "Can't get to her. Not from here, hooodoo man. She no good to you here."

The Raven King smiled. "Perhaps. But I'm willing to bet you are." Then the old bird reached out with a single finger and touched Julio's temple as he began to scream in the waking world. The old woman stumbled out from a back room, and The Raven King turned to her.

"It's you," she said.

The Raven King smiled. "You've been meddling."

"He's just a boy."

"I wasn't going to hurt him."

"Lies. All lies. I know your true name, Deceiver. Accuser of the Brethren. My God watched you fall like lightning from the heavens."

"Silence!" The Raven King squawked. "Where is he?"

She laughed. "So powerful, yet you can't find a child?"

"I found you."

She shook her head. "Do what thou will; my life is His. To take or to give."

Then the old raven turned. "And I found him."

Fear raced through the old woman. "He's a fool. Leave him be."

The Raven King held up a finger. "And there it is. Everyone wants something. How about we say, a life for a life."

"Take my life!" the woman cried.

The old raven shook his head. "Oh, you're coming with me, be certain of that. But it's not you I'm offering. It's your grandson."

Nomi swallowed. "I don't know where he is."

Her grandson screamed, and she almost fell over. "Stop, stop. I'll give you whatever you want."

"Well, well. All the fire has gone out of you, hasn't it? Give me the Human."

She leaned against a chair, her heart racing. Then she looked up as though she saw him clearly. "It's not the Human you want, is it?"

The raven did not reply.

316

"There was a Zuti with him."

The Raven King took a slow, long breath and a step towards her. "What did you say?"

She nodded. "That's who you're after. The Zuti. Give me my grandson, and I will tell you of the Zuti."

The Raven King was immediately back in the charmer's shop as the loud cry of an old woman broke through the night. He watched again in the dreaming as the old woman said, "Not you" to someone in the shop just before passing through the mortal gate. Words the old raven had initially ignored, but now he turned to see Perimas standing on the other side of the room. When he did, the feathers rose on the back of his neck. His mask became blood-red swirls, and the shop burst into flames rising so high they could be seen beyond the city walls.

Just then, something tugged at his chest. Somehow, he was being summoned.

# CHAPTER 49

Petros stood in the middle of an empty field outside Nevarii, entirely alone except for his beautiful, intuitive Nimic assistant and the old lion guard.

The Raven King stepped out of the shadows from behind a large hornbeam. "Who are you, and by what means have you summoned me?" There were not many ways in all the worlds to summon a god.

Petros smiled and held the coin up in the moonlight.

The Raven King lowered his gaze at the bald, blue man. He was only missing two coins. One was buried somewhere no one was ever likely to find, and the other had recently been gifted to a certain Human in exchange for his help. "And where did you get that?"

Petros didn't reply, but the Nimic woman stepped forward and screamed, "Jazera un-faneetoo!"

The Raven King pursed his lips. "Really? I don't have time for his," and he waved his hand as the woman turned into a pile of autumn leaves. The lion guard was startled enough to fall backward. Then suddenly, The Raven King and Petros were alone in Petros's workshop.

318

Petros held up his hand in surrender. "Forgive me, your majesty. Just a test. I had to be sure."

The Raven King perused the trinkets and treasures adorning the shelves. "I asked you a question."

Petros let the coin roll across his knuckles. "It was given to me, fair and true."

"By whom?"

"That shouldn't matter. It's still binding, isn't it?" Petros asked.

"It is..." the old raven replied, picking up a gold monkey paw from one of the shelves that held up a single finger. The Raven King chuckled. It was a knockoff of an ancient relic that granted three wishes, but all three had been foolishly waisted centuries earlier.

"Then I want immortality!" Petros cried.

"Cute. The coin is currency for a favor, and immortality isn't just a favor. It would be breaking old laws. And that one," The Raven King turned to him and held up a long, black finger, "is especially ancient. Try again."

Petros was a bit deflated. "Then limitless wealth!"

"Really?" The Raven King asked, motioning to the pile of coins on the floor. "Doable, but not terribly interesting. The last person who asked for such ended up so bored she eventually begged me to take her life." He reached for his necklace and lifted a bone. "Now she is one of my trinkets. You seem like someone a bit more creative than that." Then his eyes became starlight once again. "Tell me, Petros. What do you *really* dream about?"

Petros became entranced like he was sleepwalking, and The Raven King journeyed in a moment through all of Petros's dreams, past and present. There was anger, hunger, a lust for revenge. Then he found something else hiding far down beneath all the layers of power and wealth: A deep need to keep them safe, keep *her* safe.

The Raven King's eyes returned to white, and Petros shook off the trance. "You don't want wealth. You want this," the raven said, holding up a black card.

"What is that?"

"The location of your sister," the old raven casually replied.

Petros's eyes grew. "Lies. She's dead."

"Interesting. You thought I'd grant you immortality, but the location of your sister is too good to be true." Then he shrugged. "This, or a dragon's hoard full of platinum raichams. It's up to you."

Petros thought long. Then he held out the coin.

The Raven King took it and clearly felt it *was* the one he had given Andrew. Then he dropped it into his skin bag and was gone.

Petros turned the black card over. A single word whisked across its mirror-like surface in silver ink: Xlan.

# CHAPTER 50

As evening fell, Andrew and his party crossed the Vondermarden River at the point where Andrew had fled the Shimar Etsell—a single arrow still penetrating the trunk of a tree, reminding him of how he felt when last he had passed through.

It wasn't far before he found the hallow tree where there was just enough room for the four of them to camp for the night.

"This is it. This is where they came for me," Andrew told the woman.

She heard him, but her eyes were off somewhere in the distant canopy so high above them they could barely see it through the clouds.

"How long do you think?" Tomptee asked, who sniffed the air for danger and tightened his shawl cord beneath his neck.

"Not long. They know we're here," the woman replied.

Andrew swallowed.

She was right. As Tomptee and Perimas began to set up camp, three powerful, green tree horses broke violently through the high branches, and the woman called out with excitement. In moments, Aefook Aenoosho and two others arrived at the campsite and quickly dismounted, embracing the woman. They all shared excited words with each other Andrew didn't understand, until the woman turned to Andrew and motioned for him to join her.

"This Human saved my life."

Aefook narrowed his gaze at Andrew and drew his blade. He was taller than Andrew, with smooth, black-green hair that hung below his shoulders and loosely fitting robes that almost perfectly looked like the bark of a tree. He had two pupils in each eye.

Andrew was sure he would pass out from fear, and his top lip trembled where Aefook had kissed it with his blade when last they had seen each other.

Then Aefook did something Andrew didn't expect: He cut the tip of his finger and drew two streaks of green blood across Andrew's cheeks. Andrew couldn't be sure, but it looked like there were tears in Aefook's eyes.

"You have returned my sister to me. You are one of us now. Come." The two soldiers with Aefook drew their blades, lifted them high in the air, and let out a guttural cry that startled their horses. Aefook mounted his mighty steed and held out a hand to his sister, who laughed at him and quickly mounted the large, green horse by herself, chiding him about something Andrew didn't understand.

Andrew turned to Tomptee. "Let's go."

Aefook stopped him. "Only you."

"But my friends..."

"It is forbidden," Aefook replied.

Tomptee assured Andrew it would be alright and gave him the broken staff wrapped in the blanket. "We will make camp and wait for you here."

Andrew looked at Perimas, who nodded in agreement. "Go on then. Find a way to help Fey," and Perimas took a thin knife from his boot and handed it to Andrew, but Andrew held up a hand to stop him.

"You sure?" Perimas asked.

Andrew nodded. Then he turned to one of the riders who pulled him onto their large green horse. Tomptee watched with amazement as the three horses gripped the thick bark with split hooves and ascended the massive trees vertically until they were out of sight.

As they rode, Andrew was no longer afraid. The last time Andrew traveled through the high, vast canopy that was the Shimar Etsell's land, he was incognito. Now, he rode openly. As he passed the first homes on the outskirts of the villages, children ran to the guard's horses, stopping quickly and pointing at the sight of an outsider, a Human outsider, and one with the marks of the bloodline!

Aefook Aenoosho knew well that any outsider was absolutely forbidden, but he didn't care. This was different. His sister had practically risen from the dead! He would boldly welcome them both.

Immediately, people began to follow them, and guards mounted their horses and rode alongside, whispering and pointing. Aefook did not acknowledge them; he just kept riding, though the other two who had descended with him couldn't help themselves and shouted cries of victory at the top of their voices. People from all over the village came running as Aefook rode up to the steps of the place of the elders in the center of their village and dismounted. Three women and three men, all with greying hair, came from a building shaped like a wise and powerful tree. They stood at the top of the steps and asked Aefook something Andrew didn't understand. Aefook replied boldly. For a moment,

Andrew was sure they were arguing, but Aefook's sister dismounted and spoke to the elders calmly. As they spoke, the light of the sky turned green, and small flickering lights descended. Surprise swept across the villagers' faces. Some pointed and others hid their faces.

Andrew didn't understand what was happening, but the elders, along with every man, woman, and child in the village, prostrated themselves. Even the guards who had brought Andrew into the village climbed off their horses and bowed. To what, Andrew did not know.

"Welcome, Andrew, Son of Grace," a gentle voice spoke.

Now, standing near his horse was the Grace Giver.

Andrew recognized her. "What are you doing here?"

She was no longer in the form of a small girl but a beautiful young woman. "These are my children."

Andrew dismounted his horse. "I thought you were angry with me."

"I was. You were selfish. But then you risked yourself to save your grandmother and Teela."

Andrew looked at the woman he had freed from Petros. "Is that her name?"

The Grace Giver nodded.

"What happened to her?"

"The same that happens to so many. Someone took advantage."

"Why didn't you help her?" he asked.

"I did. By sending you."

Andrew was taken aback. "What?"

The Grace Giver smiled. "You can't understand now, but you will."

"Why do I keep getting pulled into this?"

She looked at him with compassion. "Into what? Service?"

Andrew hadn't thought of all of his heartache and pain as any form of service. "Can you save my grandmother?" he asked.

"You will find what you are looking for here, with my children."

"What about Jatoba?"

She looked away. "My brother is powerful. I cannot change his will."

"Then I'm doomed."

"It's not you who he is after."

Andrew tried to discern any meaning from the look on her face, but it was so enigmatic that he could not read it. "Tomptee?"

She did not answer. Instead, she said, "My brother can be very dangerous, but he is not evil. Not as you understand evil. He wants balance. He has lost something he needs back, but his anger grows towards you now."

"What about my family?"

She did not reply.

"Can you protect them?"

She did not reply.

"What good is all of this if you can't help those I love?"

"You cannot yet see the ripples that your choices make. You once chose other, then you chose self, you have chosen other again, but a more fateful choice still lies before you."

Andrew looked at all the Night Watchmen lying prostrate around him. "Is that why you brought me here?"

"For many reasons. One is that it is time you learn who you really are."

"As a Human."

"Yes. And as a Child of Grace."

"But what if I don't want that? What if I don't want any of this? What if I just want to go home?"

"You are free to choose."

Andrew's eyes narrowed at her. "But you said that if I return to Jatoba, I will die."

She nodded.

"Then how is that a choice?"

"Because, Andrew, Son of Grace, you are free to choose to die."

# CHAPTER 51

O nce their conversation was complete, the Grace Giver ascended through the canopy, and the sky returned to daylight. Everyone around Andrew slowly rose and looked at him like he was a god. It made him quite uncomfortable.

Teela gently ran her hand along the curves of his face, like she was touching the face of a long, lost love, and he tried to understand what he was seeing in her eyes but couldn't.

Then, a familiar voice sparked excitement within him.

"Welcome, Human!" an elderly Night Watchman said, approaching Andrew. His hair was also ashen, and his robes more ornamental than the soldiers.

"Petook!" Andrew cried and hugged the old man.

"I thought for sure you did not survive the ride across the Vondermarden."

"Then why..." Andrew stopped and shook his head, laughing. It didn't matter. He was glad to see his old friend.

"I thought I would never set eyes on you again. You look well!" Petook said.

"A lot has happened since last we spoke," Andrew replied.

Petook smiled the smile of a knowing grandfather. "I see," he replied, motioning to all the fanfare. "And a Grace Giver! Counsel with you? How extraordinary. But I knew there was something about you. Did her words comfort you?"

"You couldn't hear what she said?"

Petook shook his head.

"Well, she..."

Petook held up a hand to stop him. "Please. If her words were for my ears, I would have heard her."

Andrew nodded in respect. "I was hoping to find you again. I need your help."

Petook bowed to him, which made Andrew uncomfortable. "That's not necessary."

"Oh, but it is," Petook replied. "You have been touched by Grace. You are now consecrated, set apart, holy."

"I don't know what that means. I'm just Andrew."

Petook held up a finger. "Andrew, Son of Grace! We *all* heard that."

Andrew looked around. Now, he *really* felt everyone staring at him. "I'm not sure what that means."

Petook smiled. "It is alright. Come." And Petook approached the council of elders. He asked them something, and all six nodded. Then Petook turned to Andrew. "Please. Come with me."

Andrew followed Petook up the wide, dark-wood steps into a tall, ornate building. Teela and Aefook followed close behind.

The building looked like it had grown up along the mighty tree while also being carved, creating this incredible union of nature and craftsmanship. Inside, the ceiling was more than fifty feet high. Water flowed like a narrow stream around a large, circular table the same color as the Igbaya—Lorna's sentient chest Petook had crafted. The same tree that was on Lorna's chest—holding the raven moon—was set in relief in the center of the table.

Andrew now knew the image symbolized the Grace Giver and her brother, The Raven King, in a kind of balance between life and death, waking and dreaming.

Petook spoke to the elders in the common tongue to honor Andrew and so that he could take part in whatever fate would be decided.

"I, Petook Aenoosho Pellotuloma Pembrook, son of Avenshi Elosheema Pellotuloma Pembrook and Tereshama Hareem Lolem Aefeenoo, humbly request permission to approach the Table of Decision to discuss with the Council of Elders what is to become of this Human, Andrew, Son of Grace."

The six sat, and one of the women replied, "Permission is granted, Petook Aenoosho Pellotuloma Pembrook, son of Avenshi Elosheema Pellotuloma Pembrook and Tereshama Hareem Lolem Aefeenoo. The council recognizes your wisdom, and your family is honored within these halls. We will hear your words. Speak plainly."

"This is Andrew, once son of Lithuel, now Son of Grace. I know him, and I can vouch for his character."

One of the men spoke. "Petook, son of the honored. You need not vouch for him. We each saw our revered speak with him and give him her blessing. Though it is forbidden for any outsider to enter our lands, and doing so is punishable by death..."

"This *is* an exceptional circumstance," one of the women continued. "Never has such a holy event taken place within our lands..."

329

"And surely, it will be immortalized in story and song for epochs to come," another woman concluded, as though the council were thinking and speaking with one voice.

"We also see that he bares the marks of the bloodline," another councilman said.

Aefook stepped forward. "I, Aefook Aenoosho Imtoo Imeetauo, son of Peshosham Farem Imtoo Imeetauo and Tetaree Ha-arets Le'ulam Vayed, humbly request permission to approach the Table of Decision to discuss with the Council of Elders my experiences with this Human, Andrew, Son of Grace. I am here to bear witness."

One of the men spoke, "Permission is granted, Aefook Aenoosho Imtoo Imeetauo, son of Peshosham Farem Imtoo Imeetauo and Tetaree Ha-arets Le'ulam Vayed. The council recognizes your bravery, and your family is honored within these halls. We will hear your words. Speak plainly."

"The council knows that my twin sister, Teela Ha-efoo Le'ulam Vayed, disappeared many seasons ago and was thought lost to the world below, but Andrew, Son of Grace, has returned her to her family and this village. She was dead to us, and now she lives!" Aefook said with more passion than he had intended, and he paused to collect himself as the council slightly shifted in their seats. "I seek the council's grace," he said, hanging his head, frustrated with himself for the outburst. "It's just...I have often considered sedartis without her. The loss of her voice within me has left me in great anguish. It is true, outsiders are forbidden, but it was not always so," he looked up at them. "It was decided, to protect our homes and our way of life, but this... this... *Human* has returned to me something more precious than my own life. I have given him the marks of the bloodline."

The council considered. Then one of the women finally

spoke, "We welcome you home, Teela Ha-efoo Le'ulam Vayed. Your voice has been missed. We have not been complete without you."

Teela bowed but said nothing.

"Andrew, Son of Grace, step forward," one of the councilmen said.

Andrew took a step forward and stood between Aefook and Petook.

"It is decided. You are welcome in our lands. But you must learn our ways..."

"And respect our laws," another councilman added. "Else, you will pay as one of our own."

Andrew bowed.

Then the council spoke nothing else, and Petook took Andrew's hand and left the great hall.

Once outside, Petook held up his hands for the crowd to listen. Then he spoke something Andrew didn't understand, and the villagers slowly dispersed.

"What did you say to them?"

"That we all heard the words of our divine, and it has been decided that you are one of us now."

"What happens now?"

"Now, you will be my guest," Petook replied with a smile.

# CHAPTER 52

Aefook and Teela followed Andrew and Petook. As they walked, several villagers approached as close as Aefook would allow and bowed to Andrew. Children also began to run alongside them on the road.

"What am I supposed to do with all of this?" Andrew asked.

Petook smiled. "It is just a bit of hero adoration. It will wear off—perhaps."

Andrew shot Petook a questioning glance, but he just shrugged.

"Quite a different response than last time I was here."

Petook's eyes grew, and he glanced at Aefook, who clenched his jaw. Teela smiled. Then she pretended to misstep and bump into her brother, who tried to catch her. She laughed and hugged him. "I have missed you, brother."

This softened his demeanor just enough that Andrew thought he almost saw Aefook return her smile.

Once back at Petook's home, Aefook left them, and Teela bowed to Andrew and said, "If there is anything you need while you are here, anything at all. Please let me know. It would be my honor to serve."

Andrew rubbed the back of his neck. "Uh, thanks," and he felt himself beginning to blush, so he turned and went into Petook's house. Petook returned Teela's courtesy with a simple head bow.

"Do you still have the cloak I gave you?" Petook asked, helping Andrew with his coat.

Andrew nodded. "I did, back home, before it all burned to the ground."

Petook shook his head. "It will not burn."

Andrew did not know that.

Now that they were finally alone, Andrew asked, "What is sedartis?"

Petook motioned Andrew to remove his shoes and take a pair of cloth slippers. "To end one's own life."

Andrew was surprised. "Aefook thought about ending his life because of the loss of his sister?"

Petook nodded. "She is his twin. They are deacons. Their bond is greater than that of a brother and sister. They are spiritually connected like two sides of a coin; like two branches of the same tree. They can choose to share their thoughts, their fears."

"Could he feel her pain, down below?"

Petook shook his head. "No. Something kept her from him. Until yesterday."

"That's when I bartered for her freedom. She had some sort of device silencing her."

"A device, you say?"

Andrew nodded. "Yes. It was iron, strapped across her mouth. While she wore it, she was devoid of all color, but once it came off, she returned to how she is now."

"Iron," Petook spat on the ground. "A work of the deceiver."

"Why is iron such a problem?"

Petook shook his head. "I will not speak of it. When was the last time you've eaten?"

"I could eat," Andrew replied.

Petook nodded and set to work.

The last time Andrew had been through Petook's home, they were in such a hurry that Andrew hadn't had time to take much of it in. Now, it felt safe and cozy.

The main room was austere but comfortable. The polished, dark wood floor and ceiling gave the room a warmth while the few pieces of furniture present were more like works of art in a gallery than anything he had ever seen. The open layout also gave Andrew a sense of calm and order, drawing his attention to the single tiny tree, with little purple fruit, sitting in a beautiful wood pot in one corner of the room where the light fell in through a slit in the window.

The room in which Petook slept was little more than an ornate, satin green sleeping pad with a pillow and single blanket. Next to it was a white- and cream-colored water jar, a washbasin of the same design, and a single, long-stem flower with soft red petals. The kitchen was nothing more than a washbasin, a stone fire pit with a metal hook, and a few small pantries. Next to it was a dining room where a low table sat in the center of the room, surrounded by four pillows.

Petook hummed as he heated a pot of water and prepared the food. Andrew quietly watched him and thought his movements were more of a dance than food preparation.

"It looks like you enjoy cooking," Andrew said from

where he leaned against the muslin wall separating the dining room from the main room.

Petook smiled a simple smile as he slowly stirred the pot. "I enjoy cooking for others, of which I have not had the pleasure for some time."

"You live alone?"

Petook nodded. "It was not always so."

Andrew didn't push.

As Petook began to set out an array of beautifully lacquered dark-purple and blue-clay plates, he motioned Andrew to take the place of honor where one of the pillows was draped in a white and gold silk scarf. Andrew crossed his legs and took his seat.

The food was simple. There were three kinds of fragrant broth, one of which smelled like mint and another like flowers. Five or six little dishes held tiny piles of brightly colored paste. Then there were sliced fruits, boiled purple potatoes, and some kind of large colorless tuber steamed soft and sliced thin into a pile. There were also fresh mushrooms, greens, and a pile of what looked like white and purple string that Andrew had never seen before, though he could tell it was some kind of plant.

"You will have to excuse me. We have no meat here," Petook told him.

Andrew nodded that it was fine as he looked over the spread of colorful offerings and took in the rich smell of the broths. Then Petook set a small dish full of soil between him and Andrew, and he sat. He took a moment to look over everything, making sure everything was as it should be, then nodded and smiled large.

"Would you do the honors?" he asked, pointing to the small dish of soil, and bowed his head.

Andrew tried to discern what he was supposed to do but had no idea.

Petook slowly looked up.

"I'm sorry..." Andrew said, shaking his head and shrugging.

This was unexpected, but Petook was not offended. He assumed that if the Grace Giver had blessed Andrew, it was because he was devout and wise in the Ways of Grace.

"Have you seen this before?" Petook asked.

Andrew studied it. "It just looks like a bit of soil."

"It is just a bit of soil, but it is also more than that. It is what is *in* the soil that makes it special."

Petook held a hand over the soil and said something in his native tongue as a small green shoot broke through the soil and bloomed two small pink and white flowers. Then, with a smile, he plucked one of the flowers and dropped it in his empty bowl.

Somehow, Andrew felt like this was a lesson. It's not the soil on the outside that matters, but the beauty within. Perhaps this was the beginning of a great many lessons.

Andrew mimicked the ways in which his host prepared his own broth, fumbling with the long, thin pair of eating sticks he was supposed to use to navigate his meal. He felt safe with Petook and began sharing everything that had happened. He shared about the attack, the journey, and how he felt—secret shadows of details he had not divulged to anyone else. He talked about how afraid he was for Feyloren, how unsure he was of Perimas, and how he had never realized how much he felt like an outsider until he broke the Grace Giver's confidence.

Petook just listened, nodded, and enjoyed his fragrant broth, dipping the various herbs in the hot broths and taking a bite, then periodically lifting the bowl to his lips and drinking.

When Andrew was finally done with his story, he sat silently.

Petook said nothing. He didn't even look at him. He just kept dunking his vegetables and slurping his broth.

Finally, Andrew asked, "Do you have any thoughts?"

Petook looked at him. "Of course! I have many." Then, he continued eating.

Andrew set down the eating sticks. "Would you be willing to *share* any of those thoughts with me? I could use the advice."

"Ah. Very well. Trust, our divine," he said, punctuating his comment with his sticks. Then he went back to dunking and slurping.

"That's it? Trust our divine?"

Petook nodded.

"Anything more specific?"

Petook thought for a moment, letting a few mushrooms float in his bowl before plucking them out and tossing them into his mouth.

"I think this is an opportunity."

Andrew was taken aback. "An opportunity? How?"

"There is value in the struggle. It sounds like our divine brought you through this journey to my home for a reason."

"It feels like I'm being used."

This broke Petook's calm demeanor, and he thoughtfully set his utensils along the edge of his bowl. "Is it right for a hammer to say it does not want to be used by the craftsman, or should it be grateful for the honor of being chosen?"

Andrew had not thought of it that way. "But shouldn't I have some say?"

Petook did not reply to this; his last question was still valid. "Many have sought what you take for granted. To speak with the Divine. To find favor! This is no small thing."

"I could have been killed."

"You were not."

Andrew grunted. "You're starting to sound like her."

Petook was honored, and he showed it with a bright smile. Then he bowed his head low enough almost to touch the table.

"Perhaps, it is not about you. Perhaps you should stop focusing so much on self," Petook said.

"Please, explain."

"Earlier, you said you are just Andrew, which *is* true. A hammer is also just a hammer, except in the hand of the craftsman. In the hand of the master, the hammer becomes a witness to greatness. It becomes a part of something so much greater than itself. Perhaps you will *never* be more than just Andrew unless you are in the hands of the master."

This *was* a heavy note and perhaps why the Grace Giver had been so hurt when he broke her confidence.

"But how can I ever live up to that kind of love?" Andrew asked.

Petook's countenance became compassionate. "You cannot. Perhaps all you are meant to do is let go and accept her plans for you. Just lean back and let go, like a leaf on the stream. Trust the stream. Trust where the stream is taking you."

It was getting late.

Andrew tried to help clean up, but Petook wasn't having it, so he went into the back garden—a garden of tranquility that immediately calmed Andrew like warm water on a cold day.

Andrew could see why the home was so austere. Petook didn't spend most of his time in it. It was out here where Petook really lived. Beautiful wooden furniture covered in moss and vines looked like a natural part of the landscape. A gently babbling waterfall fed a lovely pond on one side of the garden. The pond was full of the most wonderful white and gold fish no bigger than Andrew's finger, swimming in lazy circles beneath floating leaves of green, red, and gold. On the other side of the garden was a path leading through well-manicured trees to the tender shoot Andrew had once given Petook, only now it was no tender shoot but a beautiful hornbeam covered in the same flowers Andrew had seen on the Grace Giver when first they met. The only thing missing were the eyes and the little girl sitting on a branch.

Andrew smiled at the memory.

Andrew approached Petook's open-air workshop, which was almost as large as the rest of the garden. It might have been a workshop, but the tools were works of art. The red and gold wood Andrew had once seen on Aefook's sword handle and the Bantam's wagon, who gave Andrew the location of the Grace Giver, was the same wood Petook carved into furniture. Nearly a dozen pieces ready for the master's hand stood on end in a rack on one side of the shop, and partially finished pieces, such as a chair and a small boat, hung from the ceiling.

"Is this where you made the Igbaya?" Andrew asked as Petook walked up behind him.

Petook nodded. "They were special pieces. Near to my heart. My Eetoona helped with the intuition. We spent nearly a century layering the chimcary. Shaping the wood. Speaking life into them. We were unsure, in the beginning, what form they would take. But once they came to life, we knew they were exceptional, exquisite, one of a kind."

"One of a kind? I thought you said that there were several."

Petook looked at him. "Only two awoke."

"Awoke?"

Petook smiled a wise smile and tapped his forehead. "The others were beautiful indeed, but those two... they were *alive*." Then Andrew watched sorrow sweep over Petook's face and realized that Petook still thought that Andrew had been forced to kill it to help Lorna.

"I never used the poison you gave me," Andrew assured him.

Surprise and relief overtook Petook, and he touched Andrew's shoulder. "You don't say."

Andrew nodded. "I almost did, but I decided to try to repair it first. It had fallen into such disrepair."

This disturbed the elder Night Watchman.

"But it changed somehow when I began to polish it and speak gently to it. It's almost like it healed and woke up. Then it opened for me."

Petook sighed a heavy sigh of relief. "You *are* touched by Grace. It would not be so with just anyone. It must have sensed something special in you."

Andrew considered this.

"May I see the broken staff?" Petook asked.

Andrew retrieved it from his bag and laid its broken pieces out on Petook's large work table.

Petook slowly moved his hands over the staff, not touching it, feeling it, trying to intuit if any life was left in it.

He nodded. "I think chimcary remains. This is good. It is faint, but it is there."

Chimcary. This is what Petook said he could see when looking at the flora surrounding the village. Chimcary was a kind of intuition that plants shared, almost like a language, and what Lorna had said Andrew must have seen in his vision when he was practicing with her, the morning before the attack.

"I will begin immediately. Are you tired? I can prepare your bed," Petook said.

Andrew shook his head. "No. I'd like to watch, if I may."

Petook gently bowed in agreement and carefully put the pieces of the staff in their proper order on his table. Then he went to rows of jars on small shelves on one side of his shop and collected two jars, with fresh wrappings and a stone statue like the ones Andrew had seen in Nomi's shop. This one was a light green stone, about the size of Andrew's hand, shaped like a young tree. It was a totem of the Grace Giver.

"Would you please light the candles and give us some light?" Petook asked, and Andrew nodded.

Into the night, Andrew watched the old man's hands gently dab liquid from one of the bottles onto each end of the staff's breakpoints and expertly align the wood so that the pieces came together as naturally as they once had. He then wrapped them in cloth and wet the fabric with oil from a second jar. Petook also sang as he worked —a kind of low chant, almost like a hum. Once finished, he held his hands on either side of the tree statue, then paused.

"Andrew, Son of Grace. Will you join me?"

Andrew sat next to Petook and held out his hands. Petook took them in his own and spoke words that Andrew thought might be a prayer, word of intuition or perhaps both.

"Mend these wounds and dispel the anger that has caused such pain. We seek restoration, reparation, and healing."

Andrew felt his hands tingle as the statue began to glow.

# CHAPTER 53

Many miles away, a young woman with skin the color of sapphire jewels heard a commotion in the hall outside her cramped and dirty bedroom that smelled of fecal matter. She pulled her bare feet up under her dirty and threadbare blanket as a chain attaching her leg to the wall pulled taunt. She winced as the iron shackle caught on a never-healing sore and stung. The young woman had been living in the tiny room, in her own waste, for so long she couldn't even remember her name. She had long given up any hope of ever leaving for the bitterness it brought with it, and now, any fragment of a memory of any life before this felt like nothing more than a distant dream. Then the door to her room opened and light spilled into her darkness, overwhelming her and causing her to shield her eyes.

"Sa-uree?"

What did he say? The voice sounded familiar, like the melody of a forgotten lullaby. She squinted and tried to see who was speaking to her, but the light blinded her.

"Sa-uree!" the voice cried, now cracked and over-whelmed with both joy and sorrow.

She instinctively pushed him away. It's too early. She isn't ready for another customer.

"Please, be gentle," she begged.

Petros slowly knelt next to his sister—tears streaming down his cheeks—removed his expensive coat and covered her nakedness.

She flinched and pulled away.

Just then, two of Petros's men looked in through the door, and Petros barked: "Get out!" causing her to flinch and try to hide beneath her blanket.

He held his hands open, wanting to comfort her but careful not to touch her. "What have they done to you?"

She tried to inch away from him. He could see that she didn't know who he was.

"It's me, Sa-uree. It's your brother, Petros."

She was confused. Petros? Her mind stumbled over his words. Was she dreaming? She hadn't dreamt this dream in longer than she could remember. But there was something about his voice that conjured her earliest memories. They were memories of laughter, memories of her father and her mother, and meals around the hearth. Memories of thick blankets. Memories of when she was safe.

She slowly looked out from underneath her piss-stained blanket. His skin was like hers. His face... something about his face seemed so familiar. He was older. But his eyes. She saw something of her father in those eyes.

"Petros?" she whispered.

He nodded, and she lunged at him and hugged him.

"Is this real? Are you real? Are you really here, or am I dreaming?"

"I'm here, little sister."

The door opened, and one of his men looked in. Then, he turned his face away. "Boss?"

"WHAT!"

"There are children back here."

Petros hung his head and wiped his wet face. "Get the boys. Go through every single paper, ledger, and book you can find. Find every single fat worm who has ever stepped foot in this place, and feed them to the zygors. Then burn it to the ground. All of it. And get me some clothes and blankets!"

Petros looked again at the face he had so often seen in his dreams and long though dead. He gently brushed a strand of ratted hair out of her face. "You are safe now, and no one will ever touch you again."

Then, together, they broke down and wept.

# CHAPTER 54

That night, Tomptee and Perimas set up camp and made a fire inside the hollow tree. They did not share many words, just a bit of bread, and Tomptee curled up under his cloak next to Nelot and feigned to fall asleep. He had several times suspected Perimas of digging through their things and leaving their camp in the middle of the night, but he had no proof. By morning, Perimas was always back and eagerly preparing breakfast or watering the horses. Tomptee knew Andrew suspected nothing, but tonight, he was determined to stay awake longer than Perimas.

It did not take long before Tomptee heard Perimas rise and leave the hollow of the tree. Tomptee waited a few extra minutes before rising, and only after he could smell that Perimas was gone. Tomptee was betting that Perimas didn't know his cloak was imbued with camouflage intuition, which let him blend into almost any environment, especially natural environments like these.

Tomptee leaned towards the tree's opening and sniffed the air. There was no sign of Perimas.

Many would have been uncomfortable in a forest as dark as this, but Tomptee felt at home. In the city, his people stayed inside after dark because the city posed a great many threats to the smaller Inkling race, but in the forest, the darkness was like a welcome cloak of protection. He and his kin thrived in the forests after hours. His sharp eyes could see clearly, and his keen nose sensed even more. He pulled off his boots and socks and let his toes grip the fusty soil, which made the fur on the backs of his hands stand on end. He sniffed the ground around the tree and picked up Perimas's trail in moments. He was not far.

Without a sound, Tomptee slipped through the underbrush without disturbing a single twig or bending a solitary leaf. His tiny feet moved as quick as a whisper until he came upon Perimas kneeling at the river's edge, watching something in the water. The Longbeard's form seemed odd in the light of the raven moon, hunched over the water's surface like some strange golem or goblin.

Suddenly, there was a splash, and Perimas lifted a writhing fish in both hands and tore out its throat with his bare teeth, startling Tomptee so much that he took a step back.

Perimas thought he heard something and looked over his shoulder, a fish fin hanging from his mouth by a long piece of pink flesh.

Tomptee held his breath. No way could Perimas find him in this darkness, with or without his cloak, but he still didn't want to be heard.

Perimas turned back to his meal and tore the fish's face off with his teeth and sucked back a long strand of lumpy, fatty innards.

Tomptee felt his stomach turn. It is true that his kin had some unusual delicacies, such as live silkworm and beetle larvae, but he preferred the food of the common man, cooked and without a face. But this looked like something else. It looked like an animal eating, not a man.

Once Perimas had finished every squirming fin, he rose, pulled down his pants, and relieved himself right there on the rock on which he stood, and with no sign of cleaning himself after, he pulled up his trousers and moved into the night.

The smell alone made Tomptee nearly vomit.

He followed Perimas for nearly an hour as he roamed aimlessly through the forest; twice it looked like he was trying to chew on a stick. Then he found a glowing night worm he smashed on a rock with his thumb, and one time he peed behind a tree and didn't pull his pants up for the better part of fifteen minutes. Tomptee wasn't sure he was ever going to.

Alone in the dark, Perimas was an entirely different person. His very movements were more beast than man. His gate was uneven when he walked, and he was restless. It didn't seem to Tomptee like Perimas was looking for anything more than an aimless exploration of the nearby woodland.

Once Tomptee perceived that Perimas was slowly returning to camp, he decided to get ahead of him and returned to the fire. Within minutes, Tomptee smelled Perimas outside of the tree, but he never came back in.

By morning, Perimas was clean, bright-eyed, and cooking breakfast.

"Mornin'," Perimas said, stirring something over their fire that smelled delicious.

Tomptee did not reply.

# CHAPTER 55

**T**eela stood on Petook's porch, holding a beautiful box on an ornate wooden tray. Neatly folded towels sat in a lacquered basin next to her on the porch, along with a small box of fragrant bath salts. The morning sun was low through the dense forest surrounding the village casting long shadows across the red, sloping roof of Petook's simple home.

As she nervously waited, she wondered about this man who had saved her life. Where did he come from? Who was he? Did he have family? How did he find her? There were days in her captivity that were so hard she wanted to kill herself, then she would fall asleep and find him waiting for her in her dreams. This Human. She had never met him before and thought he was just a figment of her imagination. She had no idea he was real until she saw him in the market, and when she did, she thought she was hallucinating until she touched him and felt grace upon him. Then she was certain Petros would kill him, but he hadn't. Andrew found a way. Not only had he walked out of Petros's presence unharmed, he convinced Petros to release her as well. Only by grace could such a thing have happened. No. She already knew this Human was exceptional, even before The Grace Giver asked her to take him to Eshooreem—a sacred pool. But did he have any idea what he meant to her? He had saved her life in so many ways. How could she possibly repay him? Her hands trembled. She had never known a man—by grace, Petros never let anyone touch her like that—but she would give herself to Andrew if he asked, and a part of her hoped he would.

Petook opened the beautifully ornate, sliding door and welcomed her into his home with a gentle bow and look of understanding. She removed her slippers, set them next to the door, and returned the courteous bow. Then he excused himself without a word.

Petook's home was the austere home of a master craftsman consisting of nothing more than a main sitting room with mat floors, a simple bedroom to the back of the building, and a side room for cooking and eating. The home's rich wood felt warm, and the few hand-carved pieces of furniture were so exquisite, they were more like pieces of art than furniture.

Teela wore a simple silk, cream-colored robe with yellow flowers over a linen wrap that could be easily removed. Her hair was pulled up into a bun, and she had prepared her skin with balms the fragrance of flowers and spice meant to calm Andrew and attract him to her.

The bedroom door where he had slept was still closed, so she stepped quietly across the mat floors in her bare feet to the simple kitchen where she set the tray on a narrow kitchen counter, opened the box, and removed several fruits, two large, bright-blue eggs and a small wooden bowl piled with purple and brown tea leaves. Then she rose to put a kettle on when she heard the bedroom door slide open and turned to find Andrew in nothing but a robe. His disheveled hair and squinting eyes suggested to her that he had just awoken, which she thought was cute but said nothing. Seeing him made her mouth go dry. She took a deep breath, composed herself and returned to preparing food.

"Teela! What are you doing here? Where is Petook?" Andrew asked.

"He has duties in the village," she replied, beginning to dice a large orange fruit.

"Where are my clothes?"

"They are being washed," she said, holding back a smile.

After a quiet moment, Teela asked, "Were you comfortable last night?" She slid the diced fruit from the cutting board onto a plate and set the plate on the low dining room table that was surrounded by sitting cushions.

Andrew approached her holding shut the top of his robe. "Yes. Very. I can't remember the last time I slept this well. It is so peaceful here."

She showed her pleasure with his comfort with a simple bow. Then she filled two cups with steaming water and set them on the table.

"How about you? I bet it's good to be home," Andrew said.

"It is, yet sleep eluded me. My mind knows I'm home, but my body does not yet."

Andrew nodded.

Teela held out the blue eggs to Andrew. "We found you some eggs. We do not eat them, so you will have to excuse me if I am unsure exactly how to..."

He took a step forward and gently touched her hand. "Allow me."

351

Warmth flushed through her at his touch, and she looked at his hand on hers. She had been trying so hard not to stare, but now she looked directly at him. He gently smiled, and she smiled back. Then she handed him the eggs and watched as he set a pan onto the already lit stove, cracked the egg into it and gently stirred them with a wooden spoon.

As they slowly began to firm, Teela watched Andrew touch his chin, then reach for a round red vegetable on the counter. "Here we go. These will do nicely."

He quickly diced the juicy vegetable and tossed it into the fragrant eggs. Then he glanced at her and slightly leaned towards her.

"May I pay you a compliment?"

Her eyes widened, and she looked away, a bit embarrassed. "You may."

"You smell wonderful."

She swallowed and touched the side of her neck.

"Here we go," he said, scooping the eggs into two separate bowls and setting them on the table.

Now that everything was in order, she motioned him to take the place of honor, a cushion Petook had draped with a white silk cloth embroidered with gold thread. She could see this made him uncomfortable.

"I wish you would all treat me like anyone else," Andrew said.

Now she bowed low—not a courtesy bow but one of reverence and great respect. "I am not here because you have been touched by grace—exceptional as that may be— but because you saved my life. You are *not* just like anyone else. You never will be again. Not to me, and not to my people."

"I didn't know I was saving your life. I saw you hurting and thought I could help. That's all."

She slowly and intentionally rose and looked into his eyes. "That is everything."

Teela watched Andrew swallow, straighten and slightly turn away, which she took as discomfort.

"If my presence offends you, I will leave."

He touched her hand.

"No. It's not that. It's just... I'm not used to being treated like this."

Teela bowed again and replied, "Perhaps you should be." And this time, she did not rise until he finally took the place of honor. Once he had, she pinched some tea leaves into his cup, then hers, and sat next to him.

She wasn't sure what to make of the eggs, but she didn't want to offend him. So, she leaned forward and smelled them. They had an odd earthy smell. Andrew chuckled.

"You might like them," he said with a smile.

This drew her heart even more to him. She picked up the spoon, scooped up a small pile and slowly took a bite.

"Well? What do you think?"

She nodded, then set the spoon in the bowl and gently pushed it away from her.

He grunted a laugh. "I don't have what I need to make them properly."

"Would you like me to find..."

He held up a hand, signaling that it wasn't necessary.

They enjoyed breakfast together in silence, but the silence never felt awkward. She had so many questions, but didn't want to be rude. Who were his people? Why had he been in the city that day? Had he ever seen her in his night visions? But she kept her questions to herself.

Several times she glanced at him and saw him watching

her, wondering what he was thinking, what he was thinking of her.

After breakfast, she invited him into the main room.

As he waited with a look of curiosity, she brought the towels in the lacquered bowl and small box of bath salts from the front porch and set them before him.

"What is this?" he asked.

Teela did not reply. Instead, she filled the basin with warm water, scooped in a small amount of the aromatic salts and reached for his robe, but Andrew pulled away.

She lowered her head and turned away. "I did not mean to displease you."

"What are you doing?"

"I am here to take you to Eshooreem, but first, I must bathe you."

"Excuse me?"

She took another step away from him and turned her back to him. "If it displeases you, I will leave."

He took a deep breath. "It's not that. It's just... I usually bathe myself. And you should know, I am betrothed."

Her head hung slightly, but she did not respond.

"It does not displease me. I'm just uncomfortable. I'm not used to... all of this," he added.

Teela thought for a moment, then she had an idea. She took the silk band from around her waist, and tied it over her eyes like a blindfold.

"Will this make you more comfortable?"

"I guess so," he replied. His voice was colored with a tinge of embarrassment.

She turned to him with her eyes covered, unable to see anything. She felt her robe now hanging inconveniently open, so she let it fall to the ground. Cloth was still tightly wrapped around her body, but she could feel the exposure of her shoulders and arms.

Then she held her hands out to him.

After a moment, he gently took her hands and led them to his robe.

"You're trembling," she whispered.

"I guess I am," he replied.

She slowly untied his robe, opened it and let it fall to the floor.

Even though she could not see anything, she was now acutely aware that he was standing before her entirely exposed. Vulnerable. Physically naked, in preparation for the emotional nakedness that was soon to come. Her body awoke to his presence in every way.

"Please kneel," she gently asked.

Andrew did, and she carefully followed his arms to his shoulders. She knew she should pull away, but she would not. Touching his face was crossing a line, but she didn't care. Now that she was this close to him, she couldn't help but touch his neck, his cheeks, his forehead, the slope of his nose, his lips. She moved slowly—seeking unspoken permission, and he did not pull away.

Teela dipped one of the towels in the warm water and rung out the excess. There was only the sound of droplets of water falling into the basin and the sound of Andrew's breathing.

She very gently began wiping his face, neck and chest.

"Do you mind if I... take care of my unspoken parts?" Andrew asked, which made Teela giggle, and she quickly covered her mouth and nodded.

She couldn't see him, but she could feel him. She had seen him so many times in her dreams, she didn't need the blindfold. Her mind brought every curve and line into vivid detail. His eyes. His lips. She felt her chest becoming warm and she swallowed. She wiped his hands with the towel and turned them over in hers. She could feel their strength. She set the towel aside, and began massaging them.

He quietly grunted with pleasure, which pleased her, and she massaged his arms.

"Please, lay," she asked. "You may rest your head on one of these," she said, pointing to the towels.

She heard him roll a towel and tuck it under his head, positioning himself within reach of her searching hands. Then he took her hand and laid it on his chest. She paused —her hand flat on his breast—and felt how quickly his heart was beating, and hers began to beat in rhythm.

She wanted to tell him everything. How she had been waiting for him all her life. How she had longed for him to come to her, yearned for him in her darkest nights, even before she knew he even existed. He was her vision of a perfect man. Even if some of what she had imagined couldn't possibly be real, it didn't matter. He was real. Really real, and finally here with her. If she had remained in her village, she would have known the touch of a man years ago, but she hadn't, and her body, her mind, her heart yearned for him.

She licked her lips and wanted desperately to kiss him, but she hesitated. He had said he was betrothed. She respected him too much to cross that line, so she pulled back.

"Will you please hand me the small jar?" she asked and held out her hand. He handed it to her.

Teela removed the lid and scooped some of the fragrant balm with her fingers and rubbed it onto her hands before beginning to massage it into his skin, starting with his feet. She pressed every strand of muscle just enough to release its tension. And once she was near his "unspoken parts" as he had called them, she moved on to a different part of his body, circumspect where and how she touched him. Her mind raced with imaginings that she fought to bury deep.

Once she was done, she asked him to put his robe back on and waited until he had. Once he had, he let her know, and she removed the wrapping over her eyes.

"That was... something else," Andrew said.

She gently bowed. "I hope it pleased you."

He took a deep breath.

"When you are ready, please follow me," she said, now standing by the front door.

"Where are we going? Should I get dressed?" he asked, looking around.

"It is not necessary. We aren't going far."

She could tell this made him nervous.

"This is why you've come," she told him and held her hand out to him.

He took it and followed her barefoot through the village and along a narrow path that disappeared into the thick forest.

As much as he wasn't ready to go out in just a robe, especially with all the gawkers around, he was acutely aware that he was in an entirely different culture than anything he had previously experienced, and the words of Petook were on his heart: "Trust the river."

So, trust the river he did.

# CHAPTER 56

ndrew followed Teela barefoot along a narrow path that disappeared into the forest. The sounds of the Kilo Kan were rich and varied. Birds sang, near and far. Something unseen whooped. The leaves of the canopy above rustled in the morning breeze. It was like another kind of intoxication. Chimcary. Perhaps this was chimcary. He had never considered walking barefoot through a forest, but somehow it made sense. He felt closer to the landscape. The soft green moss and rich soil between his toes. He felt stronger, faster. He wanted to run, to dance, to sing. It was so rich. The air smelled like life! He didn't know what else to call it. Everything around him spoke to every part of him. This is where he belonged. It was in his soul. Did the Grace Giver play a part in this? Had she somehow awoken something in him that now connected him to this place?

As much as he missed Fey, he felt at home here.

Deep in the forest, they came upon a private glade with a pool of water so still and clear it looked like glass. Andrew leaned over its edge and saw a reflection of himself looking back. There was no sign of living creatures in the water, only a blanket of light-green moss covering the ground beneath.

Teela approached its edge, removed her robe and the cloth wrapping her body, and stepped into the water.

Andrew turned his face away.

"This is Eshooreem, a sacred pool."

"I told you, I am betrothed."

There was silence, then she quietly replied, "We are not here for that. I am here to guide you. This is why you've come."

"I came to have my staff repaired," he replied.

"Have you? Is that all? Or are you here for something more?"

Andrew remembered the Grace Giver's words.

"She told you that you would find what you are looking for with her children. This is it," Teela said.

"I thought you couldn't hear her."

She smiled. "I was blessed to hear her voice. I could not hear much of what you discussed, but those words were for me. She said I was to guide you. My eyes are closed. I will not open them if it displeases you."

"Can't I just keep the robes on?" Andrew asked.

"No. We must enter Eshooreem as we entered this world. It is your choice."

He glanced at her. She was entirely under the water up to her nose, and her eyes were closed. Something in the water was now glowing green in a cloud around her, reflecting light up on her face.

He decided to approach the water's edge and tried not to pay too much attention to those naked parts of her that were visible beneath the water's surface. Then he slowly removed his robe and touched the water with a toe. Somehow, it was warm. As he stepped further in, she rose from the water, her naked body dripping with green phosphorescence, and she reached for him. He tried to turn away, but his mind was becoming noticeably hazy.

"What's happening?" he asked.

"Eshooreem," is all she said, taking his hand.

He started to pull away but didn't. He couldn't. He was losing himself. He wanted to protect Feyloren, but his reason was vanishing.

Teela led him slowly into the water until they submerged together.

And there, all things became new.

# CHAPTER 57

A ndrew is in a forest, laughing. Someone else is here. He is a child playing a game with a younger girl who giggles and touches his shoulder as she runs away. His skin is dark, forest green, and he can feel his long hair against the back of his neck. The colors of the forest around him are vivid, vibrant, vocal. This girl is hiding. Though he can't see where she's hiding, he knows she is close. He can feel her, almost hear her giggle in his mind. He runs to a nearby tree and peeks behind it, touching her shoulder and running away. He is Shimar Etsell, and he is home.

~

ANDREW IS NOW TWELVE. It is his first day of kata training—something akin to a cross between a dance and martial arts. Four rows of children stand in front of the kata master, each holding a bow staff level in front of them. Andrew's best friend, Aefook, is in the front row. Aefook is exceptionally skilled and learning quickly, but Andrew can't seem to get the stances right. Twice Andrew stumbles, but Aefook helps him to his feet and encourages him. Aefook's sister, Teela, is hiding in the forest, watching. She, too, wants to learn but isn't allowed. She has been told that some things aren't for girls, but she doesn't listen. She knows she can do anything the boys can do.

"You need to focus," Aefook tells Andrew as they walk to Andrew's home, and Teela joins them.

"I don't think this is for me," Andrew replies.

"Hi, Anduin! I saw you today," Teela says, but Andrew mostly ignores her because she is still a couple of years too young for him. Anduin is Andrew's new name.

"How? You're not supposed to be at training!" Aefook scolds.

She giggles and runs away.

Once home, Andrew goes into his kitchen to wash his hands and nurse his wounds.

"How was it?" his mother asks.

He just shakes his head.

"Don't be discouraged. It's just the first day. You'll get it."

Andrew isn't so sure.

Two months later, Andrew is standing in front of the oldest man in the village, who looks like he is falling asleep. Andrew tried learning the kata for two more weeks until his frustration grew to the point that he broke the bow staff in half and threw it at the master.

No one said a word to him that day, not even Teela.

Now, he stands before a new master, Master Utaa.

THE TINKER'S FOLLY

Andrew picks at a scab on his knee, wondering what he is doing here.

Master Utaa sits on a large tree stump in a quiet corner of the forest, eyes closed, hands open, and fingertips touching. His robes almost perfectly blend into the forest surrounding him.

"What do you feel right now?" Master Utaa asks. "Do not consider your answer; just speak."

"Bored."

Master Utaa nods. "What else?"

"Frustrated."

"Interesting. What else?"

Andrew sighs. Then he closes his eyes. Several minutes pass as the chimcary of the forest calms him. "I can feel the tree you are sitting on. And the leaves above us."

Master Utaa smiles.

"There is an ungorn falcon hunting... for... food for her chicks."

Master Utaa nods.

"An old owl is taking its last breaths, not far from us. It's alone. Scared."

"It is not alone. Go to it."

Andrew shakes his head. "But I don't know how. I can't."

Master Utaa does not reply.

Andrew considers the owl, its quick breathing, and the hollow of the tree in which it rests. He slowly reaches for it as though he were sitting right next to it, and somehow, he feels it in his hands. The owl's breathing becomes more regular until it slows, slows, slows, and eventually stops.

"How did I do that?"

Master Utaa does not reply.

363

ANDREW IS SEVENTEEN, and Teela is dressed in a beautiful white dress—Andrew's favorite.

"Happy birthday, Anduin!" she says as he finishes his lesson with Master Utaa, bows, and begins walking home.

"Thanks," Andrew replies.

She hands him a small basket of freshly baked muffins.

He's surprised to see them. Nothing like muffins or wheat exists here.

"How did you..."

She beams at him. "I described what you saw in your dream to Oona, and she helped me find a grain that might rise as you described. It's taken several months, but what do you think?"

Andrew takes one out of the basket and looks at it. Holding it feels ethereal and makes him uneasy. He has only seen them in his dreams, but here they are. It somehow feels more real than everything around him, but how can that be?

He takes a bite. It's a bit dense, but it's delicious.

Teela reads the look on his face and sees that his response isn't quite what she had hoped.

"Do you not like them?"

Andrew shakes his head. "No. It's not that. It's delicious." He looks at the muffin in his hand and considers its texture and the dark blue berries dotting the cream-colored breading.

"Then what is it?"

Andrew breaks the muffin apart in his hands. He doesn't know what he is feeling nor how to describe it to her.

She reaches out and takes his hand. "Are you still having the night visions?"

He looks at her and nods.

"But how could you be dreaming of the lands below?" she asks. "You have never been anywhere beyond our village."

"I don't know. They feel so real."

"But in them, you aren't even Shimar Etsell. What does that mean?"

Andrew shakes his head. "There are other races and cities full of buildings made of stone! And..." he stops when he sees that he is hurting her. He takes her hands in his. "I don't mean to upset you."

She looks away. "Sometimes, I wonder if you would rather be there."

He does not reply, and his hesitation leads her to question: "Is that it? You would rather be with them?"

He touches her cheek. "Of course not. This is my home. You are my home." Then he sets the basket on the ground and takes both of her hands in his. "I've been meaning to ask you something."

She holds her breath.

"Our parents have decided that we are to be one, but I wanted to ask you first. I know it is unusual, but I told them I would not agree if you did not want me. Teela, you are a part of me in a way no one else could ever be. Would you be my neekaa?"

"Yes!" She pulls him close and kisses him passionately.

But as he embraces her, another name fills his mind: Feyloren.

∽

IT IS the day of their wedding. The entire village has come to witness their union.

Those knowledgeable in the ways of chimcary have called to the lanternflies to light the forest in a beautiful, magical glow. Birds sing, and a pack of mighty elatoo— great forest gorillas the size of the village's homes—stand with their troop just through the trees, watching.

Andrew's parents walk with him from their home to the place of meeting, their path lined with smiling friends and family. Their robes are yellow, lined with blue.

Teela's parents walk with her from their home. The path is lined with their friends and family, and her robes are blue, lined with yellow.

It is a joyous day.

There are shared words and shared promises. Both sets of parents declare in covenant that they are witnesses to this union that cannot be broken, and the beautiful couple kiss.

For the rest of the day, and into the night, there is singing and dancing. Anduin is Shimar Etsell; welcome, loved, and a growing pillar in the community, but Andrew still feels like he belongs somewhere else. He doesn't understand why, but he is torn between two worlds.

That night, Teela comes to him in his bed in a home their families have built for them. She is beautiful. He has longed for this night for many years.

They say nothing to each other.

She removes her robes, blows out the candle, and touches his chest.

But in the darkness, his heart beats for someone else.

~

It is the middle of the night. Andrew wakes in a sweat. His heart is racing. This time, his dream was of a dark figure with wings outstretched. He is hunting Andrew, searching for him. He is as close as Andrew's breath.

Andrew goes into the next room, where his children sleep. They are nine and six, and they are, without question, the most beautiful thing he has ever seen. Ashela has her mother's eyes and loves playing the flute. Utaa—named after Andrew's late master—is daring and unafraid, following his older sister through the forest and straight off a cliff if they'd let him. They love doing crafts with their mother and baking kero cakes with their grandmother. Just yesterday, Teela and the children wove braided strands of their hair into a bracelet for Andrew, which they tied shut with a small, wooden, heart-shaped bead, that now wraps around Andrew's left wrist.

He waits with them for several minutes, not just checking on them but calming himself in this cozy, perfectly comfortable sanctum of happiness and peace Teela has built for them, like a comfortable nest for the littles in their home.

He thinks about the incredible joy Teela has brought into their home throughout the years. He is twenty-eight now, and the council has asked him to join them. He will be the youngest member in history and is unsure of the responsibility. They have asked because he has grown in the ways of chimcary, unlike anyone in the history of their people. He has not just learned how to hear the sounds of the forest but to actually communicate with animals. Three days earlier, he even calmed a storm, which he is still pretty sure was just a coincidence, though Teela saw him do it and isn't as sure as he is. He can feel Grace upon him. He can feel power growing within, but he doesn't know what that means or what to do with it.

Teela has always believed in him and somehow known that he was meant for something more, but he never paid much attention to those words until recently. He's starting to feel like he is meant for something else, somewhere else. However, he can't imagine any other life. This is his life. He is happiest here, with his family, his children.

ANDREW NOW STANDS in the early morning hours on the steps of the Great Hall, waiting for the rest of the elders who will not arrive for more than an hour. He loves these early hours when everything is quiet. He can see from this elevated doorway across the village and into the distant forest.

He has more than a few grey hairs now and holds a steaming cup of tea.

Ashela is happily joined now, with two children and a third on the way.

Utaa has one of his own and is quickly learning the ways of wood carving from Petook, an old family friend.

These are his people. This is his home, and everything is as it should be—for everyone except Andrew.

He does not have night visions very often anymore, except last night. Last night, he woke in the middle of the night to the vision of a bald woman with skin the color of a metal he has never seen before but somehow knows. He doesn't know who she is, but somehow, he knows she is in danger. He is drawn to her. This morning, he can't stop thinking about her.

The village is quiet, but his heart is restless. He decides it is time to tell Teela. He has shared all he is with her save for this one thing. It is the only secret between them, a secret that had gone quiet many moons ago, but now it is back stronger than ever. Perhaps it is just foolishness, perhaps the vain imaginings of the same restless spirit all men possess; either way, she deserves to know.

And he has made a decision.

AFTER DINNER THAT NIGHT, Andrew decides it is time. He asks her to join him in their garden and takes her hand, hoping to assure her, because what he has decided is unorthodox to say the least.

"Every time I see her, she is sleeping, but it's like she is waiting for me to return to her, to help her. I feel like her life is in danger. Don't you understand? I have to find her."

"No, I don't understand!" Teela snaps. "You have a life here! Isn't that enough?"

"Of course it is! But I have ignored this... this... spiritual toothache for years, and I can't ignore it any longer. I have to visit—just for a while. I will return."

"Will you?" she asks.

Andrew doesn't understand why she would ask such a question, but something tells him he can't be certain. He doesn't know why he can't be certain, but he can't.

"I'm asking you to choose me. Choose us!" Tears roll down her cheeks. "Leave this foolishness alone, once and for all, and stay." She presses his hand to her chest. "Stay with me."

Andrew kisses her one more time. "I'll be home soon."

That night, he rode out into the darkness. Teela silently watched him go.

# CHAPTER 58

S uddenly, Andrew broke through the pool's surface and gasped for air. His heart was pounding.

He struggled to the water's edge and rolled onto the mossy bank. His mind was racing.

He was back.

As Andrew struggled to catch his breath, Teela rose from the water near him and put on her robe.

Andrew turned to her. "What was that?"

She smiled a gentle smile, but there was deep sorrow in her eyes. "You have what you came for, Son of Grace."

"But... was that real?"

"What is real?" She asked with much of the same look of sorrow that was in her eyes the night he found her on the streets of the underground.

"You knew this would happen," Andrew said.

She looked away.

He rose, pulled on his robe, and knelt before her. Then he gently turned her chin towards him. "How?"

She smiled with a face wet with sorrow. "Many nights I

370

have seen you in my night visions. I thought it was foolish hoping, but then, there you were, on that street, in the flesh. I didn't believe it at first, but when I touched you and felt Grace upon you, I knew it must be true. I thought Petros would kill you, but you found a way. You spoke with words that were *ancient* in their wisdom. And you fought for me. Me. I felt so worthless for so long. So many nights I thought I would disappear in that underground world. Petros would not even use my name."

"*Was* it real? That life?" he asked, pointing to the pool. Then he saw it on his wrist. Three thin braids of hair held shut by a simple, heart-shaped, wooden bead.

He touched it. "Their names were Ashela and Utaa," he whispered.

"It was real to me," she told him.

He kissed her passionately. Then he studied the eyes of the woman he had loved for so long. The mother of his children. His best friend. His heartbeat. "I love you," and he embraced her. "But I cannot stay," he whispered into her ear.

"I know," she whispered back.

As Andrew stood, he felt power in his hands, arms, and back like never before. Though he could no longer see the chimcary, everything he had learned in that other life was still with him and would forever be etched on his heart: The names of his children and their children, an entire life well lived, being a pillar of the Shimar Etsell community, friends, festivals, laughter and dancing, his beautiful friend —this woman who now knelt before him. He *was* Shimar Etsell, even if he wasn't.

"I swear, by Grace, I will never forget." Then he rose and left.

Teela dropped her head and wept.

Andrew returned to Petook, who was finishing breakfast.

"How was your experience? Enlightening, I trust?" Petook asked with a simple smile.

"How long have I been gone?"

Petook shrugged. "An hour, maybe."

"An hour?! How can that be?" Andrew asked, sitting at the table.

Petook poured him a cup of tea. "It worked."

"What?"

Petook collected the staff from his workshop and handed it to Andrew.

Holding the staff, Andrew could feel a new kind of incredible power. It wasn't like chimcary. It was something different. It was in the wood and the air, the home, the village, and the forest surrounding them. The hair stood on the backs of his hands.

"What is happening?" he asked Petook.

Petook gently bowed. Then met his gaze, "Perhaps what you feel, Son of Grace, is the river."

Andrew's skin tingled at the thought. Then he squeezed the staff, and it changed shape in his hands. It had once been a grey, crooked staff with a cluster of branches at its end, as wild and unruly as the nightshade tree growing through Lorna's home. Now, it straightened and became a beautifully smooth and lacquered red and honey-colored staff with a filigree spindle at its end that held a glowing, green orb of swirling light. And just as Andrew was about to ask Petook another question, the sky turned crimson.

Petook and Andrew ran outside.

High above the canopy of the trees, dark red clouds

churned violently. Then, parting the clouds with his hands, The Raven King looked down upon the village. He was now many times larger than the Ki Lo Kan's mighty trees.

And now, the god of death and dreaming wore no mask.

churned violently. Then, parting the clouds with his hands,
The Raven King looked down upon the village. He was now
many times larger than the Teela had been a few trees
And now, the god of death and dreaming were no more.

# CHAPTER 59

The raven-black skull of death itself terrified the
village, and many screamed in horror.

Teela stood on the edge of the forest, holding
shut her robe, and Petook trembled in fear and fell to the
ground.

Andrew stepped forward and cried out in a loud voice,
"I am here. Leave them alone!"

The Raven King leaned forward. "I. Will. Not," he said
with a voice that shook the trees. "I see you boy, and I've
come for what is mine, else I will kill everyone you have
ever known and erase any memory of you from history."

"You have no power here!" Andrew cried as the wind
blew violently around him.

"Who do you think you are?" The Raven King asked
with a voice like a mighty hurricane.

"I am Andrew, Son of Grace! And I defy you!" he
screamed into the wind. As he spoke, bright green light
burst forth from his staff through the trees, pushing away
the darkness and causing The Raven King to screech and
shield his eyes. In moments, a cloud of ravens poured

through the forest and swarmed through the village towards Andrew, but they could not break through the light that shone brightly around him. Then, another sound echoed through the Ki Lo Kan. It was the sound of mighty beasts. A troop of elatoo—great forest gorillas—ran on all fours at Andrew in a violent and terrifying stampede, startling Andrew and diminishing his resolve. But the mighty alpha did not attack Andrew. Instead, he swiftly took Andrew up in his giant paw and tossed him onto his back, screaming a cry that bent the trees before him, carrying Andrew away. The entire troop of elatoo charged on into the forest, and the storm cloud of ravens followed close behind.

As they fled, the giant, blue-black gorilla clutched branches and swung from limbs. Ravens cried and tried pecking at their eyes and face, but the troop fought the birds, grabbing them by the fistful and tearing them into puffs of falling black feathers. The alpha did not turn back. He moved like a majestic beast born in the canopy, and his powerful back emanated incredible heat as he fled.

Andrew remembered his life as Anduin and did not slip. The many years of riding tree horses with Teela had taught him well how to stay aloft a swiftly moving animal, and within minutes, they were back at camp.

The alpha carefully helped Andrew to the ground and continued back up into the trees as a startled Tomptee ran to him. Seeing him, Andrew hugged him, which startled Tomptee even more, but he did not protest.

"He's coming. We must go! Now!" he told Tomptee and Perimas. "Leave the camp. Leave everything."

"What's happening?" Tomptee asked.

"There's no time," Andrew said, mounting Brynlee and urging her on.

Red light broke through the high canopy as the three fled through the forest.

"At least tell us where we are going," Tomptee hollered as Marta leapt to keep up with Brynlee.

"Jatoba!" Andrew cried.

Perimas tapped his nicatoo to take the lead. "I know a shortcut! Follow me!"

Andrew glanced at Tomptee, but before Tomptee could object, they pivoted left and followed Perimas into a part of the forest unknown to either of them.

# CHAPTER 60

Brynlee was sweating and breathing heavily, and Andrew was worried that if he pushed her any harder, she might collapse underneath him. A word of intuition had strengthened her and the other two mounts to ride much farther than they could have on their own strength, but they still had to stop eventually.

The red light had diminished and there was no sign of either The Raven King nor any of his wretched birds, so they stopped at a small lake they found in a clearing. Atop the hill overlooking the lake sat an old, abandoned cabin.

As Andrew and Tomptee watered their horses, Perimas slowly approached the cabin. He knew this place, but he wasn't sure how.

Hanging on a pike outside the front door was the sun-bleached skull of a nicatoo.

Andrew watched Perimas approach the house and go inside.

"What is he doing?" Andrew asked Tomptee. "We haven't the time..."

Tomptee looked at him. "There's something I need to

377

tell you about Perimas," but Andrew didn't hear him. He was already on his way up the hill to the old cabin.

Andrew could feel a darkness in this place. There was death here.

He looked at the ominous skull hanging on the pike and noticed a scattering of bones around either side of the house, like a macabre, nearly grown over garden border.

Andrew slowly pushed open the front door. The inside of the house was empty. Cold. His staff began to tingle in his hands, then something struck the back of his head and he fell to the ground.

Tomptee wasn't sure what was taking Andrew so long, so he ran up the hill and saw Perimas leave the house with something in his hands and go around back.

"What is this place?" Tomptee hollered, but Perimas did not reply. Something smelled off, like the night he followed Perimas to the river. He looked to the cabin but didn't see Andrew, so he followed Perimas.

"Where's Andrew?" Tomptee asked, but Perimas said nothing. Instead, he dropped something into what looked like an open grave and filled it with his bare hands.

"What have you done?" Tomptee asked, looking back at the abandoned shack.

"I'm sorry. I have no choice," Perimas finally replied, standing and punching Tomptee across the face, knocking him to the ground. Then Perimas disappeared around the front of the house.

There was a rumble in the distance, and the sky began turning red. A storm was coming.

Tomptee's head spun as he slowly rose, stumbled to the house, and looked through the window. Andrew was lying on his stomach, blood running from the back of his head. Tomptee pulled his cloak over his head as Perimas returned from the other side of the house. Perimas looked around but didn't see Tomptee. It didn't matter. He had done what he came to do.

Within minutes, the ground above the grave heaved and collapsed like whatever was buried within had just vanished. Then there was a commotion inside the cabin, and all four women stumbled out the front door.

Tomptee quickly climbed a woodpile to a back window and broke it open, dropping down into the cabin and running to Andrew who still lay unconscious.

"Andrew! Andrew!" he urged as firmly as he could without rousing suspicion from Perimas.

Andrew slowly started to move and touched the back of his head, which was wet with blood. "What happened?" he groaned.

"Perimas attacked you. And me. He buried the figurine in the backyard, and the witches are back."

"What?" Andrew asked, slowly struggling to his feet with Tomptee's help. "Grandmother?"

Tomptee nodded. "She's here too, but I don't know where they went."

Andrew picked up the staff and went outside.

The sky grew dark, and violent wind swept across the lake, pushing it back and forth, startling Brynlee and causing her to bolt away from the house.

Andrew steadied himself and raised his staff. "Brightness and focus," he said, as his staff began to glow brightly and the space around the cabin became calm, though Tomptee could still see the wind churning the lake's water.

The wicked sisters turned to Andrew from where they had tied Lorna to a gnarled old tree and gagged her with black fabric torn from their robes.

"We've come to finish what we've started, foolish boy," she who was deaf, cried out over the blowing wind.

"Silence!" Andrew spoke, leveling his staff at them, and all three stumbled back. Then Perimas stepped out from behind the tree, drew his bow, and leveled it at Andrew. He looked ragged and old, not the youthful Longbeard he had been just minutes before. His cheeks were sallow and his eyes pained.

Andrew widened his arms. "Perimas! What are you doing?"

"You don't understand! I can't control my hands!"

"Release him!" Andrew cried as the sound of the wind grew ever louder and light pulsed from the end of his staff.

Perimas squeezed his eyes and clenched his jaw. With terrible effort, he slowly lowered his bow. Then his hands jerked back up. He swallowed and remembered Feyloren. He did love her, and even if it was too late for him, it wasn't too late for her to be happy. He fought hard to move his bow again, this time to the side, and before it could be trained back on Andrew, he let loose the arrow, hoping he could give Andrew a few moments to flee before being forced to nock another arrow.

The arrow flew, but just as it was about to pass by safely, one of the wicked sisters flicked her wrist, and the arrow struck. Only, instead of striking Andrew, it struck Tomptee.

# CHAPTER 61

"**N**o!" Andrew screamed as Tomptee fell lifeless to the ground. Then everything became utterly still, and the old raven stood before Andrew.

Andrew lowered his staff. He felt no intuition in it, and its light had gone out. There was no more wind, and Brynlee stood frozen in mid-gallop near the lake.

"None of this was necessary, you know," The Raven King said, now wearing the mask of the mourner, black with silver eyes of feigned sorrow.

"I can't let you take him," Andrew said, standing over his fallen friend.

"Who said I came for him?"

"But if not him then..."

The Raven King pointed to Perimas, whose look of abject horror for accidentally shooting Tomptee was frozen in time.

"I don't understand," Andrew said.

The Raven King approached Perimas and touched his face like a mother touching the face of a child. "He is already mine. They took him from me. It's time he comes home," he said, nodding to the wicked sisters.

"So, it's been him all along? Why didn't you tell me?" Andrew asked.

"I tried. Perhaps you were not listening."

This was possible. Andrew tried to remember, but fear was all he could conjure of his dealings with The Raven King.

"What of Jatoba?" Andrew asked.

The Raven King turned back to him. "If you had dealt fairly with me, I would have dealt fairly with you. I would have released your family and faded into your dreams, but you played me the fool!"

"How?"

"By taking my favor and trading it for... for what? What was the favor of a god worth to you?"

"Her," Andrew said, pointing at Lorna. "I know you can't harm me. You have no power over me. But if you let Jatoba go, I will give you my life for theirs."

The Raven King approached him, trying to read any deceit in his eyes. "No tricks this time. If you choose this path, there is no turning back. Not even my sister can help you if you give yourself willingly."

Andrew nodded. "I know, but consider this: You once asked, 'What is love?' What if I told you that love is a choice?"

The old raven narrowed his gaze at Andrew.

"It is choosing other over self, time and time again. I was other, and someone chose me. I know what it is like to be different, feared, alone. If you let us all go, I will choose you. Not out of coercion but freely. You will freely be welcome at my table. Just imagine: Someone who *wants* to be with you for who you are. What say you?"

Now, a young Human boy stood before Andrew with black curly hair, olive skin, and eyes of starlight.

"But no more tricks," Andrew added.

The boy looked at his hands. "For an eternal moment, I forgot who I once was. This is my truest form."

Andrew didn't understand. How could a Human child be his truest form? And the boy heard his thoughts and laughed, which felt so good. He hadn't laughed in an eternity of nights.

"Wanna know a secret?" the boy whispered.

Andrew nodded.

"He loves you the most because you were least amongst your brethren. He knew it would be so and gave *us* this appearance. This is *His* truest form."

Andrew considered these words and remembered how The Grace Giver had also said such things.

"Wanna know what Ruach means?" the child asked.

Andrew nodded.

"Breath. The Great King's breath indwells you," the child said with a smile. Then the child approached the three women, and everything returned to its natural movement, though there was no longer any violent wind, and the sky's light was no longer angry.

The three women looked at the boy and spat, "Get away, child, or we will boil your bones for broth!"

The child's face changed to something Andrew could not see, for his back was to Andrew, and the three women fell on their faces prostrate before him. "I am Neetoo, nIchta allNeetoo, who you serve."

The women covered their faces. "Master! Command and we will kill this foolish tinker touched by..." and the words caught in their throats.

383

"Silence," a deep and terrible voice spoke. "I am pleased to give you what you desire. To be with me."

The three started laughing. "Thank you, master!" But as they did, he waved a hand over them, and their laughter turned to screaming as they hardened and turned to ash that broke apart in the passing breeze. All that was left were three tiny bones that he picked up and held in the palm of his hand. He took a string from somewhere Andrew could not see and strung the bones like beads on a bracelet. Then he approached Perimas. Without words, Perimas nodded, and the child nodded back.

Perimas approached Tomptee, and he removed the arrow from Tomptee's shoulder. Tomptee gasped for air and sat up.

"Sorry, friend. I guess you were right to distrust me. I wish we had met under different circumstances," Perimas said as a wind unfelt by either Andrew or Tomptee began to blow through Perimas' hair.

Tomptee stood and hid behind Andrew, which broke Perimas' heart, but he understood. Then he reached to his side, removed his sword, and held it out to Tomptee.

Tomptee was hesitant, but Andrew urged him on, so he stepped out and carefully took the sword.

Perimas smiled. "Take care of it. And yourself."

Tomptee nodded and held it up to the light. As he did, it shifted in size to fit his tiny hands perfectly.

Then Perimas turned to Andrew. "I was Fey's past. You are her future. I know that now. Tell her I'm sorry and that it was always her." And before Andrew could reply, Perimas was gone. All that was left was a small bone, which the child picked up and added to the others.

Andrew ran to Lorna and cut her ropes. She was shaken and a bit confused but not otherwise hurt.

As the child began to leave, he stopped and looked back at Andrew. "Did you mean what you said? That I can return to you, and we can sit and have a chat?"

Andrew smiled. "I'd like that."

The boy smiled back. "Be well, Andrew, Son of The Great Ruach." And he was gone.

Lorna looked at him, knowing what that name might mean but unsure who the child was.

"What happened?" Tomptee asked, rolling his shoulder where the arrow had landed.

Andrew smiled. "You saved the day!"

"I did?" Tomptee asked, brightening.

Andrew laughed and put his hand on Tomptee's shoulder. "Come, friend, we have people waiting for us."

# CHAPTER 62

On the road to Jatoba, Andrew told Lorna some of what had happened, but she was weak and near the very edge of exhaustion, so he took her home. As she climbed down from Brynlee, she asked, "Have you seen my staff?"

Andrew held it up to her, and her eyes grew. She took it from him and considered its new form. The green light had returned once again to its filigree spindle.

"I think this is yours now," she told him with a gentle smile and handed it back to him. "I look forward to hearing the tale. How about you return first thing tomorrow and brew me a cup of your special tea."

Andrew smiled and agreed.

As he and Tomptee approached Jatoba, there was no sign of ravens, which was a relief. Though he could no longer see chimcary as he could in his former life, he knew it was there, and he was happy to be home.

Jatoba's streets were filled with her people, and Feyloren was walking back to the Hiddy Coo rubbing her eyes. Seeing her, Andrew jumped down from Brynlee, ran to her, and warmly embraced her.

"Where have you been? I think I overslept," she told him.

He laughed and hugged her again. Then he asked, "Have you seen my father?"

"No. Why?"

Andrew quickly entered the tavern, heading up to the room where his father often stayed. But there, sitting at one of the tables and leaning against a wall near the hearth, rested Lithuel, waiting for his son to return.

"Father!" Andrew cried, running up to him, but Lithuel did not rouse.

Andrew could feel that something was wrong. "Father?" he asked again, but again, Lithuel was silent. He gently touched Lithuel's cheek and found him cold.

Feyloren covered her mouth with her hand.

Andrew sat at the table across from his father and took his hand. He considered for a silent minute.

"What is Jasper going to do without you." His eyes began to burn. "What am I going to do without you?" And he wiped away a tear.

ANDREW AND FEYLOREN stood hand-in-hand in a quiet corner of the valley where few wandered. The grasses were wild and ungrazed, with tiny white and purple flowers sprinkled across the landscape. An iridescent dire butterfly flitted about in the cool afternoon breeze. It was Jatoba's place of the dead where Feyloren's mother was buried, and a head-stone stood for her father over an empty, unclaimed plot. Andrew watched as she quietly lay a bundle of flowers on each headstone, then she went to a third. It belonged to Perimas. She knelt before it, the wild grass scratching at her legs, and on the stone she lay the binding ribbon used on their wedding day. Then she lay her hand on the headstone.

Andrew stood close enough for support but far enough to give her room to grieve.

"A part of me never let you go," she told Perimas. "Some part of me always imagined you might come strolling up one day and knock on my door. When you did, I didn't know what to do. The girl I was will always be yours. But it's time I move on. I know our baby is with you." She started to cry. "And that's as it should be. I will always remember the way we were."

There was silence.

After a few minutes, she rose, returned to Andrew, and took his hand.

"He loved you, you know. When it was time for him to go, he wanted me to give you a message. He wanted me to tell you that he was sorry and that it was always you."

At that, Feyloren broke down and wept on Andrew's shoulder.

THE MIGHTY NIGHTSHADE trees surrounding Jatoba had begun to blush, and a cool wind stirred eddies of deep-purple leaves blanketing the ground, signaling autumn was near. Horns blew across the valley, and banners waved in the wind, for there was cause for celebration in Jatoba: A daughter of the village was getting married that day.

"It looks good on you," Andrew said, referring to the ornate sword hanging at Tomptee's side. Andrew wore a brocaded, blue and white tunic. A braided band of hair wrapped around his wrist. Tomptee wore a matching, solid blue tunic his mother had sewn.

"I never knew I was a sword guy, but it's grown on me," Tomptee replied, fastening the end of his sleeve.

"It would seem things worked out in the end," Andrew said, trying to get a stray curl to tuck back behind his ear. "It's just..."

Tomptee turned to him. He was getting good at reading Andrew's body language and knew something was on his mind. Tomptee had just assumed it was the wedding. "What?"

Andrew took a deep breath. "It's taken me some time to unpack everything we went through, The Raven King, my time with the Shimar Etsell..."

"Are you afraid he won't keep his word?" Tomptee asked, referring to the old raven.

"No. It's not that. It's the Grace Giver. That first time I saw her, in my dream, she said something I can't forget. She told me that if I ever returned to Jatoba, I would surely die."

Tomptee considered. "Wasn't that before her favor returned to you?"

"I guess. But it didn't feel like a threat. It felt like a warning."

Andrew could see this talk was starting to make his friend nervous. "But hey! I'm sure it was nothing. I think I saw your parents out there," Andrew added, which made Tomptee even more nervous, and he leaned to look out through Andrew's shop doors where he and Andrew were preparing.

The village was adorned with blue and white ribbons, and the village center was bustling with everyone ready to move on from the ill fortune the summer had brought. Children ran around laughing, throwing handfuls of flower petals and handing the guests small bundles of tied flowers. Merriment was in the air.

"I can't believe they already put your shop back together," Tomptee said, looking around.

"Yeah. Things go quickly when everyone works together," Andrew replied.

Thanks to the combined efforts of the residents of Jatoba, the shop looked better than ever. Finely carved shelves lined the walls, beautiful plants from Daphnie added some color, and the local tanner had pledged to be his first customer just as soon as Andrew was back from his wedding holiday, which he was more than looking forward to. And the boy who had painted the racial epithet on Andrew's door had been forced by his mother to paint the entire front of Andrew's new store, himself, by hand, and only after making a very public apology to Andrew while standing on the edge of the fountain for all to see. No one even looked at Andrew cross-eyed since that day.

Tomptee turned to Andrew and smiled. "Are you ready?"

"Almost," he said, leaning down to Jasper and making sure the blue and white tunic Daphnie had sewn for the pup fit properly. The old dog wagged his tail with excitement, sure all the people in town were there to see him. Then Andrew stood and nodded. "Okay. Let's do this." Then he put a hand on his friend's shoulder. "Don't worry. You'll do great," he told Tomptee, who wasn't exactly one for crowds.

Tomptee took a deep breath and nodded.

Andrew noticed that a few short quills were just starting to peek through Tomptee's fur.

"So will you," Tomptee replied, and Andrew smiled.

Tomptee stepped out of the shop, cleared his throat,

and spoke with the loudest voice he could muster: "Hear this, people of Jatoba. Today is a great day, and we welcome one and all. Friends, family, and honored guests," he said, nodding to different individuals in the crowd that represented each of the named groups. "Please welcome, my friend, Andrew, Son of Lithuel, Son of Grace, Son of Jatoba." He made a simple bow as everyone clapped, then stepped out of the way.

Andrew made his way through the crowd and took his place in front of the village fountain next to Lorna. Since neither his nor Feyloren's parents were present, Lorna and Brutste had agreed to perform the ceremony. Lorna wore a magnificent, grey, crushed velvet gown that swept behind her in bustles. Brutste wore a cream-colored dress embroidered with images of farm life and a pair of brown-leather boots—though she made absolutely certain there was no ale on them. She had tried the little girly shoes but just couldn't, and after everything that had happened, neither Fey nor Andrew gave a good frog's fart.

Andrew's eyes swept the crowd, and he smiled as he found Daphnie with wildflowers braided in her tall horns, Wilkers and Nizzle with four of their children, Professor Lyra Luminara in incredible blue and gold robes, and a certain bald man with sapphire skin standing next to a beautiful bald woman with skin of the same hue, both of whom nodded and lifted a toast to Andrew as he met their eyes. And, for a moment, he remembered those who could not be there: Lithuel, his father; Petook, Teela and Aefook, Andrew's family in another life; His mother, wherever she was. The space they each left behind was heavy on his heart.

Then he saw her.

Feyloren stood at the entrance of the tavern under a

beautiful arch of pink, blue, and white flowers crafted by Daphnie. Fey's cream-colored story dress was stunning. Embroidered in yellow thread along her sides and back were the important scenes of her life: Her as a young girl holding a bow; her father and mother; her and her sister under the sign of the Hiddy Coo; her holding flowers over Perimas's grave; her standing next to a tinker's cart; Andrew, Lithuel, and Lorna on the back of horses; and room for so much more. She also had short, tight braids in her hair, which had begun growing again the day she woke from her long sleep.

A stranger no one noticed stood at the back of the crowd in a wide-brim hat and white-leather gloves.

Everyone fell silent as Feyloren stepped out from the tavern, approached the fountain, and took Andrew's hand. Together they stood next to Brutste and Lorna.

"Welcome, everyone," Lorna began. "Feyloren and Andrew have invited you here today to witness their covenant of love. It has been a long journey for both of them; however, they want you to know that if you can hear my voice, you are family."

Brutste wiped her eyes with a handkerchief and began, "Andrew. The first time I saw you in my tavern, I was sure that a slight breeze would blow you over, but you held your own, which impressed me. Then you fought for my sister, and that impressed me more. But it wasn't until I saw just how much her restless heart began to heal with you that I knew: You *are* the one. I've fought for this little girl my whole life, and for the first time, I know it's time I let her go. And that's okay because I know she is and will always be safe with you. But if I'm wrong!" she said, flexing and pointing. "I can still break you in half!" And everyone except Andrew laughed. She shook her head and looked at him again. "I see you, Andrew. I see you."

Andrew swallowed and nodded.

"Little sister, mum and da would be so proud," she said as her throat caught and tears rolled down her cheeks. "Just look at the woman you've become. What an honor, nay, privilege, it is to have been on this wild and crazy journey with you, but it's time you travel with someone anew. What a beautiful journey you are about to begin. I see you little sister. I see you." Then Brutste looked again at Lorna.

"Feyloren, every time my grandson looks at you, his eyes fill with hope and joy. I sense a spirit of strength, steadfast love, and confidence in you. My hope for you is that together, you find the strength to stand against the strongest storms, unmoved and unfazed.

"And Andrew. My grandson, who I lost, but now I've found. What Brutste said is right and just: It is an honor to be a part of your journey. Always remember: You are not alone. Not anymore. You have found family, friends, and a community of people who love you both. We are your chorus. We are your witness. We are a testament to the man you are and the man you will soon be.

"And now, I have a message for you, sent to me by a friend who will remain nameless. It says:

Andrew, Son of Grace. I am sorry that I and the rest of your chimcary family could not be with you on this day of days, but know that we celebrate you. You live in us now, and we in you. Be well."

Andrew squeezed Feyloren's hand and his eyes welled up with tears.

Brutste turned to two children standing at the edge of the crowd, who brought forward a folded, white ribbon.

Andrew and Fey turned to face each other and gripped each other's forearms.

"Now, bind them with cords that cannot be broken," Brutste said as she took the ribbon and loosely wrapped it around Fey's and Andrew's forearms. "And let any who would oppose them know, they must pass through us first!"

"Here, here!" the crowd shouted. But the stranger at the back of the crowd silently grunted a laugh.

"And now! Drinks on me!" Brutste cried out, and everyone cheered.

As the ceremony concluded and the night began to wear on, there was singing, dancing, and plenty of merriment. A table in the Hiddy Coo was set to collect gifts from anyone who might feel so led, one of which was a small wooden box made of the most beautiful red and honey-colored wood anyone in the tavern had ever seen—anyone other than Andrew, that is.

And as things began to quiet for the night, and Andrew and Fey were soon to leave, the stranger in the wide-brim hat and white leather gloves approached Andrew.

"Congratulations to the new couple," the stranger said, raising a glass, and Andrew smiled.

"Thank you. Are you a friend of my wife?"

The stranger shook his head and set his mug on the bar.

"Then what has brought you to Jatoba? Because I don't think we've met."

The stranger took a folded paper from his coat pocket, covered in ornate red, blue, and gold ink, and laid it on the bar. Then he removed his hat and gloves, revealing skin dotted with golden scales.

"Andrew, Son of Lithuel," the man said with a forked tongue. "You are under arrest, by order of the King, on the charge of iniuria intuitiva." Then he grabbed Andrew by the front of his tunic, and together, they vanished.

Brutste, standing nearest Andrew, heard the charge, saw the man grab Andrew, and lunged for him but missed him by an inch, landing on her face and pounding the tavern floor as hard as she could with her fists, knocking drinks and plates off tables that smashed to the ground.

Fey, who was outside saying goodnight to some of the guests, ran into the tavern. "What's happened? Where's Andrew?"

Brutste pounded the ground again and stood up. Then she read the ornate writ of arrest and looked at her newly married and very pregnant sister.

"Andrew's been arrested on the charges of assault with lethal intuition."

Images of Feyloren's father being arrested flooded Fey's mind, and she fell to her knees crying.